He never gave up on her.

WAKING HEARTS

Fox shifter Alison Smith gave up on happy endings when her ex-husband walked out, but that didn't mean she was allowed to give up on happy. With four growing kids, Allie is determined to look on the bright side and carry on. Luckily, Allie has the best friends a girl could ask for. Especially a certain quiet bear who's always been her rock.

Oliver Campbell knows what it means to be patient. But twenty years of wanting one unavailable woman may have pushed him to the edge. With Allie working every night at his bar, their friendship has begun to fracture. Then old ghosts offer one more kick to the little family that's already down.

Allie's ex-husband may be gone, but his actions are haunting his family. With danger licking the borders of Cambio Springs, the bear and the fox will have to work together. And twenty years of unspoken passion may finally come to light.

WAKING HEARTS is a contemporary fantasy romance novel in the Cambio Springs Mysteries series by Elizabeth Hunter, author of the Elemental Mysteries and the Irin Chronicles.

praise for elizabeth hunter

RT Magazine 2016 Award Nomination, BEST PARANORMAL ROMANCE. The relationship evolution between Ollie and Allie is a true joy to read, and the splashes of danger and suspense give it a spectacular, spicy kick!

RT Magazine

I stand by my earlier statement: IF YOU AREN'T READING ELIZABETH HUNTER THEN YOU ARE GOING TO DIE UNHAPPY AND ALONE!!! Cheese and crackers, I loved this book.

Penny Reid, NYT, USA Today, and WSJ Bestselling Author

I've said it before and it's something that I'll definitely repeat, Hunter has amazing ability to translate a complicated plot into a most enjoyable read. I'm never disappointed reading her books.

The Book Chick

I swooned over and over and over again. I'm still swooning. I'll probably be swooning tomorrow as well.

Rabid Reads

Miss Hunter manages to blend a small town contemporary romance with cozy mystery and urban fantasy, and it all works really, really well together.

Nocturnal Book Reviews

waking hearts

A Cambio Springs Mystery

Elizabeth Hunter

For my all the single mamas out there.
I see you.

Cover Design: Elizabeth Hunter
Illustrations by: Natalia Gaikova and Kathryn Bentley
Developmental Editor: Lora Gasway
Copy Editor: Anne Victory
Formatter: Elizabeth Hunter

chapter
one

Allie Smith took a deep breath and closed her eyes, trying to contain the temper threatening to burst through her calm facade. She glanced down at the plunger sitting in the clogged toilet and tried to decipher the legal gibberish of her lawyer who was on the phone.

"Wait, wait," she said, pressing the plunger down and pausing. "It's been a year. We filed this paperwork six months ago. It's not my fault the man's disappeared off the face of the earth."

She tried to keep her voice down. The boys were all in school, but Loralie was only in kindergarten Monday, Wednesday, and Friday. Today she was at home.

"I realize that," her lawyer said. "But he still has to be served with the paperwork. And since we don't have his address, we have to show the judge that we've made every attempt to find him."

"But *he* left *me*. And the kids. He's the one who took off."

"But you're the one filing for divorce. If you could hire a private investigator—"

"I don't have the money for a private investigator!"

"Then we have to wait." Her lawyer sighed. "Allison, I know it's frustrating, but he's not coming around and harassing you or the children. He's not draining your finances—"

"Because there are none."

"I'm just saying are you sure you want to proceed with the divorce when you're having so much trouble serving him the papers? He's sure to turn up at some point, so unless you have another relationship you're trying to proceed with—"

"Oh yeah." She shoved the plunger down again and pumped, hoping the clog was too much toilet paper and not another toy. How many times did she have to remind her seven-year-old, Christopher, that you don't need half a roll to be thorough? "Yeah, I'm burning up the dating scene here in the Springs, Kenny."

There! She pulled up and the water began to drain down the toilet bowl. Not a toy. Thank God. It could have been way worse.

"That's right," she continued. "I've got men lining up at the door for this hot thirty-four-year-old chick with four kids. I have to beat them off with a..." She looked at the messy thing in her hands. "Plunger. It probably wouldn't be all that hard."

Allie set the plunger in the bucket to take out to the garage and wiped the sweat off her forehead with her forearm. It was fall, wasn't it? Wasn't it supposed to be cooling off?

The town of Cambio Springs might have been hidden in a quiet corner of the Mojave, but that didn't mean it was sheltered from the relentless heat of the Southern California desert. The weather had started cooling off at night, but in September the days were still sweltering. Happy weather for the bird and reptile shifting clans. Not quite so fun for the canines, felines, and bears.

Kenneth Dwyer was a lawyer in Palm Springs and one of the many cousins she had in the sprawling wolf clan her mother had been born in. Though Allie was a fox and her mother long dead, the family connections had proven true. Otherwise she'd never have been able to afford Kenny's hourly rate.

His voice lowered. "Listen, Allie, I think you should talk to Alex about hiring a detective. It would be fairly routine. All he or she would have to do is put together a report to convince the judge that we've met the requirements for a diligent search to find Joe. Once the judge is convinced, we can serve by publication and you'll be able to proceed."

She fought back frustrated tears. Alex McCann was another distant cousin, the alpha of the wolf clan, and even more than that, a close friend. The fact that Alex was already helping her pay bills was humiliating, but she couldn't ask her dad to do more. She had two sisters. She wasn't the center of the universe.

No, she was an abandoned wife with four kids, two part-time jobs, and a load of debt she'd discovered after her ex-husband walked out the door just before she and the kids sat down for meat loaf one night.

But hey, at least her house was paid for!

"Listen, Kenny—" Her voice broke. "I can't…"

"We can wait," he said. "Or I'll see if any of my regular investigators have employees looking for license hours who might give you a lower rate. We'll figure it out, Allie."

She leaned out of the bathroom to make sure the sounds of Loralie's favorite cartoon were still bouncing down the hall.

"I just want to be done with him," she whispered. "I'm not hung up. I don't care about getting married again. I just want to be able to move on from Joe. Close the door. Figure things out with the kids without all these questions hanging over our heads."

"We'll do it. It'll happen," he promised. "This isn't going to last forever. But divorce is complicated, especially when kids are involved and you're filing for full custody. Take a deep breath and focus on your family. Let me do my thing here, and we'll make it through."

She took a deep breath and managed a smile. Choose to be happy. Just like the past fifteen years. Choose happiness and focus on the positive. She could do that. Allie was a professional optimist.

"You're the best, Kenny. I owe you brownies."

"You know I'm not turning those down."

"Say hi to Amber for me, okay?"

"Will do. We'll be back home next moon night, so we'll probably see you then."

Nights when the moon rose full were de facto holidays in Cambio Springs. When most of the town was populated by shapeshifters and the people who married them, full moons took on a carnival-like atmosphere. Even those who'd moved away to the more prosperous towns of Palm Springs and Indio for work would return to shift and celebrate with family. Canines and cats. Snakes and birds. Even the solitary bears occasionally lumbered out to hunt or fish under the moonlight before they retreated to their dens.

Bears…

 3

"Shit! Kenny, I gotta go. I'll call you next week, okay?"

"I'll let you know if I can find someone to help. Later."

Allie had just remembered she'd promised Ollie she'd come in early to help Tracey with the inventory at the bar. Oliver Campbell was the quietest man she knew and one of her closest friends. And for the past ten months, he'd also been her boss. Though she needed the extra paycheck, the strain of working with him was beginning to make Allie wonder if their friendship was too high a price to pay for the added money.

Ollie was constantly grumpy when she was around. He was sweet as pie with her kids and grumpy as hell with her.

The depressing thing was, she thought she knew why.

THURSDAY NIGHTS AT THE CAVE WEREN'T USUALLY BUSY unless they had a band.

Tonight they had a band.

They also were behind in inventory since Tracey—Ollie's head waitress for years—had been out sick earlier in the week and the delivery that was supposed to be there that morning hadn't come in because of a breakdown.

Ollie frowned down at the clipboard Tracey had handed him.

"I'll put that ale from Mesquite Brewery on special," he said. "We've got an extra keg from them. And then..." He frowned. "Push mixed drinks, I guess. And bottles."

Allie's mind raced. She knew they were low on some of the favorite drafts, and the crowd at the Cave was definitely more of a beer crowd than a cocktail crowd. "Could we do an ice trough with longnecks by the entrance?" she asked. "Cash only? It'll be quick. Lotta guys coming in after work would probably go for those just to cool off."

Tracey nodded. "That's a good idea."

"Who are we going to get to man it?" he asked.

"I'll call one of the weekend girls," Tracey said. "See if they want to pick up some extra. Or Dani. I think she's on break from school right now."

"If Dani can come in," he said, "call her. Pop said she needed some extra cash."

Dani was one of the younger members of the bear clan and, like Tracey's husband Jim Allen, worked at the Cave when she was able. The Cave wasn't only one of the music hotspots in the high desert, but it was also the unofficial gateway to Cambio Springs. And for as long as anyone could remember, the Allen-Campbell clan had guarded that gate. Bears like Ollie and Jim quietly discouraged outsiders from becoming curious while they fostered the too-cool-to-care reputation of the bar.

It probably helped that both Ollie and Jim looked like hot bikers dreamed up in Hollywood. Jim wasn't quite as tall as Ollie, but at six foot, he still packed a punch. He took after the Allen side more than Ollie, who was a lighter blend of African, Mexican, and Scots-Irish blood that made up most of the Campbells. Intricate tattoos painted both of Ollie's arms and covered his chest and back. His face, if you didn't know him, would be forbidding.

Ollie was a quiet man, but one whom very few were willing to cross.

Because of that carefully cultivated reputation, his bar had hosted some of the most popular rock, alternative, and country bands in the past ten years. It was well-known that the big man had some friends in LA who quietly steered bands his direction when they needed to toughen up their image.

It worked.

Playing at the Cave and not getting shouted down by the crowd was an accomplishment. Just the Quinns—Cambio Springs snake shifters and general mischief-makers—kept Ollie and Jim busy. Not to mention the bikers and other wanderers that were drawn off the interstate and into the dark, wood-paneled bar. Word about a new band got out and the crowds came. The bands sank or swam on their own merit. Nobody did you any favors at the Cave.

"A beer trough will work," Ollie said in a low voice. "Tracey, go call Dani in. I want her here at six to help you guys set up. Good idea, Allie."

"No problem."

Tracey disappeared to call Dani, leaving Ollie alone with Allie. He crossed his arms and stared at the small stage in the corner where the band would be setting up in a few hours.

"You're good at this," he said. "The customers and stuff. Anticipating what they want."

"Thanks."

"Good idea moving you to nights."

She nodded. "And I appreciate it."

Ollie frowned. "You don't have to… It's fine. How's it working out with the kids? With you gone at nights more."

"Kevin's my right hand. Doing great watching the younger three. My dad usually comes by for dinner." She shrugged. "He doesn't love me working nights, but he knows not to look a gift horse in the mouth."

"You're good at your job. I'm not doing you any favors."

"We both know that's not true," she said under her breath.

He took a step closer. "Al—"

"Ollie!" Tracey called from the back of the bar. "Dani can come in, but she wants to talk to you. Family stuff, I think."

Ollie muttered something under his breath but turned and walked to the back office without another word to Allie.

She let out a slow breath and watched him walk away, wishing the view wasn't quite so tempting.

It wasn't her fault really. After fifteen years with a man who equated kindness with weakness, Allie would probably be attracted to any man who was merely polite. And Ollie was more than polite. Despite his tough exterior, he was one of the kindest men she'd ever known.

And he was hot. Painfully, distractingly attractive in a way she hadn't let herself acknowledge for many, many years. Admitting her attraction to Oliver Campbell would have made her crazy when she was still tied to Joe.

Allie didn't want to get distracted by his big shoulders and gorgeous beard and overwhelming hotness, but come on! Three nights a week she waited tables for some of the roughest guys in the desert while the man behind the bar kept an eye on her. And Ollie took care of his girls. That feeling, combined with his looks, was enough to make any single mom go weak in the knees when she was used to being responsible for everything all the time.

But it was also ridiculous, because she was not the kind of woman Ollie was attracted to. Not even close. He kept things quiet, but she and her two best girlfriends, Jena and Ted, had gossiped plenty over the years. The women Ollie liked were all tall and dark and dramatically gorgeous. Nothing like her short "four kids later" body with flyaway blond waves and cheeks so round she felt like they'd never left elementary school.

Allie suspected Ollie knew about her ridiculous feelings, which probably explained the grumpiness. She did her best to hide it, but she must have done something to give it away. He knew her. They'd been friends since they were kids.

Awkward.

She had to get over it. An unrequited crush was not worth ruining a twenty-year friendship.

Jim leaned over the bar and shouted, "Do you want me to put Tracey on table five?"

She shook her head. Table five might have been irritating, but they were also tipping over twenty percent every round. If they were making a few suggestive comments, it wasn't anything she wasn't used to. "I've got it."

"You give me the word and I'll cut 'em off, honey."

She gave him her most cheerful smile. "You're the best, Jim."

"Try to move them out before Ollie—"

She shook her head as the drummer broke into a loud solo. "What?"

"He'll be back in five. They look like they're moving along?"

She shook her head. "I told you I'm fine. They're not causing trouble. Just a little annoying."

"Right."

The crowd was electric, especially for a weeknight, and Allie had to hand it to the alternative rock band from Orange County: they were good. Great rhythm and a lead singer who seemed to be as popular with the guys as with the girls. Young people had flooded in from all over the desert, and the bar was filled with a twentysomething crowd instead of the usual mix of all ages. Cocktails had been unexpectedly popular, and Ollie had been forced to run to his house to break into the Campbell bourbon and rye stash.

Table five looked like they were more interested in picking up girls than listening to the band. She guessed they were rich kids from LA slumming in the desert. They were dressed immaculately, even in the heat, with slick hair and carefully groomed facial hair they probably thought was "retro." The four men seemed to be more amused by giving her a hard time than they were by the music.

"Hey, sweetheart," the leader of the little group asked. "When can we expect those old-fashioneds?"

Allie eyed the tip of his glossy oxford as it tapped impatiently. She forced a smile as she set down a round of shots Jim had comped them because of the wait.

"Sorry, guys. The owner is on his way back with some more rye. Shouldn't be much more than ten minutes. They're the first order up."

She pretended not to notice the brush of his arm on her hip.

"You live around here?" he asked. "What time do you get off work?"

She tried not to laugh. "I'm pretty busy, guys."

"Your name's Allie, right? I'm Ryan."

"Nice to meet you, Ryan. Enjoy the band!"

Allie got two steps away before she felt a tug on her apron string. She stopped when she felt the weight of it slide off her hips. It landed with a thunk, the small bills and change she'd collected landing at the smug man's feet.

"Oops," Ryan said with what someone had probably told him was a charming grin, still holding the dangling end of her apron. His buddies laughed. Her apron had landed on the floor, right between his spread legs, dollar bills and quarters rolling out.

Refusing to let them get to her, Allie forced a smile. "You guys are such gentlemen. Would you mind picking that up for me?"

"If I do," Ryan said, "what do I get as a thank-you?"

Nothing, you little asswipe. You're the one who pulled it off in the first place.

"Guys, I'm not trying to spoil your fun, but I really don't have time for this. I'm working."

Allie could see table seven's drinks sitting on the bar, and Jim was glaring at her customers. She was now losing tips dealing with these *Mad Men* wannabes. If Ollie had been there, one of them would have already come out and given the men a warning. But with Ollie out, Jim was stuck behind the bar.

"Tell you what," Allie said, leaning down to the arrogant man's ear. "You can pick up my apron for me right now—" She heard the back door open and a moment later, Ollie walked down the back hall with a case of whiskey, Caleb Gilbert trailing behind. *Finally.* "You do that, and I'll forget you've been a pain in my ass all night." Allie looked up and glanced across the table at a younger man whose cheeks held a slight blush before she looked back at Ryan. "How's that sound, *sweetheart*? Trust me. This is Oliver Campbell's bar. You don't want to mess with his servers."

Ryan's smile was tight. His eyes held hers. "Oh, I don't think your thug boss wants to bother upstanding citizens like us."

Another one of the men at the table was starting to look embarrassed. "Ry, let it go. She's busy, and I want to listen to the band." He moved to bend over and pick up Allie's apron, but Ryan stepped on the hand that reached out.

"Ow! What the fuck, Ryan?"

He was still staring at Allie, a smile on his lips. "She can pick it up."

Allie heard a thunk as the case of whiskey hit the bar. "I warned you," she said, crossing her arms as she saw Ollie stride across the floor. There was a lull in the music, and the bar quieted as if just realizing something was going on in their midst.

Ollie jerked his chin at the band and said, "Play."

Immediately the drummer picked up again, the guitarist stepped forward, and the singer raised his hands, drawing the attention of the crowd.

Ryan had scooted back in his chair, crossing his arms and reaching for his drink as Ollie approached the table.

Ollie snagged the shot glass from Ryan's fingers and put it on the table. "You're done." He turned to Allie. "They paid up?"

"Yeah. They settled up and then this guy pulled my apron off."

Ollie scowled. "What are you, twelve?"

Ryan's eyes flashed. "Hey—"

"Pick her apron up and get out of here."

Ryan stood, deliberately kicking her apron under the table and scattering more of the cash.

"Oh, for heaven's sake," Allie said.

Ollie didn't say another word. He grabbed the man by the back of the suit and lifted him in the air.

"What the fuck?" Ryan yelped. "Put me down! Andrew, call the cops. Your bar is mine, asshole. My lawyer is going to have a field day with this."

"Shut the hell up," Ollie muttered, looking at the other men at the table with an impassive expression. "Any of you guys have manners? Pick up her apron while I go have a talk with your friend."

The whole bar watched as Ollie walked a puffing Ryan down the back hall, and the three men scrambled to pick up the money and stuff it back in Allie's apron. The band, bless their hearts, continued to play.

The blushing one handed Allie her apron with a nervous smile while the other two got out their phones. Caleb wandered over from the bar.

"Allie, you okay?"

"Yep." She smiled. "These gentlemen were just leaving me a very nice tip for making their neighbors wait on their drinks." She looked over at table seven. "Sorry, guys!"

"No problem," one shouted.

Another said, "Almost as entertaining as the band."

One of Ryan's silent friends was holding up his phone and glancing down the hall where Ollie and Ryan had disappeared. "Shouldn't one of us call the cops? What's that guy going to do to Ryan?"

Caleb hooked his hands in his pockets, his thumb behind the badge at his waist. "I am the cops. And Ollie was going to have a chat with him. Didn't you hear?"

Allie didn't have time for this.

She hustled to the bar and delivered table seven, then picked up empties on two before she took orders from the pool room. Stupid men and their stupid posturing. Her ex, Joe, was exactly the same kind of guy as that idiot, Ryan. Never knew when to just back down and let things go. Had to keep pushing until—

"Allie!"

Tracey yelled her name just as Dani came to grab her order pad.

"Go," Dani said. "Tracey says you need to calm him down."

"What?"

"Ollie lost his temper on that idiot. I'll cover your tables. Go."

What alternate dimension was this? Who decided that starting fights with a grizzly bear shifter was a good idea? Granted, the stupid human didn't know that Ollie was a grizzly, but he was clearly outmatched.

Tracey grabbed her arm as she headed down the hall that led to the bathrooms, Ollie's office, and the door to the employee parking lot. "Try to get him calmed down. We'll take care of the front. Caleb can help."

When Allie burst through the back door, she saw Ollie standing over Ryan, who was on his knees.

"Go for it," Ollie said. "Stand up again. See what happens."

His voice might have been quiet, but Allie could hear the thinly veiled rage. Ollie didn't lose his temper often. Something Ryan said must have really set him off.

"Ollie!" Allie saw how far gone he really was when he glanced over his shoulder. Combined with the look of quiet rage was a split cheek that made Allie's temper spike. "Did he hit you?"

"Sucker punch." He turned and grabbed Ryan by the hair to pull him to his feet. "Apologize to her. Now."

Tugging him to his feet brought the man's face into the light. Ollie had been careful. There was only a shadow of a bruise by Ryan's jaw and his lip was split, but Allie could see the pale skin and hunched shoulders that told her his ribs were more battered than his pretty face.

"Sorry," the once-arrogant man said through bloody teeth. "I'm sorry. Didn't… didn't know about your kids or anything, okay? Just thought we were having fun."

"Fun? You've got a messed-up sense of fun, mister."

Ryan watched Ollie, who hadn't said another word. "I'm sorry. I didn't know she was your girl, all right?"

"I'm not his girl," Allie yelled. "And that doesn't matter anyway."

Ryan glanced nervously at Ollie again.

"What matters," Allie continued, "is you don't treat a woman like that. You don't treat *anyone* like that. Learn some manners and don't come back here. Ever."

"Okay. I won't. I promise."

Ollie dropped him, and Ryan scrambled toward the front of the bar, kicking up dust in the cold light of the parking lot as Allie turned to Ollie.

She put a hand on his chest. "Let me see."

"It's nothing."

She grabbed his chin to angle his head down, and he winced.

"Allie-girl—"

"Was he wearing a ring or something? How did he open up your cheek like this? You look like you might need stitches."

"He was talking shit. I got distracted. I'll go to Ted's and have her patch me up."

Her other hand rose to his shoulder, and her fingers stroked the beard over his jaw before she could think. His shoulders were rock hard with adrenaline. Sometimes Allie forgot how big he really was. She barely came to his chest.

"Ollie…"

She ached. She wanted to slip her arms around his waist and lean into him. Press her face into his chest until he settled down and hugged her back. Make him laugh and smile and erase the awful wall that had risen between them. Allie could feel her heartbeat pick up as she leaned closer.

Without a word, Ollie grabbed her wrist and pulled it away from his jaw, looking back toward the bar as he said, "We need to get back inside. Talk to Caleb and make sure that punk doesn't cause any problems."

Humiliation colored her cheeks red as she dropped her hands. "Right. Sorry. It's still busy. I'll go back inside and get back to work. Why don't you run to Ted's house and have her look at your cheek? Caleb can help at the bar. Dani's station has cooled off, so she can help on the floor. We'll take care of it."

He gave her a brittle laugh. "Organizing the world again, Allison?"

Ollie was the only one who called her Allison anymore. Not since her mom died. And he hadn't done it in months.

She forced a smile past the burn of embarrassment and the memory of his jaw under her fingertips.

"Well, you know me. That's what I do. Can't turn off the mom after fifteen years, you know?"

"I guess not."

Damn men with their damn inscrutable expressions. Allie tried not to run back into the bar. She headed straight for the women's restroom and leaned against the door, pressing her hands to hot cheeks.

Get a grip, you idiot. Oliver Campbell is not for you.

chapter
two

"You're an idiot." Teodora "Ted" Vasquez slapped a bandage onto his cheek and shoved him out of the chair. "I'm tempted to tell Tia Maria how big an idiot you really are, but even I'm not that mean."

The last thing Ollie needed was his cousin tattling on him to his grandmother like they were still ten years old. He glared at Alex McCann, Ted's husband, across the room. "A little help here?"

"Sorry, man. I think you're being an idiot too."

Ollie shook his head and tried to banish the memory of Allie's soft hands on his chest. Her fingers brushing his jaw. With the bear riding him, pumped full of adrenaline and still pissed at that sorry little puke of an investment banker, he'd been seconds away from taking what he'd wanted for years.

Years.

"How long are you going to wait?" Alex was talking again.

Ted was muttering under her breath in Spanish. She was family, but damn, the woman could be annoying as hell sometimes. She was best friends with the coy little fox, but Ollie knew she was also trustworthy.

"She's not even divorced yet."

"She filed six months ago," Alex said.

"But it's not final."

"'Cause she can't find the bastard!" Ted yelled. "You really think if Joe comes waltzing back into town she's gonna give him the time of day?"

"No." He paused. "I don't know. They have four kids and fifteen years together. She's not the kind of woman who just dismisses that."

Ted froze. "I'm going to forget you said that so I don't have to give you a matching bruise on your right cheek. After everything she's found out about him? The drugs. The debt he piled up and left her with. Added to that the way he completely abandoned his kids? She's done with him. Trust me. Done."

"Even if she is definitely done with Joe, I have no interest in being her rebound."

Ted froze and across the room Alex visibly winced.

"What did you just say?"

"Rebound." He didn't back down from her glare. "What do you think? She's going to want to settle down with some asshole a year after her deadbeat husband left her? Yeah, I'm seeing that working out great."

"So you're an asshole now?"

"That's not what I said."

"Yes, it is," Ted said, ice dripping from her words. "You said 'settle down with some asshole,' implying that one, you're an asshole, and two, she'd settle down with one again. I'm not talking about the bullshit you hear at your bar, Ollie. I'm not talking about some theoretical relationship between two people who just met. I'm talking about *you*. You and Allie. Two people who should have been together from the beginning if you hadn't dragged your ass in high school and let Joe I'm-a-lazy-ass-who-can't-be-bothered-to-take-care-of-my-family   Russell sweep in and convince her he'd give her the moon and stars!"

Alex bit his lip, clearly trying not to laugh. "That's a long nickname, baby."

Ted shot a glare at her husband and turned back to Ollie, shaking her head. "You have no idea."

"No idea about what?"

"How bad it was."

Ollie could swear his heart stopped beating for a second. "How bad was it?"

"You have your secrets. She has hers. You want to know? You want to get real with her? You ask Allie, not me."

Ollie stopped talking. It was what he usually did when he didn't want to discuss feelings with his cousin, of all people. His cousin, who seemed determined to drive him crazy.

He had a plan. He'd waited for Allie Smith for twenty years, and he could wait a little longer if it meant she came to him with a whole heart.

Ollie couldn't handle being a way station for her. He wasn't being dramatic. He just knew that he'd break if she tried him on and discarded him because she wasn't ready. He'd held his peace for fifteen years, and once he had her, he wouldn't be able to let go.

"Tell me something, *Oso*." Ted used his childhood nickname, but it did little to soften her words. "So what if she does end up having a rebound relationship, huh? You think you're going to be able to handle seeing her go out with another guy under your nose? And what if it turns serious? What happens then?"

Gut-churning rage in his stomach. Ollie stood without thinking, his hands clenched at his sides. His eyes narrowed at Ted when she sighed.

"Yeah, that's what I thought."

IT WAS JUST HIS LUCK THAT TRACEY HAD CALLED ALLIE IN to work early on Friday afternoon. Just his luck he'd have to watch her bustling around his bar in her skinny blue jeans and fitted black T-shirt, her apron tied at the waist and the bow perched at the top of her ass. Four kids had added to her figure since high school, but not in any way Ollie would complain about.

When she'd been younger, she'd been so tiny his awkward teenage self had nightmares about finally getting up the guts to make a move, only to end up breaking something. Fifteen years had made her no less attractive but a little more substantial. The bear in him approved.

When she'd been married and the torment of her had been a constant ache in his gut, he'd dated. He'd dated plenty. But not anyone who would remind him of Allie. Tall, slim girls with dark hair and barely there smiles. No blondes. No short, curvy temptations. Dating anyone who even resembled her was completely off-limits.

She was filling out the specials board, her back to him, that little bow taunting him. "Ollie, did we get everything in the delivery this morning?"

He tore his eyes away from her ass and back to the newspaper. "Yeah."

"You want to put the Firestone DBA back on special then? That was selling really well last weekend."

"Sure."

"Or do you want me to try a different ale and leave the DBA at regular price?"

"Whatever you think."

She shot him a tight smile and put the Firestone back on special before she quickly filled out the rest of the board with the regular weekend deals.

Her instincts were good, and he probably should have given her better feedback, but he was trying not to stare at her. Or glare. He couldn't *not* notice her, but he knew he'd been acting like a Neanderthal. He didn't want to be such a bastard, but he couldn't find his balance with her anymore.

When Allie had been married, it hadn't been an issue. She was off-limits. Not even a possibility on the horizon. Because she wasn't that kind of woman, and he wasn't that kind of man. Because of that, he'd been able to be her friend, cherish her and her kids, and ignore the slowly degenerating asshole she'd hooked herself to when she was sixteen.

But now...

"What if she does end up having a rebound relationship, huh? You think you're going to be able to handle seeing her go out with another guy under your nose?"

Ollie knew the answer to that. He'd go insane. But he also didn't know what to do about it. He couldn't think of a way to broach the topic without coming across as a presumptuous asshole.

Morning, Allison. I've been in love with you for about twenty years now. Would you like to go out for coffee? Or maybe just marry me and put me out of my misery?

Hey, Allie. I know you're still in the middle of a divorce, but how about coming over for dinner? Bring the kids. Feel free to have them pick out rooms while they're here.

Allie was frowning as she looked out the window. "Ollie?"

"Yeah?" he growled. Yes, growled. His grandmother would have slapped the back of his head if she'd heard him.

"Caleb is coming up the road."

Well, shit. It would be just his luck if that little asswipe from the night before decided to file charges that Caleb couldn't ignore. To be fair, the surveillance camera would have picked up that the banker swung first. Unfortunately, it would also pick up that Ollie busted his ribs more than was strictly necessary.

He folded the paper and put it under the bar, surprised that Caleb hadn't called. They'd been friends for two years now. Ollie was godfather to Jena and Caleb's little girl. If anyone had made a complaint, Caleb would have called, which left Ollie wondering why the chief of police was really coming up the road at four in the afternoon on a Friday.

He heard Jim bang the kitchen door and start the prep for dinner, heard him and Tracey chatting and flirting. Nearly twenty years and the two of them were still nuts about each other.

Yeah, he was jealous.

Allie was refilling napkins and glancing at the door with a small frown on her face. Worried, probably. Worried for him.

He wanted to pick her up, cart her to his office, and kiss the frown off her little mouth. He wanted to carry her back to his house, gather her kids up, and fold them into the close-knit Campbell clan so she'd never have to worry about anything again.

He knew she *could* handle all the shit life had thrown at her. It just pissed him off that she *had* to.

Caleb pushed the door open, and a quick wash of heat entered the bar before he could shut the door.

"Hey, Caleb!" Allie said. "Get you a water? A Coke?"

Caleb wiped his forehead, his face carefully blank. "Iced tea?"

She smiled. "Tracey's making some in back. I'll see if it's ready."

Allie slipped to the back, and Caleb's face shot to Ollie's, thinly veiled anxiety written on his face.

"Hey, man. What's up?"

Caleb glanced from Ollie to the hallway where Allison had disappeared, and Ollie's stomach dropped.

"Joe?"

Caleb nodded just as Allie came back with a tall glass of iced tea.

"Just ready," she said with a smile. "So how's everything going with you today?"

"Allie," Caleb started, "why don't you sit at the bar with me?"

Her smile fell. Ollie watched as the color drained from her face, and he wanted to roar. Wanted to throw Caleb out of the bar. Instead, he lifted up the pass and went to stand behind her as she and Caleb sat down. He put his arm on the bar beside her and waited.

"What's going on?" she asked, her voice wooden.

"I... Have you heard from Joe since the last time I asked you?"

She shook her head.

"Are you sure? Not even a call that hung up? Kevin's got a cell phone now, right?"

"Yeah," she said quietly. "But he'd tell me if his dad called."

"You're sure?"

"Caleb," she said. "Just tell me what this is about."

Caleb put his hand over Allie's and Ollie knew. It was bad.

"Yesterday a rancher out near Twentynine Palms found a body on his property."

Damn you, Joe Russell.

Ollie put a hand on her shoulder and left it there.

"It had... been there for a while. There wasn't much left, but there was a pawn ticket in the pocket and they traced it back to a shop in Indio. It was for an antique Bowie knife, and the name on the ticket was Joe Russell."

Allie tore her hand from Caleb's and covered her face. Without a word, Ollie turned her on the stool and pulled her into his arms, wrapping her up as her shoulders began to shake with inaudible sobs. She threw her arms around his neck and squeezed, her cries still silent, her tears running down his neck.

Caleb had gone to the back, and he could hear Tracey, Jim, and the chief talking quietly. Then Tracey's quiet gasp and Jim's concerned rumble of a voice.

Ollie held on to her until her shoulders stopped shaking. He didn't say anything until she pulled away and wiped her cheeks.

"You're gonna be okay," he said, leaving one hand on her shoulder. "You hear me? You're gonna make it through this."

Her face was stricken. "He's their daddy."

"Allie-girl—"

"No matter what he became to me, he's their *daddy*," she whispered. "My babies, Ollie."

Caleb came back before Ollie could clear the lump in his throat from seeing her in so much pain. The police officer set a box of Kleenex on the bar and handed one to Allie, glancing at Ollie's arm, which was still around her shoulders. She took a tissue, blew her nose, and grabbed another for her eyes.

Then, in a surprisingly clear voice, she asked, "Are they sure it's him? Or could someone have stolen that ticket?"

"They're not sure," Caleb said, "which is why I need you to come with me. Did Joe go to the dentist regularly?"

She nodded. "Same one as me and the kids in Indio. He hadn't gone for a few years though. Once money started getting tight, we skipped and just made the kids get checked up."

"It shouldn't matter. If there are X-rays on file, the pathologist can use them to identify him or rule him out as a victim."

"A victim?"

Caleb paused. "It's possible it was an accident or something like that. But there are also signs that there was violence. Ted's going to call her pathologist friend in San Bernardino. See what he can share with her. The remains were taken to the county lab."

Allie nodded. "You need me to sign some forms or something? For the dentist?"

Ollie could tell Caleb hated to be asking her, but Allie was all business.

"Yeah," Caleb said. "And I need to make a proper report. You know it might take longer than you expect to identify him, right? These things don't happen right away."

"Caleb, I've watched *CSI* with Ted enough times to know it doesn't happen as fast in real life as it does on TV."

Ollie tried not to smile. "How long?" he asked Caleb.

"I don't know. I'll try to find out."

Tracey and Jim came out from the back. Ollie could see the red in

Tracey's eyes. She had married in from outside but had melted into the bear clan right away with her generous, funny nature.

She held out her arms and Allie went to her.

"What can I do to help?" she asked. "Anything you need, honey. Anything. You just ask."

Allie shook her head. "I've got to go. Kevin is watching the younger kids, but I can't... I know it's Friday, and I'm so sorry—"

"Stop," Ollie said. "Allie, it's not your job to worry about the bar. Caleb, you need her right now or can this wait?"

"She can come in on Monday if she wants, but the sooner the forms are filled out, the sooner I can send them."

"Then we'll call in someone to cover you tonight," he told her. "And you concentrate on you and the kids. Want me to call your dad?"

Caleb said, "Jena already called your dad and Beth. Hope you don't mind."

"No, it's fine," she murmured.

She looked lost. He could see her thoughts flying everywhere.

"Allie?"

"Yeah?" She was standing with her arms wrapped around herself.

"What do you need right now?"

She stared at Ollie like a lost child. "I don't... I don't know what to tell the kids. What do I tell the kids? What if I tell them and then it's not Joe?"

Ollie sat down on a barstool and pulled her toward him so they were eye to eye. "My gut instinct is you tell Kevin, but not the younger kids. Not yet. Kevin's going to know something is up though, and he'll be pissed if you don't say something." Ollie looked at Caleb. "What do you think?"

"I think that's the right move," Caleb said. "The younger three—"

"Mark is only ten, but he sees everything," Allie said. "He's the joker, but... he'll know. He's the one that stopped asking about Joe first. He knew he wasn't coming back."

Ollie nodded. "Then you tell Kevin and Mark. Leave Chris and Loralie alone for now. You'll tell them if and when you need to."

"Okay." She nodded, and he could see a hint of relief that she at least had a plan. "Okay."

Caleb pulled out his phone. "Want me to see if Jena can take the younger two tonight? We could do a sleepover at our house or something."

Tracey tossed in her house as an alternate if Jena couldn't take the kids, while Jim suggested calling Jena's parents if that didn't work out. As plans swirled around them, Ollie brushed his thumb over Allie's cheek. It was still red from crying.

"Hey," he said.

"Hey."

"It's gonna be okay. The kids are gonna be okay. And you will too."

She tried to smile, but it came out as a grimace. "You don't know that. I wish you did."

"I do know that."

"How?"

"Because no matter what," he said, "they have you. And that's a hell of a lot."

IT WAS THREE IN THE MORNING WHEN OLLIE MADE IT OVER to her house. He wasn't sure she'd be awake, but he needed to check on them. His mind had been halfway gone all night.

Allie had a little place out on the edge of town, only half a mile from his house and built at a time when there were no palatial bathrooms or master suites. The old Smith place was more of a cottage and had been a gift passed down from Allie's grandparents when she and Joe had gotten married right out of high school. Ollie remembered helping move them into it with Alex and the rest of their friends, when Allie had been a girl with a baby on the way and Joe had been the boy who loved her.

Ollie didn't know when that changed. But as he approached, he saw her sitting on the edge of the porch, looking up at a crescent moon that wiped the fine lines from between her eyes, softened the angles worry had carved, and reminded him of the girl she'd been before life had worn her down.

She angled her ear his direction, her hearing almost as keen as a human as it was in fox form. He walked slowly, allowing her time to warn him off or go inside if she didn't want company.

"It's okay," she said quietly. "No one awake but me."

"I couldn't sleep."

"Me either."

He sat on the step below her, leaning back and setting a bottle of Black Maple Hill bourbon next to her.

"Glasses?" she asked. "Or are we drinking hundred-dollar whiskey straight from the bottle?"

Ollie smiled and nodded toward the door. She got up and tiptoed in the house, emerging with two small jelly jars she set next to the bottle of bourbon.

"Hope you don't mind roughing it. I swear, every dish in the house is dirty and every one of those boys has forgotten out how to work the dishwasher."

"As long as you're not putting it on ice, nothing wrong with jelly jars."

He poured two fingers in each glass and handed one to her.

"To you." He clinked his jelly jar against hers. "One of the strongest women I know."

She tipped the glass back and drank. Then she kept drinking until the smooth, maple-soft whiskey was gone.

"Another?"

"Yep."

He poured her another two fingers, then tucked the bottle behind him and leaned back on his elbows to watch the night.

"Were you happy here?"

She tensed beside him. "What?"

"I was walking over here and remembering when we moved you guys in. You were... four or five months along with Kevin, I think? I just remember wishing you'd be happy here. That's all."

Allie was silent for a long time. "I had my babies here. And we laughed a lot, especially when the older two were little. Lots of fights, but a lot of laughs too. So yes. I was happy here."

"I'm glad." He took a deep breath and let the silent desert surround them.

"Thanks for coming by," she whispered.

 23

"How was it?"

"Not good. My dad stayed. So that helped."

"Kevin?"

"Angry."

"At you?"

"No, at his dad. That's kind of his go-to emotion about his dad lately. Also, he was pissed to know that his dad really did steal his Bowie knife, which was a gift from his grandpa and one of Kevin's prized possessions. Kev thought he had, but he didn't know for sure."

Every time Ollie thought he'd manage calm, Joe Russell just pissed him right the hell off again. "I'll make sure Caleb gets the knife back to him." *If I have to steal it back myself.*

"He'll appreciate that."

Ollie nodded and sipped his glass. Kevin Smith was a hell of a kid, but Ollie remembered his own anger when his mom had left. He'd only been seven, but he remembered. He'd split his dad's lip more than once the year after, not understanding what he'd done wrong that made his own mother abandon them.

"And Mark?"

Allie sighed. "Mark was... quiet. Kevin was asking questions one after another, but Mark was quiet."

"Mark's never quiet."

"He can be. He is when he's thinking things through. Then when you least expect it, he'll make some joke that has you laughing at the most inappropriate thing imaginable."

"That kid's smart as a whip."

She shook her head. "Some days I don't know what I'm gonna do with him."

"Pawn him off on Ted. She's smarter than all of us put together."

Allie laughed a little and sipped more of her bourbon. "This is nice."

"Yep."

"Not the bourbon—well, that's nice too—but you coming over for a drink. I feel like I never see you except at work."

Yeah, there was a reason for that, but he wasn't going to tell her the night she found out her ex-husband was possibly her dead husband.

"I've been dealing with some personal stuff. Sorry if I've been an asshole."

She shook her head, and he swore she was blushing, but it was too dark to tell. "No, I'm sorry. I... well, I've been stuck in my head lately."

"You've got a lot going on."

"World doesn't revolve around me," she said. "Never has."

"Maybe it should." He raised his glass to hide his face. "Every now and then."

She smiled. "You're sweet."

He shook his head and let out a rueful laugh. "Not really."

"Ollie?"

"Yeah?"

"I need to ask you a favor. And before you say anything, I want you to remember I grew up in this town. I know who really takes care of things and who makes sure the secrets stay secret."

Ollie narrowed his eyes. "Allie—"

"I remember before we had our own police. Before the sheriff even paid attention to us. It wasn't police who came to the door to tell Daddy that Momma had died; it was your dad."

"And?"

"And since the beginning of the Springs—before it was even founded—the Allens and the Campbells were the ones protecting us. Who kept strangers out and made bad guys go away."

"Allie, I am not the authority here. Caleb—"

"Caleb doesn't have jurisdiction. Not that far out of town. He said he can ask for information if it ends up being Joe, but he can't really stick his nose in too far without pissing people off."

"But you think I can?"

She tilted her chin up. "Are you a Campbell?"

"Of course I am."

"Then you can."

Ollie shook his head. "It might not even be him."

She sighed and a sad smile crossed her face. "I try my best to look on the bright side of things. I try to think the best of people. Because... it's easy to think the worst." She reached over and took his hand, squeezing his large paw between delicate fingers. "You and I both know it's him."

The question caught in his throat before he finally choked it out.

"Do you care that much?" *Did you still love him?* "I mean, the details… I know he wasn't good to you. And the kids—"

"The kids—especially Kevin and Mark—need to know what happened to their dad. Kevin's the one asking questions now, but eventually they'll all be asking." She shook her head. "I've been cursing him for months, and this whole time…"

"You didn't know." He tamped down his anger. "You aren't allowed to feel guilty about that, Allison."

The corner of her mouth turned up. "Not *allowed*, huh? Bossy."

"Yeah, I am. About this. You have nothing to feel guilty about. Nothing. I just don't understand why you want me to—"

"I need you to look into this because you know that the police are not going to know how or where to look for the truth about what happened. Our kind know how to keep secrets too well. And what do they really care about some small-town guy from Cambio Springs who was suspected of dealing drugs and all sorts of other shit? They're not going to care what happened to him. They probably think he had it coming. You asked me earlier what I needed? I need this."

Ollie squeezed her hand back and gave her a nod, knowing it wouldn't have mattered what she asked.

He'd give her anything.

chapter
three

S unday afternoon Allie had shoved the looming mystery to the back of her mind and taken over Ollie's kitchen to cook for all their friends. Her house was too tiny to host more than a few people, so when it came her turn to cook for their usual Sunday dinner, she imposed on Ollie.

The old Campbell house had once belonged to Ollie's grandparents. There were five bedrooms and four baths in the two-story ranch house, along with a wide porch and a barn where Ollie's grandfather had once had a blacksmith's shop. Now Ollie kept four or five project cars in the barn, but the rest of the house didn't see much company unless Ollie's friends came over.

The first time Allie had cooked in the old Campbell house, she had to force herself not to drool. It was a huge old country kitchen with room for a big table in the middle of the room, open shelves lining the back, and more cupboards on one wall than she had in her whole house. There was even room for Ollie's mastiff, Murtry, in the corner. And Murtry took up some space.

How some woman hadn't convinced Ollie to marry her solely so she could get custody of Grandma Campbell's kitchen was a mystery to Allie. It needed a little updating, but all that counter space was a cook's dream.

"I love this kitchen," Jena said, grating cheese for the tacos.

"Me too," Allie said. "Do you think Ollie would trade with me?"

Jena shot a look at Ted, who was sitting at the table, holding Baby Becca while the little one drooled on her fingers.

Ted said, "You're the one who told me to back off."

"I know," Jena said.

Allie pulled a casserole out of the oven. "Know what? That Ollie wants to trade houses with me?" She snorted. "Not likely. Ted, did you say you brought some sour cream?"

"Yeah, it's in the back of the fridge. Tell me when you want me to put the salad together and I'll hand off the baby."

Becca was chewing on Ted's fingers, but the doctor didn't seem to mind. Ted was the town's only physician, so she was a pro with babies, even if she hadn't had one of her own.

Allie winked at her. "So, has Alex convinced you yet?"

It was well known among their friends that Alex McCann, Ted's new husband, was more than eager to start a family, even if he did have final construction on the Cambio Springs Resort and Spa to finish.

Ted played with Becca's dark curls of hair and said, "I think maybe next year. This year is so busy. Once I have a nurse-practitioner hired at the clinic, I won't feel quite so crazy."

The economic revitalization that Alex McCann had planned when he started building the resort had already started. Families who had moved away for work were slowly moving back, leaving Ted with more patients than she'd ever had at her clinic. Jena too was putting together a team to work with her at the restaurant at the resort, where she would run the kitchen as head chef while her parents took over the diner.

And Allie was juggling two jobs and four kids, wondering when she'd be able to stop taking charity to pay for groceries.

Trying to convince herself the shamed flush in her cheeks was because of the stove, she ran through the menu for dinner. "Ted, I think you can put the salad together now because the meat is almost done. Jena, can you call the older boys in and have them start setting the tables? Ask the guys to oversee the kids and make sure everyone has drinks."

"Yes, ma'am." Jena walked over and picked up her daughter, blowing a raspberry on the giggling little girl's cheek.

Rebecca Doli Gilbert had been a little bit of a surprise for Allie's oldest friend. Jena hadn't expected any more babies after her husband Lowell had died. She'd been content with her two boys. But then, she'd never expected to fall head over heels in love with the town's new chief of police, either.

The kitchen door swung shut and Ted pulled out a cutting board and set it next to the stove near Allie.

"So," she said, "I wasn't able to talk to Dr. Carlisle in San Bernardino yet. He's visiting his wife's family in Denver until late next week, so I don't know much more than Caleb. Once he gets back, Larry will give me more details."

Allie nodded. "He's a friend?"

"We're friendly. He's pretty old-school. He gets it about small towns taking care of their own, you know? Even if it's not technically my jurisdiction."

"Is there anything else you can tell me?"

"One of the techs said the remains looked like they were around ten months old, but that's really hard to judge. Especially when…"

Allie squeezed her eyes shut. "Animals?"

Ted nodded.

"Not anything that would be a surprise to us," Allie said, continuing to stir the *carne asada*. "Joe's natural form was a coyote. Scavengers only seem fitting."

Ted coughed into her shoulder. "Dammit, Allie. You're not supposed to make jokes about that."

"You telling me you and Caleb missed that irony?"

"No, but he's a cop and I'm a doctor. We're supposed to be twisted."

"I wouldn't joke around the kids. You guys?" She shrugged. "I can't be his grieving widow."

"Aren't you upset?"

Was she? Ollie had asked her the other night and she'd avoided the question. She took a deep breath and turned off the heat under the meat.

"Yes. And no. I don't know how I feel. It's not *real* yet. All I can think about is the kids."

Ted's eyebrows furrowed. "Yeah, I can see that."

"Know what I felt?" She pressed her hands on the cool tile of the counter. "After I'd told Kevin and Mark? After Ollie had left with the bourbon?"

"Ollie came over for a drink?"

"Just for a bit." She shook her head. "I felt... relief. Isn't that horrible?"

Ted was quiet for a long time. Then she said in a small voice, "I don't think that's horrible."

"It *is* horrible. It's awful. He's their father. He's—he *was* my husband." Her voice dropped to a whisper. "And when I heard that he was probably dead? I felt relief. That the kids wouldn't think he'd abandoned them. That I wouldn't have to drag them through some long, awful divorce. That I wouldn't have to worry about him taking them away. And that's horrible. Because they lost their dad. And part of me hates that it didn't break my heart. I feel... sad. Horribly sad. For them."

She closed her eyes and felt Ted's arm around her shoulders.

"I think you feel however you feel," Ted said. "There's no rules for grief. There's no rules that you have to grieve a man who made your life miserable, just because he fathered your kids."

Allie wiped away her tears and went to wash her hands before she dried them on the apron she wore over her Sunday dress. "Let's talk about something else, okay? Once we know for sure, I'll talk about it. I don't want to waste any more tears on that man unless I have to."

"Fair enough." Ted started dicing tomatoes. "So, how's your love life?"

Allie laughed so hard she scared the dog.

THERE WAS A BENCH ON OLLIE'S FRONT PORCH, AN OLD swinging bench that someone had mounted years ago. The sun was setting over the mesa, and Caleb, Alex, and Sean were cleaning the kitchen when Allie finally sat in it, closing her eyes against the last rays that bathed the desert. The little boys were watching a movie in the living room while Jena and Ted let Loralie change Baby Becca's clothes like she was the best living dolly ever.

Other than scattered voices drifting from the house, it was quiet. So beautifully quiet... until she heard teenage feet shuffling up the steps, then a solid tread coming behind them. A boy and a bear.

Allie kept her eyes closed as Kevin and Ollie approached.

Kevin whispered, "Should I—"

"Leave it and ask her later. She's been working all afternoon."

"I'm awake," she said. "Just resting my eyes."

She felt Kevin sit next to her. "I have a question for you. I mean, Ollie and I have a deal, but he said that I had to check with you first."

She cracked her eyes open to see the miniature man sitting next to her. Well, kind of miniature. He was taller than her by a good eight inches, and his muscles were filling out a little more every day, but he was still her baby. Her baby that looked like he hadn't shaved since Friday morning before he went to school.

He had stubble. When did her baby get *stubble*?

"What's up?"

"You know the money I saved up from working at Grandpa's store?"

"Mm-hmm."

"Well..." Kevin glanced at Ollie and continued. "I've been doing some research online about blue book values and restoring cars. And Ollie has an old Charger in the barn that he hasn't really fixed up yet, and he agreed to sell it to me and help me work on it, but I have to ask you first, so can I?"

"Wait." She sat up at the nervous stream of words. "Okay. You've got money saved up from your job at the feed shop."

"Yes."

"And Ollie has a car that you can afford." She looked at Ollie. "A fair price? He's got to earn this. No giveaways."

Ollie nodded. "It's fair. The Dodge isn't in good shape, but it does run. He looked up the blue book value and his offer is in the range."

Allie looked at Kevin.

A car? How had that happened?

Not that having another person who could drive in the house wouldn't be a relief.

Kevin held up his hands, ticking off points he'd obviously planned out ahead of time. "I'm going to need a car to help out around the house, and spending money on this is better than buying some newer car that's only going to go down in value. With this one, the value will go up the more work I put into it. And I still have seven months before I get my license, so I have time to fix it up. Ollie says I can keep it here while I'm working on it and use his shop. By the time I get my license, it'll be mostly done. He's gonna show me how to pull out the dents and work on the engine and everything. Any parts I need he thinks I'll be able to get cheap from the wrecking yard instead of having to buy brand-new stuff."

Allie looked at Ollie. "Do you have time for all this?"

"I told him Saturday afternoons. And in exchange for my helping him, he's gonna do grunt work for me while I'm fixing up the Ford."

"The '55?"

"Mm-hmm."

There was a nearly original 1955 Ford pickup truck Ollie had been working on for almost a year. Allie drooled over that pickup, imagining it finished and painted a bright sky blue. She'd almost volunteered to work on the Ford herself.

Kevin continued. "I don't have football anymore, so I'll still be able to work at the feed shop and watch the kids on your work nights. But if I work every Saturday—"

"Kev, I think it's a great plan."

A rare smile broke out on her beautiful boy's face. "Really?"

"Really. You've planned ahead and saved up your money. I'm really proud of you. If you're willing to put in the work, then I approve. Sounds like a good deal."

He leaned over and gave her a tight squeeze. "Thanks, Mom!" Then he jumped up. "I'm gonna go tell Low. Ollie, can we—"

"You can go hang in the barn with your car," he said. "You know how to turn on the lights. Just make sure none of the little kids go exploring in there."

"Okay!"

Kevin ran around the house, and Ollie sat down next to her on the swing. It creaked ominously but held.

Allie poked at the chain. "Sturdy. Must have been made for bears."

"There is no delicate furniture in this house. Pop made sure of that."

"You sure you have time for this?"

He looked down, his arms crossed over his chest. "It's Kevin. I have time. He didn't sign up for the football team this year?"

"He gave it up so he could work more." She took a chance that her hormones wouldn't go into overdrive if she smelled him and leaned against his shoulder. It felt almost criminally good. "And to help me out. I told him he didn't have to, but..."

"The boy understands responsibility better than most grown men."

"He's such a good kid. How did I end up with the world's best teenager?"

"It's not exactly a surprise. You're a great mom. And I'm sure he still has his moments."

"He does, but not many." She relaxed into Ollie's side, grateful that he'd left his arms crossed across his chest. If he'd done anything like put an arm along the back of the bench, Allie was fairly sure she'd melt into his lap and lose whatever shreds of dignity she was clinging to around him. "Sometimes I worry I put too much on him."

Ollie paused. "He liked football, but he wasn't crazy about it. He's learning about loyalty and responsibility and taking care of the people who are important to him. That's better than football."

She didn't have anything to say to that, but his words reassured her. Murtry wandered out of the kitchen and plopped down on Allie's foot.

"Speaking of loyalty," Ollie said. "That dog has none when it's between you and me."

"He likes Loralie the best."

"That's 'cause Lala feeds him the most food and her face is right at licking level."

She laughed and felt his shoulder shaking along with her.

"Thanks for letting me use the kitchen."

"Anytime."

"I should come over and make you some real food," she said. "Thank you for all the work you do around my house."

Allie knew Ollie was the designated handyman for her since he lived so close. Sean would come by sometimes, especially if it was a problem with the old plumbing. And Alex and Caleb stopped by occasionally. But she was fairly sure that Ollie got called anytime she mentioned something wrong with the house to Jena or Ted.

"Don't mind helping out," he said quietly. "Anything you need."

 33 ✳

The corner of her mouth twitched and she peeked up at him. "Maybe start talking in complete sentences instead of grunts when you come over? If you're gonna work on that 'not being an asshole' thing with me."

His eyes slid to hers, quiet humor crinkling the corners. "I'll see what I can do."

That low rumble of a voice about did in the last of her restraint, and Allie was seconds away from blurting something ridiculous when she heard the screen door slam and Sean Quinn stepped onto the porch.

He'd returned to town the year before, right after his cousin Marcus had been killed, but Allie knew Sean was still debating whether or not he would stay in the Springs or drift away again. He wasn't a settled guy like Ollie.

What he was, was trouble.

A wicked smile curved the corners of Sean's mouth when he spotted the two of them, and he ran over, scooping Allie off the porch and into his arms.

"No!" he yelled. "She's the last single one. You can't have her, Smokey!"

Allie started laughing, half-relieved that Sean had interrupted what likely would have been an embarrassing scene, half-irritated he'd likely throw out his back carting her around.

"Sean, put me down!"

"Nope."

"I'm too heavy."

"Please." He pinched her thigh. "You're what the old man would call 'a tasty bit.'"

A low growl came from the porch.

"Sean." She dropped her voice. "Put me down."

He stopped halfway to the garage and set her on her feet. "Did I piss you off? I was just playing."

"I know." And flirting with her, making her feel like a girl instead of a mom, which was a nice change. "But I think Ollie was worried you were going to drop me."

"Sir Growls-a-Lot over there?" Another sharp grin cracked his face. "I don't think he was worried I was going to drop you, Al."

"Whatever. It's not smart to poke a bear."

"Yeah?" He bent down and wrapped an arm around her waist, dropping a kiss on her cheek in the process. "Well, it's not good to take a fox for granted, either."

Allie frowned. "I don't—"

"Think about it." He started walking back to the house. "And come back in the kitchen. Alex and Ted brought ice cream."

A door slammed in the distance, and she knew that by the time she walked back to the porch, Ollie would be gone.

THERE WAS A RAP AT THE DOOR THE NEXT DAY, JUST AFTER her dad had rolled away from the front door with all four kids on the way to school and Allie was putting another load of laundry in the wash.

"Who forgot lunch?" she muttered, checking the kitchen counters to see which lunch bag hadn't made it into a backpack. Hmm. None there. She answered the door, surprised to see Ollie on her porch.

"Hey! I was expecting a forgetful child. What's up?"

"Needed to talk to you."

The bar was closed on Mondays. And why wouldn't he have just called?

"Okay."

She was just about to motion him in when Ollie stepped back and nodded to the old Bronco in the driveway.

"What's going on?"

"Pop wants to have a word. About Joe."

She let out a breath. "Right."

"Do you have time? I thought the kids would all be in school."

She nodded. "Just give me a minute. I need to hang some laundry before it spoils."

The dryer had been one of the first things she gave up when money got tight. It only heated up the house in the summertime, and the dry air made hanging the wash more practical than wasting money on electricity.

"I'll help."

"That's all right!" *Oh, please no.* "I'll just be a minute."

"It'll be faster if I help." He stepped off the porch and headed to the backyard. "I have hung laundry before."

Allie watched him go. "Okay then."

So what if most of this load was her underwear and nightgowns? It wouldn't be the first time Ollie had seen a woman's underwear. Of course, it was the first time he'd seen *her* underwear, but she refused to be embarrassed about it.

After all, she had nothing to be ashamed of. Pretty undies were Allie's one vice. No granny panties for this girl, no matter how many kids she had. She'd thrown out every bit of underwear or lingerie that Joe had ever seen or touched, so everything she had was new, and it was all a little indulgent, thanks to her sisters and a very nice shopping spree.

Allie wore lace, and she slept in silk.

She picked up the basket of damp clothes and walked out to the clothesline to see Ollie staring at a scrap of pink lace that was fluttering in the breeze. His hands were clenched at his sides, and there was a tinge of red on his cheeks above his beard.

Allie didn't say a word, just put down the basket and grabbed one of the pins from the hanging bag. She pulled out a purple pair of panties and hung them, careful not to snag the delicate material. After a frozen minute, Ollie silently reached down and grabbed the first thing he touched, which ended up being a blue silk nightgown with white lace trim.

"Make sure you use the plastic pins, not the wooden ones."

He cleared his throat. "Okay."

"Splinters."

"Seriously?" he muttered under his breath.

"Would you like splinters in your butt when you put your undies on in the morning?"

"My boxers aren't as... tight as these."

And now she was thinking about him in boxers. *Just* boxers.

"Well, girls don't wear boxers."

"Maybe they should consider it," he growled.

"What would be the fun in that?"

Ollie pulled another nightgown from the basket as Allie hung the matching purple bra. She saw Ollie eyeing it from the side, and when he reached down, he froze. There were no more nightgowns. The only thing left in the basket was a pile of bras and panties. Mostly panties.

"Shit."

Allie bit her lip to keep from laughing. She might not have been a tall exotic beauty like the girls Ollie dated, but her lingerie game was on point. That had to count for something.

"It's just underwear, Ollie. Everybody wears it."

"No." He straightened, a pair of black lace panties dangling from one finger.

She had to admit they were small. Even by her standards.

His eyes were angry, and he sounded pissed off. "Not everyone wears *these*."

She batted her lashes. "They do if they like silk."

He glanced at the clothesline where Allie had already hung most of her bras. "Is all your underwear like this?"

"You're the one who offered to help."

"Is it?"

"Pretty much."

He took a deep breath. "So when you're at work in your jeans and T-shirts…?"

"Yep."

His eyes finally raked down her body with a surge of awareness in his eyes. She might have been wearing cutoff shorts and an old concert tee, but she'd never felt more naked in her life.

His eyes finally landed somewhere around her hips. "What—?"

"Polka dots," she whispered. "Pink."

He stopped breathing for a second, then he spun on his heel and marched out of the backyard. "I need to call my grandmother. I told her I'd pick up a pie at the diner. I should—shit!" He'd tripped over one of the kids' bikes and banged his shin. "I should… find out what kind she wants. Or something."

Well, how about that? A fox *could* make a bear run away. As long as that fox was wearing polka-dot panties.

chapter
four

There was only so much one man could take.

That... ridiculous excuse for underwear was crossing the line. Ollie stomped across the gravel driveway and slammed the door on the Bronco. He closed his eyes and willed the image of pink polka dots away while he put the key in the ignition and turned the air-conditioning up full blast.

Pink polka dots. And purple silk. Black lace.

If he'd ever imagined Allie in her underwear—which yes, he could admit happened regularly—he'd always imagined her in something sweet. Soft pastel cotton. Maybe with a little bow or two. Or... flowers. Cute, practical underwear he'd tease her about when he finally got to see it.

He groaned. "I'm screwed."

There was nothing sweet or cute or practical about the string of temptation waving in Allie's backyard. What if her neighbors saw it? If any of them were male, he might have to kill them for looking. Shouldn't she be hanging those inside or something? He lowered his head against the steering wheel.

It was useless. He was doomed. She'd come into work every night and he'd be seeing nothing but black lace under her jeans. She might as well come in naked.

And that thought wasn't helping the situation in his jeans.

He closed his eyes and took a deep breath, but every time he did, all he saw was Allie in lingerie. He'd always scoffed at men who got excited about their women in lingerie. In Ollie's opinion, there wasn't much sexier than *naked*. And lingerie got in the way of naked.

Now he realized it wasn't about the sex, it was about imagining your girl walking around all day—going to work, making dinner, running errands—with that sexy secret under her clothes, just waiting for you to unwrap it when you got her alone. Like a Christmas present you got to open every damn night.

And now she'd flashed him a peek at a present. And it wasn't his to unwrap. Torture.

His phone rang on the seat beside him.

"Yeah?"

"Is that any way to talk to your grandmother?"

Ollie winced. "Sorry, Yaya."

"Is Allie coming over?"

He gritted his teeth. "Yeah, she's hanging some wash right now."

His *abuela* gave an approving cluck. "I knew I liked that girl. Very smart. Why do people use the machines when it's so warm out? When I was a girl, no one would buy them because they were a waste of money."

When you were a girl, they didn't make underwear that only covered half your ass, was made of black lace, and needed to be hidden from the neighbors.

Or maybe they did. He really didn't want to know.

"I'm running by the diner. What kind of pie do you want me to pick up for you and Pop?"

"Coconut cream if they have it. Otherwise whatever berry pie they have."

"How about I get you both?"

"*Oso*, you'll have your grandfather losing the last of his teeth with all the sugar. It's not good for him."

Why did he find his yaya's nagging so amusing? Her natural form might have been a bobcat, but she chirped like a bird. And she was the closest thing to a mother he'd ever had.

"Love you, Yaya. I'm getting you two pies."

"Just bring Allie. Does she have the baby with her?"

He smiled. "The 'baby' is in kindergarten now."

"No!"

"Yep."

"Then swing by and get the Crowe girl too. They're friends and she has the new baby. There are too many old people around here."

"I have to go." He saw Allie come through the front door, turning and locking it before she slid her sunglasses on and walked toward the truck. "You can visit Jena and her baby another time. Pop wants to talk to Allie about her ex."

"Oh," his grandmother said. "That's a bad business."

"I know."

"I'm glad she's away from that man now. He was never good for her."

"Yaya..."

"You know what I think. Don't waste time. Some other man is going to scoop that one up. Don't be lazy again, *Oso*."

Allie was trying to open the door, but it was a sticky bastard.

"I really have to go. See you soon." He hung up and jumped out of the truck, walking around to pull the door open. "Sorry about that. I'm still working on this door."

She looked up and he could see the sheen of sweat on her upper lip. It was already well into the nineties. Despite that, her smile hinted at mischief.

"Thanks." She hopped into the Bronco. "Do you think your pop is going to want to talk long? I don't want my panties to get bleached."

Ollie muttered under his breath, glad he'd walked behind the truck so she didn't see him trip.

He put the truck in reverse and backed slowly away from her house and all her underwear.

"You enjoyed that, didn't you?"

Her cheeks were pink. "Maybe a little."

"YOU'RE PART OF THE WOLF CLAN," BEN CAMPBELL SAID gently. "But you are coming to us?"

"The McCanns are my mother's clan and... I do feel a connection with them. But Alex is already helping me with so much. And he's in the public eye now." She glanced over her shoulder at Ollie. "I trust Ollie and your family. If anyone can find out what Joe was mixed up in, it's you guys."

"You realize that what you're asking might not put your ex-husband in any kind of good light. Are you sure you want to know? Are you sure your children need that shadow over their father's memory?"

"Mr. Campbell, right now all they have is questions. The younger two don't know anything about the body yet. The older boys do. They deserve answers. Maybe not now, but someday. And I want to have answers if they ask me. I need to know."

Ollie sat back and watched his grandfather question Allie. His pop had an instinctive read on people and always had. He had known when they were seventeen that Joe Russell and Allie Smith weren't a good match. It was his pop who had come to him, comforting him when his teenage heart had been broken.

I don't know why the Good Lord allowed this, Oliver, but know that not all things last. And that boy is one of them. I don't see any kind of forever in his eyes when he looks at that girl. So don't lose hope. Be patient. You never know what might happen.

It had been his pop who realized that the devotion Ollie had felt toward Allison Smith had been far more than a teenage infatuation. His dad hadn't understood; neither had the stepmother who came later.

And Pop had been right. He only wished there was a manual for what to do next.

"Ollie can look into it," Pop said, nodding at his grandson and giving him the formal blessing of the clan's elder. "But I want you to be honest with him. Anything he wants to know, you tell him. Even if you think you or Joe could get in trouble. Remember, we aren't the police. We take care of our own."

"Thank you, Mr. Campbell."

"You call me Pop, sweet girl. We aren't so formal around here." He patted her hand. "Now, can you go help my Maria with the pie and let me talk to my boy here?"

"Yes, sir." Allie tossed him a tentative smile and walked into the small kitchen of the apartment in town where his grandparents had moved when he'd taken over their house.

Ollie lowered his voice, and asked, "Well?"

"You be careful." The sweet old man was gone and the canny elder was back. "We don't know what that man was involved in. You find answers, but you be careful. I was gonna have you look into this even if she hadn't asked."

"Why?"

"Got a feeling about things." Ben Campbell leaned back in his chair, worry lines etched in his dark brown forehead. His thick, tightly curled hair was still closely cropped to his head, but now it was a gleaming white instead of a glossy black. Most of the time, Ollie forgot how old his grandfather was. Times like this, he was reminded.

"You think Joe brought this on himself?"

"The only one responsible for that man's death is the one who killed him."

"But..."

His grandfather sighed. "The way he was darting around here after Marcus Quinn died. The way all that business about the drugs came out later? Joe Russell fell into some bad business. Then all of a sudden, he disappeared."

"And now he's back."

"Bad things happen when bones get turned up, Oliver. Don't you ever forget that."

"I won't."

"And stay close to that woman and her children. Whoever killed Joe —if it is Joe—might not even know his name. Once the newspapers identify him—"

"He had a pawn ticket in his pocket with his name on it. They have to know who he is."

"No," Pop said. "He had a ticket with 'Joe Russell' on it. But that boy changed his name when he married your girl."

Which wasn't that unusual for their kind. It was one of the reasons so many McCanns and Vasquezes existed in the Springs. When outsiders married in, they'd often took the name of whichever spouse was established in town. The Russells, who had disappeared as soon as their son married Allie Smith, had been a distant offshoot of the McCann family. So Joe had changed his name to Allie's, angry at the parents who'd never cared much for him anyway.

"His legal name was Smith," Ollie muttered, turning the thought in his head, considering what it might mean for Allie and the kids. "But if he was going by Russell…"

"If he had any enemies, the minute the papers get ahold of his name, whoever killed him is going to know where he came from and who his wife is. Do you think you could get her to move into the house with the children?"

Ollie blinked. "What? *My* house?"

"It's a clan house first, and that woman has asked us for protection. That house is the safest one in town, and you and I both know why."

Because the Allens and Campbells hadn't ever stopped serving whiskey, even during Prohibition, and they had the getaway tunnels to prove it.

"I don't think she'd move the kids," Ollie said. "Not unless there was a clear threat."

"Then you stick close. And let your other friends know too. Especially the wolves and that skinwalker. They need to know what the danger might be. I'll talk to Scott Smith and Thomas Crowe myself."

Ollie knew his grandfather would waste no time telling the older generations what was what, leaving Ollie to communicate with the younger. It wasn't spoken, but he was the oldest direct descendant of William Allen in his generation. The assumption that he'd one day lead the small bear clan was understood and accepted. His father preferred roaming the country with his new wife and their motorcycles and had no interest in leading his family.

That left Ollie with a lot more responsibility than the average thirty-five-year-old man. He owned and ran the Cave, but he was also the go-to problem solver for anyone in his clan younger than him. And more than a few who were older. He loved his family, but sometimes the amount of time they took made him a little resentful.

"Pop?" Ollie lowered his voice to just above a whisper. "About Allie… I was starting to think— But now with Joe… I think her grief is more for the kids, but…"

"Lord, son, finish one thought so I can understand what you're trying to say instead of guessing it."

"I want her," he said bluntly. "You know that. But I don't want to rush her. She's got a lot on her plate right now."

"And you wouldn't help with all that if you were her man?"

"Of course I would."

"Then what's the problem, son?"

"The problem is... the timing sucks. Even if she is over Joe, she's still got to worry about her kids. I don't want to be the jerk that takes advantage of a vulnerable woman."

"So don't be a jerk and don't take advantage. It's really not that complicated. And she's about as vulnerable as my Maria is. Good Lord," Pop said, "that girl is *tough*. She kept going through all this mess her ex-husband put her through and never once lost that sweet spirit or her smile. Any man'd be proud to have a woman with that kind of backbone."

"Pop—"

"I'll tell you right now that there's no perfect time for anything." Pop's eyes bore into him, making Ollie feel like he was about ten years old again. "That was always the problem with you, Oliver. You kept waiting for the perfect time to speak your mind or make your move."

"I know."

"Sometimes you need to meet a person where they are. Even when things are messy."

Ollie rubbed a hand over his face and listened to the friendly chatter of his grandmother and Allie as they made coffee in the kitchen.

"But right now—"

"There is no perfect time," Pop repeated.

"Fine," Ollie said. "There is no perfect time."

"You don't think that woman could use a man who loves her to help her through this mess?" His grandfather leaned over and put a still-firm hand on his shoulder. "You got a heart as big as the sky, son. Who's gonna be better for that woman and those children than you?"

Ollie stood and walked to the kitchen door when he heard the women approaching. He could smell the sweet scent of pie and the bite of cinnamon coffee his grandmother always made.

He held the door open, only to have Allie almost stumble through.

"Oh," she said with a smile. "Didn't expect anyone to get the door. Thank you."

I didn't expect anyone to help. It was such a little thing. And Ollie wanted to do so much more.

"You're welcome," he said softly. "Let me get those plates."

He held his hands out.

Who's gonna be better for that woman and those kids than you?

No one.

THE BAR WAS CLOSED ON MONDAY NIGHTS, BUT THAT DIDN'T mean it was empty. Ollie heard the roar of bikes driving up the road, then the bang of the door as Tony Razio and his boys entered.

Red Rock Drifters was a relatively harmless motorcycle club as far as most motorcycle clubs went. Not that any of them—save the casual ones made of retired professionals—were really guys Ollie would want to hang out with. There were bikers like his dad—who had always had motorcycles and liked to work and ride them, mostly on their own— and then there were guys who bought into the lifestyle.

Tony Razio bought into the lifestyle. Big-time. The Drifters dealt drugs and treated the groupies that hung on them like they were disposable. Unfortunately, they'd gained a weird kind of glamour hanging out at the Cave where the new bands from LA thought they were the shit.

Damn television shows.

But guys like Tony also had their uses. They were dangerous enough to keep the nastier clubs away, and they lived up to their name. The Drifters rode all over the high desert, though their house was in Blythe, and they were good at keeping their eyes and ears open when Ollie asked them to.

While most of the club greeted him with a shout or a wave and wandered over to the pool table or the dartboard, Razio sat at the bar and waited while Ollie pulled beers for the older club members and the younger ones hustled them out on the floor. The Drifters didn't keep a tab, so to speak, but they'd leave enough to cover most of the beer and still owe Ollie a favor or two.

"I was surprised you called," Razio said. "Haven't heard from you in a while."

"It's been quiet." Ollie leaned his forearms on the bar. "The town's almost getting respectable with this resort coming in."

"And there goes another good hangout," Razio said. "Lost to the kids with money."

Ollie said, "I didn't say the Cave was getting respectable."

"Probably won't ever get respectable if you keep beating up stock-brokers."

"He was an investment banker," Ollie said with a grim smile. "And he was asking for it."

"Heard he was messing with your girl."

"Something like that."

Razio took a long pull from the longneck that Ollie had given him. "So what can I do for an old friend, Campbell?"

"There's a guy who has family here in town. Went missing a while back."

The biker sat up a bit straighter. "How long?"

"'Bout a year. Went by Joe Russell. If he was a player, he was a minor one. Maybe some drugs. Probably gambling. I'm looking for the story on him. Can you ask around?"

"When was the last time anyone seen him? Where?"

"Hotel in Barstow. Like I said, about a year ago."

"Okay." Razio took another drink. "This have anything to do with that body out in Twentynine Palms?"

Ollie paused. "Maybe."

"And he's got family here?" Razio's eyes spoke caution. He knew enough not to ask many questions about the Springs.

"No one that's gonna come after you for asking around. At least not right now. That's why I'm asking. Trying to... defuse the situation before it gets out of hand."

Let Tony Razio think there was someone more dangerous than Ollie looking out for Joe Russell's family. Razio already feared him, and if the old biker thought there was someone even more dangerous waiting...

In truth, Alex and the wolf clan *were* more dangerous, if only because of numbers and money. They had both in spades, and more than that, Alex could be vicious when his people were at risk. The wolves did not mess around. If Allie had gone to them—and Ollie hadn't ruled out bringing the McCanns in if he needed them—then blood would spill. Better for the town if they could avoid forcing Caleb to file police reports or asking the Quinns to get rid of bodies.

"I get you," Razio finally said. "I'll ask around. See what I hear. Joe Russell, eh?"

"I'll text you a picture."

"You do that. What was his poison?"

"Whiskey and cards. He was a pretty good cardplayer, but he got worse when he drank."

"He stay around here, or would he go up to Vegas?"

Ollie thought. "Vegas is a possibility, but I think he mostly hung local."

"Fair enough. We'll see what we see." Razio banged his hand on the bar. "No girls tonight?"

"Like I'd trust my servers around your boys."

Razio laughed. "Come on, man. We mostly behave."

"Only because I'm bigger and meaner than you," Ollie said with a reluctant smile.

"But isn't that the way of things?" Razio's black eyes gleamed. "Isn't that just the way of the world?"

Ollie paused, wary of Razio's smile. "Drink up," he finally said. "Tonight's my night off, and I got nicer things to look at than you and your boys."

chapter
five

"Are you sure you only need one roll of chicken wire?" Allie asked, eyeing the plans Henry Quinn had laid out on the counter at Smith's Feed. She ignored the obvious snake bites on the man's arms and mentally calculated the perimeter of the enclosure he was building.

For what? She wasn't going to ask.

"Ya know, I think you're right. Maybe one more'll do."

"Maybe two, and you'll have a little extra," she said, glancing at his hands. "Just in case."

He squinted and gave her a nod. "I see your meaning."

"Okay then. You want some help with that? Dad's out back."

"I got it," Henry said, picking up the roll and walking toward the door. "I'll bring the truck around back and pull up. Just ring me up and—"

"Henry."

"Yeah?"

She smiled. "You know Dad's gonna ask for the receipt before he loads you up."

"That was one time I forgot to pay!" He walked back to the counter. "One time."

"One time last month. It was another time six months ago."

Muttering, Henry pulled out cash and slapped it on the counter.

"Hey now," Allie said. "Don't make me the bad guy. I'm just following the rules."

The grubby, middle-aged man leaned his elbow on the counter and winked at her. "Ever tempted to not follow the rules, Miss Allie?"

She schooled her face and handed him his change. "I don't know what you mean."

Henry scowled but grabbed the clutch of bills and stuffed them in his coveralls. "See ya later."

"Bye."

Ted walked in right as the older man was walking out. "Hey, Henry."

"Hey, Dr. Ted."

"You make that appointment yet?"

He grumbled and slunk out the door.

"Good prostate health is important for everyone!" she yelled out the door.

Allie leaned her elbow on the counter, trying not to laugh. "Is that part of your job description? Embarrassing patients in public?"

"One of the perks of being the only doc in town." Ted raised an assessing eyebrow. "How you doing today, *mama?*"

"Good!" She picked up the two rolls of smaller gauge wire and put them back on the shelves. Then her smile fell as she realized why Ted might be there. "Did you hear something?"

Ted shook her head. "No. That's why I wanted to come by. I know it's been almost a week, but I wanted to let you know they've been backed up because Larry was out of the office. He got a bunch of things slammed on him when he got back. He knew I requested he handle this case as a favor, but he can't ignore the other stuff. He called me to apologize. He's thinking beginning of next week they'll know for sure."

"Okay." She pressed a hand to her stomach. Not knowing if the body they'd found was Joe was giving her an ulcer. She'd been researching grief online and trying to figure out what to tell the younger kids even as she eased into the loss with the older boys.

Was it easier to give your mind time to prepare? Was it better just to know? She didn't have the answers, so how could she give them to her kids? She'd lost her own mother when she was ten, and the pain was so dull now it was hard to remember what her own father had done right or wrong. She'd just remembered feeling lonely. Desperately lonely, despite her father's and sisters' love.

"Allie?" Ted asked, putting an arm around her shoulders.

"I'm okay. I just want to *know*."

"Larry did say that the preliminary exam at the scene showed evidence of violence. He's fairly sure the sheriff is going to open a case, so they'll probably want to come talk to you."

She nodded. Caleb had already warned her about that.

"Is there anything else Jena and I can do?" Ted asked. "Do you need us to take the kids? Need any help around the house?"

Scott Smith, Allie's dad, walked through the door to the yard. "You want to help out at the counter?"

"Dad!"

Ted smiled at Scott. "I've got a couple of hours. That enough?"

"Yup. Kevin will be here after school for his shift."

"Hey," Allie said. "You can't kick me out of work. Stop ganging up on me."

Scott said, "Yes, we can. You look like you're about to fall over. I know you haven't been sleeping. Go home. Take a nap."

"But—"

"Go," Ted said, grabbing Allie's purse from behind the counter and shoving her out the door. "Head home. You do look exhausted. The kids won't be home for another two hours. Get some sleep."

"Ted—"

"Doctor's orders!"

Allie stood at the glass door they'd locked behind her until the headache began to build at the base of her skull. Then she turned and took her keys out to head to her car.

Kick her off her own job...

Well, it wasn't like she couldn't use another couple of hours at home. Even with Kevin and Mark pitching in on laundry duty, four kids and one adult still created a pile. She could start dinner in the Crock-Pot. Maybe tackle sorting through Christopher's toy box if she had time...

OR SHE COULD DOZE OFF IN THE BACKYARD. SHE BLINKED her eyes open when she felt someone shifting her off the folding chair she'd set in the shade to rest "just for a minute" she'd told herself.

"What—?"

"Go back to sleep," a low voice said in her ear. "Just going to move you into the house. The sun was getting on your legs."

It was Ollie. She turned her face into his shoulder and breathed deep, comforted by the smell of him. It was mostly soap, maybe deodorant and a bit of sweat. No cologne. Just Ollie. She'd recognize his scent anywhere.

"Smells good," she murmured, not quite awake.

They'd stepped into the kitchen. "It does smell good. What are you making for dinner?"

"Barbecue chicken sandwiches." She turned into his neck and threw a sleepy arm over his shoulder. "Come over if you want."

"Wish I could. Have to work tonight."

It almost felt like he brushed a kiss on the top of her head. Or maybe she was imagining it. She snuggled closer, too tired to be embarrassed about nuzzling him like he was a teddy bear.

"Hmm." She laughed a little.

"What's so funny?" The smile in his voice was audible as he walked down the hall.

"Teddy bear." She heard the chuckle in the ear pressed against his chest.

"Don't I get enough shit from the guys?"

Allie said, "It's nice. I miss... arms. You've got nice arms."

Her feet bumped into the doorway.

"Shit. Sorry. I'll just put you... You redid your bedroom."

"Mm-hmm." She refused to open her eyes. Yes, she was more awake, but she was going to milk the sleepy comfort of Ollie holding her as long as possible. Was that taking advantage? She didn't care. She couldn't remember the last time she'd been held like this. Surrounded by warmth and the particularly comforting scent of a man. And not just any man. Ollie. Strong arms. Deep chest. She'd pay to take a nap in Ollie's arms every day if it was an option.

"Looks nice."

"Thanks."

He laid her down on top of her bedspread.

Bummer.

Then he stroked a hand over her hair, tucking part of the fuzzy mess behind her ear.

Oh, that was nice.

"Go back to sleep. You got an alarm set for the kids?"

"Phone."

"Where's your phone, darlin'?"

Darlin'? Oh yeah. She liked that. She arched back and stretched her legs out. Okay, her bed was way more comfortable than the old chair. Not as comfortable as Ollie. Now Ollie *on* the bed—

"Allie-girl, where's your phone?"

"Kitchen."

"I'll grab it. You probably have another half hour or so. Try to go back to sleep."

Why don't you join me, big guy?

Okay, that would be bad to say aloud. Probably. That would probably be bad.

She rolled over and buried her face in the cool pillow, grateful that the fan in her room was working again. Of course, as soon as she did that, she woke up more.

Darn it.

Well, at least it had been worth waking up to remember the cuddle from Ollie. She heard his footsteps coming down the hall, pausing at the door to her room, then entering softly.

"I woke up," she said quietly.

"Shoot." He knelt down and set her phone on the nightstand. "Was hoping you'd sleep more. You looked half-dead under that tree."

"You say the sweetest things."

He chuckled.

"You want to come over for dinner with me and the kids? There's plenty."

He paused, and Allie wondered if that was too weird. Yeah, they were getting back on track to being friendly again, but did he think that a dinner invitation was a come-on now that she was single? Did Ollie consider her single? What the hell were the rules about all this? She hadn't been single in fifteen years. Surely he wouldn't see an invitation with her and her four kids—

"I have to work tonight, but thanks."

"Anytime."

She closed her eyes again, wishing he'd just go. She was too awake to not be aware of her reaction to him.

"The bedroom looks good."

Her eyes flickered open. Ollie was playing with the ragged edge of the sage-green shabby-chic bedspread she'd bought after Joe had left and she threw out all their bedding he'd ever touched.

Practical? Not in the least. But necessary.

"Thanks."

"Very girly."

"Well, I am a girl. So there's a certain logic there."

"Don't you have underwear that matches this?"

Her eyes flew open, and she saw the edge of a teasing smile hovering beneath his mustache.

She rolled over and gave him her back. "You'd know, wouldn't you?"

The low laugh came a second before she felt him tug one of her trailing curls.

"Yeah, I would." He stood up. "I gotta go. See you tomorrow night."

"See you."

She listened to him walk down the hall and out the front door, carefully setting the lock before he left. She made sure his truck kicked up gravel before she let out her groan of frustration. Then she swung out of bed and went to sort toys.

OF ALL THE SURPRISES OVER THE PAST YEAR—

Husband leaving her.

Sixty thousand dollars of debt she didn't know about.

Drugs.

Possible homicide.

Nothing surprised her quite as much as the call she got on Thursday afternoon.

"A what?" Her mouth was catching flies. "He did *what*?"

"I know." Mr. Lewis, the assistant principal at Cambio Springs High, sounded as shocked as Allie. "The boys he was beating up... Well, *they're* not really a surprise, but Kevin's never even gotten into a pushing match with another student. I have to think it was provoked, but he's not saying a thing. He asked to call someone and then hasn't said a word since."

"He didn't call *me*." Why hadn't he called her? "What do I need to do?"

"I'm trying to find out what happened, but you know the kids are reluctant to talk about fights. I'm going to need you to come to the office."

"Mama?" Loralie was tugging on the edge of her shorts. "What's wrong?"

"It's fine, baby." She reached down and smoothed the afternoon frizz back from her daughter's face. "Everyone's okay. Kev got in trouble at school, but everyone's okay." She asked Mr. Lewis, "Everyone is okay, right?"

"Kevin has a cut lip and bruised knuckles, and the other boys both have black eyes, but everything looks superficial. The nurse already sent the other boys to the clinic with their parents. We have to be cautious about concussions, even though both of the boys were born here."

Which meant they were shifters, and unless Kevin had been taking secret ninja classes, both would be fine by dinnertime.

"I'll be there as soon as I can," she said, snapping her fingers at Loralie and pointing to her sandals. "I'll need to drop my daughter off." She started racing through options. Maybe Jena could take her. Or Miss Cathy, Jena's mom, at the diner. That would be on the way to the school...

Ten minutes later, Allie was driving down the road, her mood alternating between pissed off and worried. She dropped Loralie off, waving at Cathy as her kids' adopted grandmother cuddled her girl.

For maybe the millionth time, Allie sent up a silent prayer of thanks for all the good things she had. Yes, money was almost nonexistent. Yes, her ex was a jerk. Yes, her car was probably on its last legs.

But her kids were healthy.

Her house was paid for.

And Allie had *people*. She had the best people. She had her dad and her sisters. Jena's parents had practically adopted her. She had Alex and Ted. Jena and Caleb. Sean and Ollie.

She had *people*.

Reminding herself of that loosened the clawing fear in her heart. Because just like when her own mom had died, if the kids had really and truly lost Joe, they were still surrounded by people who loved them. A whole damn town of them.

And that was what Joe had never understood. He'd always pressured her to move away, griping about all the limitations of living in a small desert town. He didn't get it. She didn't care about the run-down medical clinic or school, the constant presence of dust on anything and everything. She didn't care because Cambio Springs wasn't about the town. It was about the people.

And she had 'em. Even if her kid was beating some of them up.

She parked in the small lot and hustled into the office building where a student assistant greeted her with a bright smile before she realized why Allie was there. Then she grew wide-eyed.

"You're Kevin's mom, right?"

"Mm-hmm."

"He's in the nurse's office, but Mr. Lewis told me to tell you he'd meet you here. You can wait with Mr. Campbell."

Allie spun to see Ollie leaning against the wall, looking as awkward as he had his freshman year when he was a foot taller than every other classmate.

"What are you doing here?"

"Kevin called me."

"He called *you*?"

He shrugged. "Yep."

Allie went and leaned next to him, tapping her fingernails against the painted cinderblock wall.

"Brings back memories, huh?"

"Please. You were the good girl."

"I know. And I was working in the office every time you, Alex, and Sean got pulled in for something or other."

"It was mostly Sean."

"You went along with it," she muttered. "Why did Kevin call you?"

"I don't know."

"Did he say why he beat up those kids?"

"They were Quinns, and no, he didn't. He called me up, told me he was in trouble, and asked me to come to the office."

Allie blinked. "And you came, just like that?"

Ollie frowned. "Well... yeah."

Allie faced the opposite wall, her heart racing. "Weren't you at work?"

"Yeah. But it's Kevin. If he calls me 'cause he's in trouble, work can wait."

Allie blinked furiously so the tears wouldn't fall.

"I'm not trying to intrude." His voice dropped. "But if he wants me to be here for some reason—"

"It's fine." She reached for his hand and squeezed, resigning herself to the fact that she was going to fall at least a little in love with Oliver Campbell no matter how much she tried to resist it. "I'm glad he called you."

"You sure?"

"Yeah." She sniffed and let his hand go when she saw the assistant principal's door open. Mr. Lewis spotted her, noted Ollie with a curious smile, but waved them both in.

"Hey," Allie said, holding out her hand to shake. Arnold Lewis was one of the bird clan—a raven in natural form—and she'd taken English from him in junior high. The Edgar Allan Poe jokes had flown, every pun intended.

"Hey, Allie." Mr. Lewis kept his voice low. "I'm as shocked as you are about this. Kevin hasn't said anything, but I can't imagine this happened out of the blue."

She nodded toward Ollie. "He called... Mr. Campbell to come to the school. Kevin may want to talk to him about it."

Mr. Lewis frowned. "The boys weren't in the bear clan."

"I know," Ollie said. "But Kevin and I are working on a car together, so... yeah."

Ollie looked like he was the one who'd landed in trouble. He crossed his arms over his chest, doing nothing to hide his discomfort at being back in high school. Allie took pity on him and set her hand on his forearm.

"Mr. Lewis, Ollie has known Kevin since he was little. It may be that there's something he didn't feel comfortable discussing with his mom. Would it be possible for Ollie to talk to Kevin while we discuss what needs to happen with the school?"

Mr. Lewis nodded, fully aware that Kevin didn't have a dad around. "Of course." He motioned Allie toward the office chairs while he pointed down the hall.

"You remember where the nurse's office is?"

"Unfortunately."

Mr. Lewis smiled. "Same place."

"Am I still going to have to duck to get in?"

"I'm afraid the height of the doors has not changed, Mr. Campbell."

"Right."

Allie watched him walk down the hallway, trying to process that her son had called Ollie before he'd called her. Kevin had called Ollie, knowing that he would come.

Yeah.

Her people were the *best*.

But there might have been one that was better than the rest.

chapter
six

Why did it all smell the same? Hadn't they updated the cleansers or anything in the sixteen years since he'd graduated?

Ollie spotted the familiar bright red door of the nurse's office at the end of the hall. He cracked it open, only to see Kevin sitting on the bench with an ice pack on his hand, staring at the opposite wall like it had stolen his allowance.

"Hey."

The boy looked up. "You came."

"Did you think I wouldn't?"

Kevin shrugged, and Ollie saw the red stain on the boy's ears. All Allie's kids looked like her to his eyes. Kevin had her smile. Mark had her laugh. Christopher had Allie's vivid blue eyes and endless optimism. And Loralie... Well, she was just the spitting image of her mama from her toes up.

"Did you keep your thumb out?"

Kevin nodded.

"You ever tell your mom that I taught you and Low how to fight when you were twelve?"

"Nope."

"You planning on telling her now?"

A smile twitched at Kevin's mouth. "No reason both of us should get in trouble."

Ollie shook his head, but he couldn't hold in the smile. "What's going on?" No one else was in the nurse's small office, so he sat on the rolling stool in front of her desk and leaned against the wall. "Quinn boys?"

"Rory and Derrick."

"What was it about?"

Kevin clammed up again.

Whatever it was, Ollie'd have a talk with Sean Quinn about it. His childhood friend was slowly resigning himself to the fact that the bunch of miscreants that constituted his family needed him to stick around if they were ever going to keep the next generation alive and out of prison. Stuff like his younger cousins instigating a fight with Kevin Smith needed to be talked over before resentment had time to settle.

"Hey," Ollie said. "You asked me to come and I came. So what's going on?" He was probably being too rough, but the kid was fifteen. Ollie didn't think he needed a cuddle.

Kevin played with the ice pack covering his knuckles. "Are you looking into the stuff about my dad?"

Ollie was silent.

Kevin looked up. "I'm not stupid."

"I know you're not. Yeah, I'm looking into it."

"Was he dealing drugs?"

Well, hell. How was he supposed to answer that? Ollie decided on blunt honesty. "I don't know," he said. "It's possible."

"Did he cheat people out of money?"

"I don't know that either." But Ollie did know more than one Quinn had lost money to Joe. "Your dad gambled, Kev, but he was pretty good at it. Some people like to talk shit, even if they lose fair and square."

Kevin nodded, then looked down at his hands. "Did he beat up my mom?"

Ollie froze. "You tell me."

Kevin was silent for a long time.

"Kev, this is really important."

"I don't think so," he finally said. "He wasn't nice to her. He'd say really mean stuff. Then an hour later, he'd say all sorts of stuff to suck up to her. Talk about how much he loved her. How they were meant for each other. Stuff like that."

"You know that's not how you talk to a woman, right?"

He nodded. "Grandpa and I talked about it years ago. Even before Dad left."

"Once you say something, you can't take it back. You can apologize. Hope they forgive you. But you've still said it. You get that?"

"Yeah."

"Were the Quinn boys talking shit about your dad?"

Kevin nodded.

"What did they say?"

"That he was dealing drugs all over the place. And he stole money from people. Cheated them at cards, stuff like that."

"And the stuff about your mom?"

"They were saying she knew about it but was too scared to say anything because he was beating her up. Which is just... You know it's bullshit, Ollie. My mom would have told someone if he was doing all that stuff."

"I know."

"She stood up to him, you know? He said something bad to Mark one time when he was drunk. And Mom dragged him out of the room and tore into him. He never did it again. She'd never let him."

If he wasn't fairly sure Joe Russell was already dead, Ollie would have had a hard time not going hunting. But Kevin didn't need to hear about that. The poor kid was already too grown-up for his age.

"Your mom," Ollie said, "is one of the strongest women I know, and she loves you guys more than her own life. She'd never let anyone touch you or hurt you. She also cares too much about this town and the people here to let any of that go without telling someone. She might let your dad hurt himself, but she wouldn't let him hurt other people. So yeah, those guys were full of shit, and I'm gonna be talking to Sean and Old Quinn about them."

Kevin opened his mouth to object, but Ollie just held up a hand.

"Don't argue. This isn't you being a rat. If those boys have any real information—or more likely it's something they overheard one of the adults saying—I need to know."

"Are you going to tell my mom?"

"Do you want her to know?"

"No."

"You sure?" Ollie raised an eyebrow. "It sure sounds like they were trying to start a fight."

Kevin shrugged.

"Who threw the first punch?"

"Me."

He sighed. "Should have walked away, Kev."

"I know."

"You're gonna get in trouble. Rory and Derrick are gonna get in trouble too. Pretty sure that's how it works."

"I know."

"I better not hear you bitching about it."

His cheeks reddened with anger. "I won't."

"And we're not working on your car this Saturday. You're gonna clean the shop."

Kevin slouched against the wall and dropped his head.

"You regret calling me now?" Ollie asked.

The boy looked up, and Ollie could see the tears in the corner of his eyes, but the proud fifteen-year-old didn't let them fall.

"No."

Ollie leaned forward, putting his elbows on his knees. "You're a good kid, Kevin Smith. I'm glad you called me."

"Yeah," Kevin said. "Me too."

"I'm his mother," Allie hissed when she dropped Kevin off at his barn Saturday morning. "I need to know what happened."

"Why?"

She put her hand on her hips, and he knew she wanted to look intimidating, but she mostly looked cute as hell.

"Because—"

"You know what?" Ollie held up a hand. "I get it. I'm not his father, but he confided in me. If one of Jena's boys came to you and confided something that *wasn't* going to affect their safety, would you say anything?"

She tapped her foot, but he knew she'd do exactly the same thing he was. Ollie might not have any kids of his own, but his friends' kids were his responsibility, just like the younger members of his clan. He didn't take it lightly, and he knew Allie didn't either.

"Fine," she finally said. "But the school is going to suspend him. One day and a citation in his permanent record."

Oooh, a citation. Scary.

"He won't complain. And he's not working on his car today," Ollie said. "He's only cleaning the shop."

Her shoulders drooped. "You don't have to do that. He's been looking forward to this all week."

"He needs to learn how to keep his temper." Ollie shrugged. "He'll forget a citation. He won't forget missing out on the first day working on his new car."

"Don't be a hard-ass," she said quietly. "He's a good kid."

The corner of his mouth kicked up. "Me? You said it yourself. I'm a teddy bear."

Her cheeks turned a bright pink. "I was asleep."

"You were *sleepy*," he said. "Not asleep." And she'd also said he had nice arms. He crossed his arms over his chest, making sure to flex his biceps.

Juvenile? Possibly.

But she looked.

Ollie tried not to grin as Allie backed out of the garage. Kevin was already in there, putting on a pair of coveralls Ollie had found for him and banging around with the wide broom he'd use to sweep the floor.

"Okay, I'm just gonna... go." Her cheeks were still pink.

He went to the doorway and stretched his arms up, bracing his arms on the door and watching her walk away.

"Bye." His eyes dropped to her legs, which still carried a little tan from the summer. Allie turned and tripped a little when she saw where he was looking. "Um... you're gonna drop him off when you guys are done, right?"

"Yeah. What time?"

She fiddled with the ragged hem of her shorts.

Go ahead. They could be shorter.

"Five? Is that too early? I usually give them dinner early on nights I'm working so we can eat together. If I'm going in at six—"

"I'll drop him off at four thirty. Give him time to clean up before supper."

"Thanks." She licked her lips, bringing his eyes right to her mouth. "Did you want— I mean, if you're gonna be working with him all day, you're welcome to join us for dinner so you don't have to cook."

He leaned forward in the doorway and saw her eyes go right to his arms again.

Yeah, he was gonna be using that to his advantage regularly.

"That sounds good," he said. "I'll drop him off. We can eat and I'll drive you to work."

"Oh." She stopped walking again. "You don't have to do that."

"We're driving from the same place, Allie. Seems a little foolish to take two cars."

"Right." She nodded. "Okay, sure."

"Great." He banged the side of the barn. "I'll see you at four thirty then. Better get to work."

He watched her until she drove away, giving him a cute little wave while she crawled out of the driveway, trying not to kick up dust. Ollie picked up a wrench and turned to see Kevin frowning at him.

"What?"

"Were you hitting on my mom?"

How did he answer that question?

Ollie turned toward the old pickup, determined to get some work done on it if he wasn't working on the Charger.

"Your mom and I are friends, Kev." This was true. He also had intentions that Kevin didn't need to think about, but he would always be Allie's friend.

"Yeah, she's friends with Sean and Alex and Caleb too."

"Exactly."

"But she doesn't blush like that around any of them."

Ollie frowned. "Kevin..."

"I'm just saying." Kevin turned and started pulling dust from the corner with the wide broom. "If she didn't have four kids, you'd probably ask her out."

"Hey!" Ollie tried to control the spike of temper. "Turn around if you're gonna say something like that. And don't mutter."

Kevin turned around, his mouth tight. "She's still really pretty, even with four kids. And she's nice."

"Your mom's way more than pretty. She's beautiful."

"But she's just your friend."

Ollie tossed the rag he'd picked up onto the rolling tray. "One, there's nothing *just* about being a friend. I've been your mom's friend since she was younger than you. That's not something I take lightly."

Kevin looked off to the corner. "I've seen the way you look at her."

"And two—since I wasn't finished—her life is a little complicated right now. She's got a lot on her plate."

"Yeah, she does," Kevin said. "She works, like, twice as hard as everyone else's mom I know. But you know, you being around and maybe taking her out every now and then so she's not working all the time, that's probably too *complicated*, right?"

What the hell?

Ollie's anger must have shown on his face, because Kevin looked embarrassed. "I'm just saying I think she likes you, and I'm pretty sure—"

"Your mom's and my relationship is not your business, Kevin."

"So you and my mom have a relationship?"

Ollie crossed his arms and glared at the teenager. "Do you think this floor is gonna sweep itself?"

Kevin started sweeping, but he still had a scowl. "If you like a girl, you should ask her out. Then you both know what's up. If you just mess around with her, that's like playing a game and that's not cool."

"Who told you that?"

"Dude... seriously? *You* did. Last year when I was waiting around to ask Kristy Mackenzie to the homecoming dance."

Shit. He did remember saying that.

"Get back to work."

Kevin picked up the dustpan and started collecting the pile he'd gathered. "Uncle Alex says you haven't gone out with anyone since my Mom and Dad split up."

"Kid, do you want me to teach you how to fix your car in this century or do you want to keep pissing me off?"

"Bear pile!"

Christopher and Loralie leapt on him from over the back of the couch as Ollie and Kevin were playing a football game on the Xbox. The two kids tumbled over his shoulders, Chris falling between Kevin and Ollie while Loralie snuggled under his right arm and made herself at home.

"Dude!" Mark yelled. "Stop it. You're messing up the game."

"You're not even playing, Marky. You're just watching," Christopher, who was seven and completely uninterested in video games, complained.

Kevin reached over and smacked Christopher on the back of the head. "Stop calling him Marky. I told you."

"Oh my gosh," Mark hissed out. "Just stop. You're so annoying."

"Well, you're stupid," Chris said.

"And you're a fart-face."

"Mo-om! Marky said I'm a fart—mmfph."

Kevin slapped one hand over Chris's mouth, still attempting to play with the other. "Dude, be quiet. We only have ten minutes before Ollie and Mom have to go to work."

Loralie giggled and covered her mouth when Ollie looked down at her.

"Fart-face," she lisped through two missing front teeth.

"Don't say fart-face," Ollie said, making her giggle again.

Chris broke into more giggles behind Kevin's hand, his little body shaking.

"But you just said it!"

Even Mark couldn't keep from smiling. "Dude," he said. "Just be cool or we won't be able to play."

"Yeah, Ollie," Kevin said, letting his younger brother go. "You should be a good example. Don't say fart-face."

Which sent Mark, Chris, and Loralie back into fits of giggles. Even Ollie couldn't keep from smiling.

Especially when Allie came in from the kitchen, leaned over the back of the couch, and said in a loud whisper, "Ollie, did one of my kids say fart-face again?"

He busted up laughing, as much at the uncontrollable giggles surrounding him as the serious look on her face.

Mark said, "Dude, just stop saying it. I can't stop laughing."

Chris gasped. "I can't either, dude."

"They can have whole conversations in 'dude,'" Allie said, still leaning over his shoulder.

Ollie was tempted to call "bear pile" and tug her onto his lap.

"Fluency in 'dude'"—he turned his head so their lips were only inches away from each other—"is a gift of all seven- and ten-year-old boys."

He saw her eyes flicker down to his mouth, and he wanted more than anything to have the right—the simple right—to lean over and kiss her. Tuck her hair behind her ear and whisper something silly to make her laugh. Her eyes never left his mouth, even when the kids started jabbering again.

Kevin said, "Just don't say fart-face, whatever you do."

Allie busted up laughing. She might have even snorted.

Ollie couldn't remember when he'd had a better time. He hated—absolutely hated—that he had to leave for work. He looked at Allie, who nodded and headed toward her room, probably to change.

Ollie stood, holding on to Loralie when she clung to his neck. "We gotta go, guys."

"Nooooo!" Chris wailed dramatically, clutching Ollie's leg.

"Do you work all the nights, Ollie?" Loralie asked.

"Yeah," Mark said, glancing at Ollie from the corner of his eye when Kevin tossed him the spare controller. "You should come back on a night you're not working and hang out. We could play Xbox again."

Ollie tried not to react as his heart lurched in his chest. "That's up to your mom."

Allie ran back in the living room, slipping on her shoes by the door. "Okay, guys. Not too late. Kev, you know where the ice cream is."

"Ice cream!" Chris screamed.

Mark covered his ears. "Dude!"

Loralie ran a tiny hand down Ollie's beard. "Your hair is curly like mine."

"But not as pretty." He blew a raspberry on her cheek and handed her over to Allie, who kissed her and handed her over to Kevin who was already nodding as Allie gave him instructions about the younger kids.

Amazingly, they were in the car with five minutes to spare.

Ollie looked over his shoulder at the glowing lights of the house. "How do you *do* that?"

Allie was texting on her phone. "Do what?"

"Juggle the madness."

"Well," she said, "the madness doesn't come all at once. It slowly builds until you don't remember when there *wasn't* madness."

"Like the story about boiling a frog?"

"Exactly. How to boil a fox: add one child every three years until her brain is entirely gone."

Ollie chuckled and pulled out of the drive. "Dinner was fun."

"The kids enjoyed having you over."

"Just the kids?" He glanced sideways at her.

She was smiling a little. "I did too."

"Good."

She leaned back and closed her eyes. Ollie watched her in the oncoming lights as he headed toward the bar. He wanted to bypass work and take her to his place. Roll her onto his king-sized bed and let her sleep.

For a while.

"Maybe another time."

"What?"

He didn't realize he'd spoken aloud. "Uh, maybe I can come over another time when I don't have to work. Play video games with the boys again."

"They'd love that."

"Also what are you doing after church tomorrow?"

"Nothing much, I don't think." She was texting on her phone again.

"Everything all right?" he asked.

"Yeah, just letting my dad know that the kids are with Kevin and I'm at work. He'll go by later."

"Tell him he might see Elijah and Paul around too."

Allie frowned. "Your younger cousins?"

Ollie nodded. "Pop put them on alternating nights hanging around your place until we figure out what's going on with Joe."

"You don't have to do that, Ollie. Those boys are just in high school."

"Do you remember how big I was at their age?"

"Not much smaller than now," she muttered. "Still, I don't think—"

"Pop isn't going to argue with you on this one. He's worried about you and the kids, so his boys are going to be there. They're both smart, and they're not impulsive. Plus they know I'm only a few miles away. I only told you so you don't worry if you see them hanging around."

"What about church tomorrow? Why were you asking?"

They were just pulling into the Cave. Ollie parked in his spot by the back door, happy to see the lot already filling.

"We need to go up and talk to Old Quinn. If we catch him Sunday afternoon, Sean will be there too."

"About the boys Kevin fought with?"

How much to tell her without spilling the information Kevin asked him to keep private?

"About that. But also because I think some of the snakes might know something about Joe."

Allie sighed. "Why is this not surprising?"

"We need to ask. Old Quinn doesn't like me much—"

"You have filed charges against more than one of his nephews."

"Only when they break furniture or faces at my bar. But if I bring you, he'll talk."

Allie grinned. "Because he loves me."

"Everybody loves you, Allie-girl."

Her smile fell, but she rallied as she opened her door. "Not everyone. I better get in, or Tracey's gonna put me on lunch shift again."

Ollie nodded. "I'll be right in. Gonna... call Sean about tomorrow."

Man, he could be stupid sometimes.

"Everybody loves you..."

Clearly not. The person who was supposed to love her the most had up and left.

Nice reminder, asshole.

Ollie didn't know what the hell he was doing. He had teenage kids telling him off and hormones jumping like he was still in high school.

He wanted Allie. And her kids. The whole damn package. But he didn't know how to tell her, and he didn't really know whether she was flirting with him to flex newly single muscles or whether it meant something more.

"Stop thinking." He finally pushed open the door. "The drinks won't pour themselves."

chapter
seven

An hour after church, Allie had gotten her four kids situated at Cathy and Thomas Crowe's house, where Jena, Caleb, and their brood were also hanging out. Ollie had picked her up there and was driving them up into the canyon and over to the old Quinn place where Sean had been staying.

"You talked to Sean last night, right?" she asked.

"Yeah, he said he needed to work today, so he'd be around."

Sean was a freelance photographer who had roamed the world until only last year. He'd also been one of the last of her friends to see her ex-husband.

"What's he working on?"

Ollie frowned. "I don't know. Editing, he said? I think he's helping a friend out, doing the digital editing for a shoot while she's out on location."

"She, huh?" Allie grinned. "So is this a friend, or a *girl*friend?"

Ollie kept his eyes on the road. "You think me and Sean sit around painting our nails or something?"

"Of course not," she said. "I thought you two were getting together for beard-care spa days or something."

"Please," Ollie grumbled. "Sean only wishes he could grow a beard like me."

Allie laughed. Sean and Alex had both been growing their beards out and had taken more than a little teasing from their friends about competing with Ollie for the mountain man look.

She turned toward him, watching his profile. "Your beard is a thing of manly magnificence, Oliver Campbell."

The corner of his mouth twitched up. "Don't be jealous just because you can't grow one."

"But I am. So jealous."

"I can tell. If you make me brownies, I might tell you my conditioning secrets."

"Motor oil and hamburger grease?"

"Damn it," he said. "Who told you?"

"I'll never tell."

He chuckled, and Allie realized she'd heard him laugh more in the past few days with her and her kids than she had in the past year.

The road to the Quinn place took a sharp left after Sandy Wash, then they were crawling up an even steeper hill with rocks dotting the road, so she had to keep her eyes straight ahead or get really carsick as Ollie swerved to avoid them.

Ollie had always been a quiet man, but the past couple of years, he'd been heading almost into antisocial territory. He was discreet about his dating life, worked a lot, and kept busy taking care of his extended family. Though he was an only child, he had first and second cousins who were all close. The bear clan wasn't big—not anywhere near the size of the Quinn or McCann clans—but it tended to stick closer to home. Anyone who didn't live in the Springs lived in Palm Desert, Indio, Barstow, or Vegas at the outside.

"How's your family?"

He glanced over. "My dad and Ashley?"

"Mm-hmm." She didn't know what had happened to Ollie's mom, other than that she'd left the Springs when Ollie was young, but Nathan Campbell had met his new wife when Ollie was a teenager.

"They're fine," he said. "Roaming around in Canada right now. They'll point the bikes south now that the temperature's dropping up there."

She glanced at her phone. "One hundred and one today. It could be winter anytime now."

"I'm with you."

Yeah, I wish you were.

She sighed and tried to get her mind off it. Ollie had been flirting with her a little, but it could mean anything. He could be trying to mend the gap that had grown between them. He might just think she needed an ego boost. Sean flirted with her, but Sean flirted with everyone.

"Hey," he said. "Where'd you go?"

Nowhere. I'm going nowhere.

"Just wondering what you think the Quinns might know. And wondering when we'll know for sure. I know that's part of the reason Kevin snapped on Friday. He and Mark are both on edge, waiting to hear about their dad. I probably shouldn't have told them."

"And if they'd found out later, they'd have been angry. Your kids are smart, Allie. Give them as much honesty as they can handle."

"Yeah, I guess."

He reached over and took her hand. "You're doing great."

"There's no manual for this," she said. "I lost my own mom when I was Mark's age, and I still don't know what to tell them if Joe's really dead. It's not the same. My mom loved us and died in a car accident."

"Loss is loss, no matter what. They're already dealing with some of it with him being gone. You've done the best you could with that. Trust me, I know how hard it is when a parent leaves."

Allie bit the edge of her lip and Ollie squeezed her hand.

"What?"

"I will never in a million years understand your mother, Ollie. Never. How she could leave her own child—"

"How could Joe? How could a father leave four kids? It doesn't make sense either way."

"If she ever came back to town, I'd hit her." Allie grimaced. "Maybe Kevin got the violent tendencies from me."

He smiled. "Don't fool yourself, we all have them. And you don't have to worry about my mom coming back. She's well and gone."

"Did you wonder?"

He nodded.

"How long?"

"Years. But I always had my dad, Pop, and Yaya. And I always knew they loved me. Then my dad met Ashley, and I saw how happy he was.

Saw how devoted she was to him. *And* me. She's not my mom, but she's family. Ashley put things in perspective."

"How?"

"Made me realize how insignificant my mother really was in my life. How she was the one missing out, not me. Ash wasn't even my mom, and she liked hanging out with me. Liked going to my football games and making cookies and doing all that 'mom stuff.' So I couldn't be all that bad, you know?"

She said nothing. Ollie was still holding her hand, and she didn't pull it away. It was too nice to let it lie there, being all big and warm and comforting. If he wasn't pulling away, she wasn't either.

The car bounced over a particularly rough patch, and she gripped his hand tighter.

"My kids will be okay," she finally said. "Whatever happens will hurt, but they'll be okay."

"Yeah, they will."

She dashed the tears from the corner of her eyes and asked, "So, the Quinns and Joe, huh? Not all that surprising, I guess. What have you heard from your biker friends?"

"Nothing yet." He glanced over. "They don't really keep what you'd consider regular hours. It might be weeks before I hear anything at all."

"Weeks?"

He shrugged. "If I don't hear anything by next week, I'll give Tony a call. Maybe remind him how many free beers his boys have drunk."

Allie felt the color drain from her face. "Ollie, I didn't even think about this costing money. I don't want to cost you money—that's not fair."

"It's not money, it's favors. Don't worry about it."

"But—"

"Pop would have asked me to look into it anyway, darlin'. Don't worry about it."

"What do you think the Quinns know?"

He cleared his throat. "You know Joe liked to gamble?"

"I have the bills to prove it."

"He didn't just like casinos. He was actually a hell of a poker player. Did you ever play with him?"

She shook her head. "Never gamble with a coyote."

Ollie laughed. "That's the truth. I did, and I lost. He was really good. He only got sloppy when he drank too much."

She leaned her head against the window. "And he was almost a full-blown alcoholic by the time he left."

Another hand squeeze. "Yeah. But the Quinns didn't care about that. I know for a fact more than one of them won money off of Joe, but even more lost it."

Her eyes went wide. "You don't think they had anything to do with his death, do you?"

"No."

"Are you sure?"

"I can't be positive until I talk to Old Quinn. But very few of them are violent. It's more... petty shit. Cons. Stuff like that. But even more..."

"What?"

"Let's face it, Allie. If the Quinns killed someone, the body would *never* be found."

ALLIE SAW SEAN QUINN STANDING IN THE FRONT YARD, tossing a baseball back and forth with a boy around Chris's age when they pulled up. Sean had the lean, whipcord-strong build typical of most of the snake clan, along with the dark Irish coloring that made him stand out like a black slash in the red rocks around his great-uncle's house. His natural form was a diamondback rattler, but Sean was one of the most versatile shifters Allie had ever known. From the time he was thirteen, he'd honed his abilities to an astonishing degree and was able to shift into more reptile forms than anyone Allie knew.

Old Quinn hadn't laid gravel in over twenty years, so they kicked up dust as soon as they pulled in. Sean and the boy turned their heads, squinting into the sun as they waited to see who had arrived.

"You gotta get the old man to lay new gravel," Ollie said.

The boy grinned up at Sean. "Told you, Uncle Sean."

"Get outta here." He batted at the brim of the boy's hat. "And make sure all your homework gets done before you open *Harry Potter*."

"Yessir."

They watched the skinny boy scramble over the rocks beside Old Quinn's house and up to the road that ran along the top of the ridge where many of the poorer Quinn families made their homes.

"Told you what?" Ollie asked.

"That's Aiden." Sean tapped his temple. "Let's just say he's... perceptive."

Allie's eyebrows rose. "Like Bear?"

Jena's youngest boy, Aaron, was called Bear, even though everyone suspected he'd shift toward his father's clan, which had been wolf. The boy also had an uncanny way of perceiving things that he shouldn't have known.

"Maybe a little," Sean said. "He said we'd have visitors today and one of them would be a bear." He winked at Allie. "And the other one would be a fox."

Allie smiled and took the arm Sean held out. "You're making that up."

"Only a little. He mentioned the bear. And I'm taking note of the fox." He nudged her shoulder with his. "You look gorgeous today."

"That's 'cause I got dressed up for church, you heathen. You should try it sometime."

"Quinns get struck by lightning if they enter that chapel anytime Father Heney isn't in residence," he said. "Everyone knows that."

"Lying's a sin, Sean Quinn."

"Good thing I'm not lying about how pretty you are." He looked over his shoulder. "Hey, Ollie."

"Oh, am I here?" the man growled.

"Yeah, but you're not as cute as Allie." He grinned at her. "Where're the kids, gorgeous? You finally leave them with their grandpa so we could run away together?"

"Sure. Right after we question your uncle about what my cheating, lying ex-husband was up to and why my son started beating up your cousins over it at school."

Allie heard Ollie stop behind them, and she turned her head. "What? Did you think I wouldn't figure it out after you decided we needed to come up here? I know my son, and I know what sets him off. Those boys were talking about his dad, right?"

Ollie pursed his lips together. "I can't say."

"I can," Sean said. "I already talked to them. Uncle Joe had them cleaning out their grandmother's attic yesterday. Hot. As. Hell. They won't say another word to any of your boys."

Allie hugged his arm. "Thanks, Sean."

"Now, let's go get some sweet tea and talk to the old man."

OLLIE HAD BEEN RIGHT. IF ALLIE HADN'T BEEN WITH THEM, Old Quinn probably wouldn't have let them through the door. There was a natural animosity between the bears, the largest and most protective of the shifters, and the Quinns, the smallest in shifted form and also the most frequent troublemakers. The fact that Ollie and Sean had remained friends through high school was considered something of a miracle. And a scandal.

"Okay," Old Quinn settled into his seat with a mason jar of sweet tea in his hand. "What do you want?"

Ollie said, "Be polite, old man."

"Why am I interested in doing your work for you?"

"Please." Allie leaned forward. "Uncle Joe, if you know anything about what my ex was doing, I really need to know."

Old Quinn looked kindly at her. "You're better off without him. You can start over. Bright young thing like you—"

"He's my kids' dad," she said. "We need to know what happened."

The old man scratched his chin, thinking. "It's not good, Allie."

"You think you're gonna surprise me at this point?"

He frowned. "Probably."

Allie sat back in her seat, knowing that yeah, there was probably stuff she didn't want to know about her ex-husband, especially if it involved what he'd gotten up to after he left her, but that didn't mean she didn't need to know.

"You think I'm gonna break down or something?"

Old Quinn leaned forward, elbows on his knees. "You? No, you wouldn't break down. Still hate being the one to put that burden on you. There are some things a woman doesn't want to know about her man, even if he isn't her man anymore."

She glanced over at Ollie. "Would you tell Ollie?"

Old Quinn sneered.

"Please?"

Old Quinn tapped his foot. "You should let things lie, Campbell."

Ollie said, "I know you don't like me, but Allie came to us for protection. You know that means we're looking out for her and her family. If you know anything that might help us keep those kids safe—"

"Fine," Old Quinn said. "I'll talk to the bear."

Allie smiled. "You can talk to us both."

"Nope." Old Quinn shook his head.

"Seriously?"

"Sean, take Miss Allie out on the front porch. Keep her company while Campbell and I talk."

Allie narrowed her eyes. "You're an old sexist, Joe Quinn."

"Never claimed different. I'm as scared of an angry woman as any old man, but there are things you don't need to know, and I'm not gonna tell Campbell if you're here. You want the information or not?"

Allie considered whether she wanted to leave the two men alone with each of them glaring at the other, but Sean took her hand and lifted her from the couch.

"Come on. Let's go look at the fascinating rocks."

She frowned at him.

"Hey, they're kicking me out too." Sean winked at her and she let him help her up.

"Fine."

Allie cast one last look at Ollie as she headed out the door, but his eyes were glued to the arm Sean had wrapped around her waist.

The two men couldn't be more different. Sean was as charming and flirtatious as he was talkative. He'd left the Springs when he was just eighteen and hadn't been back more than a few times. Ollie was quiet and steady, his presence and reputation in Cambio Springs as solid as the rocks that surrounded them.

Sean led her onto the porch and then off it, wandering a little distance to a picnic table under a clutch of cottonwood trees. He sat down and pulled her to his side, leaning against her shoulder with his own.

"How you doing with all this?" he asked her. "I haven't talked to you in a while."

"Okay, I guess. I'm... numb. I feel like it's him. I don't know why, it might not be, but—"

"I feel the same way. And... it fits."

"What do you mean?"

"Whoever it was died about ten months ago, is that right?"

"That's what Ted thought."

"I talked to her and Alex about it."

"And?"

Sean sighed and Allie leaned her head on his shoulder, at ease with him in a way she'd never been with Ollie.

Sean wasn't like a brother—he'd always been too much of a flirt for that—but his affectionate, teasing nature made Allie comfortable. He was sweet with all his female friends, though she knew he was probably a terrible boyfriend.

"You and Joe...," he started. "It's hard. Because I got Joe, in a way. He never really wanted to be here, but unlike me, he wasn't willing to work to get out. He did love you, Allie. He just wasn't capable of being the man you deserved."

She bit her lip to keep her temper. "He hated me at the end, Sean."

"I know he wasn't a good guy. He was a jackass to you and the kids. I'm just trying to tell you that once, he did love you. And I know he loved the kids, even though he was a shit dad. In his own way, he loved them."

"What does that have to do with the body?"

He put his arm around her and said quietly, "Because I don't think Joe would have left them for this long if he could have come back."

Allie closed her eyes because it was the truth that had been lurking in the back of her mind that she didn't want to admit.

Yes, her ex was a bastard. Yes, he was a crap husband.

But he did love his kids.

She blinked back tears and felt Sean's arm squeeze her shoulders.

"You know that, right?" he asked.

"Yeah."

"I think he knew you guys were through. But he'd have come back to see the kids if he could have."

She nodded and saw Ollie coming through the front door, eyes searching for her. He spotted them under the cottonwood trees and marched over.

"Why's she upset, Sean?"

Sean's back went straight. "We're talking."

"Yeah? That doesn't answer my question."

Allie wiped back tears. "Ollie, stop."

"You're laughing and teasing her all the time, but the minute you get her alone, she's crying. So what the hell is going on?"

Sean shook his head. "You really are boneheaded, aren't you?"

Ollie planted one hand on the table and leaned over. "You and your stinking family—"

"Watch it, bear." Sean's lip curled up, and she saw the edge of a fang.

"Did you know and not tell me? Did your own pathetic need to be the hero—?"

"Hey!" Allie stood up. "What is wrong with you?"

Ollie glared at her. "He's what's wrong. Him and his entire back-stabbing clan."

"You don't know what you're talking about," Sean said. "Why don't you use your brain instead of your brawn for once in your life? Or are you jealous I can put a smile on her face when you can't?"

"Both of you, stop!"

Sean stood up and pulled his keys from his pocket. "Come on, Allie. I'll take you home."

"I'm taking her home," Ollie said.

"Neither one of you is taking me home." She grabbed Sean's keys and marched toward the pickup truck she knew he'd been driving around town.

"Allie," Sean called. "Stop!"

She heard scuffling behind her, but she didn't stop walking.

"Ollie," she yelled, "you can give Sean a ride to pick up his truck and sort things out. Stop being jerks, both of you. You're friends."

Old Quinn was leaning on one of the porch rails, watching her with a smirk on his face. "Give 'em hell, girl."

"You"—she pointed an accusing finger at him—"are probably the one that started this somehow, Joe Quinn. I hope you're proud of yourself."

"I usually am."

"If either of them comes back to town with broken bones or poison in his system, I'm gonna be pissed."

He shrugged. "Just start driving. I have a feeling that bear ain't gonna wait long to chase you."

"Troublemaker."

Old Quinn winked at her. "And that would be the pot calling the kettle black, sweetheart."

chapter
eight

"You are a moron," Sean said.

"Shut up."

"Seriously, why is it taking you so long?"

Ollie slammed his hand down on the steering wheel, gritting his teeth when he heard the crack.

"Oh, *that* was smart," Sean said.

"Why are you in my truck?"

"Because your girlfriend stole mine." Sean frowned. "That seems wrong somehow. I usually get at least a kiss before they steal my car."

Ollie shook his head. "You're a… putz."

"A putz?" Sean laughed. "Did your grandpa teach you that word, old sport?"

"Yeah, he did. And it fits."

"I'm a putz? Why the hell aren't you and Allie starting your happily-ever-after yet, huh? I don't think I'm the one who's a putz here."

"She's still grieving over her husband, Sean. Her kids are wrecked, and it's only going to get worse when they find out that body is Joe."

"She's not hung up on *Joe*. She's grieving the father of her children. She's in pain for *them*. But yeah, I'm sure having you around—*you*, who loves her kids and adores her—that would be such a bad thing, right? I mean, that would make life so much worse to know that they had a good guy who loved them backing them up while they go through all this shit. That would be awful."

"Yeah, so maybe I can help. And then maybe she makes it through this crisis and discovers she's not ready for a relationship, or that she doesn't want one with me. What do I do then, Sean?"

"So this isn't about her. This is about you being a chickenshit."

Ollie pulled over to grab Sean by the neck, only to find the man had disappeared into the floorboard. Ollie heard the whisper of a rattle somewhere in the truck, but couldn't see his old friend anywhere. The sudden chill of a brush against his ankle brought him back to sanity.

He took a deep breath. "I hate it when you do that."

Ollie reached over and shoved open the Bronco door, tossing Sean's empty clothes out the door.

"Shift and get back in the car. I'm not driving into town with your naked ass next to me."

Another, stronger rattle and Ollie took the keys out of the ignition.

"Fine. I won't leave you on the side of the road."

There was a flash at his shoulder, and when Ollie turned his head, he was greeted with the flare of a frilled lizard cape flashing in his face while Sean hissed, inches from his face.

"Dammit!" He brought his elbow up to smack it, but it had already darted away. "I hate that one, Sean."

A ripple of air outside his truck, and Sean's pale arm grabbed for his jeans.

"Hey, I could have scared you as a horned lizard."

"What does that one do?"

"Spits blood out of its eye."

Ollie grimaced as Sean hopped back in the truck.

"You do the weirdest shit."

"Because hibernation isn't odd."

"I don't hibernate."

"But you could."

Ollie shook his head and started the Bronco back up.

They rode in silence until Sean started talking again. "You think she's still in love with Joe?"

"I don't know."

"She hasn't loved him for years. You ought to know that by now."

"The timing still sucks."

"Yeah, it does. But the timing is never going to be perfect.

She's got four kids, two sisters, one father, two jobs. Her life is crazy. But being with you could help with that. She loves you, Ollie."

"As a friend."

"So show her it's more! She can't keep her eyes off you. Anytime you're nearby, she watches you. Attraction is not the problem."

"I don't want to talk about this with you."

"And I don't even want to think about how wound up that girl is. She's a fox and she's been alone for how long? She's got to be frustrated out of her mind."

"Don't make me kill you. You know I can."

"Hey." Sean grinned. "This is only good news for you, my friend. Everyone knows vixens are freaks."

"Shut. Up."

"Just saying, when this has been settled, you will be the envy of us all."

"She is a *mother of four*, you asshole."

Sean burst into laughter. "Yeah. You ever wonder why?"

No, he didn't need to. A long clothesline of lace panties spoke for itself.

A headache started building behind his eyes. "Seriously, we need to change the subject."

Sean fell silent just as Ollie turned onto the main road and headed toward Allie's house.

Ollie asked, "Did you know? About the shit your uncle told me?"

"I knew about the poker game in Palm Springs. Maggie told me one of her brothers set it up for him, but it sounds like she's the one who really did. I'm the one who told my uncle."

"Why the hell would your sister vouch for a gambling addict in a high-stakes game, Sean? Why would she even—"

"Joe owed her money, okay?" Sean raked a hand through his hair. "Listen, I'm not saying I approve. I don't. But Joe came to Maggie and asked for the introduction. The man knew his cards. She and a couple other people staked him for it and expected Joe to be able to walk away with at least enough to pay them back."

"And then he disappeared."

"Maggie's a bitch, but she wouldn't set him up if she thought it was someone violent. Joe was one of us. She wouldn't have done it. If nothing else, the old man would have killed her."

Ollie ground his teeth. "I'm going to talk to Alex."

Sean winced. "Oh, you hate me. You know he's going to blame me."

"I have to. He's the only one who's ever run in that crowd. He'll know who we can talk to. We need to find out who was at that game."

"You think they had something to do with it?"

"According to your uncle, the game was set up for a night almost exactly ten months ago, the same age as the body. You telling me you think that's a coincidence?"

Sean sighed. "No."

"Yeah, I don't either." He turned right, toward the house, only to see Caleb's police truck turn in behind him. "What the...?"

He cleared the line of willow trees that bordered the road to see Sean's truck sitting in front of Allie's house next to Ted's Jeep.

Ted's Jeep at Allie's house. Caleb's truck behind them.

"Shit," Sean whispered.

No.

Ollie parked and jumped out of the Bronco, running toward Allie, who had her arms wrapped around herself. Her face was leached of color.

No no no no.

"Allie?"

Hollow eyes turned toward him, and he opened his arms, grabbing her and lifting her up as her arms went around his neck, holding so tight she threatened to choke him.

"Ted's friend decided to work the weekend," she whispered. "Trying to catch up. He called her..."

Ollie turned toward Ted, whose eyes were red. Alex stood with a hand at the small of her back as Caleb and Sean came walking toward them.

"It's him," Ted said. "Larry said the dental work was conclusive. He called as soon as he knew."

Ollie turned his head, pressing his cheek to Allie's temple, his hand against the back of her head, holding her to him.

"Okay." He took a deep breath. "It'll be okay. What do you want us to do?"

She was shaking. Ollie took her to the porch steps and sat down, holding her on his lap, her arms still around his neck.

"Allie-girl, what do you need?"

"I can't think," she said. "I can't…"

"Do you want the kids here? Do you want us to take you over to Cathy and Tom's?"

"Ollie—" His name was a choked cry when she broke.

He held her, stroking a hand over her hair, their earlier anger forgotten. He didn't know what he whispered to her as she cried, but he felt Ted when she came to sit beside them and put her arm around Allie's waist. He heard Alex sit beside his wife. Heard Sean pacing back and forth as Caleb murmured quietly on his phone.

The wind had picked up by the time her crying stopped. Allie lifted her head and wiped the tears from her cheeks, leaving one arm on Ollie's shoulder as she blinked.

"Ted," she said in a hoarse voice, "can you call Jena? Have her call my dad and get them to bring the kids home. My car is at the Crowe's house."

"Okay, *mama*."

"In fact, see if Tom and Cathy can come over too." She sniffed. "And I need you guys to stay."

"Anything you need," Alex said. "The kids—"

"Caleb?"

The lean man knelt next to Allie, worry creasing his tan face. "What's up?"

"Can you bring Low and Bear too?"

Ollie frowned. "You sure you want so many people here when you tell them?"

"I need…" Her breath hitched. "I want everyone *here*. Everyone close. They need to know they're not alone. I want them surrounded. Want everyone… everyone who loves them—"

"You got it." Caleb's eyes filled with tears. "We'll take care of it, Allie. We'll get everyone here."

She nodded and Ollie drew her to his chest again, wrapping both arms tight around her. He could feel her heart racing against his chest.

"Take a breath," he whispered.

"Ollie, my babies."

 85

"Take a breath, darlin'. We'll keep things together."

"Stay."

"As long as you want me to." He hitched her tighter into his embrace, felt her hands move down and wrap around his waist. "I've got you, Allie. Just breathe."

THE OLDER BOYS KNEW AS SOON AS THEY PULLED UP TO THE house and saw everyone there. Ollie could tell by the look in Kevin's and Mark's eyes. Kevin didn't say a thing, just put his arm around Mark's shoulders and led him into the house. Mark's face was frozen, a blank mask as he watched Chris and Loralie hop up the front steps.

Telling the younger kids was... confusing.

Kevin sat next to Caleb in chairs brought from the dining room, his best friend Low on his other side. Mark, despite being ten, was sitting with Allie's dad, squished beside his grandpa in the old recliner. Allie had Christopher on her lap, and Ollie sat next to her on the couch, Loralie hanging around his neck.

"Dead?" Christopher asked. "Like Bandit?"

Allie and Joe's old dog had passed away two years before from old age and a love of chasing cars.

"Well," Allie said. "Yes. I guess like Bandit."

"Why?" Loralie asked. "Why isn't he gonna come home anymore?"

"Because he can't, baby," Allie said. "Sometimes, if your body is hurt too badly—"

"Ollie?" Loralie put her thumb in her mouth and leaned on his chest. "Can I have a Popsicle?"

"Yep." He stood, still holding the little girl to his chest.

"Can I have one too?" Chris said.

"Blue or red?"

"Red."

Mark huffed out a breath, and Ollie saw him on his Grandpa Scott's lap, blinking back tears. Scott leaned down and whispered something to him.

The house was bursting with people. Jena's parents. Ollie's grandparents. Jena's kids and Allie's friends. Ted's mom had come over, along with Alex's mother and grandmother. The busy hum surrounded him.

Ollie passed Alex and Sean coming out of the kitchen, and he suddenly realized why Allie had been so insistent that everyone come to the house.

Love *surrounded* him. Pressed into him. He could feel the weight of it like one of the heavy, pieced-together quilts his yaya made. Parents and grandparents. Children and friends. His cousin Paul had even brought Ollie's dog over to the house, and Murtry planted himself at Allie's feet.

"Ollie?" Loralie whispered into his shoulder, her thumb still in her mouth.

"What's up, baby girl?"

"Will you stay here when I go to bed?"

"If you want me to."

She draped her little arms around his neck. "Can you be your bear?"

"Yep."

So apparently he was staying the night in Allie's living room in his shifted form. He'd had stranger requests.

He grabbed two Popsicles, making sure one was red and one was green, Loralie's favorite. Then he carried her past all the grandmas and back into the living room, settling next to Allie again.

"I'm staying the night," he said, handing the red Popsicle to Chris. "Lala wants the bear."

Allie nodded. "Okay then."

"Mama," Chris asked. "Was daddy a coyote when he died? Did someone hit him with their car?"

Allie's eyes went wide. "No, buddy. Why would you think that?"

"I saw a coyote when I was driving to Indio with Grandpa. It was dead like Bandit, and I wondered if it was daddy."

Allie sucked in a sharp breath, and Ollie grabbed her hand.

"That wasn't Dad, stupid," Mark said. "That was just a dumb regular coyote."

"Marky," Allie's dad said, brushing the boy's hair back from his eyes. "Remember what I told you."

Mark crossed his arms and settled into sullen silence again while

Chris and Loralie ate their Popsicles. Ollie heard Kevin sigh deeply and lean his head against the wall.

Low tugged on his sleeve and said, "Hey, let's go outside."

"Okay."

The older boys left, and then the adults began to disperse, but nobody went home. Ollie smelled food drifting in from the kitchen and someone put some quiet gospel music on the radio. Pretty soon, Loralie was wiggling off his lap and asking Jena if she could play with the baby while Chris asked Caleb if he wanted to shoot Nerf guns. Mark went to the boys' room with Bear. Ted came in the room and refilled everyone's iced tea.

Ollie put his arm on the back of the sofa, and Allie leaned into his side.

"He wanted to play Nerf guns," she said to Ted.

Ted crouched down next to her. "Children process grief differently."

Caleb, who had probably dealt with more grieving families than any of them when he was working as a homicide detective, moved closer to Allie and Ted.

"It's going to come up at odd times," he said. "Kids don't always recognize what they're feeling."

"Loralie hasn't sucked her thumb in years," Allie murmured.

"She wanted me to stay the night here," Ollie said. "As a bear."

Ted smiled. "Bears are so cuddly."

"And scary," Allie said, nudging his side. "Sometimes it's good knowing there's something scary guarding the door."

"It's good she felt comfortable asking Ollie to stay," Caleb said. "She knows the adults around her are dependable. Allie, I *am* worried about safety though. The papers will get ahold of Joe's name tomorrow. We don't know why he was murdered, or if anyone is still—"

"Are they sure he was?" Ollie asked.

Ted nodded. "They found blunt-force trauma to his skull, but also a rib that was cracked. They missed it on the first pass, but Larry is fairly sure it was broken by a bullet." She glanced at Allie. "Is this too much?"

Allie took a deep breath. "No, it's fine. I'm kinda... I knew it was him, Ted. I knew."

"I think the older boys did too," Ollie said. "And Caleb, we're watching the house."

"By 'we,' you mean—"

"Bears." He nudged Allie's knee with his. "It's good to have something scary guarding the door, remember? My clan is around. No one's gonna touch the kids."

EVEN WHEN NIGHT FELL, IT SEEMED THAT ALLIE'S HOUSE was still surrounded. Tom and Cathy had driven their motor home over and parked it so Allie's dad could stay the night. Ollie's cousin took his grandparents to his house, leaving Ollie in the living room staring at a tiny girl in a princess nightgown who was holding a green stuffed dinosaur and staring at him with large blue eyes while her mother oversaw the boys getting ready for bed.

"What?" he said. "Now?"

She nodded, her thumb in her mouth.

"Okay, well…" None of the rooms in Allie's house were big enough to shift in except the living room, and he didn't want to strip down to his skin in front of a five-year-old.

He held up a hand. "I'll be right back."

Ollie went out to the front porch and off to the side yard, undressing quickly and stowing his clothes on a porch chair. He shifted, his body growing and flowing into his natural grizzly form, the hump rising on his back, his paws spreading to the size of dinner plates. He was the largest bear in his clan; he could hear the smaller creatures in the desert night skittering away when they scented him.

Senses keener, he did one wide circuit around the house, running in a burst of speed to work off some of the tension from the day. Then he shook off as much dust as he could and walked to Allie's house, climbing the porch and scratching low on the door where Ollie could see other animals had scratched before him. Allie's and Kevin's foxes. Joe's coyote. Even Ted's cougar.

Allie opened the door. "This must be the bear she's insisting on before she goes to bed."

He grunted and squeezed through the door, only to see Loralie still standing with her dinosaur, her thumb in her mouth.

She grinned behind her thumb and held out her arms. "Up."

Allie sighed. "Do you mind?"

Ollie lowered himself to the ground, and Allie lifted Loralie onto his back, settling her to sit just behind his hump. He felt her tiny hands tangle in his fur and knew she'd hold on. He lumbered down the hall and into the room decorated with mermaids and princesses, with a few random dinosaurs thrown in. Or were they dragons? He grunted and leaned against her little bed; Loralie scrambled onto the mattress and bounced a little, still grinning.

"Can you stay in my room, Ollie?"

Noooo. He had visions of waking up with pink ribbons in his fur and a tiara perched between his ears.

"No, baby." Allie tucked her under the covers. "Your room is too small for a bear. Ollie's going to stay out in the living room."

He huffed out a breath and leaned his muzzle on the side of her bed.

Loralie bent over his snout and gave him a kiss on the nose. "Thank you," she whispered.

One more contented rumble later, and he was shuffling back down the hall where he ran into Mark.

"Whoa." Mark smiled, and it was the first true smile he'd seen from the boy all day. "Hey, Ollie."

He grunted at Mark and nudged him with his massive head. The boy's hand landed on Ollie's neck, and he leaned into him. Mark had been reluctant to accept affection from anyone but his grandfather all day. Ollie was hoping he wouldn't be as reluctant with the animal.

He dug his fingers into Ollie's fur and kneaded, testing out the weight and texture of the thick pelt.

"You're, like, the biggest thing I've ever seen."

A chuffed breath.

"I wish I could be a bear," Mark whispered. "I don't want to be a coyote."

A growl from Ollie.

"I know," Mark said sadly. "We are the animal we are."

And Ollie knew that though Mark might have put on the best face, the boy felt deeply, and he would need to be watched. Mark might not be the one to act out, but he would carry his pain like silent armor if he didn't allow the wound to heal. He leaned into Ollie, pressing his body weight against the grizzly, and Ollie felt a bit of the tension seep away.

"Thanks for staying," he said. "I feel better knowing you're here."

Another light growl.

"Hey, Mark, have you seen—" Kevin stepped into the hall. "Oh. Hey, Ollie."

A low grunt.

"Mark, did you take my deodorant again?"

"I couldn't find mine."

"Dude, not cool." Kevin hooked his younger brother around the neck and dragged him back down the hall. "You cannot go and steal a man's deodorant like that."

Letting the affectionate bickering of the boys fade back, he headed toward the living room and lay down next to Murtry, who was sprawled on his back, head lying on a Little Mermaid pillow Loralie had given him, clearly unworried about his dignity. The mastiff already had a purple bow clipped to one of his ears.

Sucker.

Ollie dozed, naturally lazy in bear form, and wondered in the back of his mind if there were any leftovers from the lasagnas that Cathy and his yaya had made earlier. It didn't matter how recently he'd eaten as a human; when he shifted to his bear, he was *always* hungry.

He started a bit when he felt bare feet kneading his back, but relaxed again when he caught her scent.

"Hey, big guy," she whispered.

A low rumble. He wished she'd shift and cuddle next to him. Her fox was a little bit of a thing, but sleek and quick in her natural form. And she'd probably sleep better. Sometimes human emotions were too complicated. Sinking into their animals was a way to relax.

As if reading his mind, she cocked her head and looked at Murtry. "Would he bother me?"

Ollie reached over and shoved a giant bear paw at Murtry, who merely flopped over and let out a loud snore.

Allie laughed. "Okay then. Probably not."

She wandered back down the hall and, minutes later, he sensed her. The bright canine scent and the pad of delicate feet as the ashen silver fox trotted into the room. She sniffed around the house, inspecting the doors and even hopping up on the back of the couch to peer out the front window. After she'd inspected the perimeter of her territory, she circled around the bear warily before coming closer to investigate. Her nose tickled his nearest ear, and he flicked it at her and let out a deep rumbling sigh. Reassured, she snuggled down in the space between his head and his front paws, flicking his nose once with her fluffy grey tail.

A few minutes later, he heard her breathing slow and smooth into sleep.

It wasn't the way he'd planned to spend his first night with Allison Smith, but Ollie couldn't find it in him to complain.

chapter
nine

A llie felt the warmth before she opened her eyes. Surrounding her.
She snuggled back when it hugged her tighter. It breathed—

Her eyes flew open.

It breathed?

The last thing she remembered was her fox curling up with Ollie's
bear. They must have both shifted back to their human forms as they
slept.

Oh no.

She looked down to see a light brown, tattooed arm wrapped
around her waist.

Naked waist.

Naked Allie.

Ollie was behind her, a quiet snore rumbling from him as he held
her. He was curled around her, one arm under her head and the other
one circling her waist, his huge hand spread over her ribs, inches from
her breast. They were plastered, his front to her back, and Allie felt
every inch of him pressed against her.

As she'd always suspected, there was a lot of Ollie.

A lot.

Oh... my.

The house was silent. The dog and the man were both snoring.

Allie let herself have one moment of silent whining that she couldn't
throw caution to the wind and enjoy the moment more, but if the sun

was up, then her children would be soon. And the last thing she wanted to explain was why Mom was naked in the living room with Ollie.

She took a deep breath.

One more second. Maybe ten seconds. She didn't hear any little feet yet.

He felt so good.

Like insanely good. Big and warm and... everywhere.

It had been so long since someone held her.

With a barely audible groan, she tried to ease his arm up. He gave a low growl and hugged her closer, nudging one thigh between her legs as his arm moved up and his hand closed possessively around a full breast.

Oh dear Lord.

Allie's body heated in response.

So the bear liked cuddling. Clearly, there would be no escaping this without abject humiliation.

"Ollie?" she whispered.

He grumbled and nudged her hair to the side, burying his face at the nape of her neck.

"Ollie, you *really* need to wake up."

"Hmm," he mumbled and she felt teeth—teeth!—scrape her shoulder in a gentle bite. "Few more minutes, baby."

He stretched and pressed against her, and Allie's heart rate went into overdrive when she felt *every* inch of Ollie.

Kill me. Kill me now.

Or... in an hour or two. If that's an option.

"Ollie!" She pinched the arm wrapped around her and his hand tightened around her breast.

"Ow." He started awake behind her. "Wha—?"

"Naked. Living room. Four curious children."

And he still wasn't moving!

"Oliver Campbell, let me go."

"Okay," he said but didn't lift his arm.

"Are you awake?"

"I don't want to be."

A slight easing of the arm holding her down and she managed to wiggle away just as she heard little footsteps hit the floor in the back bedrooms.

"Now I'm cold," he said with a yawn, his eyes drifting lazily over her in the morning light. "Hey, you."

Allie suddenly realized Ollie was looking at her naked. They were both naked. But she felt way more naked than him. The only man who'd ever seen her naked was Joe. And now Ollie.

Part of her wanted to be embarrassed about that, except that sleepy Ollie didn't seem to mind the view. He wasn't looking at the belly she carried or the stretch marks she was self-conscious about.

No, he was looking at her boobs.

She grabbed a throw from the back of the sofa and wrapped it around herself. "Where are your clothes?"

He smiled and his eyes slipped closed. "Where are yours?"

"You are really not a morning person, are you?"

He stretched his arms up and out and—wow, he was a big man—he rolled over, his body bared to the sun, acting like he was going back to bed.

Yeah, she looked.

"Ollie, unless you want a five-year-old asking why your naked butt isn't a bear, you better go get your clothes."

Murtry, who had been snoring, suddenly rolled over and let out a *whoof* loud enough to wake the dead.

Ollie rolled back over and reached an arm out, slapping the ground before he rose up on one arm and blinked at her.

"Allie?"

"Are you really awake this time?"

He looked around the room and Murtry walked over and gave the side of his face a sloppy lick. "Dog…"

A small voice called from the back of the house. "Maa-ma!"

Ollie's eyes flew open, and he looked down. "Oh shit."

"Go get dressed," she hissed.

"Were we—"

"Dressed! Now!" She started down the hall. "Coming, Lala. Let mama get dressed. I'll be right there."

She ran into her bedroom and leaned against the door, the throw still wrapped around her. She heard the front door slam and figured Ollie was finding his clothes wherever he'd stashed them.

Then the reason he had stayed the night hit her, and she slid down to the floor.

Covering her face, she let a few tears fall before she wiped them away and took a deep breath.

It was going to be another long day.

HE WAS WATCHING HER. ALLIE COULD FEEL HIS EYES, AND she felt like she was still naked. Did he remember, or was he one of those men who had whole conversations in his sleep and then didn't remember a thing later?

She poured the pancake batter onto the electric griddle and waited for the cakes to bubble up before she could turn them. Ollie had figured out how to work her coffeemaker, and he set a full mug beside her on the counter. Kevin and Mark were both sitting at the table. Chris and Loralie were watching cartoons on the TV in the living room.

"Are we going to school?" Kevin asked.

"No. I thought we'd go to Aunt Beth's for a few days."

She flipped the pancakes and watched the steam rise like she had a thousand mornings before. Everything felt the same, and nothing was.

Mark crossed his arms on the table and slid down to rest his chin on them. "Aunt Beth has a pool."

Aunt Beth was also a social worker and her closest sister. She and her husband had a big house in Palm Desert where Allie often took the kids when it was time to do shopping or just to get away for a few days.

Beth and Brian, a contract attorney, just had their first baby a year before, but they loved having the older cousins come visit. Brian wasn't a shifter, but he came from a big Scottish family, was oddly blasé about his wife turning into a Mexican grey wolf on full moons, and he loved spending time with the boys. Her dad had called Beth last night, explained what had happened, and Beth and Brian immediately extended the invitation.

"Is Ollie coming with us?" Mark asked.

She glanced at the big man, who was back to being clothed, while she took the first batch of pancakes from the griddle.

"Oh, honey, Ollie has to work."

Ollie reached over and mussed Mark's hair. "You'll only be gone a few days. I'll keep an eye on things while you visit your auntie."

"'Kay."

The boys and Ollie distributed the first batch of pancakes, spreading butter and pouring syrup before they fell on them with enthusiasm. If there was one thing that never changed, it was her boys' appetites.

"Hey, Mom," Kevin said. "Should I call the school?"

"I think Caleb or Ted already did, but thanks for thinking of it."

She poured another batch of pancakes and called the younger kids, who scrambled in, Loralie immediately going to Ollie's lap. He scooted back to make room for her and started feeding her bites from his plate.

Allie tried to ignore the flutter in her chest watching them. She turned back to the griddle, her heart in her throat.

Joe never ate breakfast with the kids.

When he was working at the base, he'd been gone before they woke. On weekends, he slept in, and when he'd lost his job, he'd done the same. Mostly, he just got frustrated with how messy they were. Even eating dinner together hadn't been something he enjoyed.

Allie felt guilty comparing the two, but the thought wouldn't leave her alone. Ollie talked with all the kids, asking quiet questions and then letting them talk. He wasn't a chatty man and never had been, but he seemed to enjoy listening to them jabber at each other, his patience an endless well.

She wasn't used to it.

It was wonderful and it hurt, all at the same time.

When she turned to refill his coffee cup, she saw him frowning at her, but he didn't say anything in front of the kids. After the pancakes had been demolished, Kevin took the younger kids back to their rooms. She could hear him directing them to pack their bags to go to Aunt Beth's as she cleaned the kitchen.

"Want some help with that?"

No. How else am I going to avoid you?

"I've got it. But thanks."

"The pancakes were great."

"Thank you." She scrubbed the griddle. Scruuuuuuubbed it with all her concentration. It would be the cleanest griddle in the western United States. "Thanks for staying last night. I know it made the kids feel better having you here."

"About this morning—"

"It's fine!" Allie spun when she felt him behind her. "Really. Slightly embarrassing, but the kids didn't catch—"

"I don't remember..." A faint flush on his cheeks. "I didn't do anything inappropriate, did I?"

Do you always wake up with that much morning wood? Because I would call that very appropriate.

"No, of course not."

Also, feel free to put your hand on my boob anytime.

"Good."

"Yeah. Good." She was holding a dirty spatula in front of her like a sword. She'd resorted to rubber kitchen implements as defensive weaponry. Ollie was making her crazy. "So... I'll call Tracey and let her know I'll be gone a few days."

He was eyeing her dangerous spatula with a furrowed brow. "Please don't worry about the bar. We'll manage. Take your time with your sister, okay?"

"It'll only be a few days. I can't miss too much work. I can't afford it. And the kids shouldn't be out of school too long."

He put his hand around her wrist and lowered the spatula. "Take the time you need, darlin'."

"Why do you do that?" she murmured before she could stop herself.

"Do what?"

"Call me darling. You don't call anyone else darling. Just me."

A hint of dimples behind the beard. "Because you are." He tucked a flyaway lock of hair behind her ear, then bent to kiss her forehead. "I'm gonna go say bye to the kids, and then I'll head home. Text me when you get to your sister's, okay?"

Allie stood frozen, watching Ollie leave the kitchen. Something had shifted, and it had a little to do with waking up with the man naked and a lot to do with him feeding Loralie bites of pancake while she sat on his lap.

And one of these days, when she had an hour or two to think, she'd figure it out. Until then, there was way too much to do.

Most of the time, the weather in the California desert sucked. But there were times, like this one, that it didn't. Because while most of the country was feeling the first tinges of fall and preparing for winter, Allie and her sister Beth were sitting on the back patio, watching the kids jump and play in the pool while the baby took a nap.

"Tell me your secrets," Beth said, watching the kids.

"Secrets?"

"It's almost unnatural how nice your children are. And it's a damn miracle how well-adjusted they've turned out with their dad."

Allie shrugged. "I have people."

Beth laughed, familiar with most of Allie's "people." "You do," she said. "The kids sure mentioned that bear a lot."

Allie closed her eyes and leaned back in the lounge chair. "Ollie's a good friend."

"Oh, I've noticed how *friendly* he is for years."

Allie opened her eyes. "What is that supposed to mean?"

"It means, dear clueless sister, that man is hot for you and has been for ages."

She waved a hand and tried to calm her racing heart. "I'm not his type."

"Really? Because I'm fairly sure that man's type is *you*."

"You haven't seen the women he's dated, okay?" She closed her eyes again and concentrated on the warmth of the sun, trying not to think about how warm he'd felt around her. "Besides, what single thirty-five-year-old man is going to be willing to take on a woman with four kids? He's not insane."

Beth scoffed. "You're acting like he'd be doing you a favor."

"Yeah, 'cause I'm such a catch."

"Will you stop?" Beth tore off her sunglasses, scowling at her. "What makes you think you aren't?"

Allie held up fingers. "Poor. Single mother. Dead husband who was probably a criminal. Stretch marks."

"I will hit you if you mention your four stretch marks again. Do you know how many humans usually get? We're shifters. We're lucky as it is."

"It's more than four," Allie grumbled. "And it's just so unfair that I got them and you didn't."

"Yeah, but you have a burly, tattooed giant who's hot for you."

"And your husband wears a kilt on formal occasions."

Beth grinned. "Yes, he does. And he has great legs."

"Ollie has great legs," Allie said under her breath.

"So you've noticed?"

"Of *course* I've noticed. I'm not dead."

"But you're not pursuing him because…"

"Seriously?" Allie said, turning to her sister. "You're asking me this *now*? When you've been dealing with our emotional baggage for the past two days?"

"Well, I've kind of been wondering for months. And grief is not emotional baggage, it's a natural part of life. Do not stigmatize a completely natural part of living, Allie."

She took a deep breath. "Fine. But do you really think my kids are ready to deal with mommy having a boyfriend? Or even thinking about that?"

Beth paused, and Allie could tell she was truly thinking it over.

"Normally," her sister started, "I would say no. If you were a stranger I was counseling, I'd tell you to back off and let yourself heal. I suspect that's what Ollie is thinking as well, especially now. But you're not a stranger, and your situation isn't normal."

"You have to be clearer, because my brain has way too much going on to interpret that. Nothing about this is normal."

Beth kept her voice low, but the kids were shouting and laughing too much to pay attention.

"You had emotionally separated from Joe long before he left. You are very far from hung up on him. The grief you're feeling is the kind of grief you would feel even if this had happened ten years from now, Allie. Because you didn't lose a husband you loved, you lost the father of your children whom you *once* loved, and it's a different kind of grief."

Allie nodded. That made sense to her. "But the kids—"

"If this was a new guy who had just come into the picture, I'd warn you off. You know I don't give a shit about being polite when it comes to the well-being of my nephews and niece."

"But?"

"But Ollie isn't new. He's been a part of your life—and a part of theirs—since they were born. Having him around, whether it's as your friend or even possibly your boyfriend, is not going to hurt them. It might even help. Especially if it makes you more emotionally fulfilled. Because sister, I love you, but you have looked wrung out for months."

Allie took a deep breath and tried to reconcile what her sister was saying with the guilt that was eating her heart. Guilt for thinking of herself instead of her kids. Guilt over feeling attracted to Ollie when Joe was dead.

"Listen," Beth said, "I'm not saying you should start rubbing up on the man in front of your five-year-old. I'm just saying that if something happens because your relationship with Ollie goes in a new direction—one that I've seen the potential of for years, I might add—it's not going to hurt your kids. So get that out of your head."

"Am I a bad mother?" she asked. "For even thinking about this stuff?"

"Nope. You're a normal woman who's been alone a long time and now has a good man giving indications that he'd like to be a bigger part of her life."

Allie took a deep breath. "He is a good man."

"He's a really good man. If he wasn't, you wouldn't have him around your kids anyway."

"Okay." She relaxed a little. "I still don't think I'm his type."

"I'm going to throw you in the pool if you mention the stretch marks again, fart-face."

ALLIE AND THE KIDS ONLY STAYED AT BETH AND BRIAN'S house a few nights. In the end, she could tell that all of them wanted to get home. They needed their friends and their grandparents. Needed the routine of school and sports, even if their dad was really and truly gone. Loralie had been sleeping in Allie's bed at night, and neither one was getting much rest.

It was almost bedtime by the time they managed to pack everything in the car and head back to the Springs.

"Mom." Kevin sat up straighter next to her in the minivan. "There's something not right."

She peered into the darkness. She'd just pulled off the main road and rumbled over the cattle grate by their fence. The front porch lights were on, and she wondered if she'd forgotten to turn them off or if her dad had come over to check the house.

"Kevin, what—"

"Stop the car," he said. The unexpected command in her son's voice shocked her enough that she stopped. "I saw something." In a second, the passenger door was open and she sensed his shift.

"Kevin!"

Dammit. What was she supposed to do? She couldn't leave the younger kids alone to chase after him.

Mark unbuckled his belt and leaned forward. "What's going on?"

"I don't know."

She rolled down her window and smelled the breeze, but it was coming from the other direction. A sharp, vulpine whine came from the back of her throat.

Her son was out there, and he'd shifted because he sensed danger. She reached for her phone to call Caleb just as Kevin trotted back. He scampered behind the car and shifted back, buttoning up his jeans as he walked back to the open door.

"Kevin, what happened?" Mark shouted.

"Keep your voice down," he hissed. "Someone's in the house, Mom. I thought I saw one of the curtains move, and when I went closer, I could see flashlights."

She stifled her instinctual snarl and reached for the door. "Stay with your brothers and sister." She handed him her phone. "Call Ollie and Caleb. Now."

"Mom—"

"Stay in the car!" She handed him the keys. "Lock it. And if anyone but me comes nearby, you take off and drive to Ollie's house."

She got out and listened until the doors locked behind her. Then she walked to the back and removed her clothes, a faint shiver chasing her spine as she bent and shifted.

A tug in her belly, a tingling in her nose.

She was her fox.

Allie let out a howling bark, well aware of the chilling nature of her call. She dashed to the house, slinking between the scrub and creeping forward unnoticed. If the intruders saw anything, it would be the flash of eyes in the half-moon.

Low to the ground, the scents could be overwhelming, but the fox sifted through the layers until she scented *other* in the air, a discordant thread in the familiar tapestry of the desert.

There were two.

She crept around the back, pausing under a window where she could hear them moving. They did not speak, but she could hear ripping and tearing in her bedroom. Two grown humans were far too big for her to hunt, but she could do her best to scare them away. Away from her home and children.

Allie barked again and all sound stopped.

"What was that?"

"Sounded like a scream."

"All the way out here?"

More silence. The men moved through the house, and Allie could hear them kicking things out of their way.

"You think someone found the car?"

"Who the hell knows?" A thumping, as if the man had dropped something. "We should go. There's nothing here. Maybe when Russell's wife…"

Their voices became muffled as they headed toward the back door. Allie followed them, slinking along the edges of the house. There was a cold, foreign scent coming from under the kitchen. She poked her head in a space, only to pull it out when she caught a more threatening scent in the wind.

Bear.

She could feel the vibrations in the sand beneath her paws. The humans didn't feel it. Didn't see it. But as she watched them jog down the porch steps and into the night, she followed.

They were headed to the back of her property and the tail end of Emmet Wash. Allie was guessing that was where they left their car. On the other side of the wash was a thick stand of cottonwood on an old farm road. It was little more than a dirt track but wide enough to take a vehicle and far enough from her house that it wouldn't be noticeable.

The bear was getting closer.

"What was that?" one of the men asked.

"I don't know. This whole fucking place gives me the creeps. Let's go."

Bears weren't known for stealth. Allie couldn't believe the humans missed the crashing through the brush. A pause as the bear leapt over the fence on the border of her property. A heavy thunk.

The humans stopped.

"There's something out there."

"Probably a coyote."

"Are they dangerous?" A thread of panic.

You're not panicking enough. Not nearly enough.

The bear was getting closer.

"They're coyotes, dumbass. They're smaller than most dogs."

Ollie paused, probably twenty meters away. His shaggy brown coat would be invisible in the night. She heard the huffing pants. Then a draw of breath before the bear let out a terrifying roar.

"What the hell was that?"

The humans were running now, but so was Ollie. She could hear them scrambling through the brush.

"Was that a bear?"

"Holy shit! Run. *Run!*"

He chased them over the small hill and across the wash as Allie hurried to keep up. Ollie could run faster than most humans realized, but foxes were faster and more agile.

Crossing the wash slowed Ollie down just enough to let the humans jump in their car, but he quickly caught up to them. He reared to his full height, put both giant paws on the hood of the sedan, and silently stared through the windshield.

Allie smelled urine and adrenaline. The humans were scrambling inside the vehicle, looking for keys and yelling at each other.

The bear paused, took a huffing breath, and roared again, his fangs gleaming in the moonlight.

Every instinct in the fox told her to run. Only the human mind calmed her. This was Ollie. He would never hurt her or her young.

The grizzly slowly dug four-inch claws into the car's hood, tearing metal and drawing back before he reared up again, bouncing on the front of the luxury vehicle like it was no more than a child's playground toy.

The humans screamed, but one of them managed to turn the key in the ignition and the car started.

Allie barked again. Short, high-pitched barks designed to grab the bear's attention. If the humans rammed him, they could hurt him. Not mortally, but a car could do some damage.

With one last roar and a shove, he backed away. The humans reversed the car, kicking up dust and almost running off the road in their attempts to escape. The bear paced along the edge of the wash, huffing until the lights disappeared.

Then he turned with a low, rumbling growl and started running back to the house. Allie ran with him, darting her tail out to brush his shoulder as she passed him. She reached the minivan and circled it, checking for any unfamiliar scents before she went to the back and shifted to her human form again, pulling on her clothes as quickly as possible.

Kevin rolled down the window. "Mom?"

"I'm fine, Kevin. Stay in the car."

"What the fuck did you think you were you doing?" Human again, Ollie roared at her, striding out of the shadows and marching to the back of the van stark-naked while she was still pulling on her pants.

"Hey!" she barked. "Calm down. You think my kids can't hear you?"

"I get a panicked call from Kevin and race over here to find you playing detective in the bushes? Why the hell didn't you stay in the car?"

"Those jerks were in my house! I wasn't going to sit there and—"

"Yes, you damn well should have sat there!" he yelled again. "What if they'd seen the van? What if there'd been more of them?"

"I have a nose, Ollie. I'm perfectly capable of using it. There were two. They were in my house. And Kevin was with the younger kids."

The adrenaline crash was coming, and she could see Mark's and Chris's little faces pressed up to the glass at the back of the van, watching with eyes the size of saucers as the irate, naked man yelled at their mother.

"They had weapons, Allie! Did you smell that?"

"Stop yelling at me and put some clothes on."

"I don't have any clothes." He was still yelling. "I ran from my house."

"And you can go right back to it if you're going to keep roaring."

Allie spotted lights in the distance, and she was hoping it was Caleb. Maybe the chief of police could calm Ollie down.

"Mom?" It was Kevin, calling from the car. "That's probably Caleb coming up the road. He texted a few minutes ago."

"Are your brothers and sister okay?"

"They're tired and whiny. And wondering why Ollie is so mad."

She glared at him. "Get it together," she hissed.

Ollie put his hands on his hips and his nostrils flared, but he kept his mouth shut.

"Mom?" It was Mark.

"Yeah?" She turned around so she didn't have to watch Ollie standing there naked. She might have been angry with him, but the shift always roused her. Made her hungry. For food and… other things.

"Who were those guys?"

"I don't know, buddy."

Ollie growled behind her, "You're not staying in that house tonight."

She spun. "Says who? You?"

"Says Caleb, I'm guessing. Someone broke into your house. It's a crime scene. He's going to have to look at it."

She put a hand over her eyes. The exhaustion was starting to hit. "I'll call my dad."

"You and the kids are staying with me."

Amazingly, she still had energy to be mad at him. "You just decided that, did you?"

"Stop arguing!"

"Then stop dictating!"

Why was he still so hot? The madder he got, the more she wanted to jump him. Allie decided a visit to a psychologist might be a good idea.

Caleb pulled up in a cloud of dust and immediately got out of the car.

"Hey. Looks like someone pissed off the bear." He opened the back door of his truck and grabbed a blanket out of the back seat. "Try not to scare the kids, Campbell."

Ollie caught it and wrapped it around his waist.

Great. Now he looked like he was wearing a kilt. Because *that* wasn't hot at all.

Not the time, Allie!

"Two guys in my house," she said, ignoring Ollie. "They didn't talk much. I scared them away."

"With your creepy horror-movie bark?" Caleb asked.

"It works," she said. "They were walking back to their car when Grumpy the Bear here scared them off. I wasn't able to get their license plate."

Caleb grunted and looked at Ollie. "You?"

"No." He flexed his shoulders, probably still feeling sore from his shift. "I wasn't thinking. They just needed to get away from the kids."

It was his voice that softened her. Ollie had yelled because he was worried. Bears weren't the most rational about their young. Females in the bear clan often kept their children home or with close family for a full year, not because they were being antisocial but because they knew they could easily attack with other predators in the vicinity. It was one of the reasons the Campbell clan was so insular.

His protectiveness made Allie's stomach flip. Ollie considered her children his own; otherwise, he'd be behaving more rationally. The thought was both nerve-racking and comforting.

But he'd also questioned her judgment, which still ticked her off.

"Allie and the kids are staying with me for a while," Ollie said to Caleb.

"Ollie—"

"Don't. Argue." He glared at her. "Let me go through the house with Caleb. You get the kids settled. They're probably tired and freaked out."

Caleb's eyes pleaded with her to be reasonable. She saw Loralie yawning from the corner of her eye.

"Fine." She marched back to the driver's door and opened it.

"Mama," Loralie whined. "What's wrong with our house?"

Mark asked, "Why is Ollie mad at us?"

"He's not mad at us. He's worried because someone was in our house who shouldn't have been."

"Who?" Loralie's eyes were wide in the interior lights. "Was it Daddy?"

"No," Mark said. "Dad's not coming back, remember? He's dead."

It was a punch to the gut. Every single time. Were all children so blunt, or was it just Mark?

Loralie stuck her thumb in her mouth and leaned on Mark's arm, curling into her big brother, who picked up her hand and held it.

"When I get big," Chris said, "I don't want to shift to a coyote, because then someone might hit me with a truck. I want to be a fox, because they're little and fast. Or maybe a bear."

Mark sneered. "You can't be a bear, stupid."

"Everyone needs to be quiet and think about sleep!" Allie said, taking a deep breath as Ollie rounded the car, still wearing that stupid blanket around his waist. He bent down and she cracked open the window.

"What?"

"You got clothes?" he asked, his voice pitched carefully low.

"Of course we do. We were at my sister's."

"I'm going to look around the house with Caleb. You drive over to my place. I already called your dad and told him you were staying with me."

"Yay!" Chris yelled from the back. "We're sleeping at Ollie's house!"

Allie's eyes were blazing. "That is not your decision."

"You can't go back to your place tonight, and I have more room than your dad. Don't argue."

She felt her kids' eyes on her back. Someone yawned, and Loralie started to whine again.

"Mom—"

"Fine," she said. "We'll go to Ollie's and get you guys in bed."

Allie put the car in reverse and was about to back out when he rapped on her window.

She stopped and rolled the window down more. "What?"

He stuck a hand in her face. "Here's a spare key. Caleb had one for the back door. I'll get you a full set when I get home."

She grabbed the key and tried to roll the window up, but he put his hand on the door and leaned down to her.

"What now?"

"I know you're pissed at me, but don't drive mad." His voice had lost the authoritarian bark.

"We'll see you at your house."

Ollie frowned. That was fine. He could frown all he wanted, but she was still angry.

"There's plenty of bedrooms. Let the kids pick the one they want. They can sleep wherever, but you might have to change the sheets in some of the rooms. Elijah is already headed over there to help you out. I'll be there as soon as I can."

"Ollie, you don't have to go to a bunch of trouble. We're just crashing one night."

"We'll see." He patted the top of the car as he straightened and said, "I'll be as quick as I can. See you at home."

Allie pulled away and wondered just what he meant by "We'll see."

chapter
ten

Oh yeah. Ollie watched the taillights disappear into the desert. Allie was pissed.

He was more pissed.

Two strange humans in her home. Violating her territory. Violating *his* territory.

Because yes, he considered the small house and the children living there his to protect.

He wished he'd crushed more of the car.

Ollie crossed his arms, glaring at the mess of Allie's living room with Caleb at his side.

"They were looking for something." The former detective and chief of police walked to the kitchen and crouched by the door. He touched the crumbled soil in the footprints the intruders had left, then brought his fingers up to his nose and sniffed. "New asphalt."

"They ran like city boys."

"Okay."

If there was one thing Ollie liked about the chief, it was that he rarely said anything he didn't have to. He had made the Springs his home and had a reasonably good understanding of shifters. He also understood body language.

"Allie mad at you?"

"Yep."

Caleb stood. "She'll get over it when she realizes they were in the kids' bedrooms."

"Those mattresses salvageable?"

Caleb shook his head.

"Shit," he growled. "They're gonna need all new stuff."

"They're going to need a place to stay first."

"They're staying with me."

Caleb raised an eyebrow. "You sure she's going to be okay with that?"

"I'll make her okay with it." He shrugged. "The kids like my house anyway. I'll convince them."

"Making the kids your allies, huh?" Caleb smiled a little. "Tricky. But effective when it works."

Turning his attention back to the mess they were standing in, Ollie asked, "What's your best guess on what they were looking for?"

"I don't know." Caleb paused. "Not yet. Probably gonna have to call the sheriff's office. There's no way this isn't related to Joe's murder. Might get me more access to the investigation though. You said your boys have been covering the place?"

"I let 'em go home when she went to her sister's. My mistake."

"She was only there two nights." Caleb tapped his fingers against his leg. "They either knew she was gone or they were taking a chance. I'm betting they knew she was gone."

"Someone in town tell them?"

Caleb shrugged. "Maybe."

"Probably."

"Don't go breaking heads until we know which ones to break," Caleb said. "There's not much we can do tonight. Why don't you head back to your place and see to Allie and the kids?"

"I will."

Jim was waiting in the driveway with a change of clothes, ready to take Ollie home since he ran over in fur. Ollie dressed and filled his cousin in on what had happened, but before he left, Ollie walked back to Allie's room.

Her pretty sage-green room, so carefully decorated just the way she liked, was trashed. Clothes pulled out of the closets and jewelry spilled on the ground. He saw a necklace he knew was real gold because she told him once it had belonged to her mom. The intruders didn't seem to have taken any of her stuff, just combed through, looking for something. The backs of the toilets were even tossed off and there were holes in a couple of the walls.

Bastards.

Then he noticed a whole pile of her pretty lingerie dumped on the floor, pawed through and stepped on.

Oh yeah. He definitely should have crushed the car.

He pushed a few of her drawers back in place and tried to put some of her things in order; then he grabbed the small jewelry box with her mom's necklace and headed home.

THE HOUSE WAS MOSTLY DARK, BUT OLLIE SAW HER SITTING on the porch as Jim pulled away. Elijah was on his phone, sitting in the bed of his pickup truck, and Ollie could see Paul walking around from the back.

Elijah lifted his chin at him, then whistled for Paul, and the two clambered into the truck to head home. It was a school night after all, and once Ollie was home, there wasn't a predator alive who could get into his house without being torn limb from limb.

Allie had a jelly jar filled with what looked like his good bourbon and a weary look on her face.

She lifted the jar. "Seemed like a decent tradition to keep up."

"Allie-girl, I'm sorry I—"

"It's fine." She waved a hand. "I mean, it's not. Someone broke into my house. But I know why you were ordering me around. Just don't act like I'm being irresponsible with my kids. I'm not stupid."

"I know you're not."

"But I also know bears aren't the most rational when children are involved."

That was a severe understatement, but he didn't feel like explaining more. Ollie sat down on the other end of the top step and handed over the small jewelry box.

"I found this in your room."

The last bit of hardness flew from her face. "Oh. They didn't take it."

"It didn't look like they took anything, but you'll have to check to be sure."

She clipped the necklace around her neck. "It's just a little thing. Probably not all that valuable. My dad got it for my mom when I was born. It has my birthstone."

"I remember."

"You're good at that."

"What?" He leaned back onto his elbows. "Remembering stuff?"

"Yes. No. That's not what I mean. Knowing what's important to a person. You notice things."

He shrugged.

"It's a good trait," she said quietly. She held out the glass. "Drink?"

He took it, just to be able to put his lips were hers had been.

Yeah, he was kind of pathetic at this point.

"You and the kids should stay here until this is all over."

She looked uncomfortable at the thought.

"I know it's not ideal," he said. "I realize the kids would be better off in their own house with all their own stuff. Especially right now. But this place is big, and it's secure. Think of it like... a vacation."

"A vacation?" She looked over her shoulder at the giant house. "I can clean my house in a little under three hours if I'm in a hurry. How many bathrooms does this place have?"

"Five if you count the barn. And you're not cleaning a single one."

Her back went up. "If I'm staying here, I'm gonna pick up after my kids."

"The kids can pick up after themselves, and I have a cleaning lady to do the bathrooms."

"I can do the cleaning while I'm here, Ollie."

"And put Vicky out of work so you can prove a point and run yourself ragged?" He raised an eyebrow. "I'll let you cook, but that's it and only because I'm crap at it."

She snorted. "You'll *let* me, will you?"

"Know what?" He banged the jelly jar down between them. "Someone needs to make sure you take care of yourself."

"I'm fine."

"You're exhausted. In fact—" He stood and held out a hand. "Come on. Bedtime."

Allie scowled. "You're not my father."

"Thank God for that." When she didn't move, he leaned down and put his shoulder under her belly, lifting her in one quick sweep.

"Ollie!" she hissed as he walked into the house. "Put me down."

"It's been a hell of a week. We're all going to bed. You. Me. The kids. The dog. Everyone."

As if on cue, Murtry followed them into the house and slumped by the fireplace in the front room with a low groan.

Allie clearly didn't share the dog's need to relax.

"Oliver Campbell, I do not need you to tell me—"

"Which bedroom did you pick?"

She stubbornly refused to answer him. "I'm not going to wiggle around and make a fool out of myself," she said. "Just put me down."

"I'm guessing..." He walked up the stairs and down the right hallway, pushing open a door at the end. "Yep. Yellow bedroom with the four-poster bed. Yaya's favorite."

"Put me down!" she said again just as quietly. Just as angrily.

"Okay." He walked over and dumped her on the mattress, careful not to bang her head on the old posts. "Good night. You know where the bathroom is, right?"

"If you think being a caveman is charming, you're very mistaken."

She sounded like a pissed-off kitten. He laughed.

"I don't care about being charming," Ollie said. "I care about you having a little less stress in your life and getting more sleep. I'll see you in the morning."

He walked out and shut the door before he did something really stupid like try to crawl in bed with her. She'd most likely hurt him if he tried. He walked down the hall and saw the bathroom door crack open.

Kevin was standing at the sink, brushing his teeth. Without a word, he held his hand out for a fist bump. Ollie silently met the boy's knuckles, then went downstairs to lock up the house.

He wasn't going to lie. It felt good to order her around. But only because he finally had an excuse to take care of her. Allie was used to doing everything on her own, and she was damn good at it. But it was about time she learned that other people could and would help her out when she was at the end of her rope.

And if that made him a caveman, he could live with that.

HIS ALARM WENT OFF AT SIX A.M. OLLIE RUBBED HIS HAND over his face and was tempted to go back to sleep. But there were four children in the house, and all of them needed to get dressed, fed, and onto the bus before he could go back to sleep. He rolled out of bed and pulled on some pants and a shirt that was mostly clean.

He tapped on the doors and cracked them open when no one answered. He'd guessed right on which room Kevin had picked, which was his old one from high school, which he'd decorated in car posters. The boy was sitting on the edge of the bed, scrubbing his eyes with the heel of his hand.

"Hey," Ollie said. "Think you and me can get all the little ones off to school without waking your mom up?"

Kevin didn't say anything, but he gave Ollie a thumbs-up.

"Cool. You hop in the shower, and I'll go make breakfast."

"Okay," he said with a yawn. "I'll go wake up Thing One and Thing Two."

"Be nice."

Ollie stepped into the hall only to almost trip over a fuzzy-haired princess rubbing her eyes. Loralie held up her arms, and Ollie picked her up and brought her downstairs. He let Murtry out to do his business, then walked to the massive kitchen and opened the fridge, glad that Vicky had just gone shopping. He'd have to send her on another trip that afternoon, because he'd seen how those boys ate.

Loralie seemed to have no desire to let go of his neck, so he grabbed what he could with one hand and had to make a few trips.

He could cook eggs and toast with one arm. Sure he could. Bacon was probably a bad idea though.

With some effort, he got the coffee started and was even working on cracking the eggs when Kevin came into the kitchen.

"There she is." He moved to grab Loralie, but she grabbed tighter on to Ollie's neck. "Come on, Lala. We need to get you dressed for school."

"I want Ollie to get me dressed."

"He's fixing breakfast. Let me get you dressed."

"Nooo," she whined, but Ollie kissed the top of her head and untangled her.

"Let go, baby girl. I'll make you eggs while Kevin gets you dressed."

With a pout, she let go. Chris and Mark stumbled into the kitchen and went directly for the fridge.

"Sit," he barked. "I'm making breakfast."

"But I don't like eggs," Chris said.

"You do today."

He sighed and laid his head down on the table. "Okay."

"Ollie?" Mark said quietly. "Can I help?"

"Can you go let Murtry in? I think he's scratching at the door."

"Okay."

Juggle this task. Don't forget that one. He couldn't have done it without Kevin's help. But at seven thirty the kids were fed and the five of them headed to the bus stop a half mile from Allie's house, Ollie managing to just barely squeeze into her minivan with all four kids piled in back.

"Backpacks!" Mark yelled just as they arrived at the bus stop.

Kevin's eyes went wide. "They're all at the house."

"Shit."

"That's a bad word," Loralie lisped. "You'll get in trouble if you say that at school."

"Don't I know it," Ollie said. "Okay, you guys get on the bus. I'll grab the backpacks—"

"They'll all be on the hooks by the door in the kitchen," Kevin said. "They should be packed, 'cause we left them there on Friday."

"I'll grab them and drive them to school. They might be a little late, but they'll be there."

"What are we going to eat for lunch?" Chris asked.

"Shit!"

"You said it again, Ollie!" Loralie yelped.

"Don't tell your mom. And... I'll bring lunch too. With the backpacks. I'll make sandwiches or something."

He could see the dust from the school bus coming down the road. "Okay, you guys better get out of the car." There were already three or four kids gathered and peering curiously at the large man in the mini-van. Ollie got out and helped Loralie unbuckle her booster seat, then the four kids tumbled out of the van and onto the bus just before it sped off again.

It was only seven thirty a.m. and Ollie was already winded.

"How does she do this?"

He drove to Allie's house and used her key to grab the four back-packs from the kitchen, along with two athletic bags that smelled suspiciously like his high school football locker. They'd been opened and rifled through, which pissed Ollie off all over again.

He took a deep breath and zipped them shut. He wasn't sure what was in them, but judging from the smell, they were used regularly. Once he had everything he thought the kids might need for school, he threw it all in the minivan and headed back to his house.

He was halfway through four mangled PB&Js when he heard the door slam on the second floor. Feet skidded down the hallway and into the kitchen.

"What time is it and where are my children?" Allie stared at him with wide eyes. "What are you doing?"

"Making lunch. The kids are already on the bus, but their backpacks are in the car and I have to make their lunches."

She glanced at the counter with a frown. "You're making lunch?"

"I don't have any fruit, so it's sandwiches and chips, but I'll ask Vicky to pick up some apples or something when she goes to the store today."

Why did the bread keep tearing? Was he buying the wrong kind of peanut butter? Was it expired? Could peanut butter expire? He'd never noticed because he only used it to give the dog his pills.

He probably better not tell Allie that.

"You're making them lunch." Her voice had a distinctly watery sound, so he turned.

"I told you you needed to sleep more."

"Ollie." She walked over in her pj's and wrapped her arms around his waist. "Thank you."

He wanted to hug her back, but he was pretty sure his hands were sticky, though he had no idea how the peanut butter got everywhere like that. "You're welcome."

"Let me…" She attempted to take the knife from him. "I'll finish. You have strawberry jelly in your beard."

"That's probably from Loralie at breakfast. She insisted on sharing her toast."

Damn, she was beautiful like that, with her hair all fuzzy and piled on the top of her head, her smile crooked and sweet. He really wanted to kiss her.

"You made them breakfast."

"I'm not helpless. I can make eggs. Anyone can scramble an egg."

She wet a paper towel and cleaned off the spot of strawberry jelly before she tugged him down by the beard and laid a kiss on his cheek.

"Sweet man," she murmured. "Chris can't have peanut butter. There's a boy in his class who's allergic. Do you have any turkey?"

Totally worth it. Ollie stood frozen in his kitchen, still feeling her soft lips against his cheek.

Lack of sleep. Crazy rush. Shamefully cold cup of coffee reheated twice and *still* not drank.

Totally worth it all for that sleepy kiss.

"Ollie?"

"Huh?"

"Do you have any turkey or bologna or anything else we could use for Chris's sandwich? He can't have peanut butter."

He filed the information away for future reference and went to the fridge. "Um… I have some leftover tri-tip?"

"Lucky boy," she said, holding her hand out. "Tri-tip it is."

He handed her the meat and went to look for some paper bags he remembered Jena leaving over one time. He found them in the pantry and set them on the counter next to the sandwich bags.

"How do you do this every day?" he asked, watching her cute little ass dance around his kitchen in her sleep shorts as she finished her kids' lunches.

Yeah, he'd get up early to see that in the morning.

"You get used to it," she said. "And Kevin's a great helper."

"I couldn't have survived this morning without him."

She looked over her shoulder and narrowed her eyes. "Scheming against me, huh?"

"Your oldest son and I have similar goals. He thinks you need to rest more too."

"Hmm."

He grabbed another mug and poured her a cup of coffee. "I called the school and explained about the house and the backpacks."

"Thank you."

"Told them you and the kids were staying with me for a while."

Allie sighed. "I wish you hadn't done that."

"Why?"

"One, I don't know how long we're staying here. And two, do you know that Eula Quinn is the secretary there?"

"I thought the voice sounded familiar."

"Everyone in town is going to know I'm staying here by the end of the school day."

"And?"

She blushed. "People talk. That's all."

"Ignore people."

"Easy to say when you've never been in the middle of nasty rumors, Ollie."

She'd been the grist of the rumor mill before. Once, when she graduated high school pregnant with Joe's baby, and again when her husband left her high and dry just as she'd pulled a meat loaf out of the oven.

Which told you everything you needed to know about Joe Russell, in Ollie's opinion, because Allie's meat loaf was awesome.

"What are they going to say?" he asked, curious to see what would bother her most.

"You know exactly what they're going to say."

"That we're shacking up?" he said with a grin. "Or that we're fooling around so much in the mornings we're forgetting to feed the children?"

"Ollie!"

He chuckled at her bright pink cheeks. "They can say what they want to say. And frankly, I'd rather the kids hear rumors about you and me than have kids gossiping about their dad."

She grew quiet, and Ollie wished he hadn't brought it up.

"Hey," he said. "Know one of the great things about living in a small town?"

"What?"

"Everyone at that school knows about Joe by now. All the teachers. All the secretaries. You don't have to repeat the story over and over. They got it. And while they might gossip behind their hands, they also care about your kids. So no sorry little snot is going to say anything mean to Mark or Chris or Loralie without a teacher or someone else smacking them for it."

She nodded. "Good point."

"And if they feel the need to gossip about me finally succumbing to your feminine wiles, that makes a much more interesting story, doesn't it?"

"Ha!" She barked out a laugh and clapped a hand over her mouth when she snorted. "Feminine wiles. Right."

"Don't underestimate yourself." He dropped his voice, reached behind her, and grabbed the lunches off the counter. "You've got plenty of wiles."

chapter
eleven

Allie stood in the wreck of her living room with Jena at her back and decided she'd had quite enough. Enough heartache. Enough grief. And enough with the damn toilet in the kids bathroom that never seemed to flush.

Seeing two rolls of toilet paper carelessly tossed into the bowl by the intruders had been the last straw.

Allie turned to Jena. "Fuck Joe and all the criminals he hung out with."

Jena bit her lip and put a hand over Becca's ear. "Don't make me get the swear jar."

Allie threw her head back and yelled at the ceiling. "Have we hit the limit yet? Does it start to get better now? I'm ready *anytime!*"

"Allie—"

"Seriously?" She kicked a pile of papers that had been pulled off her desk in the living room. "I'm done. Done. These guys were probably looking for something Joe stole or... who knows? That man hadn't been back to the house in a year. He hasn't even been slinking around. I'd have smelled him."

"Do you want to look on the bright side?"

"Not really. I always look on the bright side, and it doesn't seem to get me anywhere."

"You guys were gone," Jena said quietly. "Allie, I don't even want to think of what could have happened if—"

"No." She held up a hand. "No no no. Okay. Bright side. You're right. It could have been worse. And…" She kicked at the old couch which had been completely torn apart. "I hated that couch. Joe wanted to get it because it was on sale, but blue and yellow flowers? I mean, honestly. It was so ugly."

"See? Another bright side."

A memory tugged at the back of her mind. "I missed something last night."

"What are you talking about?"

With a quick shiver, Allie shifted. She crawled out of the sundress that had piled on the floor and darted out the door.

"Allie, what…?"

She didn't pause to explain. There had been something she sensed the night before. Something before she'd had to rush after the bear who'd charged in to rescue her.

Trotting around the edge of her property, she scented the humans again but got nothing more than she had the night before. Bad cologne, sweat, urine, and gunpowder.

She paused and listened to the wind. She could hear Jena setting up the portable play yard she'd brought for the baby before she started sorting through the trashed house. Allie scampered back, running along the foundation of the house.

There.

That cold, foreign scent ran under the porch. Allie followed it. She could hear Jena's footsteps above her, hear the batting of Becca's toys on the old hardwood floor.

The smell curled in one corner, just like the shifter had. Allie sniffed all around, then let out a low growl.

Snake.

Why wasn't she surprised?

ALLIE'S OLD MINIVAN PROTESTED AS SHE MADE THE SHARP left that would take her up to Old Quinn's place. She was furious, and the old man wasn't going to brush her off this time, woman or not.

She pulled into his driveway, not caring how much dust she kicked up. Sean was sitting on the front porch when she marched up to it, covered in a fine layer of sand.

"Hey, Allie," he sputtered out.

"Where is he?"

Sean raised an eyebrow but said nothing else. Just nodded toward the door.

Allie didn't knock. She marched in and went straight to the television, which was tuned to CNN. She stood in front of it and glared at Old Quinn.

Quinn calmly picked up the remote and turned off the TV.

"Miss Allie, I heard about the kids' daddy. Very sorry to hear about that."

"You knew it was him."

Old Quinn said nothing.

"What did you talk to Ollie about?"

"That's between me and the bear."

"No, it's not. Not when my house was trashed last night and I found the scent of one of your clan lurking under it."

His eyes narrowed. "How old was the scent?"

It was a fair question. On moon nights, the snakes hid everywhere. They would crawl anywhere they could get comfortable; it wasn't the first time she'd smelled a snake under her house.

"New. She might have been there last night, but I was chasing humans away."

"Species?"

She heard the screen door open and Sean walk in. Allie paused when she heard him.

"Who was it, Allie?" Sean asked in a low voice.

"Boa," she said.

With a muttered curse, Sean slammed out of the house. A few minutes later, she heard his truck peel out.

"What did Maggie have to do with Joe?" she asked. "And why did she lead those men to my house?"

"How do you know she did?"

"Seems a little too much of a coincidence. What did you tell Ollie?"

Old Quinn sighed. "Maggie wasn't fooling around with Joe. Not like that."

"I don't care if she was. What was she doing at my house?"

"Don't rightly know. Expect Sean will figure that one out."

"But you do know something."

Old Quinn paused, his mouth turned down at the corners. "There was a poker game," he finally said. "Humans in Palm Springs. High stakes. Maggie set it up for Joe to go."

"A high-stakes game? Joe was good, but he didn't have any money."

Or had he? Had Joe been hiding money while she was forced to beg? The thought made her sick to her stomach.

Old Quinn shook his head. "Maggie and a couple of her cousins staked Joe because he owed them money."

"How much was it?"

"Fifty-thousand-dollar buy-in."

Allie's eyes bugged out. "Are you kidding me?"

"Nope."

Her knees gave out and she collapsed into the old recliner. "Joe owed Maggie that much?"

Where the hell had Maggie Quinn gotten fifty grand? Allie decided she probably didn't want to know.

"Joe didn't owe her that much, but that was the buy-in, so that's what she staked him. If he'd won, he could have paid her back the stake, the money he owed her, and he'd still have a lot left over. Maggie said he wanted to give some of it to the kids, then he wanted to go to the East Coast. Start over."

Allie's heart sank again. So he *had* been planning to abandon the kids. "How much do I owe Maggie?"

"This is why I didn't want to tell you," Old Quinn said with a glare. "You don't owe her a damn thing. She's done enough, and she won't be bothering you for the money, you have my word on that."

She could feel the headache threatening. "If Joe owed her—"

"Allison Smith, stop being a damn martyr."

She blinked and stopped rubbing her forehead. "It's not being a martyr to pay what you owe."

"You didn't create that debt, and you don't owe her a damn thing."

"I'm his widow."

Old Quinn laughed. "You think Maggie was going to put that money on her taxes? Maybe take Joe to small-claims court if he didn't pay up? She'd have done no such thing. I don't know why she was at your house, but Maggie knows she did something stupid and Joe got killed because of it. I don't think my niece is dumb enough to approach the men who might have killed him."

"You're sure it was because of that game?" Allie tapped her nails together.

"I'm sure it's related. The problem is, not one of us"—Old Quinn leaned forward—"saw Joe again after that night. Not one of us knows what happened at that game. And no one, human or shifter, is talking."

She didn't see Sean before she left, and she wondered what special kind of torture his sister was putting him through. They weren't full-blooded siblings, but they had the same father, even if he was a piece of shit. Sean had felt responsible for Maggie until he'd had to finish her fights one too many times.

He'd bugged out. Taken off in the night and gotten as far from Cambio Springs as he could. And now he was back. For how long, nobody—including Sean, she suspected—knew.

She drove to the bar, curious what Ollie would have to say about the game. She'd been mad at first but then realized the day that he'd learned about the poker game from Old Quinn was the very same day they'd learned that Joe was dead. It seemed so much longer, but really, it had only been five days.

Five gut-wrenching, horrifying, emotionally draining days.

Ollie's truck was in the parking lot, along with a bike she didn't recognize. She thought it might have been Jim's, but she couldn't be sure. She only knew she had limited time before she needed to get back to her wreck of a house if she was going to salvage enough of the kids' clothes to make things livable at Ollie's house.

Allie walked in the back door and heard voices, but they didn't belong to Ollie and Jim.

"—know for sure."

"I don't want to hear maybes, Razio." Ollie's voice was so cold he sounded like a stranger.

"Well, maybes are all I got right now. The guy wasn't a big player. No one gossips about the little fish."

Ollie paused, and Allie suspected he'd heard her coming down the hall.

"Hey, babe."

Babe?

She emerged from the dark hallway to see Ollie sitting at a table with a burly biker slumped across from him. Ollie's face was blank, and he had a notebook in front of him that he was scribbling in, but he held a hand out to her.

"Hey," she said, walking toward the table. "I don't want to interrupt. I just—"

Without warning, Ollie pulled her onto his lap and perched her there, wrapping an arm around her waist and laying a hand possessively over one thigh. She tried not to gasp.

The man Ollie had called Razio smirked. "Didn't you know you had an old lady, Campbell."

"Apparently there's a lot you don't know."

The smirk fell. "Give me another week. We're riding down to Palm Desert to meet with some guys on Tuesday. I'll see what they've heard."

"Call me." Ollie never looked up, still making scratches in that notebook. He didn't look at Razio as he left the bar. Didn't look at Allie when she tried to wriggle free. He only relaxed the grip on her thigh when the sound of the motorcycle faded away.

"Who was that?"

"I didn't know you were coming by," he growled.

"I didn't know I was coming by until I talked to Old Quinn today."

He dropped the pencil and tried to turn her, but Allie took the opportunity to slide off his lap.

"And what was that about? 'Babe?' Your old lady?"

Ollie glared at her. "That guy doesn't need to know who you are. I'd rather he thought you were my girl than anyone he was allowed to pay attention to. Why did you go talk to Old Quinn?"

"Because there was a rosy boa curled up under my house last night.

Quinn told me everything. You were going to tell me about that game, right?"

A cheek muscle jumping under his beard told Allie that no, Oliver Campbell probably had no plans to share what her ex-husband was getting into. He'd planned on sheltering her and softening things like everything else.

"You *were* going to tell me, right, Ollie? I asked you to look into things, not hide them from me. This was my ex-husband, and you don't get to shield me from his shit."

He stood up. "I get to shield you from whatever the hell I want. You're a mom, Allie, but you're not *my* mom. Stop trying to boss me around."

"Stop trying to keep me in the dark."

"Stop trying to take on every damn thing in the world, then!" Ollie threw out his hand. "You've got the kids, two jobs, dealing with all of Joe's shit, which I know has been stressing you out. You asked me to look into this, so let me look into it."

"I need to know what's happening."

"Why?"

"Because it's my house that's getting broken into! It's my kids whose mattresses got ripped apart!" She felt the tears in her eyes and hated them. "It's my life, Ollie. It's my messed-up disaster of a life, and I'm the one who has to pick up the pieces when things fall apart. I'm the one who takes care of things, so I need to know when the next disaster is going to hit. At least give me that."

His mouth was a hard line. "What's wrong with letting me take care of this? What's wrong with—"

"Because it's not your mess. This. Is not. Your problem. And you're not going to be there every time things fall apart, so you need to let me—"

"I'm not going to be there?" A low growl rose from his chest. "Allie, I have *been here* for twenty years. I have stood by and watched you take on more and more until I didn't know how you stayed standing under the weight of it. I have been here..." He stepped forward and grabbed her shoulders. "*Right here.*"

Allie closed her eyes and felt the guilt eating her. He'd help. He'd take on her problems, and eventually, when it all became too much, he'd start resenting her. Resenting her kids. And she couldn't...

She couldn't bear the thought of Ollie looking at her with bitterness in his eyes.

"Allie-girl?" A warm thumb brushed over her cheek. "Don't cry, darlin'. I can't handle seeing you cry."

"I'm not sad, I'm mad."

"I know you're mad. And overwhelmed. But I'm trying to help."

"Why? We've already taken over your house."

He wrapped his big arms around her. "It survived me and my cousins. The house'll be fine."

Allie put her arms around his waist and let herself lean. "If you want me to not stress so much, you need to tell me what's going on. *Not* knowing stresses me out more than anything."

He paused to think. "Okay. That makes sense. How much time do you have this afternoon?"

"None." She let out a cynical laugh. "I need to get back to the house and sort through all the mess. Jena was going to do the kitchen, but then she had to go work at the resort. She and Alex are ordering stuff for the restaurant."

"Why don't you let me send Vicky over to the house? She's always looking for extra work."

"I can't pay her for that."

"I'll pay her," Ollie said.

"You can't—"

He put a quick hand over her mouth. "Yes, I can."

Allie glared at him until he removed his hand. "You're awfully presumptuous, Oliver Campbell."

"Keep watching." His mouth twitched. "I'm about to get a lot worse."

WITH THREE QUICK PHONE CALLS, OLLIE HAD VICKY cleaning at her house, his cousins picking up the younger kids from the bus while Kevin did his shift at the feed store, and Jim covering the bar until Ollie and Allie could get there at six. Then he'd piled her in the truck and headed toward the Blackbird Diner.

"I'm guessing you haven't eaten today."

"I've had coffee."

"Coffee is not a meal, Allison."

"Now who's acting like a mom?"

He smiled. "Don't pout. Or do. It's kinda cute."

Allie couldn't help that her body heated—she just hoped he didn't notice. "You need to stop. Talking like that is just going to fuel the rumors that are probably already flying."

He shrugged. "Let 'em fly. I don't care."

"Men never do."

"And women care too much." He parked at the diner and turned to her with a gleam of mischief in his eyes. "Tell the truth: are you ashamed of me, Allie? Is it my... rough reputation?"

"Oh please..." She reached for the door handle, only to have Ollie grab her hand. "Ollie, what—"

He'd leaned across the cab of the Bronco, reaching one tattooed arm to the door while he grabbed her other hand and held it between them. She was trapped against him, her mouth inches from his and his chest pressed up against her racing heart.

"What are you doing?" she gasped.

"You should let me open the door for you."

Breathe, breathe, breathe, Allie. Do not tackle the giant grizzly and wrestle him into the backseat to have your way with him.

"Why? I can open my own door."

"Because it's nice. I like being nice to you," he said a moment before he brushed a featherlight kiss over the corner of her mouth. "And that door can stick."

With a hard shove that pressed their bodies even closer, he opened the passenger door.

But he didn't move away.

"Ollie," she said, glancing at a couple walking into the diner that had stopped to watch the show.

"Yeah," he whispered, "you definitely care too much what other people think."

"We can't all be big bad grizzly bears like you."

 129

The corner of his mouth curled up. "Who said I was bad?"

"I did."

"And I haven't even done anything to earn it." He leaned back to his side of the truck. "Yet."

Allie escaped the cab of the Bronco and leaned against the side, trying to calm her heart.

Calm. So he's flirting with you. Or something. Sean flirts with you too. It doesn't mean—

She almost yelped when he grabbed her hand.

"Come on," he said. "Let's go ambush Ted."

"What? Why?"

"Because I heard an interesting rumor today, and I'm hoping Ted can explain it. She's family, and I'd really hate to maul her. You wanted me to keep you informed? You're informed."

"I'm gonna say my job might also be keeping you from mauling your cousin and one of my best friends."

"Yep." He held the door open. "That's probably a good idea too."

Still clasping her hand, Ollie walked them down the middle of the diner, having already spotted Ted at her usual booth in the corner.

"Hey, Mr. Crowe," Ollie said. "Can Allie and I get two hamburgers to go?"

"Sure thing, son." Thomas Crowe, Jena's father and adopted grandparent to Allie's kids, watched them with narrowed eyes. "Hey there, Allie."

"Hi, Tom."

"Finally cooling off out there, huh?"

"Yep!" Had it gotten cooler? Allie hadn't noticed.

Ollie pushed through the whispering lunchtime crowd and walked to Ted's corner.

"Hey, cuz," he said, gently pushing Allie into the booth before he slid in. "How's lunch?"

"The pot roast sandwich is good." Ted was eyeing their joined hands with definite interest. "But maybe I should be asking you the questions."

"You could." Ollie lowered his voice. "Or maybe you can explain why there's a group of bikers who transport weed for the Di Stefano crew who told me they don't have to worry about getting shot anymore, because isn't it nice they have a doctor right here in Cambio Springs?"

Ted muttered, "Shit."

Allie was blinking, trying to catch up. "Wait, what? Who are the... who's selling weed? Someone was shot?"

"No one's been shot," Ted said. "Yet."

"But if they do?" Ollie's face was like granite.

Ted leaned back and set the rest of her sandwich down. "Why don't we wait for your lunch? Then we can head over to my office for a more... private chat."

"Yeah," Ollie said. "That sounds like a really good idea."

chapter
twelve

Ollie had forgotten his hamburger about three justifications ago.

"Cam already knew something was different about the town. I figured... if he had a vested interest in keeping people away—"

"Except the criminals he'd be giving your name to," Ollie said. "Keep everyone away except for them, right, Ted?"

Ted turned to Alex. The wolf alpha had driven over from the building site of the new Cambio Springs Resort and Spa. The resort that was promising to bring hundreds of jobs to the small town and possibly save it from ruin. The resort that was also threatening to expose the one place in the world where their people had been safe.

"Listen, Ollie." Alex sat down next to Ted, still clad in dusty work clothes. "I wasn't thrilled about it, either. But Ted's right. With the resort going in, the town will be under scrutiny."

"Right," he bit out. "That tiny little private resort that was going to be so exclusive that barely anything was going to change at all, right Alex? That resort? The resort that's already led to two murders?"

Alex's face paled, but his eyes narrowed and he did not look away from his old friend.

Ted hissed, "That's not fair. Alex is not responsible for those deaths."

The resentment that had been simmering for months between Ollie and Alex finally boiled over.

"Don't ever think," Ollie told him, "that you have my approval in this idiocy. I held my tongue because my grandfather abstained from the vote. But my silence does not mean approval. This hotel will change everything."

"The town was dying."

"So you say."

"It was." Alex glanced at Allie, who was sitting next to the angry bear. "How many times did Joe ask you to move your kids, Allie? Because he couldn't find work."

"Joe's dead," Allie said quietly. "Our problems started way before he lost his job. Don't bring him into this."

"He's one example," Ted said. "I see them every day. This town was dying. The resort gave it a future. We had to do something."

"Maybe," Ollie said. "But we didn't have to invite the damn mafia in, Ted."

"Cam isn't the mafia," she mumbled.

"Oh yeah! I'm sure he's the kinder, gentler gang leader. Who only runs illegal gambling and drugs and not human trafficking and weapons. Let's invite him over for coffee with Yaya."

Alex squeezed Ted's hand. "Careful, bear. I'll give you some latitude because you're family, but watch your tone when you're talking to my mate."

"She invited them in!" he exploded. "The Campbells have worked for a hundred and fifty years to keep this town safe, and she invited them in and offered them sanctuary."

He felt Allie's hand on his shoulder, but he could barely think past his rage. All he could think of were hardened criminals driving to Ted's clinic in the middle of the night, eyeing the sleepy town and its citizens. People he was responsible for. People who were family and friends. Vulnerable people he loved.

"I will never understand why you would do this," Ollie said. "Stop trying to justify it."

Ted, an apex predator herself, didn't give an inch. "We needed an ally. And I'm not offering sanctuary. I'm offering medical care. Nothing less than I'd offer a wounded person who showed up at my door right now. It doesn't matter who they are, I'd treat them because I made a promise when I became a doctor. I serve this town, but I don't belong to it."

Ollie lowered his voice. "You're impulsive as shit, and you did not think this through. You don't know these people."

"And you do?" Ted asked. "Cam is Alex's friend."

"Yeah, I know these people. And not from the country club. I see the bruises and the busted knuckles and the guns. These are not people you mess with. Not people you make friendly agreements with."

"Like you don't have agreements with people?" Alex asked. "That's a little hypocritical, don't you think?"

"If things get messy at the bar, they *don't* come into town. And if I have to get dirty to keep people safe, that's one thing. But Ted is a doctor. And you're the leader of the most powerful clan in the Springs. How could you back her up on this, Alex?"

"Don't act like he owns me," Ted said. "You know better."

"Ollie," Allie whispered into his shoulder. "It's done. Arguing about it isn't going to do anything. Cam's people aren't going to let them renege on the deal, are they?"

"No." He took a deep breath.

"Then it's done." She squeezed his hand. "We make the best of it. That's all we can do."

He squeezed her hand back and held it, unwilling to let go of the softness she offered. It calmed the predatory instincts in him like nothing ever had.

And if the Di Stefano family was going to use the Springs, then he was going to use the Di Stefanos.

"Since you and Cameron Di Stefano are such great buddies now," Ollie said, "then I want you to ask him for some information."

Alex's hard eyes flicked to Allie and softened. "About Joe?"

Ollie nodded. "There was a private poker game in Palm Springs last year. Happened just after Joe left. The Quinns backed him, but we don't know who was there or what happened."

"What kind of stakes?" Alex asked.

"According to Maggie Quinn, the winner would have taken two hundred grand home."

"Holy shit," Ted said. "And someone let Joe enter that?"

Alex and Ollie exchanged glances, but it was Allie who spoke.

"Oh, he might have taken it," she said. "Joe was damn good. I'd never play with him. Neither would my dad."

"So why all the gambling debt?" Ted asked.

"Because he drank," Allie said. "And the more he drank, the stupider he got. But the more he won, the more he drank. I'm sure the casinos loved him."

Ollie looked down at Allie's hand in his and thought what a monumental idiot Joe Russell had been. To have this woman and risk her respect because of cards disgusted him.

"I'll ask Cam," Alex said. "With stakes like that, he'd know who hosted it or know who to ask."

"And what will he want in exchange for the information?"

"Nothing. We're friends."

"Wrong," Ollie said. "You may be friends, but he'll want something. If nothing else, it's a mark that's gonna sit in his ledger. But don't ever think he'll forget."

Alex was still pissed. "He's trying to go straight. Make his whole family legitimate. You think that happens overnight? Happens without effort?"

"Don't know," Ollie said. "And I don't care. That's not my problem. This town is my problem. Feel free to worry about Cameron Di Stefano and his ethical dilemmas, Alex. But don't expect me to care. If he's a threat to this town, you know what my clan will do. And the Elder Council won't say a word."

ALLIE SAT SILENT IN THE TRUCK WHILE HE DROVE HER BACK to the Cave where her van was parked. That car was on its last legs. He needed to take a look at it and make sure it wasn't going to fall apart while she was driving the kids, but he'd probably have to argue with her about paying him.

"Hey," he said. "You still working tonight?"

She frowned. "Of course. It's Friday. Best tips."

"You've had a hell of a week. If you don't want to put up with all the crowds, I can call someone else in."

She shook her head. "I need to work."

"This isn't about money, is it?"

"I've got bills to pay, Ollie. That doesn't change because I'm staying with you. And you need to let me chip in for groceries. I heard you tell Vicky this morning to buy enough food for an army."

"You're not paying for groceries," he growled.

"Then we're going to my dad's."

He glared. "The hell you are."

Ollie had plenty of money, and he liked spending it on her and the kids. Why did she have to argue with him?

"If you don't let me pay my way, we are." She glared at him right back. "My family is not some kind of charity case. I refuse to—"

"What was that envelope Alex gave you, huh?"

Bright red streaked her cheeks. "He heard about the kids' rooms," she whispered. "Gave me some money to replace their stuff. He wouldn't let me say no. It wasn't from him, it was clan money."

"So the wolves can help you out, but I can't?"

"They're family. You're my friend. It's different. You already gave me a job."

Her *friend*. For the first time, the label grated. He was tired of being her damn friend. If he had a greater claim on her, she wouldn't be able to argue.

Okay, she'd argue, but he'd have better leverage.

"I know you don't like it," she continued over his silence, "but it's different. When my mom was alive, she contributed to the clan. Not a lot, but some. But if you give me money—"

"You might have to relax about it and maybe say thank you," he said. "That would be *horrible*."

Her eyes were bright with tears, but he knew they were the angry variety. He shut up. She cried when she got angry, and he knew she hated it. He didn't want to provoke her.

"I see we're back to Ollie being an asshole," she said. "Good to know."

She leaned back, crossed her arms, and they didn't say another word the entire way home.

THE SILENCE CONTINUED AT THE BAR. THE CAVE WAS hopping with a popular cover band from Coachella, and most of the tables were happy and shouting. A few couples were dancing, and the drinks were flowing. Even the Quinns were behaving, other than a group of the younger cousins trying to charm a few girls passing through on their way to the river.

It wasn't Ollie's job to prevent poor judgment.

It was the kind of night he normally loved. Mostly locals with a few visitors mixed in. Heads thrown back and a few playful howls the full humans laughed off. But Ollie couldn't shake his foul mood.

"You have been glaring daggers at her all night," Tracey said when she sidled up to him behind the bar. "What happened? I thought you two—"

"Leave it."

Tracey's eyebrows flew up her forehead. It was a warning shot that made every Campbell or Allen man wary. "Oh, I don't think so, Oliver Campbell. Don't make me have my man beat your ass for being rude to me. I am not your cute little fox, too polite to argue with you."

"She argues with me plenty."

"So that's what's up your butt?" Tracey rolled her eyes. "Get over it. She knows her own mind, and there is nothing wrong with that. If you're lucky, you'll spend the next fifty years arguing with that woman. Better get used to it now."

"It's so strange," he said. "It's almost like I pay you to stand around and interfere in my personal life."

She laughed. "Cranky old man."

"Younger than you."

"Doesn't make you any less of a cranky old man." She leaned toward him and smiled. "I know how to work the cranky out of my old man. Bet she does too."

He put a hand on Tracey's shoulder and turned her one hundred eighty degrees, pointing her back to the loaded tray she needed to carry out to table two. She laughed at him and took off, but he worried she'd do something to interfere.

Was he worried she'd interfere or hopeful?

He had silently filled four more orders for the frustrating fox by the time he noticed her red cheeks and bright eyes.

"What?" he asked.

She looked up, her blush only growing brighter. "What what?"

He scowled and she took off with her tray, only to deliver it to a booth with four guys, two of whom were smiling and laughing as she approached. For a second, he was about to go out to the floor, then he saw Tracey approach.

He settled. Tracey was a pro and she was able to defuse most situations with a laugh or a sharp word.

But...

She wasn't diverting the men's attention. She put one arm around Allie's waist and leaned in, teasing her about something before Tracey pinched the cheek of the youngest-looking guy.

What the...?

When one of the guys offered Allie a card, his cousin's wife took it and put it Allie's apron before she walked off laughing. Then she turned back to the bar and raised a single, challenging eyebrow.

Ollie scowled. Tracey could try to interfere, but he knew Allie wasn't the kind of waitress who picked up customers.

His eyes went back to her. She was still at the table, but now the other three men were watching the band and drinking while the one who'd given Allie his card chatted with her. And the look on her face...

She was smiling. Her eyes were relaxed, and he could see the usual tension she always carried in her shoulders was gone. Her cheeks still carried a faint blush, but she was talking with the guy, who didn't appear to be an asshole. He was looking at her eyes, not her breasts.

Shit.

You think you're going to be able to handle seeing her go out with another guy under your nose?

What if she did? What if this asshole came and picked her up *at his house* for a date?

She finally left the table and moved through her section, picking up empties and taking orders while she chatted with customers. The bright, sweet look on her face never left, and Ollie knew she was having fun. Allie was one of the rare people who actually liked helping customers. It was tiring, sure, but she thrived on the energy too.

"Ollie." She was at the bar. "I need four DBAs, a glass of merlot, two Pinot Grigios. And two Jack and Cokes when you get a chance."

He started pulling pints while she unloaded her empties. He was making the mixed drinks when she came behind the bar.

"I'll get the wine."

"Having fun?"

Her smile lit up her face. "I am. Feels good to be busy, and the band's good, right? I remember them from last time. Fun night."

"Yeah."

She finished pouring the red and opened the white.

"I don't pay you to flirt with customers, Allie."

She splashed the white wine over her hand. Then she set the bottle down on the bar and put her hands on her hips.

"You—"

"Hey!" Tracey said, leaning over the bar and grabbing Allie's tray. "I'll get this. Allie, take a break. I think the guy at five just went out for a smoke."

Allie's eyes met his in challenge, and before she could walk away, Ollie grabbed her arm.

"I don't think so."

He marched her back to his office and slammed the door as Allie shook off his hand.

"What. The. Hell?" She was furious. "What do you think you're doing?"

"If you go out with that guy, I'll break his arms."

"You asshole!" she yelled. "He was being nice!"

"He was not just being nice, Allie. Are you that naive?"

She sneered. "Do I look like a little girl? I'm not stupid, Ollie, even though you think I'm still some kind of innocent teenager."

Ollie crossed his arms. "Yeah, no. That's not it."

"He was being nice to me. He's sweet. He's a real estate agent from Indio who likes music. And yeah! He *was* flirting with me. It felt nice!"

Nice? Fuck nice. He wasn't ever going to be *nice*.

"And you know what?" She continued to rail at him. "There's nothing wrong with my feeling nice. Nothing wrong with my feeling like a woman instead of a worn-out wreck all the time. You and Sean joke and tease me, but at the end of the day, you still see me as Poor Little Allie with all her kids and her prob— What are you doing?"

Ollie was done. He stalked over to her until she was backed against

Elizabeth Hunter

the door. Then he leaned down, put his hands on that perfect ass, and lifted her until they were face-to-face.

"This"—he pressed her against the back of the door and wrapped her legs around his waist—"is me setting you straight, Allison Smith."

He kissed her.

It started out simple. He didn't want to lose control. He needed to be careful—

Then her mouth parted in shock, she let out a little gasp, and he felt her breath on his lips.

Her head hit the door when his mouth took hers. He reached one hand up and cradled her head, angling her mouth so he could take her deeper. She tasted like sweet tea. She smelled like heaven.

Ollie lost it.

His hips pressed forward to pin her to the wall, the hand on her ass squeezed and held, her body a delicious handful he wanted to eat up. Her arms wrapped around his neck and her mouth opened to his, her tongue driving deep in his mouth on a moan. One hand gripped a handful of the hair at his nape, raising every hair on his body as he tried to ignore the scent of her arousal as it grew lush between them.

It was everything.

He'd spent years imagining what it would be to kiss her. Hold her in his arms. But the violence of his possession shocked him into drawing back.

"No," she breathed out, pulling his mouth back to hers.

He groaned and leaned in. The hand that had cradled her head caressed her cheek, and she let his mouth go, moving to kiss his palm, her head tilting to the side and exposing her neck. Ollie bent down and put his mouth at the soft skin there, flicking his tongue against the pounding pulse. Allie drew his thumb into her mouth and sucked hard, then slid her teeth across the callused flesh. Ollie pulled her head to the side to expose more of her neck.

She tilted her head back and let out a gasp when he bit down on her collarbone, the soft wing of it something he'd wanted to bite for years.

"Ollie—"

"No." He took her mouth again. He didn't want to stop. Didn't want her to start talking again. Didn't even want her thinking. He wanted only this. The liquid heat between them and the promise of

* 140 *

satisfaction so near he could taste it in the give of her flesh and her welcoming lips.

He bit down on her lower lip, then sucked it into his mouth when she gasped. He shifted her closer, letting her feel the solid arousal that pulsed between them. Hard against soft. He squeezed and angled her hips like he would when he took her.

The tiny, begging moans from her throat were enough to make him forget everything.

He wanted her. Only her.

She pulled away from his mouth, gasping. "Ollie!"

"I do not"—he scraped his teeth along her jawline—"want you flirting..."

"What?" Her head fell back and hit against the door.

"...with anyone but me."

Ollie captured her earlobe, determined to taste everything. Sample every bit of her he'd dreamed about. He wanted to know the flavor of her belly and the taste of her breasts. He'd savor the smooth skin at her ankle and feast on the spice of the flesh between her thighs. He would know every inch of her. Because she would be his.

"No one but me," he said, pressing his hips closer and squeezing his hand on her backside. "And I will never be nice."

"Nice?" Her head fell back and her eyelashes fluttered. "What...?"

Ollie feathered his lips over hers and whispered, "But, Allison, I will rock you like—"

A loud bang came at the door.

"Hey, lovebirds!" Tracey shouted. "We're dying out here. Break's over."

They froze. Ollie realized he still had a handful of Allie's ass and her legs were locked around his hips in a very promising position.

"Allie?"

She slapped his shoulder. "Let me down!"

Her heart pounded against his chest. He didn't want to let her down. If he let her down and she ran—

"Please." Her head fell against his chest. "I can't... I can't think about this right now. I need to go back to work. I won't flirt with that guy, okay? Lesson learned."

Wait... what?

"Allie—"

"Please let me go," she whispered. "I need to get back to work."

Without another word, he released her, carefully sliding her down his body. She let out a small breath when her belly raked against his erection, but he stepped back and let her straighten her clothes before she slipped out the door.

What had just happened?

chapter
thirteen

Avoiding someone in a small town was difficult. Avoiding someone when you lived in their house was darn near impossible.

Allie had never been so grateful she had four noisy, time-sucking children.

"Allie?"

Ollie almost caught her in the hallway, but she slammed Loralie's door closed. "Gotta get the baby dressed!"

Loralie looked up at her with wide eyes. "That wasn't nice, Mama."

"I know it wasn't. I'll say sorry later."

Much later. Possibly never if she could manage it.

She went to the dresser and pulled out some grub clothes for Loralie that wouldn't be ruined at Allie's dad's store while she heard Ollie pace for a few minutes before he walked away.

Tracey had taken mercy on her the night before and given her a ride home so she wouldn't have to wait for Ollie to close up. By the time she heard his boots on the front porch, she was in bed. And she ignored the quiet tap at her door.

Saturday morning, she had the excuse of heading to the feed store with Chris and Loralie while Kevin and Mark worked in the shop with Ollie.

Saturday was her father's busiest day because Smith Feed doubled

Elizabeth Hunter

as the local garden shop. It had been Allie's idea to expand the ornamental plant section and sell more than vegetable starts. Because of it, her father's shop was busy every weekend, and he sold more pet food too.

Of course, it also meant he always needed extra help. Some days it grated on her that every Saturday was spent working. Today it was a relief, even if she was exhausted.

Large hands cupping her backside. Her cheek. The bite of his teeth at her shoulder as he held her against the door.

"Allison, I will rock you…"

She stepped away from the memory that had kept her up all night and dressed Loralie. Then she snuck to the door and listened.

"Mama, what are you doing?"

"What?"

Loralie giggled. "Are we playing?" Her little girl put her ear to the door. "I'll play too."

Sighing, Allie realized that she was being ridiculous. She cracked the door open, only to see Ollie leaning against the opposite wall, his arms crossed over his chest and his mouth set in a firm line.

"Good morning, Ollie!" Loralie ran to give his legs a quick hug. "I'm hungry," she said, then ran down the stairs.

Deserter.

"Morning."

"Hey." She waved at him. Because she was lame. "I, um…"

It never paid to forget how quick bears could be despite their size. With a quick shove at the wall, he was on her, pressing her back and planting his lips on hers like he owned them.

Every single thought fled.

So… he maybe owned them a little.

"I wanted"—two quick kisses and a sucking taste of her earlobe as he whispered—"to talk to you. And you ran off."

"This isn't talking," she managed to gasp out.

"Mo-om!"

Allie shoved him back a second before Chris and Mark's door flew open.

Saved by the second grader.

"Why can't I stay and work in the barn?"

Mark yelled from behind him, "'Cause you're too little, dork!"

"Do not call your brother a dork," Allie snapped.

Ollie asked, "Hey, Mark, you want to be sweeping with the little broom all day?"

"Sorry, Chris," Mark mumbled a second before he slipped out the door and headed toward the stairs.

The one thing Chris was horrible at doing was sitting still. If he was let loose in Ollie's barn without strict supervision, the seventy-year-old building might just come crashing down.

Allie tried to find a better excuse. "Chris, if you stay with the older boys, then no one will be at the store to play with Loralie. That's no fun for her."

His lower lip trembled. "But—"

"You love Grandpa's store. And you're always such a good helper, telling people where things are and how they work."

"But Kevin and Mark—"

"Hey." Ollie reached over and mussed Chris's hair. "You need to help your mom with the baby today. You and me will do something later, okay?"

Chris considered this. "Just you and me?"

"Yep. Today's going to be all work anyway. It won't be any fun. But I'll throw the ball with you later if you want."

"Okay!" Chris bounced down the hallway with Allie following at his heels.

The coward's way out?

Allie preferred to think of it as a strategic retreat.

Breakfast passed in much of the same blur. Allie made a quick batch of pancakes for the kids while Ollie watched her with heated eyes. With four children around, he couldn't say anything, and yes, she absolutely took advantage of that.

"See you later!" she called as she herded the younger kids to the car. "Kevin, make sure you help with your brother. Mark, listen to Kevin."

Ollie leaned against a porch post, and she could have sworn there was a hint of a smile on his face. But what worried her wasn't the smile, it was his eyes. They were amused. Like he was enjoying this. As if this was a game.

The problem was, Allie was worried it *was* a game. One that she had no idea how to play.

"Hey!" Jena waved at her when she pulled up. "How are you?"

Allie was in the front, watering the bedding plants that everyone would be planting soon. Fall rolling around meant that daytime temperatures dropped and people could finally plant cool-weather plants and fill pots with something other than cactus.

"I'm fine," she said, staring at the stream of water. "Just... fine. What are Caleb and the boys doing today?"

Her best friend walked over with Becca babbling on her hip. "Bear has a science project due on Monday that he conveniently forgot about until last night."

"Of course."

"I think Low is heading over to Ollie's place to work on the car with Kev." Jena hiked the baby higher. "You look weird."

Her eyes darted up. "What? No. No, I don't. I don't look weird."

"Yep. Now you look even weirder. What happened?"

Allie blinked. "You mean, other than my ex-husband being killed, my house being broken into, and me being forced to take up residence with my boss?"

Jena pursed her lips. "You're right. Look as weird as you want. You've had a long week."

"Ollie kissed me last night. And this morning." A burst of hysterical laughter left her throat, and Allie slapped a hand over her mouth.

"Whoa." Jena's eyes popped open. "What? Back up. Kissing?"

Allie nodded.

"Like *kissing* kissing? Or on the cheek? A slight... brush?"

She shook her head. "Hike me up against a wall, grab my ass, and pull my hair kissing."

"Nice!" Jena grinned.

"No! Not nice. Not..." She pulled her friend to the side and shut off the hose that was, at this point, only wasting water. "This is *not nice*. This is... confusing. And not well-timed. Probably completely irresponsible."

"Allie"—Jena patted her cheek—"the rest of us have been waiting for this since Joe left. You're living in the man's house. He's only got so much self-restraint, even if he is Ollie. I'm only surprised it didn't happen sooner."

Allie fell silent and went back to watering the plants. She walked away and continued on the next rack.

"Allie?"

Nothing. She had absolutely nothing to say. Her brain was mush, and it was all Ollie's fault.

"Allie." Jena sounded more concerned and less amused. "Did you not want him to? Did he—"

"I kissed him back. *Trust me*, I kissed him back. I just don't know what to do with this." She shut off the hose again. "He's Ollie. He's been my friend since we were kids. And he always... He's always been there."

Her heart was pounding. Just thinking about changing the boundaries with Ollie had her panicked.

Jena asked, "Are you not attracted to him?"

Allie gave a startled laugh. "No, that's not the problem. Why do you think Joe hated Ollie so much? I'm sure he knew..." She squeezed her eyes tight. "I tried not to think about it. I *couldn't* think about it, you know? But you can be sure attraction has never been the problem."

"Then what?"

"My *life*." She started to roll up the hose. She took a few minutes, concentrating on the routine movement. Feeling the heat. Getting out of her head for a precious moments.

"Your life?"

Allie walked to a row of garden benches her dad had placed under a shade cover and sat down. Absently, she noted a car in the parking lot with two guys inside. They were just sitting there. Weren't they going to get out? They must have been baking out there.

Jena asked, "What about your life?"

"It's crazy. I work all the time. I have four kids. My ex-husband was murdered by mobsters... maybe? And they broke into my house looking for something." She looked up helplessly. "This doesn't happen to real people. This is a bad movie. And then, here comes this guy— this amazing guy!—who has been my friend for years. And now he wants... I don't know!"

Jena smiled softly. "Did you ask him?"

"No! Because he kissed me. And it was amazing. And I freaked out."

Jena sat down next to her and bounced the baby on her knee while Becca babbled and swung her little arms. "Freaking out is kind of understandable. The first time I had sex with Caleb, I turned into a hawk and left him in the middle of the desert right afterward."

Allie blinked. "That was stupid."

"It really was. But... I panicked." Jena shrugged. "There had only ever been Lowell. I didn't know how to be with anyone else. So I get the fear."

That car was still sitting there. What the hell?

"I am fully aware that I have baggage," Allie said. "I know how to survive in a bad relationship; I don't know how to be in a good one. And Ollie deserves to have someone amazing." Her throat started to close up. "He *is* amazing. He deserves a lot more than a messed-up woman with four kids."

"You're not messed up. You're Allie. You're awesome. Strong and smart and funny. A great mom. One of the most optimistic people I've ever met, even when things are falling apart."

Allie let out a watery laugh. "Does that make me optimistic or just stupid?"

"Not stupid. And your kids are great." She kept bouncing the baby as Becca let out a burp that would make a prizefighter proud. "They're like a bonus prize with all your awesome."

"Four kids are a bonus prize?" Allie glanced at the baby. "You do realize she's got spit-up all down her front, right?"

"I feel it dripping on my arm. I'm aware. Don't distract me."

"Okay."

Jena bumped Allie's shoulder. "Allison Smith, you are a gift. And one seriously hot mama. You think Ollie doesn't see that? I think he knows exactly what he wants. The only question is: are you brave enough to ask?"

Allie wasn't listening to her anymore. There was something about that car that was making her nose twitch. She glanced back at her dad's shop. She could hear Loralie and Chris playing a game behind the large terra-cotta pots in the landscape supplies and the low drone of conversation from her father and a farmer who'd come in a few minutes before.

She took a step toward the parking lot, but the minute she did, the dark sedan peeled out, raising dust as it roared back down the road.

"Who was that?" Jena rose to her feet, wiping Becca's chin with a cloth diaper.

"I have no idea."

BY THE TIME SHE GOT HOME FROM HER JOB AT THE FEED store, Allie was exhausted. Physically, yes. But emotionally, she was wrecked. She'd been thinking about what to do with Ollie all afternoon between juggling two kids, a constant stream of customers, and a dark luxury sedan that was eerily similar to the one driven by the men who'd broken into her house.

She'd also come to a sad but obvious conclusion.

She didn't have time.

Just thinking about a new relationship was exhausting. She didn't have the emotional energy to devote to someone who tore her up as much as Oliver Campbell did. If *thinking* about being with him stressed her out this much, then *being* with him was out of the question. Getting through every day as things were was barely manageable.

He must have caught a hint of her mood when she walked in, because the playful expression on his face fell and he looked back to the television where the older boys were watching a football game.

She hated that too. Hated that she'd disappointed him. He deserved so much better.

"Hey, baby." She went over to brush a hand over Kevin's damp hair. He'd always be her baby, even if he was taller than her. "How's your car?"

His smile lit her up. "Awesome."

"And the shop is superclean, Mom," Mark said. "I even organized all the spare parts in the junk drawer. Ollie gave me twenty bucks."

Her eyes darted to him. "You didn't have to do that."

"He earned it." Ollie's eyes never left the television.

Allie paused. "Okay. I'm going to start dinner so we'll have plenty of time to eat before work."

"We're not going to the bar tonight. I called Alex and Ted to help fill in. They owe me."

Her heart began to pound. Just because she was living in his house didn't mean she didn't have her own bills to pay. "Ollie—"

"You're staying home?" Chris said, bouncing into the room. "Can we go play catch then?"

"Yep."

Ollie rose from the couch and walked out with Chris as Loralie snuggled next to Kevin, leaving Allie to stand in the entryway with her argument dying on her lips. She choked on her own frustration. Here she was, complaining about missing a night at work while Ollie kept a promise to her son.

Always practical. Never fun. She couldn't remember the last time she'd had fun. She'd become a picture of the harried single mother, and she hated it. Wiping away an angry tear, she went to the kitchen and pulled out the chicken she'd defrosted for dinner.

The world does not revolve around you, Allison Smith.

"Maybe it should. Every now and then."

DINNER PASSED IN MUCH THE SAME WAY, THE KIDS HAPPY and chattering while Ollie listened silently and avoided looking at her. Which was only fair as she was avoiding looking at him too. Not that she was very successful.

"Hey!" Kevin said. "What movie do you guys want to watch?"

"*Transformers!*" Chris screamed.

"No," Loralie whined. "I want Merida!"

"Not again," Mark groaned.

Allie was just about to interrupt and settle things when Ollie stood and grabbed her hand.

"Let them figure it out," he said roughly. "We need to talk. Kevin, we'll be out in the barn if there's blood."

Kevin glanced at Ollie's hand holding hers, his lips showing the edge of a smile. "Okay."

Allie sighed and walked out, mentally preparing for the inevitable confrontation while her children argued in the background. Every step away from the house, she grew more nervous.

Would this ruin their friendship?

Would Ollie stop spending time with the kids?

She couldn't handle not having him in her life, and her kids practically worshipped him. Allie was almost in tears when they finally reached the barn.

Before he even flipped on the lights, Ollie turned and bent down, cupping her cheeks and looking into her eyes.

"Stop," he whispered. "Just stop. I can hear you arguing already, and I want you to listen."

Heart pounding, she put her hand on his shoulder while he brushed away the tears that were falling down her face.

"Ollie, I can't."

"Stop." He kissed her. No ravenous kiss this time, but a tender brush of lips. Over and over. His lips pressing against hers. His hands on her cheeks. Her neck. Stroking over her shoulders—

"No!" She shoved him away. "I told you I can't."

He walked over and silently punched a fist into the barn wall, breaking clear through without so much as a snarl. Then he turned his back and braced his arms on the hood of the old truck.

"Why?" His voice was frighteningly calm. "Do you not want me?"

"Of course I want you," she said, her whole body trembling. "Do you know how hard it is to stay away from you?"

He spun around. "Yeah, I do know."

"Right," she scoffed. "I hardly think—"

"Think what?" He took a step closer. "Do you think this just came out of nowhere, Allie? That suddenly I decided a few days ago I wanted more?"

Elizabeth Hunter

Her anger piqued, she said, "You know what? That's kind of what it seems like to me."

"Are you kidding me?" The look on his face was shock mixed with a healthy amount of anger. "Seriously?"

"Yeah, Ollie. How long has this been on your mind?" She put her hands on her hips. "Because last I remembered, you were seeing that girl from LA."

He spat out, "I haven't been with anyone since before Joe left you, Allie."

She took a step back. No, it couldn't have been that long. She'd seen him...

Allie realized she couldn't remember the last time she'd seen him with a woman. And she saw them. Every single one.

"It seemed stupid to even try anymore." He crossed his arms over his chest. "Not when the only person I could think about was you."

No. He couldn't have been...

"You're—"

"Hung up on you? Bet your ass I am."

Her heart felt like it stopped, then it began to race.

Ollie couldn't have had feelings for her. Not this whole time. Not since before...

"How long?" she whispered.

"How long do you think?"

She shook her head. "How long, Ollie?"

His face was a mask. Only his eyes gave her any clue what he was feeling, and the look in them was enough to make her cry.

"High school." His voice broke a little. "I guess. Around then."

The pressure in her chest was painful. "Then why... You never said anything. Not once. In all these years."

"What was I going to say?" He cleared his throat. "Honestly, Allie, what was I supposed to do?"

She didn't know. But something keen and painful and maybe even a little angry broke inside her.

So *many* years.

"Even when we were kids?" She dashed a tear from her cheek. "Why didn't you ever—"

"I was big and awkward and quiet. And you were... you. You made me nervous." He let out a bitter laugh. "So damn nervous. And then... He made you happy. I thought he made you happy."

She shook her head. "I can't... Ollie, *all this time?*"

His mouth said nothing, but his silence said all.

He'd cared for her. *Wanted* her. Her friend. All these years. Through everything. During the *years* of pain and the loneliness and heartache... Allie couldn't wrap her brain around it. She turned and started walking to the door. It was too much. Too—

Ollie reached around her and slammed the door shut.

"No. Not anymore. Don't walk away. We're finishing this. I'm done being patient, and you said you want me."

"We're not kids anymore," she said. "Wanting isn't the only thing that matters."

"No, but it's pretty damn important. Give me one good reason why we shouldn't be together, Allie."

She spun around, throwing her hands up. *"Don't you get it?* I'm tapped out! I'm done. I have nothing left. I was exhausted today just thinking about last night. I am tired and short-tempered all the time. I have nothing left in me, Oliver Campbell. Everyone needs something from me, and I don't have anything more to give."

"Allie, you don't—"

"That's not fair to you. I don't know much about healthy relationships, but I know that's not the way it's supposed to work."

He crossed his arms and watched her, but Allie had nothing left to say.

She was tired and unbearably sad. She wanted to run away, but she couldn't do that to him when he'd already bared himself to her the way he had.

"I'm trying to do the right thing," Allie whispered. "I don't want to be selfish."

"And I'm trying to do the right thing too," he said. "For both of us. I don't want to make your life harder. I've been trying to show you that I can make it better. I'm standing here with my hands out, asking you to let me make life easier, and you fight me every way."

"I can't repay—"

"What the fuck kind of man would I be if I kept score like that?" he yelled. He stepped closer and grabbed her shoulders. "Yes, I want more.

But I am your *friend*. I will *always* be your friend. No matter what happens. You wouldn't do the same for me or Jena or any of our friends if life got crazy?"

"Of course I would. If I *could*."

"Well, I *can*." His fingers clenched on her shoulders before they softened. "I don't need you to pay me back with anything but *you*. Give me your smile. Let me see you laugh again. Let me—" His voice broke. "Let me enjoy having your kids around this big empty house. It's too damn quiet with just me and my dog. Let me help, Allie. I know you're tapped out. Fuck, you were running on empty five years ago."

"I can't be what you need," she whispered.

"You let *me* be the judge of that."

"But—"

"Has it been so hard being here?"

"Of course not." Being in his house with him and the kids was almost too easy.

He casually brushed a tear that had fallen down her cheek. "Are the kids comfortable? Are you?"

"Of course we are. You've been great."

"Then what has to change? What's going to be so much different if we try this?"

"What would *change*?" Her face heated. "Ollie, you know..."

"This?" He slid a hand around her waist and pulled her closer. "You and me kissing a little?"

Allie put a hand on his chest, but she didn't push away. "Yeah."

He put his hands on her waist and lifted, turning to put her on the hood of the Ford and stepping between her thighs so they were face-to-face. The lights were still off in the barn, so the only shadows cast were from the cool light of the security lamp and the waxing moon hanging low in the sky.

Ollie placed his hands on either side of her and leaned in. "This have you worried?"

Her heart began to pound. "Maybe."

"Nothing to worry about." Ollie's lips brushed hers with a whisper-soft kiss. "Stay here. Let me help you," he said softly. "And we just... try." He brushed her lips again. "Try things on. See how they fit. How *we* fit."

Her hands rose to his shoulders, but Ollie grabbed them and put them full around his neck.

"We'll go as slow as you need," he said, running his fingertips down her arms until she shivered. "But please don't back away."

More kisses along her lips. Her cheek. Allie's head fell back at the beauty of his mouth. The full lips that were the only soft part of him. They whispered down her neck and teased her ear as his hands ran up and down her back.

"Let me make things sweet for you again," he whispered. "I promise it'll be so good."

"Ollie." She gave in and pressed his face into her neck, tangling her fingers in his hair as he groaned and slid his arms around her waist to hug her close. Allie felt his massive body settle into hers, and he sighed as if he'd come home.

A small hope settled inside her. She didn't have much to give, but she could do that—be that—for him. She was good at making a home.

"Are you sure you want to do this?"

"Yes." More kisses along her neck. "I love the way you smell."

"The way I smell?" She started laughing. "I smell like dinner."

"I know; it was delicious. Thank you." He smiled a little and nibbled her shoulder. "You don't smell like dinner right here."

"You realize you and me starting something is the definition of bad timing, right?"

He pulled away from her neck and tucked one of her flyaway curls behind an ear. "The world doesn't stop so you can get your shit together," he said. "There's never going to be a perfect time. You grab the time you have, and you make it right."

"Is that what you're doing?"

His deep brown eyes were wicked. "I'm going after you. Finally. I'm willing to go slow, but I'm not gonna put on the brakes unless you tell me. Loud and clear, Allie-girl. We both know I'm not smart enough for hints."

In response, she lifted her legs and wrapped them around his waist, pulling him closer.

"You really want all this drama?" she asked. "Mobsters. Gamblers. And even worse: four kids running around your house making messes and breaking your stuff?"

"Yep."

Her heart fluttered. Nothing flowery. No grand declaration. Allie handed him all her crazy, and the quiet man said yep.

Allie tugged gently on his beard and drew him down for another kiss. "Then what kind of fool would I be," she asked, "to say no to the offer of you?"

chapter
fourteen

If there was anything that could distract Ollie from the memory of the sweet kisses he'd managed to sneak with Allie before she took the kids to the bus stop, it was an ugly biker sitting across from him, giving him news he didn't want to hear.

"It was a private game," Tony Razio said. "Guys like me aren't usually invited to shit like that."

"It was in Palm Springs."

"Yeah, but that's about all I know, man."

Razio was looking worn, and Ollie wondered if the man was tired or strung out. He gulped the coffee Ollie had set in front of him as he sat at the bar.

Ollie picked up a bar towel and started polishing the pint glasses he pulled out of the washer. "So Russell sits in on this game with four other guys..."

"Fancy game. High stakes," Razio said. "And then three days later... he's a ghost."

"Literally?" Had whoever killed Joe advertised it? It might not be legitimate enough for the police, but Ollie wasn't the police. If he found out who'd killed Joe, he'd find out how much they knew and then he'd take them out. Ollie knew Joe wouldn't have started anything, which meant it wasn't self-defense. Killing his murderer would be justified.

The Campbell clan was old school. An eye for an eye. Sometimes that was how things needed to be done. The justice system had never watched out for black freemen like his ancestor William Allen, so the Campbells and Allens took care of themselves and those who belonged to them. The town of Cambio Springs belonged to them.

"Was someone shooting off their mouth about killing Russell?" Ollie asked again. "If they were—"

"Nothing like that. Just whispers."

"About?"

Razio squirmed. "About who was at the game. It wasn't just yuppies with too much money."

"Who?"

The biker shrugged "Bad dudes, man."

"No shit." Ollie crossed his arms and stared at the man. The silent stare was usually pretty effective at making people spill their guts.

Razio was quiet. Then he picked up his coffee cup. Set it down.

"Listen," he finally said, "if you want my boys looking into this, I need more than just a favor or two. I need to get paid. Asking questions about this guy brings attention we don't want."

Bingo.

"What guy?"

The dusky-skinned biker grew a little paler. "They call him Lobo."

"Lobo?" Ollie rolled his eyes. "Motorcycle clubs and their bullshit nicknames—"

"This guy does not ride. He's from Mexico. I know he's got money, but I don't know how he gets it. Rumors say he's got cartel backing."

"Is that so?"

"Rumors." Razio shrugged. "I don't know nothing for sure about Lobo."

Lobo. Spanish for wolf. It was probably a coincidence. Lobo was the kind of nickname assholes gave themselves when they wanted to seem mysterious. It probably had nothing to do with the shifters in the Springs.

"Razio, someone broke into Russell's ex-wife's house last week. In *my* town. You know anything about that? We think they were guys from the city."

The man looked encouraged. High-stakes poker games were a little above his pay grade, but breaking and entering was right up his alley. "No, but that's something I can look into. What'd they take?"

"Nothing. Seemed like they were looking for something."

"Really?" His greedy eyes gleamed.

"Yeah," Ollie said. "There any word on who took the pot in that game?"

"Nope."

"So it's possible Joe Russell took it?"

Razio shrugged. "Anything's possible."

"Find out. About the money if you can and about who might have come looking for it."

The biker stood and finished his coffee. "I'll see what I can do."

"And I'll take care of you. I know it's more than just asking around."

"I don't mind you owing me a favor, Campbell."

Ollie grunted and returned to polishing glasses as Razio walked toward the door.

"Hey." The biker turned before he walked back into the heat. "I heard Russell's wife was a sweet little blonde. Curly hair. Nice ass."

Ollie stopped polishing and reined in the violent urge to throw the man out the door. "And?"

Razio shrugged. "Thought it sounded a lot like your old lady."

"Did I give you permission to be curious about my woman?"

Razio laughed. "Nah, man."

"Then I don't know why we're having this conversation, Tony."

"Yeah, okay." Razio put on his shades and pulled the door open. It was almost noon, and the late-September sun was already baking the ground. A dust devil kicked up in the parking lot. "I'll see you, Campbell."

"You have my number if you find anything. Use it."

"ALLIE?"

Ollie walked into Allie's house, trying not to panic about the open front door. It was hot as hell in the sun, but the breeze was probably keeping the house cool. All the windows were open too. She was fine. No one had broken in again. He sniffed the air and looked around.

Allie was still sorting out the wreck of her old house, and he was trying his best not to be a Neanderthal. She'd had to remind him several times that morning that she was a predator herself and perfectly capable of cleaning and sorting the house without a bodyguard.

"Hey!" Allie called from the back. "I'm in my bedroom."

He closed the front door and walked down the hall, not scenting anything unfamiliar. She'd gotten the kids' rooms sorted last week with his housekeeper Vicky, but she probably wanted to do her own room by herself.

Walking in, it almost looked back to normal save for the deep rips in the sides of the mattress and the piles of laundry everywhere.

"Hey."

"Hey." She smiled while she tossed rumpled clothes into different piles. "How was the meeting with the biker dude?"

He sat in the rocking chair in the corner. "He knew about the game, but not much. Gave me a name. Someone I can ask Alex about." He watched her work. "Do you want to know?"

"The name?" She shrugged. "I don't think it would mean anything to me, but sure."

"Lobo. Sound familiar?"

She wrinkled her nose. "Is that a first name or a last name?"

Ollie laughed. "It's a nickname. Probably someone thought it sounded cool."

"Like *Oso*?" She winked.

"You can blame my cousins for that one. I did not give myself a nickname."

"No." She tossed a pair of her next-to-nothing panties into a pile of lingerie. "Lobo doesn't sound familiar. And you didn't need any nicknames to be a badass, Oliver Campbell."

"I'm not a badass."

She laughed and untangled a sundress from a pile of stockings. "Right." With a sharp tug she finally got the dress free and threw it on the bed, only to sigh and cover her face. "I have to wash it all. Even my clothes that were clean. They went through my whole closet. It's like they touched everything I own, and it feels so gross." She reached a leg out and stuck her toes in the pile of lingerie. "It's creepy knowing they pawed through my lingerie. My jeans are bad enough. I'm tempted to throw all my underwear away, but I can't really afford to buy new ones."

He slid to the floor. "Don't do that." He held up a certain very small pair made of black lace. "I've been thinking about some of these for weeks now."

That made her smile. "I might make you help me hang them again."

"Fine by me." He leaned against the dresser. "I'll put a clothesline in my bedroom."

That had her blushing bright pink. "So helpful."

"I live to please." He eyed her mouth. Her lips were flushed like they had been this morning when he pulled her into his bedroom to steal a kiss before she went to make lunches. "Come here."

She shook her head. "I'm trying to work."

"Break time." He scooted over to her side of the laundry pile and leaned against the bed.

"Ollie..." She sighed.

"Come on now," he said, pulling her to straddle his lap. "This *is* work. We're having a conference."

She laughed and gave in, settling her sweet backside on his lap and putting her hands on his shoulders. "What are we having a conference about, Mr. Campbell?"

"Your underwear."

"Oh really?"

"Yes." He put his hands at her waist and teased the small of her back with his fingers, tugging at the edge of lace he felt beneath her waistband. "I think you need to consider the effect of your underwear on your housemates."

She nodded solemnly. "Is that why you want me to hang it in your room?"

"Yes." He leaned forward and nosed at the underside of her chin. "If any of your housemates—"

"You mean my children?"

"Yes, them. If they saw your underwear, they might be scandalized. They're young and impressionable."

"So..." She sighed in pleasure and leaned closer to him, pressing her breasts into the solid wall of his chest. "You want me to keep my panties in your room to... protect the children?"

Allie was driving him crazy, but it was the best kind of crazy. Her scent surrounded him, and her fingers played in the curls at the back of his neck. Also, she should always say panties that way, her voice a little breathless and soft. It was really, really hot. His hand slipped lower and he felt satin beneath the lace. He gripped her thigh harder, and her fingers twisted in his hair.

"Love the feeling," she panted, "of your beard on my neck."

"Yeah?" He brushed his cheek along her neck and tasted her ear. *It's gonna feel even better other places, baby.*

She groaned. "So much."

"I love the weight of you on me," he murmured. "Love holding you."

"I'm heavy."

He laughed loud. "Right."

"I am."

"Thank God." He pulled his hand out of the waistband of her panties and grabbed two nice handfuls of her backside. "You were so tiny when you were young, I worried I'd break you. Now you feel just right."

She froze, her cheek pressed to his temple.

"Allie?" He relaxed his hands and smoothed them up her back. "What's wrong?"

"Don't tease."

Her voice was wrong. Ollie grabbed her ponytail and tugged her back so he could see her face.

"Hey. Talk to me."

She only shook her head. She looked embarrassed, but there was no change in her scent. If anything, the wave of her arousal was even richer. Headier.

"Allie—"

"After Loralie, I mean... I didn't bounce back, you know? It was easier with the boys, but..."

It took him a second to figure out she was talking about her body. Of all the things to be worried about, he would never have picked that one.

"Darlin', you've had four kids. That's normal."

"Joe didn't like it."

He buried the flare of anger when a suspicion snuck up on him. "How long's it been?"

She groaned. "Ollie, I don't want to talk about this."

"I do."

She tried to squirm off his lap, but he held her tighter.

"Forget it." She stopped squirming. "We're just... You don't need to know. It's embarrassing. And nothing to do with us." She smoothed her hands over his shoulders. "This is you and me. I need to let go of stuff and forget it."

"And I need to know how long it's been since you've had a man hold you," he said.

It was true. Fox shifters were highly sensual. It was one of the reasons so many boys selfishly had the hots for Allie in high school. Foxes craved touch and affection. If Joe had denied touch to Allie for his own bullshit reasons, the animal in her would be starving.

"Allie?"

She rolled her eyes back in frustration and clamped them closed. "A few years, okay?"

"*Years?*"

"Yes."

"When you were still married? You were sleeping in his bed, and he didn't—"

She pushed his shoulders. "I'm not talking about this anymore."

"Okay." He brought his knees up, trapping her on his lap. "But I'm not letting you go. Not right now."

He could tell she was embarrassed and ready to run. Ollie was pretty sure that her running away from him wasn't really an option anymore.

"I need to get back to work," she said.

"And I need to take care of you." He ran a single finger down her throat and delighted in the shiver.

He stood, still holding her tightly. Then he pushed the pile of laundry off the edge of the bed and laid her on it, settling down beside her.

Allie's eyes went wide and her breath came faster. "I thought we were going slow."

"We are." He stroked a hand down her side. "Relax. I'm just touching you."

"Ollie—"

He took her lips and drew the sweetness into his mouth. There it was again. The tang of tea on her tongue overlaying the wild hunger in her scent.

"Just touching you," he whispered. "Just kissing. Relax."

Ollie felt her body give in. In fact, her body was screaming for him, and he was hard as a rock. It didn't matter. They were more than their animals. They were humans first, but their animal natures were a big part of them. If Allie had been touch-starved, no wonder she was so stressed out. The animal in him wanted to strip her bare and let her work out every frustration on his very willing body, but the man knew it was way more complicated and his woman wasn't ready.

So he stroked and kissed, petted her in long sweeps. Up and down her arms, down the swell of her hip and the curve of her thigh. He was a big man, and he'd never been gladder of it. He wrapped her up, throwing a leg over hers and pulling her into a full-body hug while his mouth stayed locked on hers.

One of her arms was tucked around his waist and the other was at his cheek.

"Just kissing," she murmured.

"Mm-hmm." She tasted like heaven, and he wanted to know what she tasted like everywhere. He could ignore his own body, but it was becoming harder and harder to ignore the screaming tension in hers. "Relax," he whispered.

He squeezed her tight and felt her shudder in his arms. She kissed across his cheek and over to his ear.

"Thank you," she breathed out.

"No, thank *you*." One hand stayed wrapped around her back while the other went to her bottom and pressed in. Let her see how much he wanted her. Let her see how desirable she was. She wasn't a girl anymore. Thank God. She was a full, sensuous woman aware of her body and her desires. Ollie loved it. The depth of her scent was a drug.

"Ollie." Her head fell back and her pale throat was there. He licked at it. Tasted that collarbone that was so tempting. Held back from taking her breasts, knowing he could only push his frustration so far. He felt her hips move against his and muffled a groan.

"So big," she whispered. "Everywhere."

"I'm all yours," he murmured. "You tell me when."

She let out a sigh. "I think we should wait."

"Okay." He didn't stop kissing her neck.

"I don't really want to."

"Okay."

She laughed and slapped his back playfully. Ollie grinned against her skin. He was pretty uncomfortable at that point, but he didn't want to let her go.

"I love your arms," she said, trailing her hands down his shoulders.

"You mentioned that."

"I knew you caught that. That's why you're flexing so much lately, huh?"

"Guilty." He lifted his head and laid it next to hers on the pillow. "Allie-girl?"

"Yeah." She let out a contented sigh and burrowed into his chest.

"Like I said, we'll go as slow as you want, but you need to let me touch you."

She blushed a little. "I know you're—"

"It's not about me." He stroked her arm. "It's about you not getting what you need. You know any adult female foxes?"

She shook her head. "But I know we need more touch than most shifters. Ted told me it's normal."

"It is. And it's also part of the reason you're feeling stressed and worn out. So..." He brushed her hair back and kissed her forehead. "You need to let me touch you. A lot. I'd ask you to sleep with me at night, but I know you wouldn't with the kids in the house, and there's only so much I'm willing to torture myself while I'm trying to be good."

"But we can... cuddle?"

"As much as you want."

She paused. "I'm not sure how much I want to show the kids. About us."

Ollie tried not to let it sting and remembered that the kids had just lost their dad. Yes, Joe had been gone for a while, but Ollie didn't need to be throwing this in their faces when they might still be confused and hurting.

"It's up to you." He kissed her forehead and rolled away. "But be warned, there's probably only so long I'm gonna be able to remember not to kiss you now that I can."

Before she could protest, Ollie bent down and scooped her pile of lingerie into a nearby basket. "Now I'm going to be a stand-up guy and take these home with me so I can wash them." He smiled. "You can thank me later."

She giggled, and damn it if he didn't love that sound.

"You're going to wash all my panties for me?"

He poked through the basket. "Your nighties in here too?"

"Yes."

"Good."

"Ollie!"

"What?" He ducked away from a balled-up pair of socks she chucked at him. "You can get them later. They'll be hanging in my room."

She busted up laughing. "You will not."

"Try me." He backed out of the room. "Your panties are mine, Allison Smith. It's a good thing I like you so much."

OKAY, HE DIDN'T HAND WASH THEM; HE WASN'T SOME KIND of pervert. But he put them on the gentle cycle, and then he pulled some hamburgers out of the freezer to make dinner. It wouldn't be fancy, but if Allie could make a salad, he could grill. There should be plenty of food after the monumental shopping trip Vicky had excitedly undertaken.

He knew his clan was more than happy that Allie and the kids were staying at the house. They were all hoping it was permanent, just like he was. They'd pestered him for years to settle down, though not as persistently as some of his other cousins, as most had known his pent-up feelings for the little fox and her children.

He wasn't being dishonest when he told her he liked having them around. When he'd been a kid, the old house had been full of cousins and friends, so having it sit quiet grated on his nerves. His grandparents constantly had extra kids around, either babysitting for someone in the clan or borrowing a kid for Ollie to play with since he was an only child and had a tendency to spend too much time alone. He didn't always participate in the mayhem, but the sound of it brought happy memories.

It was one of the reasons he liked running the Cave. Ollie liked to see people having a good time, watching to make sure everyone was taken care of even if he wasn't the one participating. Heck, he didn't really like talking to people that much, but he loved watching them talk to each other. Telling jokes. Hanging with friends and listening to a great band.

With Allie's kids, the enjoyment was doubled. He felt like he was taking care of them, and he loved hearing their stories, even when they devolved into arguments. Dinners with the rowdy brood were quickly becoming one of his favorite parts of the day.

Of course, if he could get some cuddling time with Allie, that was going to end up trumping dinner, no doubt in his mind. A quick jog by the creek had gotten his mind off the frustration of holding her that afternoon, and a cold shower had finished the job, but now that he knew he had her permission to touch, the gnawing hunger would only get worse.

Hopefully she wouldn't ask him to be too patient. He'd wanted the woman for twenty years.

Ollie smiled when he heard the shouts and shrieks of the children when Allie rolled up a little after three. He'd just finished hanging her wash in his bedroom, and he currently had pink, green, and black lace underwear draped over every hook and surface in his bathroom. Which was just fine by him.

"Hey," he said, standing on the porch. "Where's Kevin?"

"Doing a few hours at my dad's store," she said, hauling a laundry basket out of the back of the minivan. "Since I'm not working tonight. Mark, get this other basket before you start your homework! What were you up to this afternoon?"

The corner of his mouth twitched up. "Laundry."

She couldn't stop the smile. "You're a bad man, Oliver Campbell."

"I'm helping." He caught Loralie before she tumbled down the stairs. "Where are you going?" He hung her upside down by her ankles. "Huh? Don't you have homework?"

She giggled until her little belly shook. "I'm only in kinnergarten, Ollie!"

"Are they slacking off at that school?" He swung her back and forth while she shrieked and laughed. Loralie weighed next to nothing. "No homework at all?"

Allie said, "If you make her puke, I'm not cleaning it up."

"Good point." Ollie carefully flipped Loralie right side up. Her eyes were still crossed, but she was grinning. "You all right?"

She nodded and Chris ran out the front door, almost slamming into Ollie's legs.

"Mom, can we play by the creek?"

"Please!" Loralie shrieked, almost blowing his eardrum. He set her down.

"That's fine," Allie said. "Stay together."

"And take the dog," Ollie added. He whistled for Murtry, who jogged out of the house and followed Loralie and Chris when they called.

"Such a good dog," Allie said, bending over to grab her purse from the car.

"Mm-hmm." He licked his lips and resisted the urge to pick her up and take a quick bite.

"You have a nice afternoon?" she asked.

"Yep."

"Did you get my text about barbecuing hamburgers?"

"Yep. Meat's defrosting on the counter unless the dog stole it." He looked down. "He's only so good when it comes to temptation."

Her mouth twitched. "Well, there's only so much you can expect out of big hungry animals. Especially when something's right in front of them." She walked into the house, and if she'd been a fox, her tail would have been twitching.

Ollie grinned. Oh yeah. This was going to be fun.

chapter
fifteen

When Allie got back to the house after dropping the kids off at the bus stop the next Monday, the last person she expected to see was Maggie Quinn. Sean's half sister was sitting on the porch with a mutinous expression on her face, her brother standing behind her talking quietly to Ollie.

Allie parked and got out, listening for what the two men were talking about. Her hearing and sense of smell were naturally heightened, especially when she was stressed. She could hear the two men's voices, even from a distance.

Football scores. Naturally.

"Hey," she called, knowing this wasn't any old visit. Maggie was a rosy boa constrictor in her natural form, the same type of snake that had hidden under her house during the break-in. Whatever Sean had discovered about it, he felt the need to drag his sister to the Campbell house, which meant it was serious.

"Hey, honey." Sean stepped off the porch and gave her a long hug. "Am I driving him crazy?" he whispered.

"Be nice."

"It's too much fun to tease him. His scent's all over you." He winked. "What have you been doing, you vixen?"

Allie rolled her eyes but kept her face from turning red. After Ollie had stated his intention to "cuddle," he'd grabbed on to the opportunity with enthusiasm, which meant Allie spent her breaks at work making out with Ollie in his office like they were still teenagers. He even slipped into her bedroom the next morning, partly to deliver a pair of pink panties—which he might have been holding hostage in his room—and partly to slide next to her on the bed and ask her what her plans for the day were.

Kissing happened.

But he slipped out of her room long before the kids' alarms went off. So far, he was respecting her boundaries about telling the children.

He didn't, however, seem to have any problems staking his claim in front of Sean. He marched down the stairs and put his arm around Allie. "Mine."

Sean smiled. "And it's about time too."

Allie looked past their posturing to Maggie, who was looking more than a little annoyed.

"It's so nice to see your sister, Sean," Allie said. "I always miss her cheerful presence when she's not around."

"I know." He walked back to the porch. "I'm sure Maggie would say the same thing. Right, sis?"

She bared her teeth. "Can we get this over with?"

"Maggie has some information about the guys who broke into your house," Sean said. "She very graciously offered to share it."

"When you threatened me."

"I told you"—Sean's voice dropped dangerously—"I'm done cleaning up your messes, Mags. Now tell her what you told me, or I'll take you back to the old man and he can deal with you."

It was only the threat of Old Quinn that wiped the antagonistic expression off her face.

"I set up the game," she said to Allie, "but I had no idea any of the guys were dangerous."

"Bullshit," Ollie said.

"Fine." She shrugged. "Not *that* kind of dangerous. I figured, at worst, Joe would get drunk and lose. Not that he didn't have incentive to stay sober." The corner of her mouth lifted in a smirk. "He knew what I'd do to him if he drank during the game."

"Get on with it," Ollie said. "What happened?"

"I don't know," she said. "No girls allowed. I do know that Joe left the game alive. He was supposed to meet me in Palm Desert the next day, but he texted me and said everything was fine, but he'd be a day late."

"And he didn't say if he won or not?" Ollie asked.

Maggie crossed her arms. "I'll admit I was pissed. I assumed he didn't and he was trying to come up with some excuse to give him more time or find another game. I was busy. When he didn't show the next day, I texted him but never heard back."

"And that was the last you talked to him?" Allie asked.

Maggie nodded. "I was furious. But not furious enough to hurt him, you know? Besides, he owed me—"

"Maggie," Sean interrupted. "Don't start."

She lapsed into sullen silence.

"What about the break-in?" Ollie asked. "You were beneath the house."

"Yeah."

Allie asked, "Why?"

Maggie didn't want to talk, but Sean nudged her shoulder. "I was looking for cash. Jewelry. Like I said, Joe owed me."

"You bitch," Allie hissed. "I am barely scraping by and you were gonna steal from me and my kids?"

"It wasn't personal."

Allie resisted the urge to slap her. "Yeah, it was."

"Besides, I scooted out of there when the other guys showed up."

Ollie put a hand on Allie's shoulder. "Who were they?"

"Don't know—"

"Maggie!" Sean looked ready to erupt.

"—*exactly*. I don't know exactly. I'm pretty sure they worked for the one guy in the game I didn't know. The other guys…" She shrugged. "They wouldn't have hired these two."

"What did they look like?" Ollie asked.

"I was under the house, remember? I didn't see them. I heard them coming and hid."

Allie asked, "Where was your car?"

"Someone dropped me off. Someone picked me up the next morning after the bear and the cop were gone." Maggie glared at Sean. "You know how it works."

"Yeah, I know exactly how it works," Sean muttered. "But I grew out of breaking and entering. You didn't."

Maggie said, "Well, in this case, it might come in useful. The two guys mentioned a name. Wolf. Any of you know a guy with the last name Wolf?"

Wolf. *Lobo?*

Allie asked, "Was it Wolf or Lobo?"

Maggie frowned. "You're right. It was Lobo. I wasn't remembering right."

"Lobo?" Sean asked. "Gang name?"

"I guess," Maggie said. "But this game... it was supposed to be rich guys with too much money, you know? No one serious. Two real estate guys from LA. An Italian from Vegas."

"And that didn't raise any red flags?" Sean asked.

"Please," Maggie said. "I know the Italian. He's a pussycat. As long as you don't cheat, he just likes his cards. Didn't know the real estate guys, but Pinky vouched for them."

"That was the guy who organized the game?" Ollie asked. "Pinky?"

"Don't ask," Maggie said.

"I know Pinky," Sean muttered. "I'll fill you in."

"So there was the 'sweet' mafia guy," Allie said, "the two rich guys from LA, Joe, and who else?"

"I guess this Lobo guy," Maggie said. "Like I said, I didn't know him."

"Did Pinky vouch for him too?" Ollie's sarcasm was getting harder and harder to veil.

"Yeah, he did." Maggie frowned. "Kinda. He seemed... nervous. But Pinky always seems nervous."

Sean said, "I can actually confirm that. Pinky does always seem nervous."

Maggie said, "Anyway, they broke into Allie's place, and they sounded like they were making a mess, but I don't think they took anything. They were looking for cash. I heard that much."

Allie threw up her hands. "Why does everyone seem to think I have cash? If I had cash, I wouldn't need to ask the pack for grocery money!"

"Yeah," Ollie said. "You're not doing that anymore."

Allie put her hands on her hips. "Don't start."

"I'm not starting anything," Ollie said. "I'm making a statement."

Sean said, "Getting back to the intruders, boys and girls, one thing seems pretty clear to me."

"What?" Allie said. "They were looking for cash and I don't have any. They looked everywhere. Can we assume it's safe for me to go back to my house?"

"No," Sean said. "Just because they didn't find it doesn't mean they don't think it exists. And they might think you're the one who knows where it is. You are definitely not going anywhere alone."

Ollie asked, "Are you thinking what I am?"

"Probably."

Ollie crossed his arms and muttered, "You think Joe won that game, don't you?"

Sean nodded. "Why else would guys working for this Lobo dude be looking for cash?"

"Hot damn!" Maggie was grinning. "This may turn out after all. So" —she turned to Allie—"where would he put it?"

"You're asking me?" Allie said.

"You were married to the man for fifteen years or something."

"And this is why you're not going anywhere alone," Ollie told her.

"Hold on." Sean raised both hands. "We don't even know if he actually won. It's just a theory."

"Well," Ollie said, "I have an idea about how we might confirm that."

Allie asked, "Does it involve meeting a guy named Pinky?"

"No. But it does involve your finding a babysitter tonight. I think Sean was about to volunteer."

Sean blinked. "I was?"

MONDAY LUNCH WITH JENA AND TED HAD BECOME A tradition after Becca was born. They were all busy, but the three old friends carved out time for each other, which Allie was eternally grateful for. The past few months, she'd felt like it was the only adult conversation she got all week.

She pulled into Jena's just as Caleb was driving out. He waved but didn't stop. Allie parked and grabbed a tub of homemade potato salad out of the back. She'd made enough for an army the night before. Miraculously, there were leftovers.

"Jena?" she called out from the porch. The door was open—only the screen door was closed—but Allie didn't want to intrude.

"Come on in," a quiet voice said.

Allie walked in to see Jena sneaking from the hallway where the bedrooms were. She nodded toward the kitchen door and followed Allie in.

"Baby down for a nap?"

"Mm-hmm."

Allie spotted the mismatched buttons on Jena's shirt and couldn't hold back a smile. "Caleb have an early lunch?"

"Yeah, but don't worry." Jena went to the fridge. "I didn't eat."

"Oh, I know you didn't," Allie said with a smile. "Might want to straighten that shirt, you hussy."

"Oh, for the love of…" Jena untucked her shirt as a knock came at the kitchen door.

"Knock, knock," Ted said. "I brought the sandwiches. Jena, do you have any sweet tea?"

"I don't know," Allie said. "But she's got a hickey on her shoulder."

Ted cackled. "The perks of morning naptimes and a low crime rate."

"Shut up, both of you. You're just jealous."

"No jealousy here." Ted sat at the kitchen table. "Mr. McCann gets his share of nooners."

Jena said, "You do realize that office trailer at the job site rocks, right?"

"That would imply that I care if anyone knows I'm getting laid."

"Shameless," Allie joked. "Both of you. I'm embarrassed to be friends with you."

"Oh, I don't know…" Ted looked like the cat who got the cream. "Speaking of the sexy times, I heard something interesting just this morning."

How had they heard already? Allie's cheeks pinked. "Sean Quinn has a big mouth."

"What?" Jena spun around from the counter where she'd been pouring drinks. "Sean what?"

Ted said, "Seems a certain bear is getting mighty possessive about a certain fox."

Jena's mouth dropped. "So there was more kissing?"

"Wait! There was kissing?" Ted asked. "Sean said grunting and the word "Mine" might have been mentioned. Allie, why didn't I know about the kissing?"

"What?" Allie grabbed plates from the cupboard. "I... There's nothing... I mean, it's kind of new."

"Seriously?" Jena shrieked, clearly forgetting about the baby, who started to fuss.

"It's happened," Ted said. "Oliver Campbell finally made his move."

"Finally?" Allie said. "You mean, you guys knew—"

"Wait!" Jena held up a hand. "How did Sean know about this before us?"

"Um, because I'm not twelve, and I've had a few things going on besides calling up my besties and gossiping about boys?"

Ted shook her head. "No excuses. And Jena, don't complain. You knew about the kissing."

Allie tried to distract them. "I think the baby's waking up."

"Okay, okay." Jena walked toward the bedrooms. "But when I get back, you're spilling."

As soon as they were alone, Allie grabbed Ted's wrist. "Did you know?"

"That Ollie had the hots for you?" Ted shrugged. "Of course."

"Did everyone know?"

"Pretty much."

She sat at the table and covered her face. "Am I that clueless?"

"No, *mama*. Like you said, you've had a few things going on."

"But—"

"No buts." Ted grabbed the drinks from the counter and went to sit back down. "You know this is serious, right? He's not fooling around about you. Do the kids know?"

She shook her head. "I think Kevin suspects... You know he loves Ollie. My son probably put him up to this."

"I don't think Ollie needed any help in that area." Ted grinned. "So, have you... ya know?"

"No." Okay, she couldn't stop the blush anymore. "We're taking things slow."

"You don't need slow," Ted said. "You need to get laid."

"Not all of us are as confident about that stuff as you are," Allie muttered. "I'm... I mean, there was only ever Joe, so—"

"You'll be fine," Ted said. "Don't worry. It's Ollie. He adores you."

"Yeah." She let out a slow breath. "I'm starting to get that."

"Scared?"

"A little. Maybe a lot."

Jena walked back in with a happy, red-cheeked Becca on her hip, who babbled and held her hands out for Ted.

"Did you and your Uncle Alex make a deal?" Ted asked, kissing Becca's cheek. "Convince Auntie Ted's ovaries to go into overdrive with your cuteness and he'll pay for college or something?"

Jena said, "I'd be okay with that deal. Now"—she sat down—"tell me everything. Include descriptions. And any actual words you managed to get the man to speak."

Allie groaned and put her head on the table.

"Admit it," Ted said. "There hasn't been much talking."

ALLIE COULDN'T TAKE HER EYES OFF OLLIE IN THE TRUCK.

"What?" he shifted in his seat. "I've worn dress clothes before."

"I'm trying to think of the last time."

"Yeah, well... I look weird in suits."

"No," she said carefully, sweeping her eyes from the slacks to the pressed collar of his dress shirt. "You definitely don't look weird."

He looked *hot*. She could see the edge of the bear claw tattoos at the back of his neck, and the peek of barbed wire at one wrist. He'd trimmed his beard and hair that afternoon, and the effect was that of a powerful predator on a very controlled edge.

When Ollie had called her up and told her he was taking her to dinner in Palm Springs, she'd been surprised and touched. She couldn't remember the last time she'd been out for a dinner that didn't involve the kids' menu. Even when he told her they were meeting Alex, Ted, and Alex's friend Cam, she was still excited.

The corner of his mouth creeped up. "Do you have a suit fetish or something? I might wear one if you do."

"It's not guys in suits," she said. "I think it's knowing you have all that ink *under* the suit that I like."

She did. She loved his tattoos. She had dreams about licking them.

"Oh yeah?" He glanced over at her. "I like that dress. Did I mention that?"

"Once or twice."

"Which panties are you wearing under it?"

She smiled. "The black lace."

"The tiny ones?"

"Mm-hmm."

He groaned. "There goes my concentration for the evening."

"Keep it together, bear. You're supposed to be the muscle in this gang."

He laughed and reached across the car to take her hand. Allie scooted closer and held his hand on her thigh.

Ollie was making it remarkably easy to be with him. The past few days—once she'd leaped the hurdle that was holding her back—had been like a dream. Ollie woke her in the morning with stolen kisses before the kids got up. He helped get them off to school and sometimes drove them to the bus stop. Then he'd come home and sleep a little if he'd stayed late at the bar, or he'd work on one of his cars or do something around the house. She was still working at her dad's, which was a nice distraction from the giant of a man who haunted her thoughts and was far too tempting for her own sanity.

He left daisies on her pillow one afternoon.

Allie was being quietly romanced in a very Ollie way. She was trying not to analyze it. She just wanted to enjoy.

He also wasn't joking about her taking it easier. He didn't interfere when she cleaned the kitchen or did laundry, but he protested if she tried to do any housekeeping, complaining she was taking Vicky's work. They still couldn't agree about bills. But he was as affectionate and steady with the kids as he'd always been, even if the looks he gave Allie went far beyond affection.

"You're thinking awful loud over there," he said.

"I'm thinking about you."

He looked surprised.

"Sorry," she said. "Should I not have told you that?"

"No. I mean, yes. Tell me. It's just refreshing that you're not playing games, you know?"

She laughed a little. "You've been hanging out with the wrong girls, Oliver Campbell. I don't play games. I wouldn't even know how if I wanted to."

"Good." He smiled. "About the games, I mean. But there's nothin' wrong with a little playing now and then."

"Is that so?"

"Just tell me when, darlin'."

She pressed her lips together. "Now who's trying to ruin concentration?" she asked quietly.

He laughed as they reached the edge of Palm Springs.

The restaurant where they were meeting Alex and Ted was off Palm Canyon Drive, not far from the tennis club. It was the kind of place that, even if Allie had the money, she probably wouldn't have gone. She wasn't ashamed to admit she was a burgers and pizza kind of girl. She liked pretty candles and a fancy table as much as the next woman, but it wasn't something she craved. Jena's gourmet diner food was about as adventurous as she got.

"Should have taken you out before this," he muttered as he pulled the Bronco up to the valet. "Sorry I didn't think of it."

The attendant opened her door, and she waited for Ollie on the curb. "It's no big deal. This is nice."

He stood in front of her, standing below the curb so their faces were a little closer. "We're having our first date with three other people."

"Details." She leaned forward and kissed the edge of his jaw. "Tell you what. We'll skip dessert, and you can take me out for ice cream after this. Just the two of us."

He hummed deep in his chest. "Sean is staying until we get back. Want to take off for a few days? I'm sure he won't let them starve."

She laughed. "Probably not a good idea."

"He's got a house at the beach, and Alex might have a key."

"You've been thinking about this, haven't you?"

"About getting you alone?" He kissed her temple and backed away. "Constantly."

She paused. "It's not quite as easy as other girls, is it? Dating a woman with four kids who has to live with you."

He grabbed her hand. "I like having the kids around. Doesn't mean I don't want time alone with you."

They walked in, gave their names, and were ushered to a tree-filled patio strung with little lights where faint music floated in the background and a breeze cooled the dry desert air. Ted, Alex, and a man Allie had never seen before sat at a table in the corner, drinking wine and talking intently.

"Alex," Ollie said, brushing the waiter off so he could pull Allie's chair out. "Ted. Nice to see you."

Alex and the other man both rose as Allie sat down.

"Allie," Ted said, "this is Cameron Di Stefano, a friend of Alex's and mine. Cam was down in Palm Springs on business today, so I'm glad you guys were able to meet with us."

"Miss Smith," Cam said. "It's very nice to meet you."

"You too."

Cam continued, "And Mr. Campbell I know by reputation, of course."

Ollie paused in the act of lifting his water glass. "Is that so?"

Cam's mouth twitched. "Your bar is quite well-known."

"Yeah?" He put an elbow on the table. "Well, it's a friendly place."

"I suppose that depends on who you are."

Cam smiled, and Allie couldn't decide if she trusted him or not. Of course, she often felt that way around people from outside the Springs. Unlike Ted and Jena, she'd lived her whole life in the little town. Cameron Di Stefano was a worldly man, that much she could tell. But she also got the sense he enjoyed playing the kind of games that Allie hated.

She decided to cut right to the chase.

"So, Cam, what do you know about my ex-husband's murder?"

chapter
sixteen

Ollie almost snorted water through his nose.

Lord, he adored that woman.

Cameron Di Stefano sat blinking across from Allie, clearly unaccustomed to being called out for criminal connections at five-star restaurants.

Allie quickly raised a hand. "I'm assuming you didn't have anything to do with it directly. I trust Alex and Ted aren't friends with murderers. It's just that... I don't have much experience in any kind of criminal activity, and I don't really have any interest in gaining that experience, if you know what I mean. I have four children. I don't have time."

Cam tried to break in. "Miss Smith—"

"So the whole... double-talk, innuendo, imply-things-so-we're-not-criminally-implicated thing is just going to piss me off. I prefer being told things directly. It causes a lot less confusion all around." She smiled then, her dimples peeking out. "I'm sure you understand."

Luckily, Cam seemed to be as charmed as Ollie was. He glanced across the table, saw Allie's hand in Ollie's, and gave him a look that said, *You're a lucky bastard, Campbell.*

Yes, he was.

"Miss Smith," Cam said, "I hope you take this in the best way possible, but I feel a little sorry for your kids."

"I don't let them get away with much, if that's what you mean." She sipped the white wine Alex had poured into her glass and looked around the courtyard. "This is so pretty."

Ted said, "Allie, you and Cam's mother would get along."

"Yes, they would."

Ollie saw the urbane, cautious mask fall from Cam's face, and it set him at ease. His bear didn't like enemies who camouflaged themselves. So even though Cam's eyes were a little harder, Ollie trusted him a little more. He could also see why Cam and Alex were friends. Despite the fact that the man wasn't a shifter, he and Alex were similar animals.

"I didn't know your ex-husband," Cam started, keeping his voice low, "but I know who to ask. Alex and Ted are good friends. I'm just happy I could find some answers for you, even if they're not all the answers you need."

"Any information is appreciated," Ollie said. "Like Allie said, she has four kids. They need to know what happened to their father."

Cam turned his attention to Ollie. "We all understand that the police aren't going to be involved in this, I trust?"

"Man, do I look like law enforcement?" Ollie leaned on the table and ignored the wooden groan. "This woman and her children are under my protection. I trust *you* know what that means."

"Fine." Cam glanced at Alex, then back to Allie. "Joe was invited to a private poker game. I'm not sure by whom. It wasn't hosted by one of my... friends, but it was someone who wants to stay in my good graces."

Allie sipped her wine again and picked through the olive plate the waiter had set on the table. "Would this be Pinky?"

Cam's eyes laughed. "I thought you didn't know any criminals, Miss Smith."

"I don't. I also don't know a lot of guys named Pinky. The name kind of sticks in your mind." She passed the olives to Ollie. "Did you want some? They're really good."

"That's okay, darlin'. Thanks."

"So what else do you know?" Allie said, putting the plate back. "Because we already knew about the game."

"Three of the other participants are no one you need to worry about," Cam continued. "One of them is an acquaintance of my father's, whom I've already talked to. The others were simply rich men from out of town."

"And the other?" Ollie asked.

"The other..." Cam's voice dropped even lower. "The other man is the one who you need to worry about."

"Is his name Lobo?" Ollie asked.

Cam cocked his head. "I am not overly surprised you have that information, Mr. Campbell, though I'd be curious how you heard it."

"I bet you would."

Cam waited.

"Sorry," Ollie said. "You have your sources; I have mine."

"Fair enough." Cam paused as the server came by to take their orders.

Ollie ordered a steak that didn't seem to have too much stuff on it. Allie ordered some stuffed-chicken thing, which was good. He'd noticed her losing a little weight the past couple of weeks, probably from stress. While Allie would probably complain she had the weight to lose, Ollie didn't much like her not eating.

After the server had left, Allie asked, "So do you know this Lobo guy?"

Cam shook his head. "I know of him, but he's not someone I've done any business with. In fact, some would consider our... business interests in conflict. I hope you'll excuse the double-talk a little, Miss Smith. One might say that this man's friends have certain international pharmaceutical investments, while I am currently trying to sell my pharmaceutical interests."

Her eyebrows rose. "I got that one pretty clearly. And you can call me Allie."

Ollie considered what Cam had said. If Alex and Ted were right, and the Di Stefano family was trying to bring their operations into legitimate territory, then this Lobo might be the one trying to take their place, which would leave Cam in an awkward position with some of the people who'd looked to him for protection. The bookies, club owners, and dealers had to think about their futures too.

As always, Allie asked the question. "So did Joe work for Lobo?"

Cam's eyes darted around, and Ollie had to wonder at the reputation of a guy that made a Di Stefano nervous to talk about him.

"I can't know for sure," Cam said quietly, "but I don't think so. I truly think Joe was in the wrong place at the wrong time. Or... the right place at the wrong time."

"Why do you say that?" Allie asked.

"Because he won," Cam said. "Even with what happened later, he did win."

Allie's face grew pale and she gripped Ollie's hand under the table.

"I'm sorry," Cam said, noting her expression. "I thought you knew."

Ollie put his arm around her. "We suspected, but we didn't know."

"Well, he did," Cam said. A smile briefly touched his lips. "I don't know if this will make you feel any better about your ex-husband, Allie, but my father's friend—who's been beating me since I had the guts to start playing cards with him—said it was one of the best games he's ever played. He said Joe, who was using the last name Russell, was a great competitor, and he would have loved to play him again."

Allie lifted a hand and covered her eyes for a minute, then pulled it away and dashed a few tears from the corners of her eyes. "The boys will like to hear that."

Ted murmured, "Maybe not right away. Mark can already beat Alex at cards."

That pulled a watery laugh from Allie, but for Ollie, it only made the situation that much worse. Joe Russell had won, and Lobo had probably killed him to get his money back. But Joe obviously hadn't had the money, nor had he told his murderers where to find it; otherwise, they wouldn't be tearing up Allie's house.

Of course, that didn't mean they wouldn't come after her or the kids to get it.

While it meant Allie might have a chance to pay off Joe's debt and breathe a little easier, it also meant that a criminal whom Cameron Di Stefano was afraid to talk about was after his girl and her kids.

Yeah, he was going to need to take care of that.

Ollie leaned forward. "Di Stefano," he said, "you're sure that this guy is the one responsible for Joe's death?"

"My friend is. Bull said Lobo was furious. Trying to play it off, but furious. Pinky backed up Bull. He was not surprised to hear that Joe had turned up dead."

"Pinky. Bull. Lobo." Allie sniffed. "Honestly, the names these guys think up."

Cam's mouth quirked. "You'd see the humor if you knew Bull. This Lobo character? He's another story."

"Why?" Ollie asked.

The look Cam gave him told Ollie everything he needed to know. There were old guys like the Di Stefanos and even some of his ancestors who lived in the grey areas of the world out of necessity, family tradition, or an innate distrust of the law.

Then there were others.

Some men caused suffering to make themselves feel alive. For some, violence was as much a drug as alcohol. Ollie had a feeling he knew which category Lobo fell in.

Ollie leaned forward and looked into Cam's eyes. "I want to know everything I can about this guy. If you can find information that will make my woman and her kids safer, then I'll owe you a favor."

Cam was interested. "I'll see what I can do. Alex tells me Allie and her children are family to him as well. And I have no interest in some animal going after innocent women and children."

Ollie didn't say another word.

The server was putting a steak in front of him, and it smelled as promising as it had looked on the menu. Besides, Cam didn't need to know that it was the humans Ollie found untrustworthy, not the animals.

"WAIT A SECOND." SHE REACHED UP AND DABBED THE corner of his mouth with a napkin. "Got it. I told you a cone wasn't a good idea with all this beard."

He shrugged and grabbed her hand, pulling her out of the small shop and into the warm night.

"I can't remember the last time I went out for ice cream with a cute boy," Allie said, bumping her shoulder into his arm. "Thanks."

He smiled down at her and reached for her hand. "Dinner was good."

"It was okay." She wrinkled her nose. "Too many sun-dried tomatoes in the chicken. Jena wouldn't have approved."

"I will leave the food critique to those with more discerning palates," he said. "It was a good steak."

"But the ice cream was better."

"Ice cream is always better."

They walked in silence for a little while, and Ollie had fun watching the people go by. He burned with silent pride that he was holding Allie's hand, not that he was going to say anything about it.

"I like Cam," she said. "I didn't think I would."

"Me either. But yeah, he's okay."

"I feel sorry for him."

Ollie laughed. "Oh yeah. He's a rich, good-looking dude from Vegas. Poor thing. I'm sure all the girls feel sorry for him."

"Okay." She laughed along. "I know what you mean. But... he's kind of stuck, isn't he? You can tell he loves his family, but he doesn't want to be involved in all their stuff. He's trying to make everyone happy, but it's going to be impossible, isn't it? There's no way to protect everyone."

"Darlin', these people are not upstanding citizens. You stop handing work to a bodyguard, he's just going to find some other goon to walk beside so he can look menacing. The bookies are not going to go out of business. And the drug dealers will never run out of customers."

She squeezed her eyes shut and leaned against his shoulder. "I don't want to know any of this."

"So don't." He kissed the top of her head. "Let me take care of it."

"Why? Because I'm 'your woman?'"

His lips curved up. "That gonna bother you? Because you are."

"Are you my man?"

"Yeah."

She stopped, and when Ollie looked down, her cheeks were flushed. He pulled her out of the pedestrian traffic and leaned up against a wall, resting his back on it as he pulled her between his legs.

"You knew that, right?"

"What?" She was avoiding his eyes.

"That I'm your man."

She opened her mouth to speak, then stopped. Leaning into him, she lifted her face and brushed a kiss over his cheek.

"It's not that I don't want you to be my man," she said quietly. "I do. But I feel like this is going so fast. You don't have to..."

"What?" Ollie tilted her chin up. "Make a commitment? Look after you?"

"I don't want you to just take care of me."

"Well, that's a relief."

"When this is all over, I'm just gonna be *me*," she whispered. "Nothing exciting. No danger or drama. Just a busy mom who likes going out with my friends and baking cookies and going to the river to swim. I help my dad on the weekends and eat too much chocolate when I'm stressed. And... I snore."

Ollie started laughing.

"It's true," she said. "I do. It's not super loud, but I definitely snore. I'm just telling you now so you know."

"Okay, but don't spoil all the surprises about sleeping with you, okay?"

She slapped a hand on his chest. "I'm trying to tell you—"

"What? That you're a normal person who doesn't crave violence?" Ollie raised an eyebrow. "That's a good thing, darlin'."

"I just don't think... I'm not exciting or anything."

"What...?" He couldn't help the snort of laughter. "Allie-girl, what about my life leads you to think I'm not as normal as you? Am I taking off to Australia with Sean and not remembering it? Am I building giant resorts or saving lives?"

"You... know rock stars and stuff."

He curled his lip. "Most of them are pretty miserable people when they're not on a stage."

"I'm just saying—"

"Allie, I work." He smiled. "And stare at you in your apron when I'm supposed to be paying attention to the bar. And I... bring my pop all the pies Yaya won't bake for him anymore because I like to annoy her. And I go home and work on my cars. Eat crap food. Sleep in on Sunday and forget to go to church, then have to deal with my pop yelling at me about it because I'm not setting a good example for my cousins. My life is not exciting."

She leaned into his chest and put her arms around his waist. "So we're equally boring people?"

"No. We're *normal* people who see the cool stuff about daily life, like chocolate ice cream and swimming in the river."

She said nothing else, but he could feel her shoulders relaxing.

"Know what I don't find boring?" He hugged her closer. "Coming home and smelling barbecue chicken sandwiches in my kitchen and listening to you sing along to the radio while you do dishes. You dance when you work. Do you know that? It's cute as hell. Watching my dog chase Loralie and Chris across the creek and them throwing dirt clods at each other until they're covered in mud isn't boring either."

"I told them—"

"Hush." He tapped a finger over her mouth. "I'm making a point. It's not boring to help Mark with his homework because the way that kid thinks just... blows my mind, Allie. I can't wait to see what he's gonna do. It's not boring to show Kev how to take out an engine or pull out a dent or talk to girls. Darlin', you and your kids are like... the antidote to boring."

She looked up at him, her smile radiant. "You really mean that, don't you?"

"Do I make a habit of saying shit I don't mean?"

"No."

"That's right. Don't forget it." Ollie grabbed her at the nape of her neck and pulled her mouth up to meet his. Their kiss was long, sweet, and maybe a little frustrated on his side. He was trying to be good. Really trying. But to have her so close and still not have had her sweet body under his, still not tasted her, still not felt her curl into him while she slept... It was... hard. In every meaning of the word.

His hands reached up to cradle her cheeks.

"Ollie..."

The quiet way she whispered his name killed him. He imagined her whispering his name in the dead of night. They'd have to be quiet so they didn't disturb the kids. He'd take her mouth and swallow her moans when she came. He'd be slow and careful with her.

She turned her mouth to the side and sank her teeth into the flesh of his palm.

Okay, maybe not *too* slow and careful.

 187

He broke away before he hauled her to the truck and toward the nearest hotel.

"Have we"—he took a deep breath and tried to calm his body down—"put the whole 'I'm not exciting enough' thing to rest now?"

She pushed against his chest, brushing against the steel rod in his jeans before she took a step back. "Have to admit, I'm feeling pretty exciting at the moment."

He growled. "Playing with fire, darlin'."

The smile she threw over her shoulder as she walked away could only be described as cheeky. "Maybe I'm ready to be burned."

Challenge welcome and accepted, *Miss Smith.*

JUST THE SIMPLE SLIDE OF HER THIGH AGAINST HIS IN THE truck was enough to drive Ollie crazy on the way home. Would the kids be asleep? Could he coax her to his bed? Maybe just a little fooling around in the barn? Maybe it was time to propose and hope she was too distracted to say anything but yes.

"Oh shit," Allie muttered, checking her phone and starting to text back at lightning speed.

"What?" He sat up and forced his mind off biting that freckle on her shoulder. "What's wrong? The kids okay?"

"They're mostly fine," she said. "Sean says Chris is throwing up."

"That's weird. He seemed fine earlier. What did Sean feed them for dinner?"

"See? This is why he wouldn't throw up with you. Sean said it was probably..." She read from her phone. "'...the cheese sauce on the corn dogs, since the other kids had chili. Or possibly the Cheetos. Unless there was something wrong with the rocky road ice cream, since he ate most of the carton.'" Allie shook her head. "Is he kidding?"

Ollie curled his lip. "Well done, Sean. *That* can't have upset his stomach."

"I'm never letting him watch the kids again," she said.

"You realize that's why he let them eat all that junk food, right? Sure, he might have to clean up a little puke, but that's not a big deal."

He turned off the highway and toward the house with the puking seven-year-old and no chance of alone time with Allie. "But now he's made himself the irresponsible one who can't be left alone with the children, getting him out of all future babysitting duties."

Allie narrowed her eyes. "That snake."

"Yes, he is."

"Ollie?" She grabbed his hand. "I say we institute our first tradition in this relationship. Monday date night for you and me, and Uncle Sean night for the kids."

He smiled and brought their hands up to kiss her knuckles. "He had no idea who he was tangling with, did he? Poor rattler."

chapter
seventeen

They arrived home to a sick boy and a very guilty-looking Sean.

"I'm sorry," he told them at the front door. "I really didn't think—"

"Where is he?" Allie pushed past him. "Are the other kids in bed?"

"Yeah, I—"

"I hope he doesn't have to miss school tomorrow because you thought it would be funny to let him stuff himself."

Sean's face went pale. "Allie, I am so sorry."

She was mostly giving him a hard time. Chris would puke over too much pizza at a birthday party. He always felt better within an hour, and he'd never missed school because of it.

But Sean didn't know that.

Ollie said, "Not cool, man."

Sean swore softly.

"He's just a little kid," Ollie continued. "What were you thinking?"

Allie forced herself not to laugh as she walked upstairs. Ollie was good. He was already explaining how Sean could redeem himself when he watched the kids the next week. Chris was still in the bathroom, leaning against the wall and holding his stomach. He groaned when he saw Allie.

"Too much ice cream, Mom."

Allie put one hand on her hip. "Baby boy, I thought you learned this lesson after Jeremy's birthday party."

"But it wasn't candy, it was ice cream."

A sleepy Mark wandered down the hall and leaned into her shoulder. "Hey, Mom."

She ruffled his hair gave him a little hug. "Hey, kiddo."

"Did you and Ollie have fun?"

"Yeah. How about you guys?"

He smiled, his eyes falling closed. "Yeah. Fun. Until Chris started to throw up. Kevin and me had to clean it up 'cause Sean didn't know where anything was."

"I think I drank too much water." Chris bent over the toilet and puked again.

"Gross," Mark moaned. "I'm going back to bed. If I smell it, I'll puke too."

She patted Mark's back. "We don't need more puke. He'll be fine. Go to sleep."

"Night." Shuffling footsteps down the hall. "Hey, Ollie."

"Night, bud. Get to bed."

She looked over her shoulder. "You put the fear of vomit into Sean?"

"Yes." He peeked over to frown at Chris on the floor. "He going to be all right?"

"He should be." She rinsed out a washcloth and put it on Chris's neck. "His stomach is just sensitive, right, baby?"

Chris groaned. "No more ice cream. Ever."

She patted his back. "He's a puker. Has been since he was a baby."

Ollie looked like he was trying to hold in a laugh.

"What?"

He cleared his throat and flipped on the fan in the bathroom.

"Opposite of boring."

"Mo—oom!"

"What?" Allie stumbled through the front door with the first of the grocery bags as Loralie, Chris, and Mark ran into the house, dumped their backpacks, and headed for the kitchen because they were starving.

Elizabeth Hunter

Her children were voracious, hence the extra trip to the grocery store on Tuesday afternoon.

"Look!" Loralie burst through the swinging kitchen door to the left. "Ollie got you something!"

Allie frowned. "What?"

She heard the younger boys chattering in the kitchen.

"Whoa, cool."

"Try the crushed. Here, check it out."

"That is awesome."

Allie walked into the old kitchen to see Chris and Mark playing with a giant, stainless steel, french-door fridge where the old GE had once stood. It was the exact fridge she'd mentioned to Jena when she was talking about her dream kitchen.

"Oh my—"

"Mom, isn't it cool?" Mark said. "It makes ice and crushed ice and has water and everything."

Chris pulled open the freezer on the bottom. "Ice cream!"

"Don't even think about it."

Ollie walked in the back door only a few minutes later while the kids were still playing with the various ice settings and ignoring their homework.

"Hey," he said. "How was school?"

Loralie ran over, and he bent down so she could jump on his back like the monkey she was.

"We colored new name tags, Ollie! For our desks."

"That sounds fun."

Allie said, "You got a new fridge."

He shrugged and went to the sink to scrub his hands, Loralie still clinging to his back. "Been wanting to move that old one to the barn for a while. Keep drinks and stuff out there and get something bigger for the house."

"Did you know this is the exact one I've been wanting?"

He was smiling when he turned around. "Is it?"

She couldn't keep from smiling back. "Jena's been telling stories."

"Who better to ask about buying a new fridge than a chef, right?" He winked at her, then plucked Loralie from his back. "Hey, guys. Did I see groceries in the car?"

Oh, for heaven's sake. Allie had completely forgotten about the four bags of groceries left in the minivan. She rose to her feet.

"We'll get them," Mark said, grabbing Chris's arm and pulling him out the door.

"I'll help!" Loralie ran after her brothers.

"You," she whispered. "Did you buy this fridge for me?"

He swiftly walked to her and slid an arm around her waist. Allie went up on her toes and met his mouth in a scorching kiss.

"Absolutely not," he murmured against her mouth. "A refrigerator is a terrible first present."

"Mmm." She kissed him again and slid one leg up to wrap around his thigh. "That's too bad. It's a very nice fridge."

"I just happened to be in Palm Desert today getting your actual first present—which is very small, very lacy, and hidden under your bed—and I remembered I needed a new fridge. This is"—he nipped at her lips, then kissed her again—"purely a coincidence."

She slid her hand down the firm muscles at the small of his back and into one of his jean pockets. She heard the kids shouting on the porch. Allie squeezed once before she sneaked in another kiss. "Thank you."

"Thank me when you see your real present," he muttered before he slipped out the back door.

Chris yelled, "It is not!"

"Is too. You always grab the lightest ones."

"I have two. You have one."

Chris and Mark barreled into the kitchen with Loralie trailing behind. The baby, of course, had the bag with the eggs.

"Look, Mama! I helped."

Allie quickly grabbed the bag before it could fall. "Thank you!"

"I like our new 'frigerator."

"It's not ours, baby. Ollie got it for his house."

Loralie cocked her head. "I know."

Leaving her with a quizzical look, her youngest ran outside, yelling for the dog.

"ALLIE!"

She heard Ollie calling from outside the barn after school on Wednesday. He was worried about the minivan. He'd taken to muttering "catastrophic engine failure" or "don't forget your Triple A card" under his breath every time she left to take the kids to school.

Allie walked out the kitchen door, leaving the kids doing their homework while she walked to the barn.

"Let me guess," she said, walking in and sliding the old door closed to block the glaring sun. "It needs something that costs several thousand dollars and really, can I just get something that's not going to blow—what are you—?"

Ollie swung her around and planted a kiss on her mouth as he lifted Allie to the hood of the old truck.

"Hey," he murmured. "How are you?"

Turned on. Frustrated. She gripped his hair in her hands and pulled his mouth back to hers.

"Better now," she said between kisses. "You?"

"Doing just fine." He stepped between her legs and leaned in, making her feel surrounded in the very best way.

The hood of the old Ford put her and Ollie face-to-face, which was definitely one of the challenges with a man over a foot taller than you. He liked to pick her up and cart her around, which made Allie feel ridiculous. Still, it was practical if they wanted to avoid neck injuries.

After his initial fierce kiss, he slowed and savored.

Oh, the man could savor.

The innate patience Ollie had always exhibited in life told her he'd probably drive her crazy in bed. She'd want fast. He'd go slow. But the hand kneading her hip told her it would be the best kind of slow. The devastating kind that—

She gasped when his hand closed over her breast.

"This okay?" he whispered in her ear, sliding a finger along the curve of one breast while his thumb teased her nipple over her shirt.

"You getting grease on my shirt?"

He smiled. "I washed up before I called you."

"Then it's awesome." She pressed into his hand and let her head fall back when he dragged his lips along her neck.

They made out like teenagers until she heard a little voice calling her name from the house.

Allie pulled away with flushed lips, dragging her nails lightly down his cheeks, his soft growl of approval vibrating against her chest.

"I better get back. Dinner will be at six. Jim and Tracey said they'd open tonight so we can go in a little later."

He helped her off the truck. "I get your breaks tonight, woman, so don't plan on gossiping with the girls."

"Bossy." She laughed. "Oh, so what's the damage on my car? New transmission? Let me know and I'll see if my dad can—"

"Oh, I fixed the van already," he said, waving her off. "I just called you out here so I could kiss you. Car's fine."

SEAN WAS SITTING ACROSS FROM HER AT THE BAR THURSDAY night, talking quietly so they couldn't be overheard.

"According to Connor, there isn't a bank within a hundred miles that rented Joe a safe-deposit box. He hasn't been able to check all the private storage facilities, but he'll keep looking."

"What if he used a different name?"

"You do actually have to provide ID to rent one," Sean said. "So unless he had a bunch of good fakes lying around—"

"He might have." Allie glanced around at her tables, but everyone was watching the musician on the small stage. It was an older blues guitarist, not the Cave's usual hard-rocking sound, but it suited the quieter midweek crowd.

Sean said, "Good fakes are expensive, especially these days. But it's possible. Connor will keep looking."

Her eyes cut to Ollie, who was watching them carefully, then back to Sean. "You do realize your cousin probably uses those computer skills for more than just studying and looking up information about rotten ex-husbands, right?"

"I don't ask questions when I don't want to know the answer," Sean said. "He's an adult. Kind of. And hopefully college will civilize him."

"Well, I'll owe him one if he can find anything."

"You don't owe him. *I'll* owe him. 'Cause he'll be a lot more cautious about what he tried to collect with me, so don't argue." Sean scratched his chin. "You know, even if you find it, you can't just deposit all that cash in your checking account, right? Have you thought about that yet?"

"No." She grabbed three more longnecks when table seven held up their empties and nodded at her. They were regulars, so she popped off the caps and loaded her tray. "The first step is finding the money. Then I can worry about what to do with it. I just don't want this Lobo guy to get it first."

She could tell Sean didn't like that answer. His mouth turned down in a frown.

"Allie—"

"Don't tell me to keep my head down and forget about the cash, Sean Quinn. I may not have approved of Joe's gambling, but the fact is, he won that pot fair and square. His kids deserve to have his share of it." She blinked back the unexpected tears. "Damn it, he died for that stupid game. It shouldn't be for nothing."

"I get it," Sean said, brushing a hand over her shoulder and kissing her cheek. "We'll keep looking."

She nudged him back. "You trying to cause drama?"

"I can't help it. You're so damn cute when you're happy."

She could feel a bit of a blush, but she didn't care. She was happy, and she was glad her friends could tell.

"He treating you right?"

She glanced down the bar at Ollie, blowing him a kiss before she picked up her tray.

"Course he is," Allie said. "He's Ollie."

HE'D CAUGHT HER DOING THE DISHES THE FIRST TIME IT happened. Allie was cleaning up on Friday night, rushing around so they wouldn't be late for work while Ollie settled the younger kids in with a movie in the family room. He snuck up behind her and wrapped his arms around her waist, pulling her back against his chest and teasing his beard against her neck.

"It tickles," she said, laughing and trying to wiggle away.

"Kiss me."

"The kids—"

"Are staring at the TV. Kiss me."

She turned her head and kissed him. He drew it out, teasing her lips until she opened for him, then she turned, her hands still soapy, and leaned into him, her arms resting on his shoulders while he made her head spin.

"Need to get some alone time," he said quietly.

"Agreed."

"Want you something fierce, Allie-girl."

"I want you too." She sighed and closed her eyes, drifting into the warm happy place he took her.

"It's not gonna be at the bar, and that's the only time we're alone," he whispered. "Maybe if we—"

He broke off when he heard the giggle.

Allie's eyes went wide as she turned her head to see Loralie in the doorway, giggling behind her hands.

"Ollie," the little girl whispered. "You're kissing Mama."

He cleared his throat and took a step back. "Uh... yep."

Allie's heart was beating out of her chest. "Hey, baby."

Loralie ran over and help up her arms to Allie. "I want a kiss too."

"Okay," She picked Loralie up and kissed her little bow of a mouth while Ollie smacked a kiss on her cheek. Then she wiggled and Allie put her down.

"I don't wanna miss Merida. Ollie, kiss Mama again!"

Of course she had to shout that. Of course she did.

And yet... there were no shocked gasps from the boys. No apparent signs of emotional trauma.

"Well," Ollie said, sounding way more cheerful than she felt. "I guess the kids know."

"Apparently, yes."

"Good." He leaned down and gave her one last kiss before he smiled and smacked her backside. "That'll make life easier."

Then the man walked out to the family room—whistling!—and said in a loud, cheerful voice, "Guys, I'm kissing your mom now."

Loralie giggled, and Chris asked, "Why?"

She heard Kevin say, "I'm shocked. So shocked."

"Ew. Gross," Mark added. "Just don't do it in front of us."

Allie covered her face with her hands only to realize they still had soap all over them.

"Hmmm." She started awake when she heard the door slam. She'd been resting her eyes on the couch in Ollie's office while he closed up the bar. "Hey."

"Hey." He sat down next to her, let out a deep breath, and leaned his head back. "Long week."

She scooted over and snuggled into his side when he put his arm around her. "Two days off."

"I checked with Kevin and Eli. Kids are asleep. House is quiet."

"Good."

"We doing Sunday dinner at my place tomorrow?"

"Mm-hmm."

"Come on." He turned toward her. "We should get you home. You're exhausted. You've got to get your dad to hire someone on Saturdays. You work way too much."

She burrowed into his side. "Snuggle."

He sighed. "I've only got so much self-control, woman."

Allie's breath caught, and her sleepy languor took on an entirely more heated tone. She stretched against him, throwing one arm over his shoulder and one leg over his thigh before she scooted onto his lap and nuzzled into his chest.

"Allie…" He let out a breath and put his hands on the small of her back, teasing the sensitive skin there with rough fingertips. "We should get home. You're worn out."

Yeah, but she wasn't dead. And they were alone in the bar. Really and truly alone.

With a lazy stretch, Allie pressed her body into his. Her breasts against his chest. Her heat against his hips. She felt him, hard and swollen between her thighs, and she let the animal in her out to play, overwhelmed by the scent and feel of the male beneath her.

Allie rocked into him, laying her head on his shoulder and pressing lazy kisses to his neck. She licked at the edge of the flames that marked his chest, pulling his collar down so she could taste more.

"Off." Her voice was thick with need. "Want your skin." She slid her hand under the edge of his shirt, shivering at the feel of the hair trailing down his abdomen.

"Allie—"

"Need it." She breathed the words against his neck as her hand continued to pet him. "Need you."

With a soft curse, Ollie sat up and pulled his shirt off. Allie was roused by a violent wave of desire she had no intention of quelling. Ollie tugged at her shirt, pulling it up and over her head before he tossed it across the room. Then his eyes were on her, fixed on the soft blue lace covering her breasts.

He bent down and grazed his teeth over the rise of her left breast, then he licked at her, sliding his tongue under the edge of lace that shielded the last bit of her from his eyes.

Allie reached back to unclip her bra. This was Ollie. She didn't care about caution anymore. She only wanted to know him. Know his touch. Feel his heat.

"Allie," he groaned, pressing his cheek to her neck, his left hand reaching up to gently cradle her breast. "Not in the bar. I don't want us—"

"Not..." She took his mouth and drank him in, desperate for more. "Not everything. I just... I need a taste. Give me something."

The little voice in the back of her head reminded her of Joe's scorn. Reminded her of the marks of age and children. Marks that younger, fitter women wouldn't carry.

She froze. "Please, Ollie."

If he rejected her, she'd crumble.

With a fierce growl, he flipped them over, pressing her back into the couch as his mouth descended on her breasts. There was no more coaxing. No teasing. His mouth covered one nipple, his teeth scraped over her, and he sucked hard.

It wasn't the first time a man had touched her like that, but it was the first time *he* had. The first time she'd felt the fire of him taking her over. She cried out, digging her nails into his shoulders.

He swore softly. "Harder," he growled. Then his mouth was on her again, licking and biting down her body. Her mind was too swamped with the feel of him to be self-conscious. There was only Ollie. Only her. She felt his teeth at her waist and was jolted by a moment of panic.

"Ollie." She grabbed a handful of his hair. "I didn't mean... I don't know—"

"What?" He pressed himself up, his massive shoulders hovering over her. "Didn't you say I could have a taste?"

His eyes were pure evil. He knew that wasn't what she'd said, but he licked his lips and let the corner inch up in a wicked smile.

"I didn't..." *Damn, damn, damn.* Of all the times for her inexperience to show, it had to be the first time her shirt was off. She tried to turn to her side, but Ollie was already tugging at her jeans.

"Let me guess." His voice was low and rough. "Joe didn't like doing this."

"Ollie, maybe we should just—"

"He was an idiot." Ollie yanked her jeans off and stopped a moment, just to stare. "Damn, you're pretty." Then he knelt next to her on the couch, sliding one hand down to her bottom as he took her mouth. "Let me," he whispered against her mouth, stroking long fingers up and down the back of her thigh, barely brushing over the lace of her panties. "Please."

Allie said, "I feel stupid."

"Why?"

"Because I don't know what I'm doing. It's not that I don't want to. Of course I do. It's just... I'm thirty-four, for heaven's sake. Not some stupid girl."

"Want to know how big a bastard I am?"

"You're not a bastard."

"Yeah, I am. Because there's a pretty big part of me that's glad he never did this with you. That he never kissed you there. That I'm the only one who will."

"Ollie—"

"And that's a bastard thing to think, because you should have had this, baby."

His voice was so deep and soft Allie felt it on her skin.

"You should have had a man who loved you like that," he continued, bringing his mouth back to her body. "Wanted to kiss you all over." He brushed his lips over her breasts. "Wanted to know you." Kissed down her soft belly. "Wanted to know every inch of you."

Allie melted into the sofa when he used his teeth to drag her panties down.

"Especially these inches." He tossed the blue lace over his shoulder. "They're pretty much my favorite."

She couldn't stop the low laugh. "Wicked."

"Nope. Greedy."

Then he was between her thighs, the rough man who was so unutterably gentle that, when he finally put his mouth on her, he reached up and grasped her hands, knitting their fingers together while he tasted her.

He held her hands, and Allie flew.

chapter
eighteen

"I hate you!"

Ollie paused on the top step of the porch when he heard Mark's voice. He heard Allie's softer one responding and Chris crying in the background.

"I do!" Mark yelled again. "I hate him. He takes my stuff and he breaks it. And he's so stupid, Mom!"

He thought about going in but waited, never sure how much he should insert himself into the kids and their fights. He was even less sure now that he and Allie were together.

He couldn't hear exactly what she said, but whatever it was made someone—he was guessing Mark—storm up the stairs even while Chris still hiccupped and sniffed. He could hear Allie talking to her youngest son, so he took a seat on the porch and waited to give them some privacy.

Living with four grieving kids was kind of like walking through a minefield. Most of the ground was safe, but every now and then the most random thing would cause an explosion.

He heard the side door open, and Kevin and Loralie came around the corner. The baby, her face covered in jam, immediately ran over to crawl on the swing next to him.

"Hey," Kevin said. "You taking shelter too?"

"What's going on?"

"Chris broke Mark's yo-yo."

Ollie's eyes widened. "His yo-yo?"

Kevin rolled his eyes. "It's the big thing in fourth and fifth this year. All the kids have yo-yos."

"Huh. And breaking one…?"

The teenager leaned against the porch railing. "Is cause for disowning your little brother, yes."

"What part did he break?"

"The string."

Ollie made a mental note to look up how to restring a yo-yo. "That seems like a bit of an overreaction."

Kevin shrugged. "He has more at home, but Mom only let him bring one over here."

Ollie would have to talk to Allie about that. Mark wasn't going ballistic over a broken yo-yo string. He was going ballistic because he didn't have his stuff. He remembered being a little boy. Having your stuff safe and within reach was important.

For the first time, Ollie reconsidered whether it was best to keep Allie and the kids here.

Was he being selfish? He loved having them around. Kevin was mature enough that they could have real conversations, and he was a breeze to teach because he was such a hard worker. Mark had a sly humor and delighted in making his mother laugh. Chris was boundless energy and unflagging optimism, and Loralie was sweetness in dinosaur princess form.

Naughty too. With three doting older brothers, Loralie had plenty of naughty. And Ollie was probably a bad adult, because the naughty mostly made him laugh.

Besides, knowing Allie was within easy reach every single day…

He forced his mind away from the memories of the night before while the kids were sitting with him.

Kevin said, "We still need to stay here, don't we?"

Tony Razio hadn't located the guys who'd broken into her house. Ollie knew leaving her unprotected wasn't an option. His house was still, undoubtedly, the safest place for them. But he needed to talk to Allie about letting the kids bring more of their stuff.

Ollie nodded slowly. "I think you guys need to stay until we find out who broke into your house. I know it's rough being away from home, but—"

"It'd be rough being home too." Kevin's eyes were too old for his face. "Most of the time I forget about it. He was already gone in my head, you know? I was so… pissed at him."

"Kevin, you said pissed," Loralie whispered.

"I know. Don't tell Mom on me, okay?"

The baby nodded quickly.

"But then he was really gone," Ollie said.

"Yeah." Kevin looked away. "Which makes me… I don't know. Still pissed. Mark's angrier than me though. He hit Chris the other day when Chris said that Dad didn't leave us. That he would have come back if he hadn't died."

Loralie cuddled into his side. "I miss Daddy. He reads me stories."

"Grandpa reads you stories, Lala. Dad didn't read much."

"Oh." She stuck her thumb in her mouth.

Ollie nudged her little shoulder. "Want me to read to you when Grandpa can't?"

"Yes," she said behind her thumb. "At bedtime."

"Okay."

Kevin sighed. "Lala, Ollie has to work at your bedtime."

"I'll come home for a few minutes," he said. "They can spare me."

Loralie lifted her head and took her thumb out of her mouth. "Will you get in trouble?"

"Nope. I'm the boss."

Loralie leaned a little closer and Ollie saw calculation in her sky-blue eyes. "Can you be your bear when you read to me?"

Ollie threw his head back and laughed.

IN THE END, THE FESTERING ARGUMENT WAS ENDED BY THE figurative hand of God.

"Enough!" Allie finally yelled. "We are getting ready for church, so both of you need to stop and get dressed. I don't want to hear another word. After church, we'll run by the house and you can get another yo-yo, Mark."

Sullen silence from the boys.

"And you're both going to pray for each other during silent prayers."

Ollie—still eavesdropping from the porch—bit his lip to keep from smiling, but Kevin couldn't disguise his snort.

"What?" Mark yelled. "Why? Should I pray for Chris not to be so stupid? Is that even possible?"

"Mo-om!"

Ollie stood, picked up Loralie, and walked in the front door.

"You're gonna pray for your brother," he said, mussing Mark's hair, "because it's harder to be mad at 'em when you're praying for them. And stop calling your brother stupid."

Grumbling, both boys dragged themselves up the stairs, and Allie came over to take Loralie from him.

"Lala, go clean your face and then pick out two dresses for church. I'll come up in a minute."

"Okay!" Unlike her brothers, Loralie bounced up the stairs.

"And Kevin—"

"I got it, *mamita*." Kevin walked past Allie and patted the top of her head while Allie, laughing, tried to smack his hand away. "I'll let you know if there's any blood."

She took a deep breath and turned to him. "Enjoy the morning show?"

"Probably more than I should have. A yo-yo string?"

She just closed her eyes and shook her head.

"The forced brotherly prayers were a stroke of genius though. My yaya used to do the same thing to me and my cousins, only it was out loud and in front of whoever we'd been hitting."

"I might try that." She glanced at his grubby jeans and T-shirt. "Did you want to come to church with us?"

He'd gotten up early to check the barn and property line. There had been no signs of intruders, but he still checked every morning to be safe and relieve his cousins of duty.

"I got time to take a shower?"

"Yep."

"Cool." He bent down and gave her the good-morning kiss he'd been thinking about before the boys started World War Yo-Yo.

"Mmm," she murmured, her hands going up around his neck. "Good morning to you too."

He nipped at her lips. "After last night, I probably need to go confess a few things anyway."

The blush was immediate. "Ollie—"

"You better not," he said quietly. "I'm teasing you. There was nothing wrong with what we did."

She closed her eyes and shook her head. "Sorry. You know my family's traditional. There's still a lot of voices in my head from the last time I fooled around with a boy I wasn't married to."

"Allie-girl, where exactly do you think this is heading?" He kissed her one last time, pinched her bottom, and headed up the stairs before he had time to see her reaction.

In case she'd been wondering about his intentions, she probably wouldn't be now.

Ollie headed toward his bathroom and pretended his heart wasn't racing with fear.

BETWEEN CHURCH, RUNNING TO THE MARKET FOR SUNDAY dinner supplies, and driving by the house to pack up more toys, they were home with barely enough time to start the barbecue before their friends showed up.

The toys had been a challenge. Allie kept saying no, so the kids stopped asking their mom and started asking Ollie. He pretended he didn't know what they were doing and just kept loading things in the back of the van. She'd probably be mad at him, but the kids seemed happy, so he figured she'd get over it.

Sunday supper passed with the usual parade of kids and dogs and animals. When the sun started to go down and the baby had fallen asleep in the house, Kevin and Low, both old enough to shift to their natural forms, made a game of hunting down the younger kids outside while they were in their fox and owl forms. Low, as a near-silent barn owl, was impressively sneaky. The yard around Ollie's house was filled with delighted shrieks, the occasional eerie fox howl, and the low rumble from Ollie's cousins who were guarding them in bear form to give the kids a thrill.

Ted shivered and moved closer to the fire pit Ollie had lit in the front yard.

"What is it about fox calls?" she asked.

Allie scooted her chair closer to Ollie and he put his arm across the back.

"Horror movies," he said. "They sound like horror movies."

Allie laughed. "We do not."

"Going to disagree," Jena said. "That scream you make? Definitely horror movie creepy."

Sean said, "I know it makes me hide on moon nights."

"Everything makes a snake hide on moon nights," Alex said. "But I agree about the fox calls. Totally creepy."

"I object to this anti-fox bigotry!" Allie protested with a laugh. "We are small but fierce predators. Worthy of respect for more than our creepy calls."

"Small and fierce." Ollie's hand slid down her back and grabbed a handful of her backside. "With cute fluffy tails."

She narrowed her eyes. "Careful what you say about my tail, mister."

"You know I love your tail."

"As disgustingly cute as you two are," Caleb broke in, "Allie mentioned something to Jena about needing help. What's up, sweetheart?"

Allie perched forward on her chair. "Okay. Here's the thing. You all knew Joe, in some way or another. And according to Alex and Ted's friend Cam, we now know he won that game of poker fair and square. So the help I want from you guys is... finding the cash."

The whole circle was silent.

Ollie cursed silently, wishing she'd talked to him about this before she brought it up. He didn't much relish all their friends searching out places Joe Russell might have been hanging, looking for clues like this was a Scooby-Doo mystery while there were guys connected to drug cartels roaming around.

"Allie-girl—"

"Don't." She held up a hand. "I know you don't want us going to seedy hotels or bars or anything. But listen to me. I don't think that's where he would have hidden it."

Ollie thought that was exactly where Joe would have hidden it, but he shut up. The most likely answer was that Joe Russell, a coyote shifter who knew he was in trouble, would have dug a hole in the desert someplace only he knew about and hidden the money where no humans would ever look. Which meant it would never be found.

Sean was the first one to speak again. "Is there any way we could get some kind of scent on it?"

Ollie shook his head. "I don't think so. It's two hundred grand in cash that was won at a poker game in a private club. It's going to smell like paper, ink, sweat, alcohol, and tobacco smoke."

"So basically, it's going to smell like all cash everywhere." Ted wrinkled her nose.

"Yep," Ollie said.

"Your only option is to forget about tracking the cash and try to track the man," Caleb said. "I've been trying to put Joe's movements together in the days before he was killed, but I'm not having much luck. He didn't use hotels. Or not hotels that kept records."

Sean said, "Maggie told me she checked with the hotel where they were supposed to meet after the game. Cash only. He'd been staying there, but he packed up and left in the middle of the night according to the clerk. Didn't even check out. Just left the keys in the room."

"So he left town as soon as he won?" Ollie asked.

"That's what it sounds like. He was smart. Probably knew the guys he beat weren't going to let things go."

Alex said, "According to Cam, the only one we really need to be looking at is this Lobo guy. He's the one who was a sore loser. He's also the one with a drug cartel backing him, if you believe the rumors. He'd have access to people who would have no problem killing someone so Lobo could get his money back."

"I've got some guys poking around," Ollie said. "We'll see what they can turn up about the break-in at Allie's place. My guys weren't real happy about it. This is not a criminal you mess with, according to them."

Ollie watched everyone nod in agreement, and he was glad. He wanted all of them to realize how serious this was.

"Well," Allie said. "Then we don't go where Lobo might be looking. We go where Joe might have hidden it. We knew Joe better than anyone else."

"And I'll smell anyone familiar who comes back," Ollie said. "I won't forget the scent of those two anytime soon."

Jena asked, "What were they driving?"

"We didn't get the plates."

"'Cause someone lost his temper," Allie quipped. "And had to tear things up and roar a lot."

He tugged on a piece of her hair. "Behave."

Allie snorted. "Like that's ever worked." She patted his knee. "Nice try."

"What about Joe?" Jena asked. "What was he driving?"

"He took his old truck when he left," Allie said. "When he left us, I mean. I don't know if he was still driving it months later."

"Maggie said he was," Sean said.

"It was a solid truck. And it was four-wheel drive," Allie said.

A thought occurred to Ollie. "Alex, what's the status at the base?"

"What do you mean?"

The old air base where Joe and most of the rest of the town had been employed up until a few years ago was still sitting there. Guarded by soldiers but, as far as Ollie knew, intact. Joe had been an electrician.

"They haven't torn anything down at the base, have they?"

"Not as far as I know," Alex said. "It's protected though. Gates all chained up."

"Please," Sean said. "That perimeter fence is about as secure as my grandma's wallet. Joe wouldn't have any trouble breaking in, especially not in his coyote form."

Jena frowned at Sean. "Please tell me that's a figure of speech and you don't actually steal money from your grandmother."

"Do you remember how mean my grandma is?"

Jena shrugged. "True."

"I don't do it anymore," he muttered. "But Joe could easily have hidden something on the base. He worked all over the place. Knew all the maintenance areas and lots of spots to hide things. I'd check there first."

"Could you?" Allie asked.

"Search the base?" Sean nodded. "Sure. I'll take some of my cousins. We can cover it pretty quickly. No one will see us."

Allie nodded. "I'll go with you."

The "no" came from Sean and Ollie at the same time.

"Guys, I'll go as my fox. They're not going to see me. But I know how the man thought. The search will go faster if I'm along."

She was right, but Ollie really didn't want her there.

"Allie," Sean said reasonably, "why double up like that? We don't need that many people searching the base. Why don't you and Ted search somewhere else in town?"

He was going to have to thank Sean later. Once he got past visions of Allie trying to explain to military police officers why she was naked and running around an old air base.

"Where else do you think we should look?" she asked.

Jena said, "What about his old house?"

"His parents' old place?"

Ted nodded. "Or the feed shop. He worked there with your dad."

Jena said, "It's like you said. You know how the man thought. I agree that the base is the most likely place, but think about Joe's routine. What other places could he have hidden a pile of cash where he'd think you could find it?"

"The house?"

"Too obvious and goons already searched there. If it was there, they would have found it."

"What about the high school?" Alex asked. "Joe was good at sneaking around there."

Allie groaned. "Joe was good at sneaking around everywhere. Why do you think I ended up pregnant at seventeen?"

Ted cracked a laugh before she cleared her throat. "Sorry."

"Laugh." Allie threw up a hand. "That's the only way I'm dealing with all this."

"Hey." Ollie reached over and grabbed her hand.

She turned her face to smile. "You're right. Not the *only* way."

Ollie tugged on her arm until she rose and went to sit on his lap. He wrapped his arms around her as she put her head on his chest and let out a deep breath.

"This is overwhelming," she said.

"One piece at a time, darlin'. I'll ask Jim and Tracey if they can help out at the bar more in the next couple of weeks so I can help you look. They won't mind."

She settled into his chest as Ollie heard a sigh coming from his left. He turned to see Jena staring at them with tears in her eyes.

"You all right?" he asked.

"I love this," she said, nodding toward Allie. "I love this so much."

"Ignore her," Allie whispered. "She's super hormonal right now. New baby."

Jena threw a wadded-up napkin at Allie. "Whatever, super-breeder. I remember how weepy you were when you had newborns. Shut it."

"She's not a newborn," Ted said. "She's ten months old. Should your boobs still be that big?"

"At least I have boobs, Ted."

"Not for long," Allie said. "Mine are the only ones that stick around past the breast-feeding."

"Thinking of ways to hurt you both right now," Jena said.

Caleb reached around and squeezed his wife's shoulder. "Ah, the delicate, warm love of female friendship."

IT WAS A THREE-DAY WEEKEND, SO THEY'D LET THE KIDS play late. After eyes started drooping and fights started breaking out between siblings, everyone packed up and made their way back to their cars, leaving Allie and Ollie standing on the porch watching dust.

She turned her head toward the house. "Where's Mark and Kevin?"

Ollie frowned. "With Jena and Caleb. Went to spend the night. They told me, but I thought they cleared it with you."

"Oh." She blinked. "Jena mentioned the boys coming over earlier, but I forgot about it. I guess they just assumed it was okay."

"Should I call Caleb?"

"No, it's fine. They spend the night over there all the time."

"Wait." Ollie cocked his head, listening.

Silence. Complete and utter... *silence*.

"Where are Loralie and Chris?" he asked.

"Ted asked if they could spend the night because she's watching her niece and nephew tomorrow and wanted the kids to have someone..." Her eyes went wide at the realization.

"Allie." He turned and gripped her shoulders. "Are you telling me there are no children in this house tonight?"

Her mouth dropped open. "There are no children in this house tonight."

Without another word, Ollie bent down and lifted Allie over his shoulder, marching into the silent—and miraculously child-free —house.

chapter
nineteen

Allie watched the living room recede as Ollie sprinted up the stairs. She was breathless with excitement. And also because his shoulder was digging into her diaphragm, but she'd survive.

He put one hand on her bottom to hold her as he turned the corner, then he gave a long, luxurious squeeze that had her eyes rolling back.

No children.

Ollie.

Bedroom.

No children.

"How long...?" she wheezed.

"Allie?"

"Can't breathe."

He stopped immediately and set her down. "Sorry."

Then he bent and scooped her up, lifting her until her legs were wrapped around his waist. He kissed her, somehow managing to walk the last steps to his bedroom while their lips were plastered together.

"How long can we leave them with other people?" she asked between kisses.

"We'll just"—they bumped through the doorway—"wait for someone to call. They're nice kids. Our friends won't let them starve. We might be able to"—he kicked the door shut—"stretch this out for a couple of days if we're lucky."

"I haven't"—frantic kisses along the line of his throat—"done this in a while."

His head fell back when she closed her lips over his pounding pulse. "I have protection."

"I'm on... the pill." Allie felt like her skin was burning from the inside. "Have been since Loralie."

"I'm good, but do you want—"

"I'm good if you are." She trusted Ollie more than anyone.

He sat on the edge of the bed, still holding her; they were tugging at each other's clothes. Allie heard his old T-shirt rip when she pulled it off. She reached down and palmed him through his jeans.

Ollie let out a long groan.

"I never got to return the favor last night," she whispered. She bit his earlobe before she bent to kiss his neck. "I really want to do that."

"Later." He fell back on the bed and pulled her shirt over her head, scooting her up so that his mouth closed around one breast.

"Ollie!"

"Baby, I am going to make you scream," he said, his voice rough with need. He started to fumble with her bra. "Do you know how long I've been dreaming about this?"

Nerves twisted her stomach. Years? *Decades?*

Oh shit.

No actual sexual experience was going to be able to live up to that kind of hype! It had been a pretty long time for her. What if she'd forgotten how to do things? What if Ollie didn't like the way she did the things she knew? What if—

"You're thinking too damn loud again." He pulled off her bra and rolled over so she was under him. Then he kissed her hard. "What are you getting twisted about, huh?"

Allie took a deep breath. "You're good at this, aren't you?"

"What?"

"Sex."

He pulled away from her and blinked. "I... don't know how to answer that."

"You are."

He frowned, and dammit, even his frown had her body heating up. "Who've you been talking to?"

"I don't need to talk to anyone. I've seen the way your old girl-friends look at you."

"What are you talking about?"

He was so big and so hard and so sweet and so... everything. She wanted him like her next breath. Ollie braced himself over her, propped up on one arm and looking down at her like he wanted to eat her alive. She should have shut up and sent an enthusiastic "thank you!" to the universe, but she just kept talking. The nervous blather spilled out of her mouth.

She had some kind of verbal disease. It was the only explanation.

"Your old girlfriends. They always came back to the Cave after you broke up with them, like they were just hoping you'd reconsider. And you'd be really nice, but they always had the same look on their face. Like someone gave them a big bite of chocolate cake, then told them they'd never have another one and all chocolate was off-limits forever."

He looked at her like she'd grown a third eye.

"It's true. Jena and I used to joke about it. 'There goes another one. The bear ruined her for all other men.'"

The corner of his mouth twitched. "So you're worried I'm going to ruin you for all other men?"

Her breath caught and her mouth dropped open, but no words came out.

Allie was already ruined for all other men.

Because she loved him.

"That's not what I meant," she whispered.

"Because let me tell you something..." He began kissing her face softly. Her cheek. Her lips. He nudged her chin up and tasted her neck. "There aren't going to be any other men for you. And there aren't going to be any other women for me." His big heart pounded against her chest as he lowered his head. "In case you didn't catch it earlier, my plans are more of the permanent kind."

She'd caught it. She just didn't believe it.

"Ollie," she whispered. She didn't know what else to say. He was everything she'd ever wanted, but more than she'd let herself hope. Allie had given up on happy endings coming her way. To have the possibility of one dangling in front of her was terrifying.

He put a hand on her cheek, stroking a thumb over her flushed face.

"I love you," he said simply. "I don't remember a time I haven't loved you, Allison Smith."

For once, she had no words. She reached up and pulled him down, kissing his lips as he gathered her up in his big arms and rolled them across the bed. Then the sweetness turned hotter as he tugged on her jeans. She was already aching for him, ridiculously aroused by the scent and taste of the man who held her. His beard rasped over skin that felt electrified. Every touch set off another spark.

Before she could get her hands on his jeans, he was thrusting up, the harsh denim scraping against the inside of her bare thighs.

"Chocolate cake, huh?" He bit her lower lip. "Woman, I hope you're hungry."

"Starved," she gasped, reaching for the button of his jeans. She managed to get them open and shove his jeans down his hips, taking over with her feet as her hands closed over something far more important.

He swore silently, but Allie wanted to purr.

It was one thing to suspect. Far more satisfying to know.

He pushed himself into her hands. "You know, it's a good thing I like these panties, or they'd be ripped off."

"Respect the lingerie, bear."

"Oh, I do," he growled. "But right now?" He scooted down the bed and pulled slowly as he kicked off his jeans. "They're just in my way."

And then there was nothing between them. He crawled over her, nudging her legs apart so he could settle his body over hers.

The heat was all she could feel. And the solid weight of him. The brush of his chest hair against her breasts. His arms braced beside her shoulders. The heavy weight of his thighs between her knees. The hard hot length of him...

"Allie?" He arched over her, holding her close, his breath against her temple as he slid inside. "*Allie,*" he whispered again.

His chest was a bellows. She reached her arms around his body and held on, pressing kiss after kiss into his shoulder.

Yes, yes, yes.

He was all the way inside, and Allie realized she'd never felt safer. Never felt more at home.

And holy hell, he felt amazing.

"I love you," she said, letting out a slow breath. "So much."

It snapped whatever leash had been holding him back, and Ollie began to *move*.

And Allie? She just held on tight.

She dug her nails into his back, but that only seemed to excite him more. He fisted a hand in her hair and thrust, his hips working in a rhythm that lifted her like a wave. Within minutes, she was cresting, lights bursting behind her eyes as she cried out, only to realize he wasn't stopping.

A roll to the side and he grabbed her leg, hooking it over his elbow and opening her wider.

He groaned when he slid deeper. "Flexible."

"Yoga."

"Still hungry?"

"Uh-huh."

He reached a callused hand between her thighs and set her off again.

Now Allie was the one cursing.

"Baby…" Ollie grinned at her. "You got a dirty mouth."

"You like it."

"Bet your ass I do." He reached behind her and slapped her bottom, making her jerk and him moan.

Ollie rolled to his back and sat up, lifting her, then setting her down hard as he took her mouth. In that position they were face-to-face, and she realized what he wanted.

She wrapped her arms around his neck and leaned close, taking his lips in a sizzling kiss as she moved over him. It was slower and achingly intimate.

One hand splayed across the small of her back and the other brushed the hair from her eyes.

"You love me?" he asked in a low voice.

"Yes."

The new angle stroked already-sensitized nerves. Allie felt like she was moments away from snapping.

"How much?"

A press of his hand, and she was gasping into his neck with another release.

 217

"I love you... like crazy, Oliver Campbell."

"Like crazy," he panted into her ear. "Yeah. That's how it is."

Then Allie smiled because there was nothing else to say in that perfect moment when Ollie closed his eyes, let his head fall back, and she felt him let go.

SHE WOKE SLOWLY, THE MORNING SUN PEEKING THROUGH the drawn shades in his bedroom.

Ollie was snoring behind her, having exhausted both of them in one very long night. She glanced at the clock.

Ten thirty a.m.

Her eyes went wide. The fact that no phone was ringing was evidence that their friends knew exactly what they'd been doing the night before. That had clearly been a coordinated intervention on the part of Jena and Ted.

Man, she loved those girls.

And Ollie.

Her heart fluttered.

I don't remember a time I haven't loved you, Allison Smith.

As if reading her mind, the arm around her tightened a little and hugged her closer to his chest.

He'd woken her twice during the night, clearly as starved for connection as she was. Allie's body felt deliciously used. Worn out and limber with the loose-jointed exhaustion that was only produced by a long night of really good sex.

And yes, Ollie was very good at it.

But she wasn't so bad herself. It really was like riding a bike.

In this case, a really big, bearded, heavily tattooed bike who liked to use his teeth in all the right places.

He made a noise behind her and Allie had to smile, because it sounded so much like a bear that she almost laughed. It was a low, rumbly, almost grumpy sound he made in his chest when he was sleeping, and she loved that she knew that now. Loved that she would recognize it anywhere.

"Cake," he mumbled, tightening his arm when she started to giggle. "Allie?"

"Mm-hmm?"

"Thank fuck," he mumbled. "Wasn't a dream."

"You said cake in your sleep."

"Really good dream…"

His hand slid from her waist down her hip, and he lifted her knee, working his thigh between her legs.

"You aren't good at waking up in the morning, are you?"

"Mmm. Cake…"

She laughed louder and grabbed the hand that had wandered up to her breast. "No cake. We're taking a break from cake, or I'll be walking funny."

He hitched her closer and buried his face in her hair. She could feel his beard tickling the back of her neck.

"Love you, Allie-girl."

Her heart was so full she thought it might just be possible for it to burst.

She loved her children. Adored them. But… they were her kids. And they needed so much from her.

Ollie filled her up. She felt like she'd been walking through the desert only to find she'd been circling an oasis the whole time. And now that she'd wandered in, leaving its cool shelter might just kill her.

But what if she never had to leave?

There aren't going to be any other men for you. And there aren't going to be any other women for me. In case you didn't catch it earlier, my plans are more of the permanent kind.

Some animal instinct urged her to run. It was happening too fast. It wasn't the right time. He could break her heart. Break her children's hearts. Leave a hole even bigger than Joe had left because Ollie was everything Joe was supposed to have been and wasn't.

He would get bored eventually. Get frustrated with her and the kids. The cutting remarks would start, and then the coldness. She could handle anger, but if Ollie turned from her like Joe had—

He made the rumbly bear noise behind her and she stilled. He pressed his hand over her racing heart and she knew he was really awake.

"Stop arguing when I can't fight back," he said quietly.

She hugged his arm with both of her own. "I'm panicking."

"Okay." He took a deep breath, but he didn't sound angry. "Why?"

"Because… it's fast."

"We've known each other our whole lives."

"But the kids—"

"I love your kids," he said softly, playing with a piece of her hair that was lying on the pillow. "I really do. I loved them before, but having them here… They're really cool people. And they're funny as hell. Even when they're fighting."

"They'll wear on you eventually, Ollie."

"Like they never wear on you?"

He was right. Ollie was way more patient than she was. Always had been.

"Kids try your patience. They get annoying," he said. "Then you send them off to someone else's house for the night and hopefully you like them better when they come back. Some of my younger cousins make me want to leave them out in Sandy Wash and hope a flash flood takes them away. But I get over it. Usually after I've made them clean my shop or the bar." He pinched her belly.

"Stop." She slapped his hand.

"No." He laughed. "I like your belly. It's soft."

"I hate my stretch marks."

He laughed harder.

"What?"

"Baby, I didn't even notice you had them. Were you checking out all my scars?"

"No. Most of them are covered by tattoos anyway."

His voice dropped. "Want to cover up yours?" His hand spread over her bare hip. "I could definitely see some ink on this pretty curve right here." He flipped her over, and his fingers teased her lower back. "Or maybe something here."

"Like Property of Oliver Campbell?"

"You read my mind," he said, dipping his mouth to taste hers.

Their kiss was long and lazy. If Ollie noticed her morning breath, he didn't mention it.

"So," he murmured against her lips, "still panicking?"

 220

"Not so much. You muddled my mind with thoughts of cake."

"That is now my favorite sex-euphemism. Thank you."

"I'm glad you approve."

He laid his head on the pillow next to hers. "Tell me what you're really scared of, Allison."

Oh, he saw her. Saw right to the heart of her. It was glorious and terrifying, all at the same time.

"Don't hurt me."

His eyes softened and his hand came to her cheek. "Allie—"

"I never felt this way about Joe. I can admit that. I never... It wasn't this big, overwhelming thing. I loved him. I was... content. Even happy for a while. But—"

"Am I a bastard again for admitting I'm glad?"

She shook her head. "I made my own bed and got four great kids out of the deal. But you..." She took a deep breath. "You're everything I've ever wanted. You're steady and honest. Affectionate. Funny. If you hurt me, I'd break. Really, really break. And I don't know how I'd put myself back together for my family. So yeah. You terrify me, Ollie."

She could see him thinking, but his eyes never left hers.

"I can't promise you I'll never hurt you," he said quietly. "'Cause... I'm a guy. And all this is new for me. Your being here. The kids. Everything. I'll probably get impatient. Or get jealous of your time. I work too much. My family..." He let out a long sigh.

"You are kind of a pushover about fixing their problems for them."

"Yeah. And I'm really bad about leaving laundry lying on the floor."

"I noticed that."

"But I'd never hurt you on purpose. I don't know if I even could; I can't imagine wanting to."

"I'll mess up too. I don't know how to be with a good guy. I might walk on eggshells for a while. Overreact to some things."

Ollie nodded. "Then like I said before, we'll take as much time as you need. You know what I want." He paused. "I guess I need to know if that's what you want too. Eventually. When all this shit is over. When things are safe and you can go back home. I need to know you're not gonna be done with me."

She smiled, oddly relieved that he had his own insecurities about them when he always seemed so cool and confident. "You think I'd pass on the best man I've ever known? You're stuck now, Ollie Campbell. I never was very good at turning down cake."

He kissed her, and it was a promise. And that was all she needed right then. She'd still panic at times, but she knew that Ollie would be there to talk her down in his quiet, methodical way.

"Just so you know," she said when they came up for breath, "I'm not sleeping in your bed when the kids are in the house."

He groaned. "Please?"

"No way, mister."

"Not even every now and then?"

"I have a teenage son. Forget it. We'll figure something out."

"Fine." He rolled over on top of her. "Better enjoy the bed while you can, Allie-girl, because your back is gonna be feeling a lot of my desk at the bar from now on."

She laughed and slapped his back, but Ollie just grinned.

"Time for cake."

chapter
twenty

Alex, Caleb, and Sean arrived at the bar just as Ollie finished the books for the week before. Tuesday always ended up being a catch-up day, which worked because it was the slowest night at the Cave. He heard the front door open and caught the familiar smells of his friends.

"He's whistling," Sean said. "It finally happened."

"It better have," Alex added. "Do you know what four kids did to my coffee table? Ted was no help. She just laughed at them. In fact, she might have helped."

Ollie stood and walked to his office door.

"It's disturbing that you two are even discussing this," Caleb said. "Besides, we all knew—"

Ollie shut the door in their faces. Then he locked it and walked back to his desk.

Whistling.

"Hey." Someone—probably Sean—pounded on the door. "This isn't cool."

"We watched all your kids, man. Where's the love?"

"Ollie"—Caleb rapped his knuckles on the door—"I actually do have some new information I wanted to run by you."

He stood and walked to the door, silently opening it and staring down at his three friends.

"Well?" Alex asked.

Ollie said nothing, just pushed his way past them, grabbed a bottle of water from behind the bar, and went to one of the larger tables to sit down.

"Seriously, man." Alex sat down across from him. "So did you and Allie—"

"Do I ask you about your sex life with my cousin?" he asked Alex.

"No."

"Then shut the fuck up."

Alex rolled his eyes. "Fine. But we all know why you're whistling."

Sean said, "I no longer have a sex life because I live in this town. Feel free to ask me anything."

Caleb narrowed his eyes at Sean. "Can you really shift just enough so that you have fangs?"

"Yes, but I don't know why and not even Ted can figure it out."

"Are they poisonous?"

"If I want them to be," Sean said. "Can you really turn into anyone you've seen?"

From one blink to the next, there were two Seans sitting at the table.

"Yes."

Sean just stared at his mirror image, even when it spoke with Caleb's voice. "That is *so* weird."

Caleb shifted back and cracked his jaw. "You're telling me. Are we done with gossip?"

"Men don't gossip," Alex said. "We discuss."

Ollie laughed, and Caleb shoved a file folder across to him. He flipped it open to see Tony Razio's mug shot looking back at him.

"You know these guys?"

Ollie flipped through the pages. Photos of Tony Razio and three of the Red Rock Drifters stared up at him, along with a couple of men he didn't recognize.

"Yeah," he said.

"They got picked up at a bar fight last Saturday. They were dead twelve hours later."

Shit. Well, that explained why Razio wasn't returning his calls.

Ollie's eyes darted to Caleb. "Other prisoners?"

"No one's talking. Whoever did it knew the county jail well enough to avoid the cameras."

"Guards?"

"They got nothing. They're writing it off as a scuffle between gangs."

"It probably was," Alex said.

Ollie turned to him. "What do you know?"

"I know there are certain people who are going out of business—voluntarily—and others moving in. And the ones moving in are a lot more brutal than the ones going out."

"Mexican cartel?" Caleb asked.

"The big boss is," Alex said. "North of the border doesn't sound quite as organized. Smuggling weapons. Moving people. Drugs, obviously."

Sean leafed through the black-and-white mug shots. "These are the guys that Maggie set Joe up with for a poker game? I'm gonna kill her."

"No," Alex said, pulling out his phone. "This is the guy—I think—that played with Joe." He handed the phone to Ollie first, and he peered at the small picture of a dark-haired man in a business suit.

"He looks like a lawyer," Ollie said. The man even wore wire-rimmed glasses.

"He's not. This, according to Cam, is the Lobo guy everyone seems to be avoiding. He's very well funded. Very smart. And very cool."

"What's his real name?" Caleb asked.

"Don't know. Neither does Cam."

Caleb reached for the phone. "Is this someone San Bernardino Sheriff's Office is going to know?"

"You can ask Dev the next time you see him," Alex said. "But I'm guessing no. The FBI might know about the people backing him, but he sounds very new and very brutal."

Sean plucked the phone from Caleb's fingers and studied the photo. "Joe was nothing to him then. Why even bother?"

Caleb shrugged. "Ego? Maybe he just wanted his money back."

"His name is Lobo," Ollie said, staring at Alex. "Is that a coincidence?"

"You mean, could he be one of us?" Alex asked. "Not likely."

"But not impossible."

"I've never met any others," Sean said quietly. He passed the phone back to Ollie. "Everywhere I've traveled. Europe and South America. Asia. Africa. The Pacific. I've never met any others like us. And I've looked."

Caleb said, "Lobo is not an uncommon nickname in Spanish. Hell, don't they call one of the Leon boys Lobo? The sophomore on the varsity team?"

Ollie ignored the question. He was staring at Alex's phone again.

If Cameron Di Stefano was right, this was the bastard who'd killed Joe over a lost poker game. He couldn't picture the cool, urbane man on the screen even holding a gun. But maybe others did that for him.

"Alex," Ollie asked, "do the Di Stefanos have anyone in county right now?"

"Probably."

Sean stood abruptly. "Hey, Caleb. I have to go take a piss, don't you?"

The police chief stood too. "Hate it when that coffee catches up with you."

The two men walked down the hall, and Ollie leaned toward Alex.

"Tell Cam to find out who killed Razio, and I'll owe him a favor."

"You think it'll be the same ones who killed Joe?"

"Probably not. But it could be the people who broke into Allie's place. That's who Razio was looking for."

"So they'll be Lobo's men."

He nodded.

"I'll ask," Alex said. "I can't guarantee."

"Give me somewhere to start," Ollie said. "I can take care of the rest."

"Just take care of yourself," Alex said. "I don't even want to think about what it would do to Allie and the kids if something happened to you."

It gave him pause. Ollie's clan had always depended on him, but not like Allie and her kids. He might get his cousins out of trouble, but he didn't tuck them into their beds at night.

With that realization, personal safety took on a whole new meaning.

"I'll be careful."

"What you'll do is you'll call me before you do anything. No lone-wolf moves, okay?"

He sat back and crossed his arms over his chest. "Do I look like a wolf?"

"No, you look like a stubborn-ass bear, which makes you even worse than a lone wolf. I know you're pissed at me. Call me anyway."

"Fine."

"And Ollie? You hurt Allison Smith by being stupid brave, I'll tear you limb from limb."

"I'm sure you'd try, puppy."

"I'm sure I have a whole pack behind me, and every single one of them adores that girl."

"She doesn't belong to your pack," Ollie said quietly. "She belongs to me. Don't forget it. I'll let you know when your people are needed."

ALLIE WAS PANTING AND SATED ON HIS LAP, HER HEAD resting over his heart while Ollie drifted, somewhat mindless, musing over how he'd mark her on his skin. It was no question Allie would be added somewhere, he just had to decide what. A fox? Most of his ink tended toward Native American designs, so he'd have to look for something that captured the brightness of her.

Whatever it ended up being, he wanted it right over his heart so her cheek would rest against it when they made love like this.

They'd managed to sneak in a few kisses throughout the night, but Ollie tugged her into his office after the bar closed, his need for her too overwhelming to resist. She'd come to him eager and laughing, kissing his face and chest despite her own exhaustion.

She owned him. Completely.

Allie was light and laughter. Even when his arms were around her, he still wanted to pinch himself to make sure he wasn't dreaming. Because... she was everything he'd ever dreamed.

And she was also exhausted. He could feel her breathing change on his chest and knew she was minutes away from sleep.

"Darlin'?" He stroked her back. "Come on, Allie-girl. Need to get you home."

"Hmm?" She sat up and Ollie forced his eyes away from her chest.

Her clothes were scattered around his office, so he stood and turned, setting her on the couch before he started to gather their things. She rubbed her eyes, looking more like a girl than the grown woman she was.

"What?" she mumbled. "Sorry, I should help."

"You got up early and you didn't get a nap this afternoon," he said. "Relax."

He had to figure out a way to get her more sleep. If he gave her a raise at the bar, she'd refuse it. He wanted her to stop working at her dad's store—there were more than enough people moving back to town who could take her place—but he knew she needed the money.

If she found Joe's stash, she'd have it. Maybe the idea of searching for it wasn't so bad after all.

That didn't mean he wasn't going to ride herd on Alex to get him the name of whoever had killed Razio and his men. He was getting nervous about the kids' safety. So was his pop. He'd upped the number of bears around his house while the kids were alone at night. Allie and the children might not realize it, but there were four bears patrolling the property every night, including one camped out in the tunnels between the house and the outbuildings.

They'd been dug during Prohibition when distilling whiskey was a crime, even in the remote California desert. Did they get raided? Only once. But bears were cautious by nature. Having escape routes was something they appreciated. They didn't like having to fight their way out of a situation, even when they were almost guaranteed to win. No, avoiding the fight in the first place was far more desirable and safer for the cubs.

This needed to end, whether they found Joe's money or not. The amount of attention being drawn to their small corner of the desert was making his bear itch.

"You're so quiet," she said. "Are you happy?"

He jerked up from gathering their clothes. "Am I what?"

"I can feel your frown from over here. I know you want me to stay in your room at night, but I just can't, Ollie. It would feel too awkward—"

"Allie, I'm happy. I am the happiest I can ever remember being in my life."

It was the simple truth, but he was glad it made her eyes sparkle like that. It was the way she used to look in high school and when the boys were little.

"I love you," she said.

He felt his mouth curve up a little. "You sure about that?"

God, please let her be sure.

"Yep."

"Good." He gathered a bundle of their clothes in his arms and walked back to the couch.

"You missed my bra," she said.

"I did?" He looked around.

"It's on the light-up beer sign with the armadillo."

"Huh." He cocked his head. "I think it improves it."

"Ollie!" She laughed. "You can't keep my bra in your office."

"Fine." He grabbed it and tossed it to her. "Spoil my fun."

They got dressed quickly, locked up, and walked to the car holding hands.

Yeah, holding hands. He felt like a kid and he didn't care.

"So the sleeping thing—"

"Told you we were going at your pace," he said. "Don't worry about it."

"So we're just going to keep fooling around on the couch in your office?"

"Clearly"—he opened her door—"you underestimate my creativity."

"Should I be worried?"

"Nope." He shut her in and took one last look at the bar before he walked to his side. There was something…

He tapped on Allie's window and she rolled it down.

"What's up?"

"You smell anything?" he murmured. Her nose was way better than his.

Allie leaned out the window and took a deep breath. "Nothing." The wind shifted and she put a hand on his arm. "Wait…"

He stood completely still, not wanting to kick up dust or anything that might distract her.

"Cat," she said quietly.

"What kind?" He heard a faint rustling in the bushes.

She shook her head. "Gone now."

Ollie walked back to his side of the Bronco while she rolled her window up.

"Who would be hanging out at the Cave like that? Hiding in the bushes?"

He shrugged. "Don't know. How old? Could you tell?"

A juvenile might worry about being caught out late and try to avoid detection by shifting. God knows he had when he'd been young. Most teenagers in the Springs spent half their nights in natural form.

"Didn't smell like a kid," Allie said. "Didn't smell like anyone familiar. It was just for a second though, so—"

"I'll ask Ted tomorrow. Or Alex. He keeps track of who's moving in and out of town better than anyone."

She must have heard the irritation in his voice, because her mouth pursed in disapproval. "When are you going to forgive him? You guys have been best friends your whole lives."

"Forgive him for what? Being friends with criminals? That'd be the pot calling the kettle black."

"For building the resort."

He bit his tongue and started the truck. Then he backed out slowly, thinking about her question.

"You guys haven't been the same since he announced the plans."

"We haven't been the same since he moved to LA."

"But you understood that. You don't understand the resort."

He said nothing. He knew her dad's store was thriving with all the new people moving back into town. And it wasn't as if his own bar hadn't benefitted.

"I didn't like the idea," she said. "Even though it probably would have meant Joe could have a steady job again."

"You were worried about the kids."

"Yep."

It was exactly what he worried about.

Cambio Springs was special. It was the only place where their odd tribe could be who and what they were without fear. He grew up cautious around outsiders, but within the town limits? Life was free. Nobody had suspicions because everyone knew their secrets. It was a safe place. The *only* safe place.

"I want your kids—*our* kids if we ever have them—to be able to grow up the way we did. Running around without having to worry. Playing games like Kevin and Low did the other night. Just free to be themselves, you know?"

She fell completely silent.

"Allie?"

"We haven't talked about kids," she said under her breath.

His heart twisted a little because yeah, he wanted kids with her. But she had four, and he knew she probably felt overwhelmed by even the idea of more kids. She was young enough, but how could he ask her to carry another baby? She was probably sick of diapers and car seats and sleepless nights.

"Do you want kids?" she asked.

He figured it was just better to be honest from the get-go. "Yeah. But it's up to you."

She leaned her head against the window. "Ollie, you can't—"

"You asked. I answered. It's not a deal-breaker for me. You have four great kids that I love. But yeah, I've got a big house and I love you, so I'd have more if you wanted to."

More silence.

"*If* you wanted, Allie." He reached for her hand. "I'm not going to put pressure on you. That would be a shit thing to do."

"Can we talk about this later?"

He squeezed her hand. "Your pace, remember?"

"Where do you think Joe hid that money?"

Since he was running on an honest streak, he just kept going. "Out in the desert somewhere only he was going to find it."

He expected her to protest or argue, but she didn't.

"I don't think he did," she said softly.

"Why?"

"Because he texted Maggie and ran. He knew someone was after him."

"And?"

"If there was anything that man was good at, it was knowing his own faults. Sometimes that's all he focused on."

Ollie said nothing. In his opinion, Joe's faults had outrun his virtues by a mile.

"But if he knew someone was after him, he'd know his chances. And it seems to me like he would have known his chances weren't good. Old Quinn said he wanted to leave money for the kids. I think he would have tried to do that. If he knew he wasn't going to make it, he would want to the kids to get that cash."

"I don't understand why he just didn't shift and run. He could have been halfway across the country if he'd done that. Come back later when things were cooled down."

"He probably didn't even think of that."

"How's that?"

She was silent for a little while. "He really didn't like being a coyote. He only shifted when he had to. If he'd been able to avoid it, he'd never have changed."

The thought staggered him. Ollie loved being a bear. Wearing that skin was as natural as breathing, and he knew Allie felt the same way about being a fox.

"So," she continued, "if he knew he wasn't going to outrun them, if he knew they'd find him, he'd put it someplace I'd find it."

"He didn't think to drop you a note?"

She shrugged. "Maybe he couldn't. Or just didn't want to."

Ollie pulled up to the dark house and scanned the yard before he exited the vehicle. "You're the one who was married to him, darlin'. You'd know way better than me."

No sign of anything out of the ordinary. Elijah was parked on the porch in human skin. Paul he could see loping toward the barn, probably ready to shift back and head home. His cousin Sandra rose to standing in the distance, a faint furry outline in the waxing moon. That meant that Dani was probably exploring the tunnels while her older cousins covered the surface.

"I'm gonna look at his parents' old place tomorrow with Jena."

He paused before he opened his door. "As long as you don't go anywhere on your own, I'm okay with it. But I don't want anyone looking for that stash by themselves. Not Sean. Not you or Jena. No one." *But especially not you.*

"I get it," she said. "I heard. We'll be smart."

"I'm probably going to Indio tomorrow." He had a couple of other strings he could tug. "Do you need anything?"

"You." She leaned over and kissed him sweetly before he got out of the truck. "Home safe at the end of the day."

"You got it."

"I'm serious."

He watched her face. The exhaustion wasn't able to mask the quiet happiness and growing contentment he saw there.

Allie was happy, but it was a fragile thing. He knew that if her trust in it broke, she might never be the same. He'd promised to make life sweet for her again and was startled to realize that part of that promise meant his own self-preservation.

"I'll be safe," he said. "I promise."

THAT PROMISE IN MIND, HE CALLED ALEX THE NEXT morning after the kids were off to school and Allie was headed over to Jena's.

He drove over to Ted and Alex's old adobe house on the other side of town and waited in the driveway while his friend kissed his new wife good-bye.

It was good to see Ted and Alex that way.

He'd been angry at Alex for what felt like years. But that didn't mean Ollie didn't want his happiness. It had been a hard road home for the young wolf alpha, but Alex had made it and was now enjoying his own measure of peace, even if he carried the mantle of responsibility for the town's economic future.

It was a heavy burden—one he didn't envy.

When are you going to forgive him?

Shit. As usual, Allie was right. It was past time. Holding on to a grudge never worked well for Ollie anyway. He was too apt to understand other people's points of view. And at the end of the day, he understood what Alex was trying to do with the resort.

"Hey." Alex popped open the door and put two travel mugs of coffee on the center console mounted between the seats. "I brought the good stuff."

If Alex wanted to share his overpriced Hawaiian coffee, Ollie was not going to argue.

"You get my message?" he asked.

"Yeah." Then Alex grinned. "But I got something better."

He raised an eyebrow and waited for Alex to speak.

"Cam came through." Alex slammed the door shut. "And it turns out even tough guys like their spa appointments in Palm Desert. Ready to get your chakras aligned?"

Ollie cracked his knuckles before he put the truck in reverse. "Oh yeah. They're all out of whack. Maybe punching something is just what my aura needs."

chapter
twenty-one

Allie wiped her hands on her jeans, a cloud of dust rising to her nose as she eyed the old attic space now owned by Josie Quinn and her family, who'd moved there after Josie's husband, Marcus, was killed.

The house, which had belonged to the wolf clan, had been given to Josie, even though she was a Quinn by marriage. But Alex and Marcus hadn't only been co-workers; they'd been friends. He took his responsibility to Marcus's widow seriously.

Jena sneezed beside her.

"I don't"— *sneeze*—"see anything that tells me Joe was here recently. You?" Jena wiped her eyes.

"Nothing," Allie said. "I can't smell anything but dust and old paper. I don't think Josie's touched it yet."

"She says she won't let the kids play up here until she can clean it out. I don't blame her for waiting until winter."

Neither did Allie. Even in the fall, the attic was sweltering.

Allie tapped her foot and remembered when the attic had been Joe's hideout. His teenage hangout he shared with Sean and Alex. Even Ollie occasionally came over. Then Allie had started coming over, and Ollie had stopped.

So many years she was seeing in a new light.

She walked over and traced initials carved into a beam.

A.S. + J.R.

He had loved her once.

Not enough.

No. Joe's love had been a shallow, struggling thing. Allie had only realized that after drinking deep with Ollie. She brushed tears from her eyes when she remembered the boy her late husband had been. There was no comparison to Ollie. It wasn't even fair.

Oliver Campbell could love her fully. Generously. Because he'd been given that love by so many in his life it practically poured off him. But the boy who'd carved hopeful initials into the old house hadn't been loved like that. He had a hope of it, but none of the determination to make that hope live.

Jena took out a Kleenex and blew the dust out. "So nothing that smells like money?"

Allie shook herself out of her memories. "No."

Jena waved a hand toward the high windows that let in light on the far wall. "There's no signs of forced entry. I didn't even notice any marks in the dust until we disturbed it."

Just as Allie's nose was keener than normal even in human form, Jena's eyes were hawklike even when she was wearing skin. Her visual acuity made her the perfect partner to search Joe's childhood home, along with the school and the tire shop where he'd once worked. So far their searches had turned up nothing.

"Let's get out of here," Allie said, moving the boxes back where the current owners had placed them. "I'm trying to think where else he might have hidden something."

Jena followed Allie when she walked down the narrow staircase. Josie was at work, borrowing salon space from Patsy on Main Street. Patsy might have shook her head at Josie's newly purple hair, but she didn't complain about the rent the vivacious stylist was bringing in from new young clients who used to travel to Indio or Palm Desert to make their appointments.

Yes, the town was changing. But as she locked up with the spare key Josie had loaned her, she thought that might not be a bad thing if it meant Josie Quinn and her small brood of snake shifters would have a safe place to be.

"So, where to next?"

Allie leaned against her minivan. "Ideas?"

"School locker?"

"Checked it."

"Gym locker?"

"Joe hated sports."

"Right." Jena closed her eyes and said, "I'm probably going to regret going there, but… first place you had sex?"

"Ha!" Allie snorted. "Um… hmm. Hadn't thought about that one."

"Do I even want to ask?"

Allie cocked her head. "I thought for sure I'd told you and Ted that one."

"Nope."

"Huh. Well"—she opened her car door—"it's not really that big a secret. Where did half the teenagers in the Springs lose it?"

"Ewww," Jena said. "Not the old cave by the fresh spring."

"It's tradition," Allie said. "Show some respect. Are you telling me you and Lowell never made out there?"

"Sure, we made out and carved our initials and everything, but we didn't actually have sex there."

"Well, we did." Allie started the car as Jena buckled herself in. "And let me tell you, that blanket was not thick enough."

"Rocks in your back?"

"So many bruises."

SHE PARKED IN THE SMALL LOT BY SPRINGS PARK AND TOOK the footpath cutting through the pools. Two of the smaller—and frankly, uglier—springs had been walled off and enclosed in the resort grounds.

The new wall that bordered the park had already been painted with the beginnings of a mural that Willow McCann, Alex's sister and famed Southwestern artist, had created. Broken tile pieces made to resemble pottery shards gave way to Spanish-style blankets and subtle animal motifs. Wolf. Bear. Cougar and bobcat. Birds of all kinds. And hidden through the swirling designs were clever serpents and darting lizards.

It was a work of art that would have paid Willow tens of thousands of dollars in any major city and been celebrated with speeches and a festival. In Cambio Springs, the children ran tiny fingers over the polished clay and poked their fingers into the mouth of the bear while their mothers gossiped near the playground and the old people wandered back to the hidden spring that refreshed them.

The fresh spring would always be hidden.

Allie and Jena took the small footpath that led behind the mineral springs and past the wall of bougainvillea that had been planted as a precaution. Only residents could know this place existed.

Jena whispered, "Have you been here since—?"

"No." Allie took a deep breath. "I need to bring Kevin here next moon night. Just him and me."

Her friend nodded but said nothing more. She waited outside when Allie went into the small cavern where a sandstone bowl had been carved into the rock. The fresh spring held the sweetest water Allie had ever tasted. It was also the secret of their transformation. Years ago, her ancestors had followed a vision into the desert, only to find themselves transformed by the water that had let them survive.

She dipped her head and reached for a gourd dipper one of the old women had set next to the basin. She lifted it to her mouth and drank, letting the water refresh her body first and then her soul. She tasted the earth on her lips and held the memory of her mother's voice in her mind, letting it wrap around her.

Taste, baby girl. No sweeter water than this.

Will it make me a wolf like you?

It'll make you whatever animal God put in you, Allison. But not for a long, long time.

Her mother had never seen her shift. It had been her poor father who'd helped her, then called her mother's cousin to come over and talk Allie back into her human form.

Confusing. Scary. Somewhat painful. And natural as breathing once she got the hang of it.

Not unlike another rite of passage she'd experienced not far from here.

"You gonna bring Ollie here?" Jena asked, leaning against one of the sandstone walls that marked the mouth of the canyon.

"Do I look like I'm still sixteen?"

Jena's eyes smiled. "I'm thinking about bringing Caleb here. Just to make out a little."

"Weirdo."

Jena walked back into the canyon and ducked under a low stone arch. Allie followed her until they stood at the mouth of a small black cave not ten feet off the main path. Taking out the flashlight she'd brought from the van, Allie clicked it on and scanned the cavern, running the light along the edges of the open space, making sure no creepy crawlies had made themselves at home.

"Anything?" Jena asked behind her.

"Nope. Doesn't smell like anyone's been here in ages."

"Oh well." Jena patted the graffiti-painted walls. "I guess all make-out spots lose their cool factor eventually."

"Probably right about the time you discover your mom's name or initials when you're trying to feel up your girlfriend."

"That might do it, yes."

Allie walked around the cave, scanning the ground to see if any places looked dug up or disturbed. Meanwhile, Jena had her own flashlight out, peeking into the many nooks and crannies that kids had carved into the wall over the years.

"Careful," Allie said, watching Jena put her hand into one. "I don't even want to think about what sixteen-year-olds might have hidden back there."

Jena pulled out a small vodka bottle. "Shocking."

"That's better than what I imagined."

Allie froze when she heard footsteps outside. She snapped her fingers once at Jena, who also turned into a statue.

There.

She couldn't smell in the still air of the cave, but she could hear when something crept closer.

Cat.

By the sound of the footsteps, not a big one. A bobcat, probably, but who would be creeping around without making themselves known? That just wasn't polite, especially in a place with only one exit.

The hair on the back of Allie's neck stood up, and she clicked off her flashlight. Something wasn't right. Was it a wild bobcat? There were plenty around, but they were more than shy. And no shifter would be

Elizabeth Hunter

slinking around outside the cave without announcing their presence unless they were up to trouble.

In the shadows, Allie slipped out of her clothes and into her natural form. The quick ache and pop, the flip of her stomach, and Allie was on the ground, her paws silent in the cool sand.

"Allie?"

She hissed silently, and Jena shut off her light, but she didn't shift. A bird in a cave was only asking for trouble.

Bobcats might be small, but they were some of the wiliest predators in the desert. In that, Allie's fox and whoever was outside were evenly matched. She crept to the door and paused, her right paw lifted. Her nose twitched when the first scent hit her nose. In a heartbeat, Allie was sure it was the same cat she'd smelled outside the Cave. But there was something...

Wrong. This scent was *wrong*. It was a shifter, no doubt, but it didn't hold the depth of scent Allie associated with their kind. Shifters, no matter their clan, smelled of the complex layers of human and animal, sand and water. This shifter, whoever he was—and she was fairly certain it was a male—smelled wrong. He was unwashed human and panicked animal. No depth. And no scent of water.

She poked her head out of the cave, wishing the sun was farther down. Her only comfort was that cat eyes were as sensitive to light as a fox's. Both were working at a disadvantage in the afternoon glare.

Allie darted out and under a rock, crouching down so her ash-grey pelt blended into the brush.

A quiet snarl.

He wasn't wild, but... he was. The shifter smelled more of the wild-cats in the canyon than anyone she knew in the Leon or Vasquez clan. And she smelled fear. A lot of fear.

Allie sat forward and shouted an alarm. The shrieking cry echoed in the canyon, resembling a woman's screams more than the call of a canid. She barked again and caught a shadow moving from the corner of her eye as the bobcat shrank back. He was crouched on an outcropping across from the cave, perched not far from the fresh spring. The cat's face kept turning toward the spring before it looked away. Then back. Then away.

Allie watched the shifter struggle to keep his eyes on the cave

※ 240 ※

opening three times before she barked again and jumped out into the canyon.

His form stuttered in the fading light, shimmering out of focus and then back. Allie barked again, louder, and the bobcat stumbled on four feet, lurching to the side while Allie jumped closer.

She had no desire to fight the small cat. She just wanted to know who it was. Had a new family moved to town and she didn't know? If he was, then why did he smell so sick? Just then, the cat turned his face full toward her and let out a wracking shiver. Right before her eyes, he transformed into a young man.

No more than seventeen or eighteen, the teenager looked more like a man than a child. His dark hair was cropped close, and ominous tattoos marked his shoulders, arms, and back. Gothic lettering was scrawled on his throat.

One word: *LOBO*.

With a howl, Allie lunged forward and nipped at the back of the naked man's ankle before she darted away. With a shiver and a groan, the man pulled his leg up and started shifting again, but not before Allie saw him spit yellow bile from his mouth. He sprang into his bobcat form and disappeared.

Jena stepped into the canyon two seconds after Allie gave a quick yip signaling all clear.

"Was that…?" Jena looked flabbergasted. "What was that?"

She shifted and rolled to sitting, holding up a hand for the clothes that Jena threw at her. "It's a shifter."

"I know that, but who? What was that on his throat? Did you see that?"

"*Lobo*," she coughed out, her stomach still wobbling a bit from the two quick shifts. "It said *Lobo* on his throat."

"The man who's after you?" Jena's eyes widened. "He has shifters? Like us?"

"I don't know any more than you, Jena. Stop yelling."

Allie was trying to sort through her memories of the young man while her head pounded. He had been young. Only a few years older than Kevin. But the scars on his body and his extensive tattoos spoke of a hard life.

"He calls himself Lobo," Allie said. "*Lobo*."

 241

"Caleb said it was a nickname," Jena said.

"Maybe it's not."

"So you're saying this new gang leader—the one who probably murdered Joe—is a shifter?"

"I don't know. Maybe." Allie pointed the direction where the young bobcat had fled. "We know he *has* shifters."

"But—"

"Jena?" A sleepy conversation from that morning filtered into the mass of confusion in her head, and Allie's stomach rolled. "Where's Ollie?"

"Caleb's not supposed to know anything about it, but I think he and Alex were going into Palm Desert to follow up a lead on someone Alex found."

"Someone to do with Lobo," Allie said, jumping to her feet and throwing on her shirt. "Someone who might not be all human. I need a phone. *Now!*"

chapter
twenty-two

Ollie turned the radio up and rolled the window down, enjoying the bite of creosote in the air. He glanced at Alex, who was drinking coffee and checking his phone.

"Work?"

"Everyone has excuses," Alex muttered. "And I don't give a shit about any of them unless Grandma died."

Ollie smiled, once again reaffirming his belief that more employees just meant more headaches. One of his promoter friends in LA had come to him five years ago, wanting to open another location for the Cave in Coachella, capitalizing on the growing music scene in the desert and taking advantage of the festival traffic in the spring. Ollie had said no for all the reasons that were giving his friend grey hairs.

There was one Cave, and he ran it. Of course, he might be asking Jim to work a few more hours in the future. After all, time with Allie was going to be scarce enough as it was. She and the kids were a package deal, and he wouldn't have it any different, but it did mean less time alone with her. At least they had their nights working together, even if he couldn't coax her into his bed. Yet.

"This guy," he said, turning his attention away from the tempting little fox and back to the goons who were threatening her. "He's the one who searched Allie's place?"

Alex tucked his phone away. "According to Cam. One of his dad's people heard the guy talking about it."

"Simon Ashford? Sounds like an accountant."

"He might be," Alex said. "The more I learn about this Lobo guy, the more I want to know. He's not what we've seen before."

"But old Simon likes his massages, huh?" Ollie cracked his knuckles.

"Try not to break anything that'll make him yell too loud. I know the manager, but we don't want panicked girls calling the cops."

"I'll be the soul of discretion."

"Right," Alex snorted. "Is it possible for you to be a little presentable? This is one of the most exclusive spas in the desert."

Ollie glanced across the car, taking in the button-down shirt and light brown pants his friend was wearing, then down at his old jeans and black concert tee. "I don't own any chinos, Biff."

"Shut up."

"You keep everyone busy. I'll ask Simon a few questions. He might need to leave before the aromatherapy."

"Bad karma, man. Interrupting a man's aromatherapy."

"What can I say? I live dangerously."

THE SPA DIDN'T HAVE A SIGN IN FRONT. IT DID HAVE VERY high walls and lush plantings that screened it from the regular mortals who drove by on the highway. From the front, you'd think it was an estate. Ollie turned in the service entrance, knowing the Bronco would raise too many eyebrows with the valet. He parked behind a pool house and hopped out, taking a moment to gauge the scents and sounds of the place.

Quiet. The grounds smelled of eucalyptus and sage.

"Do we know where he is?" Ollie asked.

"I called my friend. Massage cabanas are by the pool."

Ollie lifted his chin and headed toward the smell of chlorine. Walking along the shaded paths, he passed a few attendants who gave him curious glances, but no one spoke. This wasn't the type of place where you chatted with the clientele. He saw the blue shimmer of the pool through the trees along with two other men who stood silently nearby.

He caught Alex's eye and paused behind a screen of bamboo.

"This is not the guy who searched her house," he said in a low voice. "A grunt does not warrant two guards."

"Maybe one of the guards?"

Ollie peered through the bamboo. It was possible. He couldn't remember the faces, but he'd remember the scents. The pool was isolated, and the man in the cabana was the only guest in sight. Quiet harp music drifted through the air, and Ollie couldn't hear any attendants nearby.

"I need to get closer if I'm going to figure out who might have been at Allie's."

Alex shrugged, a calculating glint in his eye. "Or we could just grab whoever's sitting on that massage table and get curious."

The bear in Ollie liked that idea a lot. He nodded and walked around the screen, heading toward the isolated group with Alex at his back. The first guard tried to stop him, putting up a hand that barely reached Ollie's chest.

Why did they always assume he would stop when they did that? He didn't.

"Sir, this is a private—"

Ollie took a deep breath, but this man's scent wasn't familiar. He lifted an elbow to the guard's face, slamming it into his cheek. A stunned breath escaped the dark-suited man, then he crumpled under the force of the blow. The other guard came running, his hand already on a weapon as Alex cut around the lawn and toward the back of the cabana.

Well trained. The other guard had been listening for his partner, but he wasn't expecting two men.

The bear took another sniff and rumbled in satisfaction.

Oh yeah. This was one of them. The guard didn't draw fast enough. Ollie's lip curled up and he rushed him, his long legs eating up the gravel path between them before the man could get out a shout. He reached for the guard's gun first, twisting it away from the man before he grabbed the guard in a breath-stealing headlock.

"You and me," he murmured. "We're going to have a conversation while my friend talks to your boss."

The guard tried to twist around to see the man on the table, but Ollie held him in place, his elbow cutting off the man's voice. Ollie glanced over at Alex to see his friend holding a vicious-looking knife to the neck of the half-naked man. He was pale and soft. Hell, maybe he really was an accountant.

Slowly, the man rose, and Alex tossed a sage-green robe toward him. He put it on and slid into the soft slippers the spa provided.

"I hear voices," Ollie said.

"Me too. Let's get these two to the car."

The pale man put on his glasses and brushed his sandy-brown hair away from his forgettable features. Ollie was a professional observer of humans and their interactions, but he didn't think he'd ever met a man as purposefully forgettable as this one. If he'd been coming into the Cave for a month, Ollie wouldn't have noticed him.

"I do hope you know who I am." He had a slight accent Ollie thought might be British. Or possibly Australian. "Even if you don't," he continued, "this is extremely foolish."

"Yeah?" Ollie said, keeping his arm firm around the guard's neck. "It's also foolish to attract my attention."

"Who are you?" the man asked.

Ollie found no reason not to tell him. It wasn't as if they wouldn't be able to guess from a general description. "The name's Oliver Campbell."

A flicker in his eyes and a glance at the guard told Ollie that the pale man knew exactly why they'd been taken.

"And I'm gonna assume you're Simon Ashford," Alex said. "Nice to meet you, Simon. My friend and I have some questions for you."

Holding the knife at Ashford's back, Alex escorted him down the path as Ollie brought up the rear, his arm still around the shorter guard's neck. He kicked the fallen guard into the bushes as they passed him. He'd be fine, though he'd have a hell of a shiner.

A groundkeeper stepped into their path, eyes wide and holding a ladder and a rake. Without a word, the man turned and ran.

"Time to go," Alex said. "Luckily, there's more than enough room in the back of the car."

Ashford piped up. "I hope you know—"

Alex clocked him on the back of the head. The man went down and Alex hoisted him over one shoulder, carrying him in a fireman's hold. "It's not your turn to talk yet."

The frantic legs of the guard bounced off Ollie's shins.

"That's right," he said to the scrambling guard. "You get to talk first."

The man fell still.

"You get up to anything interesting lately?" Ollie growled as they reached the Bronco.

No reaction from the guard.

"Meet any bears?"

The scent of urine filled the air. Then Ollie slugged the man and tossed him in the back of the Bronco with his unconscious boss.

It was time to find a quiet place and get some answers. Ollie knew just where to go.

BOTH MEN WERE GROGGY BUT AWAKE WHEN THEY REACHED the abandoned gas station near Thermal. The guard was muttering nervously. Simon Ashford was utterly silent, watching Alex and Ollie with preternatural calm and calculating eyes.

Ollie kept Ashford in the corner of his vision but focused his attention on the guard, whose scent had been all over Allie's property. He was younger, midtwenties at most, but had deep, pitted acne scars that aged him and sharp black eyes that had given up years ago. He was Latino, and his accent said LA or Orange County.

Ollie placed a sturdy wooden chair in the center of the room and tied the guard to it with the zip ties he always left in the truck. The man's face was relatively unscathed, though there was a large knot swelling at the back of his head.

Ollie stood in front of him and kept his voice low. "What's your name?"

The guard said nothing. His eyes kept returning to the frighteningly silent man in the corner with Alex.

It was one situation where Ollie knew keeping silent wasn't going to work. He bent down and spoke directly into the guard's ear.

"You afraid he's gonna hurt you?"

An almost imperceptible nod.

"Alex." He turned to his friend. "Take Mr. Ashford out to the car, will you?"

"Sure thing." Alex nudged Ashford with the edge of hunting knife.

Then Ollie and the guard were alone.

"What's your name?" he asked.

"I don't think… I shouldn't—"

"They pay you to think or follow orders?"

The response was so quick Ollie was sure he'd answered the question more than once.

"Follow orders," he said.

"Well, your boss is gone, so now you're following mine."

Still keeping silent. Clearly he hadn't scared the man enough.

Ollie bent down, grabbed the man's hair and yanked back, almost strangling him with the sudden angle. "Does that hurt?"

A strangled sound that resembled yes.

"See, man, you're afraid of Ashford hurting you, but I think you're forgetting something."

The guard froze.

"I already hurt you," Ollie murmured. "And I'm gonna hurt you more unless you tell me why you were in my girl's house, tearing up her stuff."

The odor of adrenaline and urine colored the air.

"You get me?" Ollie asked.

The man whispered, "Yes."

"What's your name?"

"Adrian."

"Adrian, did you break into my girl's house?"

"Yes."

"You been warned about coming into our town?"

A pause. "Everyone knows not to go out there."

"But you did anyway."

Another pause.

"Did Lobo tell you to do that?"

"No."

"Did Ashford?"

Nothing.

Ollie let Adrian's hair go, stepped back, and contemplated what he'd seen of the two men. Adrian was clearly a follower, but though Ashford appeared to be an employee of this Lobo character, there was nothing of the follower in the man's demeanor. Ollie could smell the cold calculation on Ashford from a mile away. The man might look like an accountant, but he was far more than that.

"Who's your boss?" Ollie asked Adrian.

The man paused. "Lobo is."

"Who told you to search the woman's house?"

"Ashford."

Not Lobo.

Interesting.

Ollie asked, "Did you kill Joe Russell?"

"No." The answer was swift.

"You know who did?"

More silence.

Ollie asked, "What were you looking for at her house?"

"The money. Lobo wants it back."

"Says who? Ashford? Pinky said the game was a fair win. So why would your boss make Pinky look like a fool?"

"Ashford says Lobo doesn't care about—" The man cut off his own words, glancing at the closed door where Alex had led Simon Ashford.

"Care about what, Adrian?"

"I can't say."

"Lobo doesn't care about making Pinky look like a fool? What about Bull Rusconi in the Di Stefano crew? Lobo care about him? Is this really coming from your boss, or is it coming from that pasty accountant you're guarding?"

The guard began to shake his head, his body trembling. "You're killing me."

"Not yet. You keep talking, and we'll see what happens."

"Killing me, man," the guard repeated. "No way I'm leaving here alive."

"Who?" Ollie glanced at the door. "Ashford? My friend has him, and he's not the kind of guy you mess with. You just worry about me right now."

"I can't..." The guard looked at him. "I didn't want to grab your woman or those kids. Tony Razio told everyone she was yours. But he'll kill me."

"Who? Lobo?"

"He'll kill me, man!"

Ollie asked, "What about Razio?"

"You might put me in the hospital, but he'll kill me without a second thought."

Ollie's anger spiked. "Did you kill Tony Razio?"

"No! That was Lobo's boys on the inside. He's got a whole gang of them in there."

"Who else was with you that night?"

"Some guy." Adrian shook his head. "New guy. I was supposed to... but then the bear." Adrian glanced at Ollie. "I never seen a bear like that in real life. What kind of insane bitch keeps a guard bear?"

Allison Smith, dickhead. She's got a guard bear whether she likes it or not.

"Where's the other guy?"

"Chepe? He freaked, man. Never saw him again. He started spouting off to Ashford about how there was creepy shit out there. How that wasn't just a bear. Said he'd heard rumors... I didn't believe him, you know?"

The look on Adrian's face told Ollie that the guard was starting to believe all sorts of things now.

He felt his phone buzz in his pocket, but he ignored it. There was no noise from outside and no one ever came out to this old service station. It had been abandoned when his father had been a boy.

"Who wants the money back, Adrian? Is it Lobo, or is it Ashford?"

Adrian was almost crying. "I don't know, man. I've never even met Lobo. I thought I was doing a job for the Di Stefanos, but when I got to the club where I was supposed to meet one of their boys, Ashford was there. He had a better offer. That's all I know. That's all I *want* to know."

His phone buzzed again, but Ollie ignored it. He was starting to wonder who was really the brains behind this new crew. Lobo was a mythical bogeyman, and so far, Simon Ashford seemed like the more dangerous player. He was also the kind who would have pegged Joe Russell as a desperate man from a mile away.

Adrian's shoulders were slumped. His head hung, and Ollie could see the sweat lining the man's once-pristine collar.

His phone pinged with a text. Ollie finally grabbed it.

Three from Allie.

Shit.

Answer your phone.

Please pick up.

I don't think Lobo's a nickname.

Just as he read the last, a car door slammed outside the building and Ollie heard Alex start to curse.

"Oh hell no!" Adrian yelled, starting to pull on his wrists, which were zip-tied to the chair. "Let me go!"

Alex shouted, "Ollie!"

He strode out of the crumbling building, leaving Adrian tied to the chair. "What's going on?"

Alex was raging. "He fucking shifted."

"What?"

"He shifted in front of me!"

How?

Who?

A million questions shot into his mind, but Ollie's eyes swung around the barren parking lot. "What is he?"

"A damn snake. He slipped under the floorboards of your old wreck. I have no idea where he is. Just a pile of clothes in the back of the Bronco."

As soon as Alex said snake, Ollie ran for the door.

It was too late. Adrian's leg was a mass of blood and torn fabric.

Ollie couldn't see a snake anywhere, but Adrian was shaking and yelling, "I told you! I told you!"

A sheen of sweat bloomed on the man's forehead. He was panicking, and Ollie knew he'd been bitten. The poison was now surging through his bloodstream.

"Adrian, you need to calm down," Ollie said. "We'll get you some help. Alex!"

"I'm dead. I knew it. I'm so dead."

"Deep breaths, man."

They were half an hour from the nearest hospital, but even snake shifter bites, far more toxic than a wild snake, were rarely deadly unless they went untreated. The safest course would be to take him to Ted, who was rarely short of antivenin and could be discreet, but could they wait an hour and a half? His leg was bleeding profusely, almost as if the snake had bitten then torn the skin.

"Please," Adrian begged. "Please, don't let me die."

Alex stood in the doorway. "He doesn't look good. I'll call Ted."

Ollie took out his knife, and the human flinched. He bent over the man and swiftly cut the plastic strips that tied him to the chair. He cut away the pant leg from around the bites and winced.

There were four deep bites going up his leg. The shifter had aimed for the softer flesh on the interior of Adrian's legs. Luckily, the young man was muscular enough that the fangs could only go so deep. The amount of swelling around the bites told Ollie the snake had still managed to push a sizable amount of venom into the young man's system.

"Okay," he said. "I'm gonna move you, Adrian."

"Don't leave me. Please, don't—"

"We're not leaving you." He and Alex might have been fine with interrogating the man—even roughing him up if he didn't cooperate—but they weren't monsters. "We'll get you to a doctor."

"Can you call my mom?"

Christ, how old was this kid? Ollie had thought he was in his late twenties, but the look on his face put him closer to a teenager. Despite his misgivings, Ollie felt his protective nature rise.

"I'm going to pick you up, and it's gonna hurt like a bitch. Try not to pass out."

Adrian nodded, his face already pale and sweating. Ollie decided they couldn't afford to wait for Ted. He lifted Adrian up and carried him toward the Bronco.

Alex lifted the window and dropped the tailgate of the truck. "Ted said if he's already sweating to get him to the hospital."

"Got it."

Adrian started to shiver.

"What kind of snake was it, Alex?"

"I couldn't see. I just saw Ashford's clothes."

Adrian started babbling in Spanish. Ollie wasn't fluent enough to understand him, but Alex was. He got in the back seat, leaning over the bench and speaking to the man who lay in the back while Ollie started the truck.

"He's saying something about Ashford."

"What?"

A longer stream of Spanish.

"Shit," Alex said. "I think this kid was there when they killed Joe."

Did you kill Joe Russell?

No.

But he'd never said he hadn't been there.

"Find out what he knows before he passes out!"

Ollie didn't want the kid to die, but he still wasn't his best friend. Alex hammered Adrian with questions, and the kid practically wept when he answered.

"I'm pretty sure Ashford killed Joe. Lobo wasn't even there." A pause while Adrian spoke. Then Alex continued, "He didn't tell them anything. Not even where he was from. They didn't know he was from the Springs until the papers reported it. That's when they searched Allie's house."

More panicked words from Adrian. Softer questions from Alex.

"He says that Joe was laughing at Ashford. Said he'd never find the money, even when Ashford threatened his family. He said... I think Joe said something about a hotel?"

Adrian's words were more slurred. His tongue sounded like it was swelling.

"Joe laughed at Ashford and said the hotel would take care of his kids. They tore up any hotel room they could find that Joe had stayed in, but there wasn't any money. Then Ashford saw the report of the body and he sent Adrian and... some guy named Chepe to search Joe's old house." Alex growled low in his throat. "They've been watching. Waiting for a chance to grab Allie, but they couldn't get her. Ollie, I think he's losing it."

Ollie heard thumping in the back.

"He's having a seizure!"

Ollie said, "This cannot be diamondback venom."

"What the fuck does that guy shift to?"

"I don't know!" Ollie slammed his foot to the floor and the old truck roared forward. "Get in back and make sure he doesn't crack his head open."

Alex crawled into the back, but by the time he was kneeling next to the seizing human, the man had gone still.

"He's not breathing," Alex yelled.

"Try CPR." Ollie kept driving.

He pulled up in front of the big glass doors, put the truck in park, and jumped out, lifting the window and slamming the tailgate down to grab the barely breathing human.

He ran Adrian into the emergency room and yelled, "Snake bite! He's not breathing!"

A guard, an orderly, and two nurses ran to him. The orderly pushed over a bed and strapped Adrian in just as he started seizing again. The guard pulled Ollie away while the nurses started shouting in medical jargon he couldn't decipher.

The guard was asking him questions, but he kept watching Adrian's bed until it disappeared from view.

"He asked me to call his mom," Ollie muttered, turning to the guard. "I didn't get her name."

"What happened?"

"We... found him. Driving out toward the Salton Sea. I think there were four bites on his leg. My friend and I could tell it was bad, so we brought him here."

Alex was pacing in the waiting area, speaking low into his phone.

"Your friend there know the kid?"

Ollie shook his head. "Neither of us did. Alex is probably on the phone with his wife. She's a doctor."

"Oh yeah?" The guard was suddenly friendlier.

"Yeah. Ted Vasquez? I think she's here sometimes."

"I know Doctor Ted!" The guard's suspicious frown was suddenly gone. "That's her husband, huh? Never met the guy before. Sorry about that."

"Right." Ollie let out a small sigh of relief. "I, uh... better go move my truck."

"Sure thing." The guard nodded toward the door. "I'll see what I can find out about that guy. Maybe he had a wallet on him or something."

Ollie nodded and went to move the car. The police would want to question them; better to get it out of the way so he could get home. Ollie suspected Adrian wouldn't be giving his side anytime soon.

Or ever.

Two hours later, a solemn nurse broke the news that the young man they'd tried to help had died from multiple bites from an unknown snake. None of the antivenin had had any effect.

Ollie and Alex exchanged grim looks in the waiting room. Then he pulled out his phone and texted Allie.

Keep the kids in the house. This just got a whole lot worse.

chapter
twenty-three

A llie lay on the bed, Ollie's shirtless body draped over hers, his head resting in the crook of her neck and his arm wrapped around her waist. He'd stumbled home around one in the morning, obviously exhausted. Allie hadn't protested when he crawled into bed with her and passed out. She couldn't. He looked too tired and worried to send away.

She knew most of the story from his texts the night before. The young man who'd broken into her house was dead. His partner had disappeared. And Ollie had discovered, as she had the day before, that they weren't the only shifters in the desert anymore.

A snake. A vicious one. Allie had trouble sleeping, imagining her babies alone in their beds. Snakes could get anywhere. They were silent and often very hard to detect, even for someone with senses as keen as hers. She'd smelled the wolves Alex had sent to patrol the property, along with the comforting scent of familiar bears.

She wasn't going to protest. Not with her children sleeping in the house.

Ollie rumbled and nuzzled closer until she wrapped her arm around his shoulder and held him tighter. She heard a tap at the door and glanced down. She couldn't bring herself to feel any embarrassment at having him close.

"Come in," she said quietly.

Kevin poked his head through the door. "Hey."

"Hey, baby. I'll be up in a minute. Ollie got in really late."

He walked into her room, his perceptive eyes taking in Ollie's sleeping form. She saw no judgment or embarrassment from him, either. Her oldest son had a hint of a smile.

"You and Ollie, huh?"

Allie smiled. "Yeah."

Kevin shuffled his feet. "He makes you happy."

"He always has."

Kevin nodded. "I know. It's good."

Ollie let out a light snore but made no move to wake.

"I think," Allie whispered, "it's always been him, Kev. And it's always going to be him. Is that okay?"

"Course it is." A slight blush covered his cheeks. "He was always there for all of us. Even before."

Oh, her wise boy. Kevin had the whip-thin build of his father but the big heart of the man she held in her arms. She could see that now. See how Ollie had always been there. Always been the calm, steady rock they'd all depended on, even before she knew how deeply he cared.

"He loves you guys."

"Yeah, well…" Kevin shrugged, and she could see the shine in his eyes. "The feeling's mutual."

Changing the subject before she burst into tears, she asked, "Your brothers and sister up?"

"Mostly. Mark's dragging a little and Loralie's playing instead of getting dressed."

"Give me five minutes, all right? I'll be up in just a bit."

"Okay. You want me to start making breakfast?"

She nodded. "You're the best."

His smile turned into a cocky grin. "I know."

Allie laughed softly when he slipped out of the room. She brushed Ollie's thick hair back from his forehead and rubbed the stubble at the edge of his beard. He murmured something she couldn't understand, and his hand slid up to her breast.

"Okay," she said, moving it back down. "Time for me to get up, big guy. Save that thought for later."

"Later," he muttered.

Elizabeth Hunter

Allie kissed his forehead and managed to untangle herself from his grip. Ollie rolled over, stuffed his face in her pillow, and let out another snore. His back rose in a deep breath as he fell back into sleep. She looked at him, traced a finger over the line of his shoulder, following a line of ink that led down his spine. Then she traced the words she'd been thinking on the small of his back.

Property of Allison Smith.

AN HOUR LATER, ALLIE WAS DRIVING BACK FROM THE BUS stop when she saw Alex's car turning onto the road behind her. He followed her back to Ollie's place and parked near the barn.

"Hey," he said. "The bear still sleeping?"

"Yeah."

"He was tired."

"Worry will do that to you." She nodded toward the house. "Coffee?"

"I wouldn't say no."

Alex parked himself at the kitchen table while she poured two cups. The house was still quiet, so she figured Ollie was still sleeping.

"You saw the guards I sent over last night?" Alex asked.

"Yep. You ask Ollie about that?"

He nodded. "We agreed that with this many unknowns, backup around the house would be a good idea. I already talked to Ted's mom. She's on it. The cats will be guarding the schools when the kids are there."

Ted's mother was the principal of the elementary school. With so many cats as teachers, asking them to guard the children was a good idea.

"You cannot go anywhere alone," Alex said. "The man who broke into your house, the one who died, he specifically mentioned plans to grab you or the kids. We're not going to take any chances."

"Do you think I'm gonna argue?"

"I think that—despite your sweet-as-pie disposition—you're as stubborn as my wife. Maybe more."

"I've also got four kids, Alex. I'm not gonna argue with you about protecting them. Kevin will be the hardest."

"I know. But he's smart. If we explain it to him, he'll do what's best."

She nodded and drank her coffee, the sharp hit of caffeine doing nothing to dispel her exhaustion. She'd slept like shit the night before.

"Snakes," she muttered. "Damn things can get anywhere."

"But they can't travel far in their shifted form. They're not going to slither all the way from the highway, and they can't get here cross-country like a wolf or a cat might. So we'll be watching cars."

"This Ashford guy. Who is he?"

Alex paused. "My gut instinct says he's Lobo's second-in-command. He does the dirty work even though he looks like a bookkeeper. The guy was cold as ice."

"Did he kill Joe?"

Alex nodded.

"How sure are we of that?" A cold fist sat in her gut. This man had seen Ollie. Knew who she was and possibly even what she was. Knew she had children, and he'd made them a target.

"I'm pretty sure. Adrian—the man who died—was pretty out of it. He told us everything."

Allie looked up. "The money?"

He shook his head. "They didn't know where it was. Said Joe mentioned a hotel, but they couldn't find any trace of it at the places he stayed. You have any ideas?"

"A hotel?" Allie racked her brain but came up with nothing.

"There anyplace you guys went for a weekend away? A vacation or spa?"

"Joe at a spa?" She snorted. "You're joking, right? We didn't take vacations, Alex."

"Well, if you think of anything, let me know."

"I will."

Alex tucked a piece of fuzzy hair behind her ear. "You working at your dad's place today?"

She shook her head. "I called in. He said he had someone who could fill in."

"Go back to sleep. You look like you barely slept a wink."

Allie shivered. "Snakes."

"I know." Alex set down his empty mug. "But we're watching. I put my dad in charge of organizing shifts to watch this place and yours. The sergeant likes that stuff. Get some sleep. Nothing's slithering in on our watch."

And with that comforting thought, she locked the door behind him and returned to her room, slipping back into her nightgown and joining Ollie on the bed.

She was out before her head hit the pillow.

ALLIE WOKE TO THE FEEL OF OLLIE'S BEARD ON THE INSIDE of her thighs. She arched back and slid her hand down, reaching for his as he kissed her in the most intimate way. He hadn't been lying. It really was one of his favorite things to do, but she'd never woken up to it.

"Morning." His lips moved against her flesh, and she gasped. "Stay right there and relax."

She couldn't relax. He'd managed to strip off her nightgown and panties along with any stitch he'd been wearing the night before. The sight of him bent between her legs, morning sun streaming over his smooth brown back, was enough to make her come. But he didn't let her. He teased her until she was practically weeping, then he slid up her body and into her in one movement, pressing up, his arms black-inked columns surrounding her. She smoothed her hand up the corded muscle and pulled his head down to take his mouth, tasting his lips and tongue as he slowly made love to her in the morning light.

Her release was so sweet and long, Allie could only smile and sigh. Then he flipped her over and entered her again, covering her with his body as he kissed the back of her neck. Softly bit the curve of her shoulder as he surrounded her. Allie had never felt safer. More adored.

"Love you," he whispered.

She was breathless with pleasure. She sighed and turned her head to kiss him again, and when she bit his lip, he lost control and thrust into her harder. Faster. Until he came in a roaring climax that seemed to shake the bed itself. Ollie rolled to the side and pulled her back against his chest, his heart pounding against her shoulder.

"Good morning," she finally managed to say.

He laughed and turned her over to face him. "Good morning."

"You already said that," she said. "In the nicest way possible."

"There are benefits to waking up next to a hungry bear."

"I can see that."

His eyelids were drooping again, and Allie decided she could snooze a little longer with all the kids in school, so she snuggled back into him, put one of his big hands over her breast and patted it.

"Sleep," she said. "We've still got some time."

A low, satisfied rumble was the only sound he made before he smoothed his hand over the soft skin and let out a contented sigh. In a few minutes, they were both snoring.

When Allie's eyes finally opened, she could tell Ollie was already awake. He was holding her, but was propped up on the pillows, staring out the window and frowning.

She turned and lifted a hand to smooth a finger between his eyebrows. "You still look tired."

"I slept. I'm just... worried."

"About Simon Ashford?"

"Yes."

"He turns into a snake."

Ollie nodded slowly. "He does. But something tells me you already suspected that. Why did you text me yesterday about Lobo?"

"Because I saw a shifter. He was young. Maybe a few years older than Kevin. He shifted to a bobcat and tracked me and Jena into the canyon. I think it might have been the same one who was hanging around the Cave the other night."

"Shit." Ollie's mouth turned into a deeper frown. "What were you doing in the canyon?"

"Looking for Joe's money."

"No luck?"

"Nope. We were looking in that old cave when I smelled him. The bobcat. He didn't smell like us. I mean... he did. But it almost smelled sour. Unhealthy, if that makes any sense. He had trouble holding his form. Shifted out and in. Then he puked and ran away."

"And you're sure it wasn't one of the cat clan? Maybe someone you don't know who moved back to town?"

"Would one of the cat clan have a big tattoo of the word *Lobo* on his throat?"

"No." He closed his eyes and pinched the bridge of his nose like he was trying to fend off a headache. "This is bad, darlin'."

"I know."

"You and the kids don't go anywhere—"

"Without guards. I got the lecture earlier today from Alex. He came by for coffee."

"So I don't have to fight with you about it? I owe him one for that."

"I'm not gonna fight this. I'm not dumb. But I might fight you if you end up taking any stupid risks. I don't think you should be going anywhere alone either."

"Allie, I'll be fine."

"Snakes can bite anyone. Even bears."

"And I'll be careful."

Cold claws wrapped around her heart. "Ollie, please."

He put a hand on her cheek and watched her. Allie made no effort to hide the terror she felt. The Quinns were the only snakes she knew. And yes, they could be mischievous. Even vindictive at times. But they were still part of the Springs. They were still safe. This snake...

"We have no idea what he's capable of," she said. "Simon Ashford bit that man to keep him from talking. He killed Joe. He'd kill you too. And rattlesnake venom doesn't act the way you described. He's something else. Something horrible."

"I'll be careful."

"Not good enough."

"Fine." He sighed. "I won't go anywhere alone. That better?"

"Yes." She scooted up and kissed him softly. "The kids depend on you. They'd be devastated if something happened."

He grabbed a handful of her hair. "What about you?"

Those claws around her heart squeezed. "Please don't make me think about it."

He crushed her mouth to his in a powerful kiss. "Same goes for you. Don't get stubborn. Be careful. I finally have you. Don't make me imagine life without you here."

"I won't."

"We're going to be fine. We'll figure this out."

She laid her head down and rested it on his chest, listening to the steady beat of his heart. Ollie ran a hand up and down her back until her heartbeat evened out and her shoulders unknotted.

"We should take a vacation after all this is over," he finally said.

She smiled. "Where do you want to go?"

"I've always wanted to go on one of those Alaskan cruises. I've never been all the way up there. You think the kids would like that?"

"I do. But I want to take a vacation with just you and me first."

He squeezed her backside. "I like the sound of that."

"We don't have to do everything with them. We can take some time for just the two of us."

He shrugged. "I like having them around. They're fun."

"I like them too. But I also like nice hotels and movies rated more than PG."

"You should stay at the resort once it opens." Ollie grunted. "Get a massage. Facial. All that stuff. Relax a little."

"I'm pretty relaxed right now."

Ollie laughed. "Glad I could help."

"But it might be fun to stay at the spa. Maybe do a girls' weekend..."

Resort. Spa. Hotel.

Joe mentioned a hotel, but they couldn't find any trace of it at the places he stayed.

Oh.

Ohhhh. Of course. He was smart. Of course he'd think of that.

Not a hotel. A resort. One Joe had never stayed at but one with which he was still familiar. Allie sat up and grabbed for her phone on the bedside table.

"Allie?"

She held up a hand as she dialed Alex.

"Allie?" he answered. "What's—"

"Ten months ago," she interrupted. "Around the time of the poker game. What were you guys working on at the building site?"

Alex sighed. "Uh... let me think. We'd started pouring foundations on the bungalows, because the main building was pretty much finished.

They'd already done the finish work on the first story and were finishing up the drywall on the second. All the grading for the gardens had been done, but we hadn't started on the pool—"

"The main building—the one that was almost done—what's in that section?"

"The gift shop. Front desk and reception. Bell closet. Kitchen—"

"The kitchen," Ollie said, obviously catching on to her train of thought. He reached over and put Alex on speakerphone. "You guys install anything yet?"

"No. Just the walls and the counters. I wanted Jena to have a say in what appliances she worked with, so I waited until—"

"They haven't cut into the walls," Allie said. "But they will. He'd know where they'd install the vents. The microwaves. The lamps."

Ollie nodded. "And it's Jena's kitchen. And Alex's. Anything they found…"

"They'd know," Allie said. "He'd have written a note or something, but Joe knew they'd get it to me."

Alex said, "What are you guys—"

"Joe mentioned a hotel," Ollie said. "A *hotel*, Alex. Think about it."

"You think Joe's money is at the building site? Don't you think we would have found it by now?"

"Not yet," Ollie said, "But you would once you started installing the appliances in the kitchen. He would have wanted you to find it."

Allie sat up on her knees. "He was an electrician. He did installs like that all the time. He'd know where to put it so you'd find it and give it to me."

"Damn," Alex said. "I didn't give the man enough credit."

"We'll meet you at the resort in half an hour," Ollie said, already flipping back the covers and swinging his legs out of bed. "Bring a drill and a drywall saw. We can apologize to Jena later."

chapter
twenty-four

Wherever Joe had hidden the money he'd won, he'd hidden it thoroughly. Two hours after they started searching the kitchen, they still hadn't found it. Allie, Sean, and Alex were all there, tapping on walls and behind cupboards, trying to find the cache. They'd had a few false alarms, lots and lots of trash from the crew, but nothing real so far. Not even a hint of it.

Allie hopped up on an empty counter. "Maybe I was wrong."

"Maybe," Sean said. "But I agree with you. This makes sense for him."

Ollie agreed with Sean. The more he thought about it, the more Joe hiding money at the resort made perfect sense. Joe would have hidden the money if he knew he was being tracked, especially if he'd somehow found out Lobo and his men were shifters. Even if he came back for it later, there was no place safer than the Springs. That much had been drilled into every shifter kid since childhood. And he also knew that Alex McCann kept the place guarded twenty-four seven ever since one of his employees had been killed on site.

It was here. It had to be.

He carefully tapped down another foot-wide section of wall where one of the refrigerators would go.

Nothing.

He started back at the top. It was a slow process, one that Jena didn't have the patience for. She'd taken one look at a wall where

Sean had already cut several holes, covered her eyes, and walked right back out again with Alex trailing behind her, murmuring reassurances.

A dull thud met his fingertips, and everyone turned. Ollie leaned closer to the wall, reaching for the drywall saw, only to pull back.

"Sorry. Think I'm just hearing a patch."

Allie said, "Darn."

Sean turned back to his wall.

Ollie, however, leaned closer. A section had been cut out at chest height, right between two studs. It might have been nothing. Hell, a hammer could have been swung wrong or a piece could have cracked.

But maybe…

He kept staring at the section, trying to figure out why he was stuck on it. Allie stepped closer.

"What is it?"

"I don't know."

Sean looked over his shoulder. "The taping is different."

"What?"

"I'm no construction expert, but…" He nudged Ollie out of the way. "The taping here. It's a little different. Not as smooth. And the plaster's a little thicker."

"Might have been a new guy."

"A new guy repairing walls?" Sean shook his head. "Hand me the knife."

Sean tapped around the repaired site until he got the rough dimensions. Then he took the knife and slid it in. It caught on something almost immediately.

Ollie shoved him to the side. "Give me that. We need to go wider."

He carefully inserted the knife an inch to the left and pulled down.

It caught again.

"Another couple of inches," Allie said, her voice humming with excitement.

They moved the knife two more times until the seam was clear. Then they sawed across and down, an equal number of inches from the original patch, which Ollie could now see was a messier job.

Come on, Joe. Our girl needs a break.

He cut two notches in the top of the section, which ended up being about eighteen inches wide and just as many from top to bottom. Then Ollie and Sean pulled.

A dusty section of white drywall pulled away, revealing…

"Oh." Allie's shoulders slumped. "More trash."

It was a black garbage bag, but not the thick kind used at construction sites. No, this was the kind everyone with a yard had. The kind sold by the roll at the hardware store.

Sean glanced at him from the corner of his eye and Ollie knew he'd noticed the difference too.

"I think this is something," Ollie said.

"But…" Allie pulled on it. "It's just a trash bag."

As she pulled it out of the wall, a Post-it note fluttered down to the ground.

Sean picked it up and read; then he held it out for them to see.

Allison Smith.

Allie picked up the bag and held it up, but the black plastic was obviously empty. "It's gone? They found it already? But the wall—"

"The wall was patched months ago," Ollie said, wiping the dust from his palm. "Someone found this, took the money, and repatched the wall."

"But who would have guessed anything was hidden here?" Allie asked. "Who would have even known to look? Nobody knew Joe had any money."

Ollie glanced at Sean, but the snake had already come to the same conclusion Ollie had.

Sean stormed out of the kitchen, yanking the plastic bag from Allie and taking it with him. "My fucking sister!"

By the time Ollie and Allie made it up the hill and found Maggie Quinn's trailer, the two siblings were already fighting. But this wasn't the frustration or irritation that Ollie had witnessed before. No, this time Sean Quinn was in a full rage.

Unfortunately, his sister lived her life pissed off and was almost as skilled at changing animals as Sean was.

The two reptiles were a tornado; they changed so quickly Ollie could barely keep up. Maggie shifted to a cobra and so did Sean. Then he was a rattler, striking with lightning speed, only to have his target disappear and reemerge from the weeds as a venomous Gila monster. Sean shifted to an iguana, hissing and puffing his chest as he raced toward her. But Maggie melted into a puff adder and the iguana was forced to retreat.

The scales flew, but they kept returning to their natural snake forms, especially as the fight wore them down.

Ollie was tempted to shift and step on them, but he knew he'd probably take Sean out by mistake. Grizzlies weren't known for their delicate footwork.

Allie started, "Should I—"

"No."

"Probably not a good idea to get in the middle of them," she murmured.

Foxes ate snakes, but they weren't honey badgers. They could die from venom. So he gripped Allie's hand and stood back to watch the fight.

It was ironic, in a way. Sean, one of the friendliest and most well-adjusted people in his clan, wore the natural form of a diamondback rattler, a viper who struck quickly and with deadly venom. While Maggie, who was hell on wheels as a human, shifted to a rosy boa, a sociable reptile that was often kept as a pet.

Yeah, the universe missed the mark sometimes.

The boa was tiring, so Maggie did the next best thing. She shifted human and started to run.

Sean, as always, was right behind her. He tackled his sister to the ground and shoved her face in the gravel surrounding her trailer.

"You bitch!" he yelled. "What did he give you?"

"Nothing!"

"Stop lying, Maggie."

"Get the fuck off me, Sean!"

Ollie walked over and nudged Sean aside, calmly yanking Maggie up by her hair. She squealed the whole way to the truck. Allie grabbed a sheet off the line and threw it over the naked woman while Sean went to find his pants.

"I've had it," he said, buttoning up the Levi's that were brown with dust. "The old man wants me to take over this crazy family? Well, I'm making my first decision. You're gone."

"You can't do that."

Ollie shoved her against her trailer and glared. "If you have any survival instincts, don't move."

Sean walked over and put a hand around Maggie's throat when she began to shimmer again.

"You better not."

"Get your hands off me."

"Where's the money, Maggie?"

"I don't know what you're talking about."

Sean's grip tightened. "Stop lying. Where is it?"

Allie walked over, her arms crossed and her eyes cold. "You were working with Simon Ashford the whole time, weren't you?"

"You three," Maggie spit out, "have no idea how dangerous that man is. I was doing what I had to."

"By betraying one of our own?"

"He knows about us! I had to give him something."

"He *is* one of us, you idiot!" Sean yelled back. "Or did you not figure that out?"

Her eyes narrowed. "He is not."

"Yeah, he is." Sean kept his hand on her throat. "Did you tell him where Allie's house was?"

"He found it on his own. I only told him when she left town."

Ollie stepped forward, his hand fisting at his sides.

"I was trying to keep her safe, Campbell. She wasn't home when they broke in."

Sean shook his head. "You backstabbing bitch."

"It's real easy to say that, isn't it?" Maggie shoved his hand away. "High-and-mighty Sean Quinn! Famous photographer. Favorite son. *Deserter*."

"I'm back now."

"And who's gonna step in when you run away again, huh? Who's gonna keep the kids fed when the old man kicks off? You? Please."

"Don't pretend you're thinking about anyone but yourself."

Maggie screamed, "You have no idea what's going on!"

Sean took a step back. "So tell me."

"He found me months ago. He beat my name out of Pinky, then he tracked me down to try to get the money back."

"For Lobo?"

"For himself. He threatened our family, Sean. *He knew about us.* He told me he'd killed Joe. What was I supposed to tell him? Fuck off? Not likely."

"You knew he'd killed Joe," Allie said, "and you didn't say anything?"

"What was I going to tell *you*, Suzy Sunshine? Hey, Allie, your ex used to chat up skanks in Indio and run up credit card debt at the casinos. But don't worry, he's dead now!" Maggie choked. "After a game I booked him in. Yeah, that would have gone over well."

"At least I would have known where he was."

Maggie sneered. "No, you wouldn't. No one did. He was dead. I thought he'd stay buried. Then Ashford came around—the cold bastard—looking for the money. Threatening to expose us. He thought I had it. Didn't believe me when I told him Joe took off."

"So you knew he'd won?" Ollie said. "You were lying through your teeth even after you'd found the cash."

"Hey"—she shrugged—"a girl's got to have a few talents. Ashford wanted the money. Said he'd give me back my stake and he'd take the rest. Leave us alone. Leave Allie and the kids alone. Leave the *town* alone. I just pretended I believed him."

"So this was all for the good of the Springs?" Sean asked. "Yeah, I'm buying that."

"I needed the money too."

"And that's what you were thinking of," Sean spat out. "Just don't pretend otherwise. You disgust me."

"How did you find it?" Ollie asked.

"'Cause I used my *brain*. You should try it sometime. Joe was an electrician. He was smart, whether you guys saw it or not. There was only one construction project going on in town. I looked all over that site for months, but I finally found it."

"But you didn't give it to Ashford."

"And cave to his blackmail? He'd only come back for more."

"So what was your great plan, Maggie?" Sean asked. "What was your endgame? You don't do anything without an endgame in sight."

Her eye twitched.

"Was that guilt, Mags?" Sean asked. "Don't make me laugh. What was the plan?"

"I didn't have one until the body showed up. I was stalling Ashford, telling him I was still looking. Then after Joe's body was found... I knew the bear would go after them once they broke into Allie's house. He takes out Ashford, leaves me the money. Everyone's happy and no one needs to know."

"You sent them to my house," Allie said. "Those men tore up my children's mattresses, you bitch."

"And you were gone when it happened! Be grateful you never had to make a call like that, Allie Smith. Keep living your happy, shiny life and always do the right thing. Pretend there isn't a wolf just outside the door. Pretend that it's all going to be fine." Maggie lifted her chin. "Not all of us have that luxury."

Ollie shook his head. "You're so full of shit, Maggie."

"Fuck off, bear."

Sean grabbed her hair. "Watch your mouth."

"You're full of shit," Ollie said. "Because yeah, there *is* a wolf at the door. There's a bear too. And we may not like you much, but if you had come to any of us, we would have helped. Maybe then this wouldn't have gotten so out of hand. Now one of Lobo's guys is dead—probably both the guys who searched Allie's house are toast—and we've got a snake shifter and a bobcat roaming around who have four kids in their sights because they think they're leverage for finding a cache you've had the whole time."

Her eye twitched again.

"But you didn't tell any of us," Ollie continued. "Because you wanted the money for yourself. Wanted to have other people sort out your problems. Even when you end up hiding shit that could have gotten us all killed."

"How do you know Ashford's a shifter?"

"Because Alex fucking saw him shift!" Sean yelled. "He's a snake, but he's got wicked nasty venom, and this whole town is in his sights. Where is that money?"

"Let me get dressed," she muttered. "You can have it. But I want my fifty grand."

Allie said, "You're lucky I don't rip your throat out for putting my kids in danger."

Maggie leaned toward her. "Try it. It's not really a surprise, I guess. You precious McCann pups have always been more valuable than the kids on this hill. Just a bunch of dirty Quinns, right? Nothing but trouble. Who cares if the outsider threatens *them*, huh? If the Quinns lose a few, they'll only breed more."

"If you believe I'd think that way, you don't know me at all," Allie said.

Sean followed Maggie into the trailer just as Alex and Ted pulled up.

"Anyone injured?" Ted asked, stepping out of the Jeep.

"Not yet," Ollie said. "Give it a few minutes. Maggie and Sean are alone."

"What happened at the resort?" Alex asked. "You found something. I saw the hole in the wall. Might have been nice to check your phones."

"Maggie found Joe's money months ago," Allie said. "Simon Ashford was looking for it. Found her. Threatened the kids up here. Threatened to expose the town. She was stalling until Joe's body was found. She figured you and Ollie would take care of Ashford and she'd be free and clear with the cash."

Ted nodded slowly. "That sounds like a solid Maggie scheme."

Alex asked, "She didn't know Ashford was a shifter?"

Ollie shrugged. "You didn't spot it on him. Neither did I."

"You're right."

Allie said, "It's the scent. They smell different, but not like us."

Ollie could agree with that. There had been a sharp, sour smell in the old service station after Ashford had shifted and bitten his guard. Ollie had blamed it on the human at the time—panic held multiple layers of scents—but perhaps that pungent smell had been Ashford.

Maggie and Sean walked out of the trailer a few minutes later.

"Great," she said. "The wolves and the cats are here too."

Nothing else passed between them as Maggie turned to go. She walked back into the rocks behind her trailer, crouching down when she got to one shaped like a diamond at the base of a spreading Joshua tree. She rolled the rock to the side and pointed at the disturbed ground beneath.

"There. I didn't bring a shovel."

Ollie bent down and cupped his massive hands, digging into the loose dirt. Just a few inches down, he felt the cool smoothness of metal against his fingertips.

"Lockbox?" He glanced up at Maggie and she nodded.

"It was in the garbage bag. Knew I shouldn't have left that shit behind," she muttered.

"You gotta key?"

"I busted it open with an ice pick."

Ollie grunted and bent over, slowly brushing the dirt from the nondescript, black metal box buried in the soil. He dug around until he could lift it out. Then he stood, holding it carefully.

"As far as I'm concerned," he told Maggie, "you get none of this."

Maggie's eyes were bleak, but Ollie chose to ignore her. Maggie Quinn was not his problem. If she'd come to him in the beginning, he would have bent over backward to help her. But she hadn't done that. She'd put Allie and her kids in danger, and no bear would forgive a threat against his children.

He held the box out to Allie, but she shook her head. "I don't have a safe. Do you? What do I do with it? I can't take it to the bank."

Ollie glanced at Alex. "The wolves have a safe."

"We have a few of them," Alex said. "I'll keep it for you, Allie. Get it counted. We can figure out what to do about it after this is over."

She nodded and hooked her arm through Ollie's after he passed the box off to Alex. Then the six of them walked back to Maggie's trailer where Ted pushed her to sit on the old picnic table while she cleaned her split lip.

Maggie kept her eyes on her brother. "What are you going to do to me?"

"I already told you," Sean said quietly. "You're gone."

Maggie's eyes sparked fire. "You can't do that."

"Watch me." He kicked the tongue of her trailer. "Hope this thing moves, because you're not staying in the Springs, Mags. I'm serious. And the old man will back me up. You're gone."

The color drained from her face. "For how long?"

"Ask me in a year." Sean turned and started walking away.

Ollie had never seen his friend's eyes so cold. But then, he didn't have any siblings. Betrayal on the scale that Maggie had committed had a way of changing everything, even ties of blood. There was a coolness in Sean's gaze. A weariness in the set of his shoulders. Leadership was never an easy burden, but Ollie wondered if it was one that would end up breaking his friend.

ALLIE HADN'T BEEN ABLE TO KICK HIM OUT OF HER BED that night either, but she had insisted he put on a shirt with his sweatpants.

"Loralie and Chris will come barging in. It's almost a guarantee."

"There are locks on the doors for a reason," he muttered, closing his eyes and pulling her head to his shoulder.

"But not when they're away from home and there are all these guards around. Not when everything is so... chaotic."

He grunted, but he was quickly falling asleep. Ollie could hear his clan and the wolves circling the house. His bear approved. More predators in the den wasn't usually a good thing, but if it kept the children safe, it was acceptable.

"Tell me this will be over soon," she said quietly.

Ollie's heart jumped.

What? No!

Allie sighed. "Tell me we'll be able to go back to our house. Have normal lives again. You and I could... go to the movies. Take my dad's boat out to the river on a Saturday. Have regular Sunday dinner and worry about Nerf guns instead of real guns."

His heart calmed down when he realized she was just talking about the looming danger.

"It will," he said. "I'm going to take care of this, and life will go back to normal."

She snuggled in and whispered, "Okay."

"Not gonna lie though." He kissed the top of her head. "I like having you guys around."

"You might not think that when you find out Chris broke your torque wrench this afternoon while Kevin was working on the Charger."

Ollie winced. "The Craftsman?"

"The Snap-on."

"The old one or the one with the digital read out?"

"Since one of the things he was using it for was taking the dog's temperature, I'm guessing it was the digital."

Okay, he could admit it. That hurt.

"Still glad we're around?"

"Yes." He pulled her onto his chest and swatted her backside. "But I may demand repayment for the torque wrench."

She laughed. "I can live with that. For the first time in my life, I have some extra money lying around."

Ollie lifted one eyebrow and spread a broad hand over her cheek. "Oh, that wasn't the kind of repayment I had in mind."

chapter
twenty-five

Allie still hadn't wrapped her brain around the idea of having two hundred thousand dollars. She'd brought her bills over from the house but had hidden them in her room, embarrassed by how much red ink was on them. Now she spread them nervously across the kitchen table where she and Alex were drinking coffee.

"This all of them?" he asked.

She nodded.

"Have you totaled it up?"

"Around sixty grand all together. A little over that."

Alex let out a low whistle but nodded and started tapping on the calculator with almost manic glee.

Allie let out a slow breath. It felt good to plan. She'd been holding on by the skin of her teeth for so long she'd forgotten that she'd been great with budgeting when she'd had a real paycheck to work with. This was all manageable. She could pay everything off and even stop asking for charity.

And Alex loved handling money. It was the reason she'd called him. Ollie was at the Cave, trying to catch up on his own paperwork after so many days off his regular schedule. Ted and Jena were both working. Sean was holed up with his uncle. He'd said something vague about making things right, but she didn't know what that meant.

The whole town felt like it was on guard. There were extra volunteers at the schools, and ranchers and farmers had been warned to watch for any unfamiliar vehicles and call Alex or Ollie immediately.

People. She had them.

And this threat had gone far beyond her own small family. Simon Ashford, his mysterious boss, and whatever foreign shifters they had were a threat to everyone.

For now, she'd just concentrate on keeping the water running.

"So," Alex said, "the first thing we need to do is get you current and pay off the smallest creditors. These casinos... I'm going to look into what they might take as a settlement. I don't know if it'll be successful, but we can try. After that—"

"What am I going to do with all that cash?" Allie felt the anxiety rising again. "I can't just deposit it in the bank. Or can I?"

"Not if you don't want a lot of questions from the IRS," Alex said, still scribbling notes on a legal pad. "But... I think I just hired you as a consultant, so we'll figure out a salary that gets you your money and still keeps things mostly legal. Just let me figure it out."

Her eyes bugged out. "What?"

"Listen," he said, folding his hands and looking up. "I was thinking about having you working at the resort anyway. You have a natural gift for hospitality. You could easily work in event planning once Loralie is in school full time. I'll just... start paying you a little early."

Allie blinked her eyes. "But... Alex, I have no experience in that kind of stuff."

"Don't be humble. I saw Christopher's last birthday party, remember? You had thirty-two seven-year-olds at your house and no one was bleeding. That's practically a miracle according to Jena. You ran that like a drill sergeant. And I should know, I was raised by one."

"But that's kid stuff!"

"So?" He laughed. "Is a business retreat going to be more difficult than thirty seven-year-olds and assorted younger siblings?"

Allie shrugged. Since grown-ups could pour their own lemonade, Alex might have a point.

"All that cash would raise flags if you deposit it, but the pack can *always* use cash. My dad was practically salivating when he saw all those small bills. I'll pay you a regular salary starting now—you'll have to pay taxes on it, but I'll make sure you don't get slammed—and when you start working for real, you'll get the rest. It won't be a lump sum, but you won't get any inconvenient questions, either. Does that work for you? It's up to you. That was just my first thought."

"If I worked for you, I wouldn't have to work at my dad's store anymore," she mused.

"Nope. And there are plenty of people looking for jobs. He'd have a line out the door when he started hiring."

"But I might still want to work at the Cave."

Alex shrugged. "It's all details. We can work it out. The point is, Joe left you something to work with. And I'll make sure you get to keep most of it."

Allie thought for a moment. "Do you think I should pay Maggie back her fifty thousand?"

"I'm not going there. Talk to Sean."

She nodded.

"Allie, there was something else." Alex's voice dropped, and he pulled an envelope out of his pocket. "This was mixed in with the money."

He slid a battered envelope across the table. It had her name on it in Joe's handwriting.

Allie froze, staring at it.

"It hasn't been opened," he said.

"It's from Joe."

"I figured."

Her hand was trembling when she reached for it. All these months. Every harsh word she'd said to her friends about him, every resentment she'd held, it all rushed into her mind. The anger was there, but so was the confusion.

What was there left to say that he hadn't already yelled at her over the years?

Alex said, "You don't have to read it right now, but I wanted to give it to you. Want me to throw it away?"

"No." She hesitated. *Maybe.* "It's from Joe."

"I know."

The last words he would leave her with. Would they be sweet? Bitter? Angry or sorry? She didn't know. She had never known.

"Allie?"

She cleared her throat and tapped a finger on the envelope. "You know, if Ollie gave me a letter, I'd never worry about opening it. He'd never be hurtful. Not on purpose. With Joe? You just never know."

"Okay," he said softly. "So wait. Wait until life has settled down. Or don't open it at all."

"No, I have to."

"Why?"

She smiled sadly. "Because of fifteen years and four kids. This—whatever it is—is the last thing he's gonna give me. Good or bad, I'll handle it, Alex."

"You always do."

ALLIE WORE A SWEATER WHEN SHE WALKED TO THE PARK. Fall weather was finally starting to break the heat, and the change was more than welcome. She saw Jim following her from a distance, knew Ollie had assigned him to watch her when she went out, but she tried to ignore him. She sat on the benches across from Willow's mural, Joe's letter burning in one pocket and a handful of Kleenex in the other.

Trying to calm her nerves, she pulled out the letter and opened it, sliding the single sheet of lined paper from the envelope. With a deep breath, she braced herself.

Dear Allie,

If you're reading this, I'm probably dead. I'm sorry. Just another mess for you to deal with, right?

I left you too many messes.

I'm trying to do the right thing, but I've always been pretty stupid about knowing what the right thing was. I was a shit husband. A shit dad. I guess this money is my one way of paying you back for all the stuff you had to put up with.

I'm sorry, honey. I tried, but not hard enough. This is my fault. I know you tried your best. And you're such a good mom. I'm sorry that I took it out on you. I was the one who wasn't good enough, not you.

I didn't deserve you. I grabbed on to something I wanted and didn't care that I was dragging you down with me. I knew it. Everyone did. The fact that I resented how good you were is on me, not you. You were a way better wife than I deserved.

The only good thing I ever accomplished was our kids, and I know that's mostly you anyway. Tell Kevin I'm sorry about his Bowie knife. I'm going to try to get it back to him, I promise. I see so much of myself in Mark that it scares me sometimes. But I know you'll do a better job than my parents did, so he'll be fine. I'm sorry I was mean to Chris. He never deserved that. Tell him I miss reading him bedtime stories in funny voices. And the baby. God, Allie, I can still feel how small she was. She's getting so big already, and I'm going to miss it.

ALLIE SAW OLD TEARSTAINS MARKING THE PAGE. SHE pulled the Kleenex from her pocket to wipe her own away.

I'm going to miss everything. Every funny story. Every silly joke. Every football game. Their graduations. Their weddings.

I hate myself so much.

This is all I can give them. I had to do something. I knew it wasn't a good idea, but I had to do <u>something</u>.

I love them. I love you. I know it's not enough.

It wasn't all bad, was it? We had some good times, right? Can you remind the kids of that sometimes? They probably hate me. I know you do. I deserve it.

You should be with Ollie. He's loved you for years. I know nothing ever happened between you guys, but he loves you and the kids. Just let him help, because you can be stubborn as hell. I guess you had to be, being married to me. But I can't remember the last time I heard you laugh. And you have such a great laugh. Maybe he can make you laugh again.

I'm sorry. I'm sorry. I'm sorry.

I think this is the longest letter I've ever written. I don't know what else to say, but I don't want to stop writing.

Please remember when I made you laugh.

Please tell the kids how much I love them. How proud I am. How amazing they are.

Please remember our first kiss. Because it was perfect.

I didn't know how to love you right, but I loved you.

I always will.

Joe

SHE COULD BARELY SEE THE LAST WORDS HE WROTE.

Allie crumpled the letter to her chest and cried. For everything that was. For what might have been. For everything Joe would miss and for the good things he'd never seen about himself.

She remembered the hours he'd spent walking Kevin up and down the hallway when he wouldn't sleep in his crib. The way he'd laughed hysterically the first time Mark had peed on him when he changed his diaper. The way he'd tickle Chris until neither one of them could breathe. His insistence in dressing Loralie in the frilliest dresses they could find, so delighted to have a little girl after three rowdy boys.

She didn't know how long she cried, but the sun had started to go down when she felt Ollie sit down next to her. He didn't say a word, just put his arms around her and scooted her onto his lap, surrounding her with his presence. Kissing the top of her head and rocking her back and forth as he wiped her tears with the edge of his flannel shirt.

"Jim called me," he said after her tears were spent.

"There was a letter from Joe. With the money."

He paused. "Should I have left you alone?"

"Never."

"Okay."

Allie took a deep breath and rested her cheek against his chest. They were silent for a long time, but it felt good. It felt right to be there with him, mourning the past so she could move into their future.

"We never did a memorial for him. Nothing. I was so shocked... They gave me his ashes, but they're at my dad's."

"We'll plan something."

"The kids probably needed that, but I didn't even think about it. I'm a bad mom."

She felt his chest shaking with laughter.

"Stop," she said throwing a wadded-up Kleenex at his chest.

"You're not a bad mom." He tugged on her ponytail until she looked up at him. "You're an amazing mom, and they love you. So do I."

"Joe mentioned that."

Ollie frowned, so she held out the letter to let him read it. She didn't mind. She'd be feeling sore from it for a while, so he should probably know why. He read it silently and then folded it up, put it back in the envelope, and sighed.

"You'll remind the kids about the good stuff," he said softly, hugging her tighter. "When you're ready. When they need to hear it. You'll remember."

She nodded.

"You ready to go home? Eli and Paul are hanging with the kids."

"Can we keep your cousins?" she asked. "When we're no longer in mortal danger? They're great babysitters, and they have driver's licenses."

"They love your cooking. You probably won't be able to get rid of them until they leave for college."

They held hands in the car, and Ollie wasn't able to make her laugh, but he did make her smile.

The laughter could come later.

SHE SKIPPED HER SHIFT THE NIGHT SHE RECEIVED JOE'S letter, but she couldn't skip two, even if Ollie gave a token protest. She could spot a token protest from a mile away; she knew he needed her there. It was a Thursday, and there was a band coming in from San Diego. The Cave would be slammed.

Allie left Elijah and Kevin with instructions while Ollie briefed the bears and the wolves outside.

"Are you sure we should both be going?" he asked as he climbed into the truck. "It's not that I don't trust everyone, but—"

"Ted's coming over later," she said. "She'll be in the house with the kids, just in case."

Ollie said nothing.

"I know," she added, "but I'm trying not to be paranoid. Careful, but not paranoid."

"I want to go hunting," he growled. "You shouldn't have to live like this."

"Do we even know where to start looking?"

He paused. "Not really. Alex is working on it."

"And when he finds something, you'll know. Until then..." She slid his hand in hers. "...we have great people."

The corner of his mouth turned up. "You and your people."

"You're my favorite though."

"Oh yeah?"

"Yes. You're excellent people."

Ollie brought their hands up and kissed the back of her fingers. "You're making it awfully hard to take this thing slow, Allie-girl."

The new band wasn't as good as the last one, but it wasn't bad either. The drinks were flowing, and the crowd was enjoying itself.

Too bad Allie wasn't. It was the kind of night she usually loved, but there was something nagging at her.

"Darlin', I got your order up!" Ollie yelled from across the bar.

Allie shot him a smile and a wink, not missing the longing sigh of the two ladies at the table.

"That one yours?" one of the women asked.

"Yep," Allie said with a grin. "Hands off."

"Girl," the other said, "I don't blame you. That man is *fine*."

"You ladies liking the band?"

"Yeah, but I think it's the first time we had to hike so far for parking. This place is packed. We parked halfway up the road into town."

Allie froze, fumbling the glass she'd been about to pick up.

"You okay, honey?" the first woman asked.

"Yeah," she said, her heart starting to pound. "I just... I'll check back with you guys in a bit. You okay for now?"

They waved her away and Allie practically ran to the bar.

"Hey." Ollie was right there. "What's wrong?"

"All these cars," she said in a panic. "We've been watching for strange cars because this Ashford guy isn't going to be able to get close to town without a vehicle, but now there's all these cars, Ollie, and there's no way—"

"Baby, I've got twice as many men at the house for just that reason. They're watching extra close. And Sean said he was going to send some of the Quinns over later to help."

"But he's a snake!"

Ollie glanced around, and she lowered her voice.

"He's a snake, Ollie. You can't... they can get anywhere. Everywhere." She couldn't calm down. "I need to be home. I can't be here."

Ollie passed a harried gaze over the bar. "Allie—"

"Just drive me home and come right back. Or have Jim do it. I don't care. But I'm gonna be useless here. I can't stop thinking about that guy." She felt her breath coming faster. "He could sneak in the house and no one—"

"Okay." He smoothed his hands down her shoulders. "Okay, we'll get you home. Calm down. I'll... call in someone else to fill in. But I can't leave. Are you okay letting Jim take you home? The kitchen's pretty slow. Is that okay?"

She nodded, but the icy claws in her chest didn't ease. "Okay."

Ollie waved Jim over and explained the situation. Allie grabbed her purse and practically ran to Jim's truck.

There was something wrong. She just knew it.

The claws in her chest only tightened when she got back to Ollie's and saw every light on in the house and barn and half their people in shifted form.

Jim threw open the door. "What's going on?"

Elijah ran up. "We were just about to call you, Dad. We can't find Chris."

"What?" Allie shrieked.

Elijah held up a hand. "He and Mark got into a fight about some cards or something—"

"Pokémon cards?" Allie yelled. "He ran off because of Pokémon cards?" She ran toward the house, Elijah following her.

"They were fighting, and then Mark yelled something and Chris ran off. Miss Allie, he's probably just hiding."

Jim said, "Call Ollie right now."

"Dad—"

"I'm not angry. But you need to call him right now, then call some of the older cousins to go help your mom out at the bar."

"Yes, sir."

"Allie, wait!"

She heard Jim calling her, but she didn't stop. Those stupid, stupid cards! She was getting rid of every single one of them. Maybe that was going to be her policy from now on. Every time they fought over a toy, it belonged to her. She strode up the porch steps and into the house. "Kevin!"

Kevin and Mark ran down the stairs, Kevin holding Loralie.

Mark looked like he was about to puke. "Mom, I'm so sorry. He bent my cards and I lost my temper and I yelled at him."

"Buddy, don't worry about that right now." She passed Loralie to Mark. "Watch your sister. Stay upstairs and scream *really, really loud* if you see anything slithering. Kevin, shift and find your brother."

"But Eli and Mr. McCann said—"

"I know what they said." She put her hand on his cheek. "But I need to stay human so I can talk with the other grown-ups, and other than me, you know him best. I don't think anyone grabbed him." *Please, God, don't let anyone have grabbed him.* "I think he's just hiding. Shift and find him for me, baby."

Kevin nodded and ran to his room.

"Allie?" Alex's dad, Robert McCann, walked through the front door. "Why don't you stay in the house with the kids while we—"

"Kevin is shifting right now. He and I will start searching in the house. Please send someone up here to stay with Mark and Loralie."

His mouth was a thin line. "I really think you should leave the searching to us. We're probably being overcautious, but—"

"We probably are, but Mr. McCann, I know my child better than you. He ran off to hide. He does this fairly frequently. Kevin will be able to find him." Kevin trotted out to stand next to her. "We'll look around the house first. Has anyone gone down to the tunnels beneath the house?"

"What tunnels?" He glared. "Damn bears! I can't secure a perimeter if I'm not given the right information!" He spun and marched out the door.

Allie didn't have time for territorial fights. The acrid fear had eased, but she still wanted to find her youngest son. "Kevin, the door in the basement. Start there. You know Chris has been dying to go explore."

Kevin raced down the hall, nudging open the basement door that never seemed to latch correctly. He disappeared and Allie ran after him.

"Do not run so fast, Kevin Smith! I have to keep up."

Kevin was waiting at the set of shelves that hid the door to the tunnels. They were so smoothly oiled a child could swing them open. Allie was worried that Chris had done just that.

Kevin had his front paws up on the second shelf.

"Did you catch his scent?"

A high whine she thought meant yes.

"Okay." She swung open the door and grabbed a flashlight. There were only a few lights down in the tunnels, but the dirt floor was worn even by years of use. The tunnels weren't used for bootlegging anymore; they were used for storage. Ollie had shoved some of the older furniture in them, so she worried about tripping.

Kevin had no such concerns, his night vision far more acute than her human eyes. He darted ahead, then stopped.

"Do you have him?" she asked.

Kevin pawed the ground.

"No, I don't want you running ahead. Stay with me. *Chris?*"

She passed two branching passageways before she heard the sniffling. Allie let out a sigh. "Chris?"

"Mom?"

The claws around her heart eased. Kevin ran to the left.

"Hey, Kevin." Chris's small voice echoed down the passage. "Is Mark still gonna pound me?"

She pulled out her phone to call Robert McCann, but of course she had no signal.

Allie followed Kevin and swung her flashlight around. Chris was crouched in the corner, the bent Pokémon cards still clutched in his hand and dusty tear streaks down his face.

"Mama, I'm sorry. I know I'm not supposed to play with them, but... Don't let Mark pound me."

She bent down and picked him up, grunting as she put his legs around her waist. He was getting *way* too heavy to carry. "Buddy, no one's going to pound you. But don't you remember? I told all you guys you had to stay in the house. You scared me to death."

Kevin was nosing the ground, darting farther into the passageway, then running back, still whining.

"Come on, Kev," Allie said, still carrying Chris. "Help me find the way back."

Kevin waited, still whining.

"What's up?" Allie huffed out a breath. "Just shift and tell me what's going on, Kev. I'm your mom. I've seen you naked before."

Chris wiped his runny nose. "He has trouble changing back sometimes when the moon is big. I heard him telling Low."

Oh, for heaven's sake.

"Why didn't you tell me? That's not a big deal. I can help you, but not right now. Let's just head back. Ollie's probably freaking out right now." And her back was about to break. She didn't think she'd be able to pry Chris's arms from around her neck. He was hanging on like a limpet.

Kevin still wasn't moving. He blocked the passageway and let out a sharp bark.

Allie wanted to cover her ears. "It really is like a horror movie. Kevin, will you just—"

She heard another scream echo from the passageway leading back to the house.

Allie's eyes went wide.

Not a fox scream. A bobcat's.

And the fact that Kevin was dancing around her feet and whining told her that scream didn't belong to anyone familiar.

She looked over her shoulder into the darkness. She had no idea where it led, and she was carrying a child. She looked down at Kevin and whispered, "Get one of the bears who knows the tunnels. Run *now*. Fast as you can."

A desperate, high whine. He didn't want to leave her and Chris.

"Now, Kevin!"

He disappeared down the tunnel a second before she heard the footsteps.

But it wasn't the young man who'd turned into a bobcat who appeared. It was another man, pale with sandy-brown hair. He was wearing ill-fitting sweatpants and a shirt Allie thought he must have pulled out of storage.

"You must be Allison Smith," he said in a gently accented voice. "How very nice to meet you. I've been looking for you for some time."

Chris clutched her tighter. "Mama, what's wrong?"

Allie stroked his hair, her eyes never leaving the chilly face of the man who blocked her way. "Nothing, baby. Everything's going to be just fine."

chapter
twenty-six

O llie was trying hard not to burst into his fur. He pulled up to the house and jumped out, taking in the organized chaos surrounding him. Men and women were walking outward in a silent grid, looking for one small boy and keeping watch for any snakes. Sean had sent people, but he'd told them not to shift. If Ashford had taken Chris—

"I'm sorry!" Mark burst out of the house and jumped off the porch, tears streaming down his face. "I'm sorry, I'm sorry. I'm so sorry, Ollie!"

Ollie bent down and let the boy jump into his arms, pulling him into a bear hug. "This is not your fault."

"It was just some stupid cards, and he ran away. I'm so stupid. It was just a toy."

"Marky, calm down."

"I can't—" He choked on his tears. "If something happens to him—"

"Mark." Ollie set him down and put a hand on his cheek. "Nothing is going to happen to him. I'm going to find Chris. Where's your mom?"

"She went to look in the tunnels with Kevin."

Flashing red alarms blaring in his head. "Alone?"

"Mr. McCann sent someone down there with her." Mark's eyes swept the yard and he pointed. "That guy."

"That guy" was talking to Robert McCann, but Ollie didn't see Allie or Kevin with him. He stalked over.

"...pitch-black. I'll need some flashlights. It'd really help if one of the Campbells—"

"You!" Ollie shouted at him. "You're supposed to be down in the tunnels with Allie?"

The man sighed. "I tried. But I couldn't see a damn thing, and I got completely turned around. I heard her calling for the kid. Think I heard him call back. They sounded fine, but we should—"

"Where the hell are my cousins?" Ollie hadn't seen Paul or Elijah anywhere.

"The boys?" Robert McCann asked. "They're watching the road. Don't need young people—"

"You're an idiot." Ollie cut him off, not caring if he offended the man, even if he was an elder. "Those boys know this property as well as I do. You should have sent them down under the house with Allie."

He walked away. Even if the man had heard Allie and Chris talking, that didn't mean—

Panicked fox howls sounded in the distance.

He froze. "Allie?"

More howls, then Ollie saw a slim grey fox dart out of the scrub on the edge of the yard. "Allie, is that you?"

No, the markings on the face were different. Ollie bent down and the fox almost climbed up his arms.

"Kevin, calm down." Panicked howls and nips at his shirt sent Ollie's heart into overdrive. Something was very wrong. "You have to shift. Tell me what happened."

He heard someone running, then Robert McCann bent down beside him and grabbed Kevin by the scruff, picking him up with one arm and growling, "No."

Kevin went limp at the command in the older male's voice.

"Shift now, Kevin Smith."

He dropped Kevin when the fox started shimmering. Both Ollie and Robert stood back and let Kevin's body reform. Then Robert held out his hand and helped the shivering young man stand.

"Ollie"—his teeth were chattering—"he's got Mom. Some guy. White guy with brown hair. I smelled a cat—"

"In the tunnels?"

He nodded, then turned his head, bent over, and vomited.

Ollie shouted at Robert, "Stay with Kevin!" Then his clothes fell to pieces around him when he let the grizzly take over.

"VERY CONVENIENT, THESE TUNNELS," ASHFORD SAID, following Allie into the darkness as they followed the light step of the bobcat who'd remained in animal form. "Jesús found them weeks ago. There were bears around, of course, but they were looking for humans, not animals."

"Who are you?"

"My name is Simon Ashford. I suspect you've heard of me."

"No, I mean *what* are you?"

"I'm like you, of course."

"No," she said. "You don't smell like us."

Ashford laughed. "Yes, there's a very good reason for that. But I don't feel like telling stories right now. Perhaps if we have time later."

Ollie, where are you? Allie would have no objections to a big growling, marauding bear right now. Right now that sounded about perfect.

She could smell the fresh air, knew they were probably using the same route Kevin had used to escape the tunnels. If she'd been in her fox form, she'd have followed her nose to fresh air too. Ollie had told her some of the tunnels led out to old farm roads and another led toward the Cave. Was that where they were going? Had Ashford and his man parked at the bar and snuck in through the tunnels?

"Mama, I'm tired," Chris whispered.

No, he was scared, but he didn't want to say it.

"I know, baby." She kissed his head. "We'll get home as soon as we can."

"Precious," Ashford said dryly. "So many families here. It's... precious."

"Yeah, it is. What do you want, Mr. Ashford?"

"The money, of course."

"For your boss?"

"No."

So it wasn't Lobo who wanted his cash back. This sounded like one of those twisted intrigue plots that villains liked in books. But really, Allie knew it came down to one thing that even a child would understand.

"So," she said, "you're stealing your boss's toys."

Chris said, "I steal my brother's toys." Then he sighed. "I always get caught though."

"Yes," Allie continued. "People who steal things have a tendency to get caught."

Ashford chuckled. "You're delightfully simple, Mrs. Smith."

"And you're not-so-delightfully condescending. So you want the money. Then what?"

"Then I leave, of course. What happens after that is none of your concern. I have no interest in your people—no ax to grind, as they say. I'm not Efrén."

"Who's Efrén?" Was that Lobo's real name?

The bobcat had paused in front of them, and Allie remembered he had a tattoo of Lobo's name across his neck. Did the young man realize Ashford was trying to double-cross his boss? Did it matter?

"Efrén is the man you people refer to as Lobo. Ridiculous nicknames. His people like it. Efrén's cobbled-together pack wasn't something I was ever truly interested in, but they were useful."

"For what?"

"Money, of course. Then I realized that Efrén wasn't always motivated by profit. Revenge is so... inefficient. You'd hardly understand. He should have spent more time making money and less time at the poker table interrogating your husband."

Those cold claws dug deeper into Allie's heart.

Chris said, "Did you know my dad? He died."

They paused and Ashford reached out, pushing open an old wooden door. The hinges must have been recently oiled because it didn't even creak. She could finally see his face in the nearly full moon, but he wasn't looking at her, he was looking at Chris.

"Of course I knew your father, Christopher." His cold eyes rose to Allie's, and she stared in shock when the flick of a nictitating membrane slid across his eyes. "Such a tragedy for children to lose a parent when they're young. If you're not careful, they'll grow into utter monsters."

Allie held Christopher closer as they walked out of the tunnel. The tunnel faced a wall of rock, the slope hidden by the rise of a small hill and a fall of boulders on either side. But beyond the boulders, she could see the edge of Emmet Wash and knew they were closer to her house than she realized. The problem was she couldn't shift and leave Christopher. She had to hope Kevin and Ollie were fast.

An owl screeched overhead, but Allie didn't hear another sound other than the quiet, familiar calls of insects. Then there was another screech, but still no sound of wings.

Lowell.

Jena's oldest son shifted to a barn owl in his natural form. Even young, he was the most silent hunter she'd ever seen. Had they already told the Crowe clan to be on the lookout?

Ashford must have had a similar thought, because the mild expression fell from his face.

"Put the boy down," he said. "You'll shift and take me to the money. I know you have it. I've been listening."

"Forget it." She hoisted Chris up to get a better grip. "I'm not leaving my son here. And if you've been listening, you know I don't have the money. It's in a safe. Miles away from here."

"You'll leave the boy and call McCann. We're not far from your house. Tell him to come alone, and Jesús won't hurt your son. It's very simple, Mrs. Smith. Even you should be able to understand. Once I have it, Jesús and I will be gone and your children will be safe."

"And you're simple if you think I'm leaving my son alone in the desert with an animal I don't know!"

She didn't even see his arm rise before he slapped her. It was hard and sharp. The back of his hand drove her jaw into the top of Chris's head, and he started wailing in fear and pain.

"Mama!"

"Don't test me," Ashford said quietly. "You know I could do far worse. Adrian Lorra died after only an hour or so. My venom is even more effective on smaller, more delicate creatures." He ran a hand down Chris's back before she could jerk him away. "Leave your son and come with me. Or do I need to be more convincing?"

Ollie, where are you?

"You need me," Allie said softly, her eyes watering but steady. She refused to show weakness to this man. She just needed to stall him. If Low had spotted her, if Kevin had made it to Ollie, it would only be minutes before the cavalry arrived. She just had to keep her boy safe. "You'll never get that money from the McCanns on your own," she continued. "They'd squash you like the little snake you are. So don't raise your hand to me again. And don't threaten my child."

"I've been pleasant so far, Mrs. Smith. I don't think you realize just how *un*pleasant I can be."

"Yeah? Well, I'm a *waitress*. I deal with assholes professionally." She heard the distant call of another owl and the short yip of a coyote in the night. "And, mister, you have no idea what you're dealing with."

He couldn't get the scent. THE CHILDREN AND ALLIE HAD BEEN all over his property, and he was too enraged to sort through the maze of which scents were new and which were old. The bear had taken over, but without any direction, his fury and frustration only grew.

The screech sounded overhead, followed by a lower hoot. The bear stopped in its tracks and listened, huffing heated breaths into the cool night air. He turned his head to follow the screeches.

There.

The bear didn't catch the scent of his woman or child first, it was a bobcat with a sickly smell.

He didn't smell like us. ...it almost smelled sour. Unhealthy...

Allie had smelled the bobcat before. This was the shifter who'd been tracking her. If the bobcat was in his territory, Allie would be with him. And so would the snake.

A primal roar tore out of his throat, and he charged into the night. Then a wolf was at his side. Familiar. The scent told him it was Alex. The bear and the wolf ran over gullies and across the scrublands separating Ollie's property from Allie's. He launched himself over the fence, arrowing toward his woman as he felt his rage build.

Simon Ashford would die that night.

The wolf broke away and ran at an angle away from him, circling around as two other wolves joined him. The pack would cover the wash. His clan should be spreading through the tunnels. They would cut off any means of escape.

But Ashford was a snake.

They can get anywhere. Everywhere.

Not if they were dead.

Ollie let out another enraged roar when he crested the small hill and saw the two shadows. He was going by scent. His night vision was weak, but he saw one shadow break away and run toward Emmet Wash. The other ran toward him.

"Ollie!"

The running shadow was there, then it was gone.

And the snake was loose in the desert.

chapter
twenty-seven

Allie ran toward him. Chris was crying on her chest, but Allie didn't stop.

"Ollie, I need you!"

The bear stopped its rampage and jogged toward her as she heard the sound of wolf calls fill the night. The pack was hunting, but Ashford was a snake. If he burrowed, they'd be confused. If he slithered into the rocks, they'd lose him. Brute strength wasn't needed now. They needed stealth and delicacy.

They needed a fox.

The bear huffed up to her and pushed against her side, almost knocking her over.

"Take him home!"

Ollie shifted in front of her, his chest heaving, his eyes on fire. "Where's Ashford?"

"He shifted." She shoved Chris at him. "Get him out of here. Please!"

"I'll shift back. I can carry you both."

"No, take Chris. I need to hunt."

Ollie's eyes went wide. "No."

"Don't argue with me. I have his scent and I'm better at this than the wolves. You know I can find him."

"Allie!"

She grabbed his arm and pulled him down, pressing a hard kiss against his lips. "Please," she whispered. "Take care of my son. Get him home. You're the only one who can carry him that far, that fast. Then come back for me."

The growl in his throat told her he wasn't pleased, but he held Chris out to her, shifted, then waited for Allie to put the boy on his back.

"You hold on," she whispered to her son. "It's Ollie. He won't drop you no matter how hard you hold his fur. Do *not* get down. Don't put your feet on the sand until you get back to the house."

"Mama?" Her big boy had disappeared. Chris was panicked and confused.

"Christopher, you go with Ollie." She spoke firmly. "Go now. Kevin and Grandpa are waiting for you. Mama needs to hunt."

He nodded and twisted his little hands in Ollie's fur.

Then Allie bent down and kissed Ollie near his ear. "Run fast. Come back."

As soon as he took off, Allie stripped out of her clothes and looked up in the sky, hoping that the keen owls were still flying.

"Come on, Low," she yelled at the top of her lungs, not caring about stealth anymore. She didn't need stealth, she needed his eyes. "Help your auntie out!"

She shifted and immediately circled back to the place where Ashford had been, sticking her nose to the ground until she found his scent.

The bobcat had fled, the young man panicking and running as soon as he heard the pounding gallop of the grizzly bear. But Ashford...

He'd escape into the night if she didn't find him. Come back to haunt them, just because she'd pissed him off. He wanted that money. He'd killed Joe for it. Betrayed his boss. The man was desperate, despite his calm facade. She had to find him and kill him.

She caught the scent, but it went underground. She pawed at the old gopher hole for a few minutes, but the scent didn't grow stronger.

A barn owl screeched.

The fox lifted her head and waited.

Another screech, a little farther away.

Allie ran.

Her feet barely touched the sand. She ran toward the sound of the owl's call. He was circling slowly and silently, moving toward the wash.

Of course. Ashford and his man had parked at the Cave and hiked up the wash, avoiding detection from any locals who would know better and avoid it. The tunnel opening wasn't far from the crossing near her house or the old farm road where the men who'd broken into her house had parked. Ashford was heading for his vehicle. If he didn't get there before the bears, he'd survive, but he'd be stuck out in the desert for who knows how long.

Allie had a feeling the prissy man wouldn't like that.

She ran toward the wash, the wolves catching on and following after her. But she was faster than they were. She leapt over rocks and ran under fallen trees when she reached the dry waterway. Every human instinct told her to crawl away, but her fox reassured her. Flash floods were always a danger in the desert, but there was no smell of water on the wind.

Allie ran, stopping periodically to sniff. She darted back and forth. The scent of the snake was faint and foreign. She'd noticed his accent when he spoke. What kind of reptile was he? The fox was a curious hunter.

The wolves waited at her back, a few pawing and yipping as she trotted. She was far faster than a snake. She'd only lose him if he managed to sneak off out of the dry creek bed. That was why she was being so careful. As long as she stayed on track, she'd find him.

She ran forward, then halted.

Forward again.

No scent this far down the wash. Allie ran back.

She circled around a wide spot where a rusted-out car had caught bushes and even a tree as the water swept through. Everything was dry now, but it created a tangle of nooks and crannies where the snake might hide. Allie trotted around the wreck but didn't see anything.

Still, instinct and a tickle in her nose told her the snake was here.

So she sat primly, her tail flicking the sand, and she waited.

And waited.

No snake was leaving that wreck without her catching him, and the snake knew it.

The wolves stayed on the banks above her, yipping and pawing at the dirt. The night birds called and the owls hooted. She could hear

Ollie and two other bears chuffing on the edge of the wash. Soft cat paws padded through the weeds.

And still Allie waited.

The waxing moon was high in the sky when she saw movement. Ashford was moving inside the old car. Slowly. He must have been dark scaled, because she could barely see him. He slithered from under the moon shadow, hiding in the branches of an old manzanita, its reddish-brown bark smooth and its branches as twisted as the serpent.

Allie saw him from the corner of her eye, but still she waited.

The far side of the wash was in shadow. The snake would try to slither there, then flee in the darkness, past her and the wolves who were waiting on the high banks.

She waited until his forked tongue started to flicker, tasting the air. He poked his head out of the manzanita branches.

A little farther.

A little more.

Allie pounced, then darted back, avoiding the quick strike of the snake's deadly fangs. She hopped back away from it, then snarled and darted back toward its tail.

The snake was fast.

Its dark brown scales lay in a smooth chevron down its back. It was almost featureless except for the pale cream face and the flickering tongue. The snake whipped its tail away from her and slithered back as the wolves began to howl and pant. Allie lunged forward and the snake circled, striking again.

His body was twisted over itself protectively; the length behind his head twisted into a sickening S curve that warned Allie he was about to attack.

She ran.

Not away, but around. She circled the wreck on silent feet, jumping over the twisted metal and skirting the manzanita to come up behind the snake. Then she darted forward, her mouth wide, and clamped her jaws around the tail and shook.

A sharp hiss and the thunk of his body flailing, but she felt no strike. No venom entered her bloodstream.

She bit harder. Tasted blood.

Then the snake was rolling away. Growing. Her tongue tasted the bite of human flesh and she released it, running back into the safety of the twisted car. The fox knew she was no match for a full-grown man.

But the bear was.

He leapt on Simon Ashford, who was clutching his leg and vomiting. Ollie knocked the man to his stomach, put a giant paw in the center of Ashford's back, and roared.

Allie yipped and ran toward him, brushing her tail across his flank. *That's my bear.*

THE INFURIATING VIXEN BRUSHED HER TAIL OVER HIS belly, and it was all Ollie could do not to roar. He wanted to bite down, crush the soft neck of the human who'd attacked his family, but he didn't. Ashford had information, and Ollie wanted it.

With a shrug, he shifted back to human, clamping his hand around Ashford's neck.

"Don't even think about it," Ollie growled. Then he brought his fist up to the man's temple and knocked him out.

Ollie sat and leaned against the cool dirt wall, and Allie came and jumped on his legs, carefully walking across his naked skin.

"Darlin'," he said with a sigh. "I thought it'd be the kids, but I'm pretty sure you're the one who's going to give me a heart attack."

ALLIE SHIFTED AND ROLLED OFF HIS LAP, WELL AWARE THAT they had a whole audience of Cambio Springs shifters and an unconscious murderer with them, no matter how excited the shift and the fighting had made her.

"Hey."

Ollie grinned. "Hey yourself."

She couldn't help crawling toward him and pulling his mouth down to hers, but she let him go after only a few seconds.

"Told you," she whispered against his lips.

"Told me what?"

"Big. Bad. Grizzly."

chapter
twenty-eight

Ollie crossed his arms, watching the twisting brown taipan in the large chicken-wire cage behind Henry Quinn's cabin.

"How did you know this was here?" he asked Allie.

"Let's just say that large chicken-wire purchases make me suspicious. He must have gotten the screening somewhere else."

What Henry Quinn had built with all that chicken-wire was effectively a snake prison. While some of the most skilled snake shifters would be able to change to something small enough to fit through the caging, most of them wouldn't, including Simon Ashford, who hadn't shifted to anything but the six-foot-long brown snake that must have been his natural form.

Sean came to stand next to him. "Australia."

"Hmm?"

"Taipans are from Australia. I've looked there, you know? Didn't find anything."

Ollie shrugged. "The world is a big place. Never made much sense that we were alone out there."

He heard Allie giggle and turned toward her. "What's so funny?"

"Do you think there's a town in the outback with kangaroo shifters?" Her cheeks were pink. "Koalas? I'm sorry. I know this is serious."

Sean tried to control his smile and failed. "Wombats. The fearsome were-wombat. I thought it was only an urban legend."

Ollie chuckled, but his eyes never left the snake in the cage.

He was thinking more about crocodiles.

"How secure is this thing?" he asked.

"Henry put screen under it so Ashford can't burrow. As for smaller forms that could fit through the chicken wire... He hasn't tried any."

Just then, the taipan shifted back to human and leaned against a post. "I'd like some water please."

"Answer our questions," Ollie said, "and we'll give you some."

Ashford was silent.

"Fine. Just so you know, it gets pretty hot out here."

"You people are animals."

Sean said, "Well, yes, we are. And so are you."

"I'll tell you about Lobo. I'm not answering any questions about myself."

Sean exchanged a look with Ollie, who shrugged.

"Sure," Ollie said. "Tell us all about Lobo."

"His name is Efrén Abano, and he hates you all."

"Why?"

"I don't know." Ashford smiled. "He isn't one for chatting."

"What does he want?"

"Money. Power. Revenge."

"For what?"

"As I said, he isn't one for chatting." Ashford cracked his neck. "You're not going to let me go, are you?"

Allie stepped forward. "Did you kill my ex-husband?"

"Yes."

"Why?"

"Because he had something I wanted," Ashford said. "And he had information that Efrén wanted about this town. I wanted the money, and I didn't want Efrén to have the information. It was a simple calculation, really."

"Simple," Allie murmured. "Right."

Ashford started smiling. "I'm going to enjoy knowing he's out there, waiting for you all. Eager to take your territory and kill your young." Then his smile dropped. "Or maybe I won't."

With a macabre grin, Ashford opened his mouth and hissed, short venomous fangs on either side of his front teeth.

Sean shouted, "No!"

Ashford sank his teeth into the inside of his left bicep, inches from his heart. He held on, pumping venom into his own veins until his body began to twitch. His back arched and sweat bloomed over his body as the poison took hold.

Within minutes, he was unconscious. Within a half an hour, he was dead.

The Quinns hid the body. And Ollie was right.

It would never be found.

HE HELD HER ON HIS CHEST THAT NIGHT WHEN HE FELL asleep, ignoring her protests that she was too heavy.

She wasn't too heavy. She was necessary.

So was making love, even if it meant waking in the dead of night and being extra quiet. He needed to feel her alive against him. Needed to feel her heat when he sank so deep in her that he knew he'd never escape whole. She wasn't just in his heart, she *was* his heart.

He moved slowly and silently, holding her on his lap so he could touch her face. Her eyes were closed. Her head fell back. Her mouth was soft and open, swollen from his kisses, flushed with desire.

"Ollie," she whispered.

His mind flashed back to the twisting serpent who'd struck at her. The careful dance of her paws as she dodged. Her patience, waiting for the predator who had threatened her young.

She'd waited for hours.

He wrapped his arms around her, pressing her so close neither one of them could move. He held her, just like that, until his heart stopped racing. Ollie thought he'd known what fear tasted like, but he hadn't. Not until a small blond woman and four precious kids invaded his house and his heart. He'd thought he loved her before.

He had no idea.

Ollie brought his hands up to cradle her head, kissing her over and over across her face as she began to move again. He would be patient.

Love her for hours. Until the hours he'd spent waiting for the serpent to strike were washed away by her touch.

He could never, ever let her go.

One week later

OLLIE STOOD, HANDS ON HIS HIPS, WATCHING ALEX AND Kevin unload more bags. "I really don't like this."

"Ollie." She pressed her hand to his cheek. "You knew we wouldn't be staying forever."

Nope. That was actually what he'd been planning on.

"The kids need to be back in their own house," she said. "They need their rooms, and their routines, and their memories... all of that. At least for a while. They need to be able to remember their dad and grieve."

He shook his head. "If you're here, it's harder to protect you."

"We don't have any evidence—other than the threats of a dead man—that anyone is out to get us. And besides, it's not like I'm banishing you from the house. I want you here for dinner at least three times a week."

He fought back a smile. "I have a better kitchen."

"Don't remind me. I miss your refrigerator already."

"It's your fridge. I bought it for you."

She cocked an eyebrow. "You gonna deliver it over here?"

"No." He kissed her hard and fast. "I'm holding it hostage until you come home."

Then he went to help the kids unload her old, crappy minivan and move back into their house, cursing his promise to let her take everything at her own pace. As soon as she agreed to marry him, he was buying her a new car. Something with armor plating, maybe. And then he was fixing up that truck for her so she'd have a fun car too. He knew she wanted that thing. Then he was going to buy a boat and a trailer to match the Ford. Because she liked to go to the river, and because he could.

And if she tried to argue with him, he'd just kiss her. That seemed to be the most effective strategy so far.

He caught Mark sulking on the back porch.

"Hey," Ollie called. "What's up?"

"Dude, I thought we were staying with you."

Ollie sighed and sat down next to him. "I know. I was kind of hoping you were too."

"So why are we moving back? Chris's and my room at your house is way bigger. And you have a creek. And a dog. And Kevin said he'd help us build a fort down in the tunnels."

"Yeah, that's not gonna be happening anytime soon."

Mark shrugged. "Still."

Just then, Loralie's delighted squeal broke through the air.

"My dinosaurs! Mama, my dinosaurs are still here!"

Ollie looked down at Mark. "You guys need to be here a while longer."

Mark's lip pushed out in a pout. "Fine. Is my mom still your girlfriend?"

"Hell, I hope so."

"Don't say hell. You'll get in trouble."

"Thanks, bud." He put his arm around the boy. "You know I love you, right?"

Mark's little body went tense. "Yeah?"

"Like you were my own, Marky." He bent down and kissed the top of the boy's head. "And that will never change. Whether you're living in my house or not."

Mark let out a long breath. "Okay."

"You have any more questions?"

"No."

"Good. Go help your mom."

chapter
twenty-nine

Six months later

Allie pushed open the door and stepped back as if she'd been burned.

"Hey." Alex walked down the hall. "What's wrong?"

She put a hand over her mouth. "That's… um, that's an office."

Alex frowned. "Well, yeah."

"Like a real office. With a desk and a computer, and… Is that a coffee machine on the table over there?"

"Yeah," he said. "There's a little kitchenette in here. I thought since you'd be meeting with clients, especially for catered events, you might—"

"Oh my God!" Allie backed against the opposite wall. "Alex, I can't do this."

He smiled. "Of course you can. We're not even open for another six months. You have time."

"I don't even have clothes pretty enough for that office."

"So go shopping. You have the money now." He smirked. "Ollie loves it when you go shopping."

Allie stood up straight. "Alex McCann, what did he tell you?"

"Nothing."

"You are such a liar."

"Look!" He pointed at the open door. "You have your own bathroom too."

"Stop trying to distract me with..." She gasped. "I have my own little garden?"

"Yep. Walled off for privacy. All desert plantings. The fountain goes in next week." He spread his hands. "Think of this office as a small taste of the resort. When clients come to meet with you, they need to be able to experience the food. The atmosphere." A speaker crackled to life somewhere, and soft Native American flute music drifted in. "The music."

Allie started to nod and walk around. "You want them to feel at home."

"No, I want them to be more relaxed than they are at home. I want them to feel like they're already on vacation."

She nodded. "I can do that."

"I know you can." He sat in the chair across from her desk. "You can personalize the space a bit, but not too much. Sorry."

"No, don't apologize. It needs to reflect the resort and the amenities. Not my tastes. And besides, it's beautiful, Alex."

He smiled. "Thank you."

"Really." She tentatively sat in the soft brown leather chair behind the desk she didn't quite believe was hers. "It's all so beautiful. It's going to be amazing. I just know it's going to be a success, and I will help in any way I can."

"Think you can get your boyfriend to ease up on me a bit?"

"Don't ask for miracles. Besides, you know he'll come around."

There was just one more thing she had to tackle with Alex. Just one more thing she wasn't sure about.

"Alex, you know Loralie is going into school in the fall, so my hours are pretty easy because the kids are more independent. And of course my dad still helps. But... You've invested so much money and time in me taking this job. I guess I need to know that *if* something changes... Well, I mean if—"

"If you and Buster Bear end up having more kids, we'll figure it out."

She blushed. "It's not... I mean, we haven't even really talked about it. I just don't want to rule anything out. We're still young."

"I get it. Totally. And Allie, there are so many kids popping up around here, I'm thinking of building on a day care center." He looked out the window, but a furtive smile crept to his lips.

"Why..." Allie gasped and clapped her hands. "She is, isn't she?"

Alex nodded deliberately and said, "I have no idea what you're talking about. My wife would kill me if I spilled any secrets that you should not ask her about regarding things that may or may not be happening in around seven months' time."

Allie laughed. "It's absolutely killing you not to tell everyone, isn't it?"

He threw his head back and groaned. "She's going to drive me crazy."

"Good practice for when the baby comes then."

ALLIE SNUGGLED INTO OLLIE'S SIDE ON THE COUCH IN HIS office. Now that she and Ollie weren't living together, they had to grab the time they had. It was one of the reasons she'd continued working at the Cave even though her finances had eased considerably.

It was Wednesday night, and most of the regulars were gone. They weren't technically closed, but she saw his eyes drooping so she dragged him to the office and let Tracey man the bar.

"Ted is pregnant," she whispered.

His eyes flew open. "No way."

"Yep. I'm not supposed to know about it. Alex kind of spilled the beans yesterday. So don't say anything."

He rubbed his eyes and yawned. "Well, you know I have so much trouble not gossiping..."

Allie laughed.

She laughed a lot now. She laughed when her kids dog-piled Ollie on the couch. She laughed when they ate dinner at night. She even managed to laugh—and maybe shriek a little—when she was teaching Kevin to drive.

Ollie had taken over by the second lesson.

Even though they weren't living with him, the big man was so much a part of their lives, separate homes almost felt like a formality. He didn't sleep over and neither did she, except for the rare nights that the kids were all gone.

But when the oven broke, he was the one to fix it. When the car finally gave out, Ollie was the one who drove her to buy the used SUV he grudgingly approved of, even if he wanted something newer and fancier for her.

He'd been the one to hold Loralie during the small memorial service they'd held for Joe, and he'd helped to scatter his ashes by the river with the kids.

"Hey," she said, brushing her fingers against his lips as his eyes started to close. "I love you."

He smiled and kissed her fingertips. "Love you too."

Two months later

"ALLIE?"

"In the kitchen!" she yelled back, smoothing down one of the pretty dresses she'd bought for her new job and trying to ignore the butterflies in her stomach. She could hear Loralie and Chris giggling on the back porch, and she knew Kevin and Mark were probably having the devil's time keeping them outside.

"Hey." Ollie walked through the door with his toolbox, still grubby from work. He and Jim were working on revamping the pool room at the Cave. He grinned. "You look nice. Jim said it won't turn on?"

She motioned to the garbage disposal. "I think there's something stuck down there, but I can't figure out what. I already unplugged it so you can look."

He frowned and peered down into the drain. Then he opened the cupboard underneath the sink and bent down.

Allie said, "What are you doing?"

"If there's something stuck in it, I need to get it out. Don't worry. It's not a big deal."

"But can't you just..." She bit her lip. This wasn't the way it was supposed to go! "Can't you just, you know, stick your hand down there and see if you can feel anything?"

Ollie laughed and held up a giant paw. "Darlin', you really think I can fit my hand down that little drain? Don't worry. It's not a big deal. Won't take but a few minutes to get it off."

"But—"

"Allie, don't worry." He stuck his head under the sink. "Man, you have the cleanest cupboards I have ever seen. Do you dust down here? That's... kinda crazy, to be honest."

"Ollie, stop!"

"What?" He bumped his head a little when he pulled his head from under the sink. "What's wrong?"

Allie took a deep breath and plunged her hand down the garbage disposal, pulling out a small black box and holding it out to him with an embarrassed laugh.

Ollie's face went blank. "What is that?"

"I wanted to be clever. The garbage disposal was Mark's idea because you're always fixing stuff. I didn't even think about how big your hands—"

"Allie"—he came to his knees—"what is that?"

She cracked open the box to reveal the band she and the kids had picked out. Five gold strands woven together, one for her and one for each of them.

Her heart was racing. "I think, technically, I'm the one who's supposed to be on my knees right now."

"Baby—" His voice cracked.

"You said we could go at my pace," she said. "Well, this is my pace. You're already part of this family, Oliver Campbell. We all love you so much. *I* love you so much. I can't imagine..." She started to cry. "I can't imagine life without you. You promised to make my life sweet again, and you have. So much, Ollie. So much sweetness, I don't know what to do with it all except give you some back. As much as I can. So will you do me the honor of being my husband?"

He rose and took her face in his hands, kissing her with wild, joyful abandon. He wrapped her in his arms and swung her around, laughing against her mouth when he finally set her down.

He smiled and blinked hard when he looked down at the ring she still held in her hand. "But I already have yours picked out. Kevin helped me."

"Double-crossing kids." Allie laughed and wiped the tears off her cheeks. "Does that mean it's a yes?"

"Yes." He picked her up again and kissed her slower, savoring her. "Yes, yes, yes." He shouted over his shoulder. "Did you hear that? *Yes.* Now stop listening at the door and go play so I can kiss your mom."

Loralie's giggles burst through the air.

Chris shouted at the top of his lungs. "He said yes, guys!"

"I'm shocked. So shocked."

"Are they kissing again?"

"Oh yeah. Lots."

Allie ignored them and kissed her man. The finest man she had ever known. The man who loved her. Who made her heart race and her body sing. The man who lived in her heart. The brave, brave man who'd had the guts to say "Yep" to all her crazy.

The man she trusted to be hers for the rest of her life.

And that life had never looked sweeter.

epilogue

Sean Quinn walked into the quiet, velvet-walled club in Las Vegas. The soothing sounds of a quiet piano played in the corner of the room, and vintage French advertisements lined the walls. It was the kind of place that reminded visitors that once, Las Vegas had meant glamour with an edge of danger instead of giant mega malls, exploding volcanoes, and fading pop stars.

He slipped a hundred-dollar bill to the manager and hooked his thumbs in the pockets of his faded black jeans as he strolled past the booths.

Sunday afternoon was a quiet time, but there were still a few regulars. A couple of Vegas institutions, chatting over vodka tonics, and one of the headliners at a smaller casino.

And him. The man Sean had paid good money to find.

He was a man of no particular fame, of medium height and build. His face was nondescript. So were his clothes, which were fine, but not too fine. Well cut, but not particularly stylish. He was reading a newspaper and drinking a clear cocktail with three limes.

Sean slid into the booth opposite him, and the man put his newspaper down.

His eyes were notable.

Cool blue in a brown face. Notable.

"Can I help you?" His English had no accent.

"I believe we have a mutual acquaintance."

"Oh?"

"He took a wrong turn in the desert. Didn't find his way out."

The polite mask fell away from Efrén Abano's face, and the cool blue eyes turned frigid. "I see."

"He had a young man with him."

"He did," the man they called Lobo said. "He was quite forthcoming when he returned. He told an interesting story. Unfortunately, he also took a wrong turn in the desert not long after that."

An unexpected flare of anger rose in Sean. "That's too bad."

"Well," Efrén said, "the desert is a vast and dangerous place. One wrong step can lead to death."

Sean leaned his elbows on the table. "It's good that you remember that, *Lobo*."

Irritated eyes flickered around the room. "I wasn't talking about me."

"No? You should have been."

"What is your name? Since you know mine, it only seems polite."

"My name is Sean Quinn."

Efrén chuckled. "Ah. A Quinn. If they had sent the wolf, I might have taken more notice."

"I'm glad you feel that way. We prefer to be overlooked. Makes it so much easier to get what we want."

The smile fled Efrén's face. "What do you want?"

"Your man said you wanted revenge. On us. Why? As far as I've been able to find out, no one in our town has even heard your name."

Efrén pursed his lips together. He almost looked amused. "That's quite possible. But of course, you only have the word of a traitor that I want revenge, and you only have the word of old men that they've never heard of me. It's a conundrum."

Sean ignored the slight against the council. For now. "So you don't want revenge?"

"I didn't say that."

Sean was silent.

"Am I irritating you yet?" Efrén asked.

"I'm the leader of the snake clan. It takes a lot to irritate me."

"The leader?" Efrén's eyes sharpened. "So the old man has finally curled up and died, has he?"

"I didn't say that."

"Ah." Efrén smiled. "So you are his chosen successor. Interesting."

"Not really."

"What do you want, Sean Quinn? It seems only fair to return the question."

Sean leaned back. "I don't know about your organization. I don't really want to know. I just want you to leave the Springs alone."

"Is that so?" Efrén's face was a picture of innocence. "I'm sorry. There must have been a misunderstanding of some sort with our... acquaintance."

"Oh?" A faint hope rose in Sean's chest. Maybe Ashford had been exaggerating. Maybe he was just a liar. Maybe Efrén didn't care two shakes about Cambio Springs after all.

"Yes," Efrén said. "I'm afraid leaving the Springs alone is quite *impossible*."

Sean's face was a carefully impassive mask. *Damn.*

"Now," Efrén said, picking up his newspaper and his drink. "I don't have much leisure time, Mr. Quinn. I'd appreciate it if you respected that. Good-bye."

He used the drive back from Las Vegas to summon the internal fortitude to call his editor. Or his former editor? Sean wasn't sure of anything anymore, particularly his job.

His life was a damn mess.

He'd never belonged here, at least that's what he'd told himself. But with his great-uncle growing older, someone had to take over the family, and Uncle Joe preferred that it wasn't someone with a criminal record.

In his family, that was a challenge.

If his cousin Marcus hadn't been murdered, he would have been perfect. Marcus had loved his family but never deluded himself that they were upstanding citizens. He'd built a business. Had a family. Everyone had loved and respected him because he'd still been tough as nails. Marcus should have been the one.

And then he was dead.

Because of an ignorant human and fear.

It had killed a little bit of Sean inside when he'd heard Marcus died. Not only because it meant one of the few cousins he'd felt close to growing up was gone. Not only because he'd left a widow and children behind.

Selfishly, Sean knew the minute Marcus was gone, his bid for freedom was over.

He turned off the interstate and onto the state highway that would take him home.

Home.

It had always been a loaded word for Sean Quinn.

Home meant laughter and mischief and the loyalty of a hundred cousins who would have his back against anyone outside the clan. Home also meant fists and drunken fights and constantly looking over his shoulder to watch his back against those same cousins. Because while loyalty against other clans was a guarantee, within the clan, nothing was given.

And now he'd agreed to lead the rowdy lot of them.

A laughing voice in the back of his mind, overlaid by the sound of tambourines and singing.

"You'll have to deal with them eventually, Spider. Family has a way of haunting you."

He pushed the voice back into the mental box of things-no-longer-possible and called his boss.

"Rani, you've got to give me a little more time. You, of all people, understand how complicated family is."

He'd been to her wedding in Bangalore. It was possible his editor had more family than he did.

"I love you, Sean, but you know this is getting ridiculous. Shooting off for an assignment once every three months or so is not enough to keep you on staff. Even if I'm paying you a fraction of your old salary.

There are people who have been waiting years for a staff position, and you—"

"Send me more editing! I'll do it all. That leaves everyone else on assignments. I'll do all the editing you want."

It would kill part of his soul to do nothing but edit other photographers' images, but he had to do something. If all he could get was glimpses through the window of other people's adventures, he'd take it.

Rani sighed. "I know that worked well for you and Juniper. Chati might take you up on it too. But you know some of them won't let anyone edit their images, even if it is you. I'll... see what I can do."

He had great relationships with most of his colleagues, but there was always competition. No one was making a fortune, but everyone was doing what they loved.

"There's a spa resort coming to my hometown. Very exclusive. Hellacious expensive. It's beautiful, Rani. I can do a feature on that."

"A spa?" She paused. "The new Cambio Springs resort?"

"Yes!"

"I didn't know that was your town," she said.

"I know the owner. I know this area. I grew up here. I'll cover it. It'll be a great feature."

"Well... shit."

"What? Shit what?"

"That would have been perfect, but I already assigned Juniper."

He could almost hear her laughing in his ear.

"Juni?"

"Yeah. I guess she has family in that area."

"Juni's from Albuquerque. I'd hardly call that in the neighborhood."

"She's been in Southeast Asia for almost three years. She almost jumped at the chance. She probably needs the dry air."

He knew she'd been in Southeast Asia. He could still see her laughing and soaked to the skin during Songkran.

"You're saying our Juni is coming to Cambio Springs?"

"Yeah, just before the opening. She might already be there. She flew back to the States last week. You know she likes to wander."

Jena and Caleb's house came into view in the distance. The passel of kids his friends had produced were running in circles in the front.

Chasing each other. Riding bikes. It was the kind of childhood he'd always envied. One he'd only glimpsed from the edges of his life.

"Rani, I gotta go."

"Why don't you and Juniper collaborate again? Every time you do, it ends up being fantastic. Let her write and you can focus on the photography. Play to both your strengths."

"I'll call her." He parked a little ways down the street. He hated being late for Sunday dinner, even if he did feel like the odd man out these days. He needed to drag Willow to some of these things. Alex's sister could be such a hermit, but at least then he wouldn't be the only one not paired up.

"Take care, Sean. And... sort out whatever family stuff you have, okay? We miss you."

He swallowed the lump in his throat and bid farewell to everything he'd worked for. "Bye, Rani."

Sean gave himself a few minutes before he opened the truck door and stepped into the dust.

Dust. Grit. Cactus.

He missed the lush green of Yunnan Province and the flowers in Indonesia. He missed laughing and drinks with fellow wanderers and the tug of longing when he'd stayed in a place just a little too long.

Sean was grounded in the Springs. *Grounded.* It was a feeling that killed his soul.

"Hey, Uncle Sean!"

"Uncle Sean, watch this!"

"You're heeeeere."

Little bodies tumbled into him and called his attention. Christopher scrambled up his back like a monkey. Jena and Allie's kids weren't really his nieces and nephews, but they were as close as family.

Actually, no, they were closer.

He adored every single one of them. He watched skateboard tricks and yo-yo fumbles before he begged off to go grab a drink and whatever was left of Sunday dinner.

"Hey!" he called when he walked through the door. He could already hear his friends laughing and chatting in the kitchen and on the back porch. "Sorry I'm late, but I had an interesting—"

"Spider?"

He lifted his head and worlds collided when he saw her perched on the counter in Jena Crowe's kitchen.

"Juni?"

With a grin and a laugh, she jumped down, running into the living room and jumping into his arms, her currently-blue-streaked hair flying behind her. "Sean!"

"Juniper Rain Hawkins." He caught her and spun her around. Such a little thing. So young. So damn alive. He hugged her tight and took a deep breath. "Aren't you a sight for sore eyes? I just called Rani. She mentioned you were covering the… Wait, what are you doing at *Jena's*?"

She slid to the ground and pinched his cheek. "It's not *just* Jena's house, old man."

Sean lifted his face and saw Caleb Gilbert leaning in the doorway, arms crossed over his chest.

Cambio Springs' current chief of police looked grim. "So you know my baby sister, huh?"

Baby sister?

Sean looked down at Juni.

Oh yes.

Back up to Caleb.

Oh no.

DUST BORN IS COMING!
FALL 2023

Sign up for my newsletter for news about Dust Born and all new Elizabeth Hunter books.

coming 2023: dust born

S ean Quinn returned to Cambio Springs to help his family find their way out of trouble—not uncommon in this desert town of shapeshifters—but before he can hit the road again, a new threat emerges on the border of his family home, a threat that could leave Sean stuck in the Springs just when he's most desperate to leave.

And one unsuspecting human might be stuck right there with him.

Ever since Juniper Hawkins came to Cambio Springs to visit her big brother, strange things keep happening, not the least was running into the man who'd almost made her change her wandering ways. Juni wasn't the kind of woman who settled down, even when the object of her affection was a tall, dark, and handsome photographer who kissed her senseless then abandoned her in Southeast Asia.

Not that she was still irritated about that.

DUST BORN is a brand new novel in the Cambio Springs Mysteries, a paranormal romance series by ten time USA Today Bestselling author, Elizabeth Hunter.

ElizabethHunterWrites.com

acknowledgments

There are always so many people to thank, and I always seem to forget some. As a single mom, this book definitely hit home for me. Allie is a heroine I can relate to in many ways, particularly regarding her "people."

Here are some of my "people:"

My son, the most understanding ten-year-old in history. You are my favorite not-so-little dude.

My sister, who is the best assistant ever and keeps my life manageable, so I can get lost in my head and write books for you.

My parents, who are the bestest parents and grandparents ever.

My friends. Writing friends. School friends. Friends close by and halfway across the world. I love you all so much.

"Two are better than one, because they have a good reward for their toil. For if they fall, one will lift up his fellow. But woe to him who is alone when he falls and has not another to lift him up!" Ecclesiastes 4:9-10

Thanks, as well, to all the professionals who make my books shine. Thanks to Damonza.com for their amazing cover work. Thanks to Anne and Linda at Victory Editing. Thanks to Lora Gasway, my amazing developmental editor. And thanks (again!) to my sister, Gen, my first reader.

Many thanks to Jane and Lauren, my agents at Dystel and Goderich Literary Management.

Thanks most of all to my readers, who buy my books, talk about my books, and make all this possible. I have the best readers in the world, and I love bragging about you.

about the author

ELIZABETH HUNTER is a ten-time *USA Today* and international best-selling author of romance, contemporary fantasy, and paranormal mystery. Based in Central California, she travels extensively to write fantasy fiction exploring world mythologies, history, and the universal bonds of love, friendship, and family. She has published over thirty works of fiction and sold over a million books worldwide. She is the author of the Glimmer Lake series, the Elemental Legacy series, the Irin Chronicles, the Cambio Springs Mysteries, and other works of fiction.

also by elizabeth hunter

Cambio Springs

Long Ride Home*

Shifting Dreams

Five Mornings*

Desert Bound

Waking Hearts

The Elemental Mysteries

A Hidden Fire

This Same Earth

The Force of Wind

A Fall of Water

The Stars Afire

The Elemental World

Building From Ashes

Waterlocked

Blood and Sand

The Bronze Blade

The Scarlet Deep

A Very Proper Monster

A Stone-Kissed Sea

Valley of the Shadow

The Elemental Legacy

Shadows and Gold

Imitation and Alchemy

Omens and Artifacts

Obsidian's Edge (anthology)

Midnight Labyrinth

Blood Apprentice

The Devil and the Dancer

Night's Reckoning

Dawn Caravan

The Bone Scroll

The Elemental Covenant

Saint's Passage

Martyr's Promise

Paladin's Kiss

(Summer 2022)

The Irin Chronicles

The Scribe

The Singer

The Secret

The Staff and the Blade

The Silent

The Storm

The Seeker

Glimmer Lake

Suddenly Psychic

Semi-Psychic Life

Psychic Dreams

Moonstone Cove

Runaway Fate

Fate Actually

Fate Interrupted

Linx & Bogie Mysteries

A Ghost in the Glamour

A Bogie in the Boat

Contemporary Romance

The Genius and the Muse

Love Stories on 7th and Main

Ink

Hooked

Grit

Sweet

*short story